THE DANCE OF DREAMS

BOOKS BY CLARK

THE STAINS OF TIME

The Piano of Death

The Boot of Destiny

The Chains of Desire

The Elixir of Denial

The Dance of Dreams

OTHER BOOKS

Those Little Bastards

All He Left Behind

Missing Mr. Wingfield

The Seven Wives of Silver

Bad Poetry Night

Out of the Woods

Under the World

THE DANCE OF DREAMS

E. CHRISTOPHER CLARK

Published in the United States by Clarkwoods in Chelmsford, Massachusetts.

This is a work of fiction. Names, characters, places, and incidents either are the product of the author's imagination or are used fictitiously, and any resemblance to any actual persons, living or dead, events, or locales is entirely coincidental.

ISBN for the Print Edition: 978-1-952044-33-5
ISBN for the Digital Edition: 978-1-952044-32-8

Library of Congress Control Number: 2022914356

PROLOGUE

AUGUST 2010

ADA

da Coffin worked the bar inside The Strumpet's Sister, serving the weary and the brokenhearted wherever and *when*ever the tavern appeared each night. For years, the patrons' tales of woe had been a pleasant distraction from her own weariness, from her own broken heart. But now that the time of her grand revenge was at hand, the rage Ada had drowned beneath her sadness for so long was bubbling to the surface.

"Can I get a pint?" asked the next guy who sidled up to the bar, a smarmy smile upon his face. "And an appletini for my special lady friend over there?" he added, shaking his chin in the direction of the nearest table.

Ada nodded and filled a mug for him, because that was her job. She would've preferred to smack the ingratiating grin off his face with the hardest slap she could muster, and hit him upside the head with the mug for good measure, but she couldn't afford to get fired. Not now, not when she was so close to getting what she'd been after for so long.

As she made the mixed drink for Guy Smiley's companion, Ada cast a glance over his shoulder to see who this "special lady friend" might be—to see who'd been suckered into suffering this man's company for the evening. A dolled-up blonde sat at the high-top, looking bored in a dress made for dancing. She had a cell phone in one hand and was swiping a finger across its screen, absent-mindedly paging through photographs of men who looked to be—from a distance, at least—decidedly more attractive than the fellow who'd come to the bar on her behalf.

When she was younger, Ada might've offered the poor, smiling sap a bit of kind-hearted advice, or forewarned him about the reception waiting for him back at his table. Today though, she stayed blank-faced and silent as she took his money and handed him his drinks. In her head, Ada prayed the guy wouldn't notice his date's disinterest and that he wouldn't lose his cool if he did end up noticing. She imagined the young woman making it home safely, changing into a comfy set of pajamas, and texting a friend about how disastrous the date had been. Ada imagined this and willed it to be true. There was a magic in belief and in a person's will. Sometimes, Ada knew, wishes really did come true.

And sometimes they don't, she thought to herself as she sighed.

One hundred and thirty-five years ago, as her mother lay dying, Ada had been tasked with continuing their bloodline. "You are the last daughter," her mother told her, "in an unbroken line, going all the way back to the mother of us all. There is magic in our blood," said Ada's mother, "and the task falls to you, child, to make sure that this magic doesn't disappear from the earth."

Ada was ten. She was *ten* when this was left upon her shoulders, when she was told she could not buckle beneath the burden.

At twenty-five, she was married to man who had been charged by his own dying mother with continuing *their* family line. Silas Silver—the ninth in a line of Silases going back centuries—had been through three wives already in his quest to produce an heir. After learning that there was a young woman working in the local brothel who was just as desperate to have a child, he had proposed to Ada straight away.

After a quick ceremony at Town Hall, they got right to business. But after two years of trying: nothing. And so, Ada turned to desperate measures.

In 1892, she performed an arcane ritual passed down to her from the witches of old. But though it worked, though she found herself pregnant at the end of the ordeal, her horrified husband murdered her in a fit of rage. Afraid that Ada would give birth to some sort of demon's spawn, Silas had wrapped his hands around her throat and squeezed the life out of her. And yet, even murder could not stop this magic. The ritual's bending of time allowed Ada's dying body to progress through the nine months of pregnancy in mere minutes, and to deliver the baby alive and well.

Overcome by the ghastly sight, Silas passed out. This allowed Ada's ghost enough time to rescue the child and leave it on the doorstep of a family who would never learn where he had come from, nor the nature of his birth—enough time to do that, but nothing more. After her son was safe, Ada's ghost had been brought to the Strumpet's Sister and put to work. It was the closest she could get to keeping an eye on her descendants, or so the barkeep had told her. The windows of the Sister, he said, allowed the dead to look out across time and space.

"Stay here," he'd told her, "and you can stay connected with the living world." And so, instead of moving on, Ada had worked here in the Sister ever since.

She felt a tap on her shoulder as she stared off at Guy Smiley and his uninterested date, still wishing a safe evening upon the young woman. Ada turned to find Belinda, the tavern's owner, standing behind her.

"Take a break," said Belinda, who offered Ada a kind smile as she spoke. "You've earned it."

Ada nodded and made her way out from behind the bar. Then she turned to her left and pushed open the door to the alley out back. A bit of quiet would do her some good, she figured, a bit of solitude. Her life—or her *after*life, she supposed—was about to get very loud and very chaotic, assuming everything went according to plan. She might as well savor every bit of peace she could, while she could.

Sadly, there was already someone else outside—someone who caught sight of Ada before she could escape back into the bar.

"Hello, Robin," said Ada, offering the other woman the faintest hint of a wave.

Robin said nothing in reply, not at first. She just sat there on the grimy asphalt, with her back leaned against a green dumpster, and she stared. She had a bottle of beer in one hand and two more sitting on the ground beside her.

"Did you want to be alone?" asked Ada, turning her body toward the door and shaking a thumb at it. "I can go back inside."

"Did you know it's been twenty years since we first met?" asked Robin. She took a healthy swig from her bottle. "That was back when I was a kid, remember, before I was killed and stuck in this place with you. Twenty *years*."

Ada noticed now that the two beers on the ground were already open and probably empty.

"I was just hanging out with my younger brother," said Robin, "trying not to die of boredom while our mom waited tables to make ends meet."

Ada nodded. "I remember," she said. "We met the day you found your obituary."

"In a stack of newspapers *you* were supposed to throw out each time the bar moved," said Robin, with a hint of anger in her voice.

Ada nodded again. "I thought, if you found it, it might inspire you to change things," she said. "I thought leaving it there might help you avoid the inevitable."

Robin snorted back a laugh. "And then, in your desperation, you ended up *causing* the very disaster you were trying to avoid."

It was true. After learning that Robin was a descendant of hers—of the son she'd left on a stranger's doorstep—Ada had done everything in her power to keep Robin safe. She'd done *everything*—including trying to have Robin's girlfriend, one of the wicked Silvers, killed. But the assassin had bungled the assignment and shot Robin dead instead—the last of Ada's living relatives, the last hope she'd had at keeping her mother's bloodline alive.

Ada stared at Robin as the younger woman pushed herself off the ground and got to her feet. She looked deep into the eyes of the person who had been her last hope at fulfilling her mother's dream. And she tried not to smile, not even to smirk, as she did this. Because, while Robin's death had dashed any hope of keeping the family line alive, Robin was *also* the key to Ada's latest scheme.

"I don't know what you're planning," said Robin, as she stepped toward Ada, "but—"

"Who says I'm planning anything?" said Ada.

"You did," said Robin, poking Ada in the shoulder. "When I first showed up here, even though you should've felt one hundred percent defeated, there was still a flicker of hope in your eyes. And when I asked you what you were up to, you said 'Nothing yet, but give me time.' Don't think I don't remember," said Robin. "Don't think I haven't been keeping an eye on you ever since."

Ada brushed Robin aside and strode up the alley towards the street the Sister had landed upon. "I'm going for a walk," she said.

"Where?" shouted Robin. "You can't leave. Neither of us can."

Ada stopped for a moment at the far end of the alleyway, glanced over her shoulder at Robin, and said, "Watch me." Then she turned to the right and continued on her way, smiling to herself as she imagined the look of confusion that must've overtaken Robin's face in that moment—the feeling of sheer terror Robin must've felt as she, Ada, turned the corner.

Robin was right. They couldn't venture out into the living world, but The Strumpet's Sister didn't really exist in the living world anyway. The Sister that the living saw, that they walked into for a drink or three, was just the façade. The rest of the building existed in a liminal space, a purgatory, and that's where Ada was going. That's where she'd gone many times before to blow off steam, to contemplate her continued existence or at the very least grab a decent cup of coffee.

Ada walked down the Avenue of the In-Between, past the old mill and the brewery, the cookie stand and the subway station, and she stopped in front of the courthouse. The sign out front called it The Court of Memory, and it was honestly the most gorgeous thing Ada had ever seen.

She'd walked past it a thousand times over the years without paying it any mind, but now that she'd foreseen the role it would play in her plans for vengeance she was struck by the austere beauty of its brick walls and of the Doric columns which stood to either side of its front doors. She could've stared at it forever, or at least until her plans rolled into motion, but her brief respite was ruined by the sound of rushing footsteps and heavy breathing.

"Where are we?" asked Robin, as she came to a stop beside Ada and doubled over. With one hand braced against her thigh, she pointed up at the dome which sealed this place off from the rest of the world—and at the storm clouds brewing near the top. "Are we," she asked, "inside a *snow globe*?"

"Yes, on an island that sits between life and death," said Ada. "The Skerry of Souvenirs. At least that's what our friend Belinda calls it."

"Belinda is not our friend," said Robin, who was starting to catch her breath. "She's our captor."

Ada shook her head. "She may own the place, but I don't think she has any control over who's allowed to come and go. That's above her pay grade," she said.

"A higher power?" said Robin with a scoff. "Whatever. Anyway, Belinda is creepy. With that super-long hair of hers—"

"She's cut it recently."

"—and the way she looks like she's maybe 21 but she's actually—"

"Old," said Ada.

Robin stood up straight now, though she was still panting. "Why do you trust her?"

"She listens to me," said Ada. "When I caught the old barkeep breaking the rules, she got rid of him right away."

"The rules," said Robin, shaking her head. "Jakob rigged one set of dice! That was it."

Ada set a hand upon Robin's shoulder, wanting to convey the gravity of what she was about to say. She couldn't afford for Robin to ignore this or take it lightly. "You don't break rules with Belinda," she said. "You just don't. She's a lovely person, reasonable to a fault, but she has no patience for cheats and scoundrels."

"I know," said Robin. "I saw the blood on her boots a few months ago, remember? She came downstairs with blood on her shoes after a card game—a *card* game! What were the stakes, for Christ's sake? What could have possibly happened during a game of Five-Card Draw that made her feel like she had to kill someone?"

Ada turned Robin around and pointed off into the distance, past the rocky shores of the island they were trapped on, past the dome which kept them here, and to the raging celestial river which surrounded them on all sides. "Belinda pulled herself out of those rapids after bearing witness to more horror than we can possibly imagine," she said. "She clawed her way to shore, and every hard choice she's made since—the killing and the cajoling, the making of love and the making of war—*everything* she's done has been to keep us, our whole world, safe from the things she's seen."

"Is that a strip club?" said Robin, deflecting—ignoring the gravity of what Ada had just said and pointing at a distant building instead, a two-story brick affair with a flashing neon sign hanging above its front door. "Is it built into an old fire station?"

Ada nodded, annoyed and hoping that Robin had gotten the point before she changed the subject. "Yes," she said. "See," she continued with a simpering smile, "your girlfriend would've had a place to work, if only she'd taken the bullet instead of you."

Robin slapped Ada hard across the face and stalked back toward The Strumpet's Sister with tears in her eyes. Ada restrained a laugh. She knew that she deserved what she'd gotten, but it had been worth it. For years now, she'd been trying to get it through Robin's thick skull that loving a Silver never ended well. She was glad to have been given another opportunity to drive that point home before she escaped this place, before she exploited the loophole she'd found to return to the land of the living.

Before she put an end to the Silver family once and for all.

"It's almost time," she said to herself as she looked once again upon the courthouse. Then she cast a glance over her shoulder and took one more look at the retreating Robin, who would be her ticket out of here and didn't even know it. Ada smiled and nodded, then she said it again: "It's almost time."

I

TOO MUCH TIME ON MY HANDS

2010-2016

BELINDA

"Who are *you?*" That was the question on the professor's mind as Belinda walked into his classroom that first afternoon. She could hear it in his head from across the way, could hear that it was "Who are *you?*" and not "*Who* are you?" or "Who *are* you?" But she couldn't answer him, couldn't have answered him even if he asked the question aloud—not truthfully, at least—because he wouldn't believe her. How could he? So, instead, she just took a seat. At a desk near the back of the room, she tried to keep the inane thoughts of her classmates at bay, and she did her best to focus on the lesson the professor had prepared.

It was an English composition course for athletes, and Belinda knew the professor was only teaching it as a favor to the college. She knew this both because he was thinking about it right now, repeating a mantra in his head to give himself strength, and because once upon a time—in another life—he had told her.

In that other life, he had been Uncle Matt and she had been his favorite niece. "Your only niece," she used to correct him, "and technically speaking, I'm not even that."

He'd clutch his chest with both hands whenever she told him this, feign an imminent collapse, and beg to know why she sought to hurt him so.

Belinda would laugh—even when she got older, when the joke had long since stopped being funny—and she'd remind him that, technically speaking, they were first cousins once removed.

Uncle Matt would rub his forehead with the back of a forearm and slump into the nearest chair. Then he'd say, "That's right. But it's also just semantics, kiddo. You're my favorite niece, and you always will be."

Always—Belinda hated the word. It meant nothing, not a thing—not in a world that could end on a whim, that the gods would reboot whenever they were slighted, that they would transform into something altogether unrecognizable. Belinda *had* been his niece, until an old woman had meddled with time and given offense to the deities of this place. Now Belinda was nothing. It was like she didn't exist.

In fact, she wasn't supposed to.

"Welcome," Uncle Matt began. "My name is Professor Silver. I'll be your instructor for the next four months. My deepest sympathies."

Nobody laughed at his poor attempt at humor, nobody but Belinda.

She took copious notes that first day, and throughout that first course with Uncle Matt as her teacher. From that first meeting in Hasseltine Hall, with the windows open and a warm September breeze rolling across the back of her neck, through the falling of October leaves and cold November rain, to the December storms that made her thankful for the underground tunnels which connected the academic buildings to one another—through it all, she wrote and wrote and wrote. Sometimes she took down what he wrote on the board—his musings on the power of punctuation and the greater mysteries of English grammar—but mostly she just took down her own observations of him. She took note of how different he was from the man she'd known—lively instead of lethargic, loquacious instead of taciturn—and how much he was the same, despite all that had changed.

A few of them went out for drinks after the final exam, Belinda praying that Uncle Matt wouldn't ask how old she was—hoping that he'd see the fact that she'd been carded and let into the pub by the bouncer as proof that she was old enough and leave it at that. Because how would she answer? That's what she found herself thinking as they drank round after round, and her jock classmates discovered that Matt had been a star shortstop before turning to creative writing: how would she answer *any* of his questions? And—assuming he didn't just laugh her out of the building the moment she told him that, technically speaking, she was about 14 billion years old—how would she stop the questions, once they started?

That spring, she took a second course with him. It was his advanced workshop in short fiction, it met on Friday afternoons, and it was tradition to congregate after class each week for a libation or three, depending on how thoroughly they'd eviscerated the work on offer that day. An unbroken tradition, since the days when Matt himself was a student at the college.

The week that it was Belinda's turn to choose which establishment they would take their business to, she chose her own place: The Strumpet's Sister.

"You have your own bar?" asked one of her classmates.

Belinda nodded. "Been in the family for years," she told them.

Uncle Matt smiled. "Ms. Michaelson," he said, "you are just full of surprises."

THIS TIME AROUND, The Strumpet's Sister was a dive tucked into the basement of an upholsterer's warehouse on the banks of the

Merrimack River. It had been many things to many people over many years—and in many places—but Belinda had brought it here to Haverhill with the intentions of keeping it in one spot for a bit. There was a lost love to get over, and she felt like it was about time to stop putting off college.

They tucked themselves into a booth in a dimly lit corner of the main room, and all but Belinda picked up menus to peruse which pint might strike their fancy. She considered for a moment why they hadn't asked her for her recommendations. That had become the custom each week, asking the person who picked the place what they'd recommend, but alas: no one was asking. Was it *just* that she was the lone chick here, or was it something more than that? Belinda let herself drift into their minds for a moment and realized that none of them were even *thinking* about asking, which made it somehow worse.

It was as she did this that she felt a thought hammering at Uncle Matt's brain again and again, a persistent thing that was testing his defenses. She felt it first as a pure feeling of panic, only slowly coming to realize the kernel of truth at its core: Uncle Matt had a play happening down on Cape Cod this weekend, and the thought was trying to remind him that it was going to be a disaster. No ifs, ands, or buts about it. The play was going to bomb. And why wouldn't he acknowledge that? That's what the thought wanted to know. Now that Matt was done with teaching for the day and should've had time for it—the thought, that is—why wasn't he crying? Why wasn't he hanging his head in shame? Why was he daring to celebrate with his students, to honor the work of the week gone by?

"Belinda," said Uncle Matt, setting his menu aside, "what would you recommend?"

The others, prompted by their professor leading the way, set down their menus as well. And as they all set their attentions on her—their thoughts too, she realized—she blushed. Words failed her. They were cute, the lot of them—not as cute as her dearly departed Nasha, but no one was—and their lingering gazes (and thoughts) warmed her to her core. It was only a gentle hand on her shoulder that broke her from her panic—a gentle hand attached to a person who brought no thoughts with her. The gentle hand of her only true friend in the world: Ada.

"How's everyone doing tonight?" asked Ada, smiling down at the lot of them.

"Just fine," said Uncle Matt, offering up a smile of his own. Then he raised an eyebrow. "Have we met?" he asked. "You look wicked familiar."

Ada shook her head. "So," she said, "do you all know what you'd like?"

The youngest fellow in their company, a stout psychology major, sat up straight as he spoke, and tried to make himself seem taller than he was. He told Ada that they'd just been asking Belinda for her recommendations—told her this as an interior dialogue broke out in his head over the advisability of sneaking a peek, for even just a second, at Ada's ample bosom.

"Well," said Ada, "you can't go wrong with the Sister's Swill— that's our own IPA—but if you're feeling adventurous, there's always the Caffeine Coffin."

Belinda smiled. "I can vouch for that," she said. "It's a concoction of our estimable barkeep's own creation."

"What's in it?" asked the art student among them, a bearded heathen who'd made his money drawing commissions of humanoid animals in various states of undress.

Ada grinned mischievously. "Kahlua and a shot of extra dark espresso, mixed with a Canterbury dark beer."

Across the table, Uncle Matt nodded and chuckled. "Who needs sleep? Am I right?" He thumped the student sitting closest to him, a lithe gay kid who was pursuing Matt as steadily as he was pursuing his business degree. "I'll take one of those," Matt told Ada. "Anyone else?"

The boys declined and ordered a Sister's Swill each, while

Belinda went in for her standard tequila sunrise. But before Ada left to fill their orders, Belinda gave a gentle squeeze of her friend's wrist and asked if someone had called out, if that's why she was waiting tables and not behind the bar.

"Saw you come in," said Ada, giving Belinda a squeeze back. "Thought I'd say hi." And then she was off.

۞

LATER, while she danced with the Psych Major and the Art Student in turn, Belinda couldn't help but cast the occasional protective glance over at her uncle. Matt looked like had fallen into a blissful sleep. He was slouched back into the cushions of the booth's bench seat, with his eyes closed and one arm around the shoulders of Business Kid. Business Kid, meanwhile, had a pained look on his face. Pressed against the body of his professor, his nose nuzzled into Matt's armpit, Business Kid was a young man torn between lust and good sense. Thanks to the veritable castle of empties strewn across their table, he had finally acquired the company he'd been pursuing for four years of college. And yet, as much as his lascivious lizard brain wanted him to take advantage of the situation, Business Kid knew in his gut that he was no rapist. He could not and *would* not assault his inebriated professor. Nope. Not him. Not gonna happen. He kept his hands planted firmly on the table to make sure of it.

But Belinda saw the kid's fingers drumming out patterns, over and over again, and she didn't know how long his resolve would hold—so she kept an eye on the pair of them, just to be safe.

Soon enough, bewildered by the combination of the friend they swore was seconds from giving their professor a hand job and the girl who wasn't going home with either of them—no matter how well they defied the stereotype about the kinesthetic capabilities of the average white boy—the Psych Major and the Art Student said their goodbyes.

Belinda made her way back to the booth and searched the empties for a swig of something. Sure, she didn't have to pay for drinks here, but the place was hopping and she didn't want to try and flag down Ada in the middle of this chaos. She was parched, yes, but she wasn't *dying*.

"We just about done?" asked Belinda, still searching for something to sip on.

"I don't know," said Business Kid, sounding terribly depressed.

Belinda rolled her eyes at him. "He's out," she said.

Business Kid slid his pint glass toward Belinda. It was empty except for ice cubes, but ice cubes would do. They would work.

The two of them people-watched for a minute, a blissful sixty seconds of silence, before Business Kid pitched an idea Belinda's way.

"You ever seen *Wonder Boys*?" he asked. "The one about the writing professor, his agent, and his eccentric student?"

Belinda nodded. "Writers gone wild," she said. "In Pittsburgh, of all places."

Business Kid nodded back. "You've seen it then?"

She had, and she knew where he was going with this, but she was tired and she let him. She let him go there, and she let him explain—about the protagonists' drunken night at a dive bar, about the scar-faced pompadoured Vernon Hardapple, the game of telling a story about a stranger, and all of it. Business Kid didn't need to know that a game like this against a girl like Belinda was rigged, that she could read someone's mind from across a room. And he didn't need to know that once upon a time she'd played this game with her uncle on the regular—and that she'd always beaten him.

"Winner's the one who can keep a straight face for the longest," she said, making her only contribution to the conversation.

He nodded. "You first."

She let her mind reach out to find someone in the crowd who would have a laugh at their game if they found out about it, someone who could take a joke and wouldn't mind a couple of college kids fucking with them. The person she settled on was a jovial chap who'd set up shop at the bar and was talking Ada's ear off by the looks of it.

"Him," said Belinda, pointing.

Business Kid squinted, having taken off his glasses earlier to see if that would make Matt give him more of a chance. "The guy with the mullet?" he said.

Belinda scoffed. "It's not a mullet," she said, though she was unsure at this distance. "He's just sweaty. It's all slicked back."

Business Kid laughed. "Whatevs," he said. "You go first."

Belinda debated for a second about whether to go with truth or something more absurd. The truth was the guy was a trucker. They were unloading his rig right now over at the Market Basket downtown, and he was taking a well-deserved break before he got himself back on the long and lonesome highway for the next leg of his journey.

"He's a bassist," she said, "for a metal band."

"Nah," said Business Kid. "Everyone in your stories is a musician or an artist."

"Fine," said Belinda. "He's a hunter."

"Likes to use a bow and arrow," said Business Kid, nodding. "No guns for him."

Belinda nodded, though she knew the guy was packing right now—a tiny pistol tucked away inside one of the many pockets of his enormous jean jacket—then she added "He lost half a foot to a hyena on his first trip to Africa."

"Fellated his way across the country in the 70s," said Business Kid, "back when hitchhiking was still a thing."

"But he's married now," said Belinda. "To a woman."

"And he's never told her."

"But she suspects, especially on Sundays, when..."

"When he'll watch football all day, but always change the channel before the postgame interviews—"

"Because," said the apparently not-so-sleepy Matt, "he loves the look of a tight end, but he can't handle the sight of their pretty little mouths."

Belinda and Business Kid looked at each other from either side of their slumbering professor's body, trying to decide whether a laugh was in order or some other kind of reaction altogether.

"I gotta piss," said Matt, blinking his eyes as he sat up straight for the first time in a good, long while. "Then one of you has got to drive me home."

❦

IN THE PARKING LOT, buffeted by rough March winds, Belinda fumbled with the keys to Uncle Matt's car. Already slumped against the old shitbox, with Business Kid doing his best to hold him upright, Matt was gesturing wordlessly—trying to tell Belinda something. She looked into his mind to see what it was he was trying to say, but things were pretty jumbled up there.

"I'm freezing my balls off," whimpered Business Kid. "Do you want me to try?"

Belinda looked over her shoulder at the two of them, about to say something about how she had no hope of holding her tall, musclebound uncle aloft, but then she caught sight of something back by the entrance to the pub. Ada was standing there with the door ajar, staring at them. Belinda gave an exaggerated shrug in that direction, hoping the message would travel clearly across the distance, and was pleased when Ada nodded, waved, and then stepped back inside.

Finally, Belinda found the right key. But as she plunged it into the lock, she heard someone thinking nearby—someone new—and what the thinker was thinking was this: "Whose car is she driving?"

"Are we gonna play out the whole fucking movie now?" said Belinda aloud.

"Huh?" said Business Kid, looking about for who Belinda might be talking to—all the while wondering if he'd done something to make her think he was still on his *Wonder Boys* kick from earlier.

Then Captain Mullet stepped into the light of the nearby streetlamp, twirling his own set of keys around a finger. "Everything all right here?" he asked.

"It's my..." she began to say, before cutting herself off. "It's his," she said, pointing to Matt.

Captain Mullet laughed. "Not what I asked," he said with a chuckle. "But okay. I mostly just wanted to make sure y'all were good to drive."

"Why?" said Business Kid, putting on his most flirtatious voice. "You wanna take us for a ride?"

Captain Mullet laughed again, shook his head at the two men, and then returned his attention to Belinda. "You good, sweetheart?" he asked. And when she nodded, he gave the hood of the car two gentle knocks and was off—with a final tip of his cap, of course.

❦

IN THE CAR, on the way back to Uncle Matt's house on campus, Belinda and Business Kid shot the shit. Business Kid wanted to know if Belinda had heard about the play Matt had going up this weekend. She wanted to know if he thought she was an idiot, or that her ears were clogged, because how could anyone who'd been in Matt's class this semester *not* know that *The Boot* had just premiered?

"You're so delightfully bitchy," said Business Kid.

Belinda said nothing in reply. She just kept her eyes on the road, easing into a stop. Then she flipped on her blinker, signaling her intent to make a right onto South Main. She said nothing because she could hear in her head the thought and the feeling behind Business Kid's jab: he was *jealous*. He only wished he could be as assertive as she was, as sure of himself.

The light changed, Belinda turned them onto South Main Street, and soon enough they were crossing over the bridge and the churning river which divided working class Haverhill from the hilly haven of Bradford.

Business Kid fiddled with the radio, unable to bear the silence —even when Belinda reminded him that they were almost there.

"Do you really think it's going to bomb?" asked Business Kid. "His play, I mean. I mean, could it really be that bad?"

Uncle Matt mumbled something from the back seat, then feigned a crying fit.

Belinda wasn't sure what to say. She didn't know how this reality's version of *The Boot* would compare with the one she grew up with, back before her world ended. The story of their family's fall from grace, even if it was a temporary fall, was a remarkable tale. And the sheer visceral terror of watching a ghost impregnate the heroine on stage—the very willing heroine, it turned out—how could that not arrest the attention of any theater-goer, even the bluest of the blue-hairs?

"I guess it could be," said Business Kid. "Bad, that is."

Belinda nodded absentmindedly.

"It's just," said Business Kid, "he seems so good." And then, in a moment of sheer honesty—with none of the artifice he'd worn all evening—he added, "Matt's the best professor I've ever had."

As she pulled the car past the college and up to the corner of Kingsbury Avenue, Belinda took a moment to turn to Business Kid and give him a smile. "Best teacher I've ever had, too," she said, nodding. Then, checking to make sure there was no oncoming traffic, she spun the steering wheel and made the left turn.

AFTER THEY'D LAID Uncle Matt out on the divan in his parlor, after they'd left the keys on the coffee table, Belinda walked Business Kid back to his dorm across the street. He was living in one of the old Cluster Houses, ramshackle cottages built in the 1970s as temporary housing, a quintet of structures that should've been torn down a decade ago—and which had been, in the version of reality Belinda had grown up in, in the version of reality where the college had a different name and had closed a few months into the year 2000.

"Where are you living?" Business Kid finally thought to ask, once they'd made it to his threshold.

Belinda jerked a thumb in the direction of the river—in the direction of the Strumpet's Sister—and said that she had a place downtown.

"With roommates?" asked Business Kid. "Or are your parents just *that* rich?"

Belinda laughed. "Do I look like a trust-funder?"

Business Kid shrugged. "You wanna crash?" he said, as he unlocked the door. "We've got a couch upstairs that's free."

Belinda shook her head. "Nah," she said. "Besides, I could use the walk."

Business Kid shivered. "It's pretty fucking brisk," he said.

"I'll be alright," said Belinda, answering the question he'd been thinking of asking but hadn't.

৩৯৫

AS SHE WALKED the Main Street Bridge—the Merrimack heading eastward beneath her and flowing toward the sea—Belinda thought of the story Uncle Matt had assigned for them to read at the end of that afternoon's class, a yarn by the old man who had founded the college's creative writing program back in the 1960s and 70s. Part of the story was set on this very bridge. Part of it followed the long and lonely walk home of a townie turned murderer, a kid beaten down by a world that had little use for him —a kid who had lashed out with his pain and done something unspeakable.

Belinda thought of the things *she* had done because of her own pain.

At the other end of the bridge, she took a moment to stare over into the Market Basket parking lot and look for Captain Mullet's big rig. She wasn't sure why—was she going to run over there and apologize for the game she and Business Kid had played?—but it didn't matter; there was no truck nor trailer to be found. So she turned left instead, heading back downtown, back toward the Sister.

She hoped Ada would still be awake, once she got back, so there'd be someone to talk to. Ada didn't *need* to sleep—no ghost did—but sometimes she liked to let herself drift off, back toward oblivion or heaven or whatever else comes next. And it was impossible to stir her from her slumber when she pulled that trick.

Ada had kept Belinda company for nearly a hundred and twenty years now—first as the most reliable person on the Sister's waitstaff, and now as the barkeep herself—and she had always been a shoulder to cry on, despite the history of bad blood between Ada's family and Belinda's own.

From the arrival of the Silver family in 1620 upon the shores of Cape Cod, they and their fellow Europeans had caused nothing but grief for Ada's people—her mother's people, at least, who had called that place home for millennia. And though the families sometimes went a century without causing each other any direct harm, that all came to an end in the 1890s when Ada met and married Belinda's great-great-grandfather. The things Ada had suffered at the hands of Silas Silver—it was a wonder she could ever forgive them, and yet she seemed to have done just that.

They would talk for hours and hours sometimes, after Ada had closed up the bar for the night and Belinda was done with her business upstairs. It had begun with Belinda's acknowledgement of the wrongs her family had done, yes, but it had grown so much since then. Sure, they still spent an inordinate amount of time staring at the family tree Belinda had drawn up to prove the point that, though there were rotten apples everywhere, there was fresh fruit too—people who could still be saved and turned toward the path of righteousness. But they also talked about philosophy and art and whether the Bee Gees and their brother Andy were secretly the Four Horsemen of the Apocalypse.

And they talked about Belinda and Nasha, of course, and the House of Thrones that Belinda was building one chair at a time on the upper floors of the Sister. They talked about the ruthlessness it took to keep the universe from falling apart.

Lately, they talked a lot about what Belinda had done to Nasha's mother.

As she drew nearer and nearer to the Sister, Belinda wondered where they'd start their chat tonight. Would Ada listen to the tale of Uncle Matt and his worry about *The Boot*, or would that be too sensitive a topic? The play was about Ada, after all—about Ada's murder, in particular. Sure: it was Uncle Matt's own way of trying to reconcile with the horrors of their family's past, but Ada didn't know Matt. Would she care how much he was torturing himself over whether the play did Ada justice? Belinda doubted it. Ada had a soft spot for Belinda, but still didn't care much for her kin.

It was only once she'd reached the Sister's small parking lot that Belinda could sense that something was wrong.

At the doorway to the place stood a woman she'd seen Ada talk to every once in a while, a punk-looking chick who had no thoughts for Belinda to read—another ghost, it seemed. And she was waving her arms like a manic pixie, with tears streaking mascara down across her cheeks and onto her chin.

Belinda picked up the pace, dashing toward the bar to see what was the matter.

"She's gone," said the pixie. "She... she used me."

"Who's gone?" said Belinda, taking hold of the pixie by the shoulders to try and steady her. "Who used you?"

"Ada," said the pixie, in between sobs. "She finally did it. She finally escaped."

❧ 2 ❧

TRACY

When Tracy woke in the middle of that most fateful night, there was a person standing at her window. A naked person, it turned out, and not the naked person she might've expected to find there. *He* was still asleep in the bed beside her—she glanced over, just to be sure—and that meant that the naked person by her window just then was a different naked person altogether. Which, when you added Tracy to the mix, meant that there were *three* naked people in her room right now. And while she might be 18, Tracy still felt entirely too young for her first ménage à trois. After all, she was still getting the hang of the ménage à *deux*. So she scooted to the edge of her four-poster and said "Hello?"—because she needed to get this party started, and to make sure that whatever was happening here didn't get any kinkier than it was already.

The woman turned to face Tracy, bare but for a few splotches of dried mud on her legs and a blood-soaked scarf wrapped tight around her throat. And with each step she took toward Tracy's bed, each step further into the light of Tracy's Ravenclaw nightlight, the woman became a little more solid. A little more real.

"You know," said the woman, with a nod toward the boy asleep in Tracy's bed, "you can do better."

"Well, *yeah*," said Tracy. "I was a virgin like three days ago."

The woman smirked at Tracy's snark. "I meant that you can do better than him."

"I knew what you meant," said Tracy. Then she screwed up her face and asked the woman why she was naked.

"Why are *you* naked?" asked the woman.

"Because my life isn't rated PG-13," said Tracy.

The woman laughed. A bit too loudly, Tracy thought, given the situation. And yet: the boy in her bed did not stir, and there was no rush of motherly footsteps in the hall outside, so everything was going to be okay.

"For serious," said Tracy. "Why aren't you wearing anything?"

"My husband ruined my dress in his haste to bury me," said the woman. Then she ran her fingers along the fringe of the cloth tied round her thin neck. "All that was left was enough to hold together the two pieces he made of me."

Tracy saw now that this rough scrap of fabric was less a scarf than a tourniquet. It bound a neck torn open on one side, a neck covered in bruises from throat to nape.

So this one had been murdered, Tracy realized. *That* was new.

"Could you wear something of mine?" she asked the woman. "If I gave it to you?"

"I could wear anything I wanted," said the woman. "I'm no ghost," she said. "I am memory made flesh."

Tracy nodded at the phrase she'd heard half a dozen times before, from half a dozen happy haunts. Then she sighed. She sighed, uttered an exasperated "yeah-huh," and made her way to her dresser. It all made sense now. A couple of days before, she'd used an old family secret to unlock a door she shouldn't have opened. Tracy realized now that she must've forgotten, once again, to shut it tight behind her.

Tracy, she could hear her mothers saying, *do we live in a barn?*

No, but they did *own* a barn. And their dumb ancestors, those positively pea-brained pilgrims, had built it atop an ancient burial ground.

Tracy eyed the woman one more time, calculating, and then nodded. They were about the same size, Tracy decided, so she opened the third drawer down. That was where she kept old concert tees of her mothers, vintage gold that Des had begged Mom to toss after reading one too many books about minimalism.

Mom had hidden them in Tracy's room instead.

Tracy balled up a shirt and tossed it to her guest. The woman shook it out and examined the graphic on the front. "This skeleton," she said, "the chair that he's sitting in. Is that—?"

"He's riding the lightning," said Tracy, stepping into a pair of clean underwear.

"Oh," said the woman.

"Does it fit?" asked Tracy, as she pulled on a t-shirt of her own. "My mom's tall," she said. "Her t-shirts are like night gowns on anyone else."

The woman pulled the worn black garment over her head and Tracy watched it cascade over shoulders and then breasts, stomach and then hips. The woman tugged gently at the hem, reached a hand around back to see if it was covering her behind, and then—seemingly satisfied—said "Yes. This will do nicely."

"Keep it," Tracy told her.

"Why thank you," said the woman. Then she blushed and extended a hand. "But we've forgotten to introduce ourselves," she said. "How rude of us."

They laughed. Then they shook hands. Tracy gave her name, then the woman gave hers.

And it was a name Tracy was *not* ready to hear.

"Not *the* Ada?" said Tracy, as they let go of each other's hands.

Ada nodded as she said, "The very same."

❧

THE GHOSTS who had visited Tracy before had been dead and gone long before her colonizing ancestors had driven the People of the Dawn, the *Wampanoag*, toward their dusk. But this woman, she had lived here on this land little more than a century ago. In the dilapidated Victorian cottage that once stood on this very spot.

"You were," said Tracy, and she held a hand to forehead now to try and steady her thoughts, "one of my great-great-grandfather's seven wives."

"Indeed I was," said Ada.

"This is nuts," said Tracy, shaking her head as if to tell herself *nah, nope, this can't be*, except that it was, yep, for sure. "The potion that makes all my shenanigans possible—"

"Yes?" said Ada.

"It came out of *your* journal."

෴

ONCE IT HAD BEEN a sacred recipe—a cherished secret of Ada's mother, and her mother before her. But in 1892, unable to provide an heir for the husband who'd tried and failed with three wives before her, Ada had defiled her ancestors' once taintless tonic. It would no longer suffice to revisit her own past, which was all the concoction had been conceived to do. No. Her predicament called for more drastic measures. And so she fiddled and fiddled until she'd found a way to delve into the past of another.

"Do you know," Ada asked Tracy, "what your great-great-grandfather wanted, more than anything else in the world?"

Tracy laughed. "Kinda obvious," she said. "To have a kid, right?"

Ada shook her head. "No," she said. "That's what his *mother* wanted. What Silas wanted more than anything else in the world was a mother who loved him as much as his father had."

Tracy scoffed. "His father drowned at sea the year Silas was born."

"Indeed," said Ada with a nod. "But Silas felt *sure* his father had loved him. I'm not sure *how*, but he did. And he never felt sure about *anything* with his mother, least of all when it came to matters of love."

"So he wanted a kid," said Tracy, scratching at the top of her head, "because his mother wanted him to have a kid?"

Ada nodded. "It was her dying wish."

"Dying!" said Tracy, and she was scoffing again. "*Exactly*. She was dead before he even started trying. So what the hell was she going to care?"

"Wouldn't you do anything for *your* mother?" asked Ada.

Yes, thought Tracy. She'd do anything for either of her mothers: the one who gave birth to her, or the one who'd learned to love her despite the fact that Tracy's very existence had trapped Mom in a loveless marriage to a glorified sperm donor for years.

A loveless marriage which ended only when Tracy used Ada's potion to force the issue. She'd slipped it into Mom's evening tea one night, and the next morning—after a "dream" she described as one part *A Christmas Carol* and two parts *It's a Wonderful Life*— Mom decided it was high time to cut the crap and be with Des once and for all.

"Tracy?" said Ada.

"The first time I used your potion," she said, "it was to get my mothers together."

"Your mothers?" said Ada, raising an eyebrow. "Plural?"

Tracy nodded. "Welcome to the twenty-first century."

"And you're the only child?" asked Ada.

"The only child in the whole family," she said, "if you can believe that."

Ada held a hand to her chest. "That can't be true," she said. "Can it?"

Tracy nodded. "Uncle Matt is gay too, Auntie Ashley got her tubes tied the second they'd legally let her, and Uncle Michael..."

"What about Uncle Michael?" said Ada.

When you got right down to it, Uncle Michael was the reason this whole night was happening. It'd been for his sake that Tracy had opened the door that Ada snuck through.

Uncle Michael had been a father figure to Tracy for most of her life, but last year she'd uncovered some pretty unsavory secrets about him, and that had kinda pissed her off. So she'd decided to use Ada's potion again, this time to put her uncle on trial for his "crimes against femininity."

Ugh. Even just two days removed from uttering that phrase out loud, Tracy couldn't believe she'd ever said it. She couldn't believe she'd said or done *most* of what she'd done that night.

"Tracy?" said Ada.

"He's infertile," said Tracy. "We've all known that for a while, but I saw something last year that made me a bit unsure. Made me think he was *lying*, in fact."

"But he isn't?" said Ada. "He wasn't?"

Tracy shook her head. "No," said Tracy. "The baby I thought was his—it wasn't. They even did a test to be sure."

"Well," said Ada, "thank goodness for that."

Tracy frowned. "Him being infertile is *not* a good thing," she said. "He's always been like a father to me. And he would be a *great* dad to his own kids if he could have them."

Ada waved a pair of dismissive hands. "Oh," she said. "I meant no offense. I meant to say 'thank goodness' that he hadn't lied to you."

"Oh," said Tracy.

"I can see how much he means to you," she said.

"And I can see now what you meant about Silas and his mother," said Tracy. "But what I'm still wondering about is this newer version of your potion—the one I used to call the witnesses for Michael's trial, and the one that *you* used to call..."

Tracy trailed off. This part of the story about Ada was the part she'd always had the hardest time with—even now, after she'd called a bunch of people back from the dead herself.

"You have to remember," said Ada, "that I was desperate."

"I can understand desperate," said Tracy. "But don't you think that what you did went a little too far?"

What Ada had done, it turned out, was develop a version of the potion that could bring a person out of a memory and back into the real world. And all it took was a little bit of the person in question. In Ada's case, that was seven flakes scraped from the insole of a boot she'd disinterred from beneath her kitchen's floorboards.

"Was it really his father's boot?" said Tracy.

Ada nodded. "The man who walked out of the maelstrom and into our parlor that night was the spitting image of my beloved, and Silas was struck dumb by the sight. He just couldn't believe it: his father, right before his eyes. In the flesh."

"In nothing *but* the flesh," said Tracy. "Or so I've been told."

Ada shook her head. "The clothes he wore were in tatters," she said, "but he *was* clothed."

"Until you *un*clothed him," said Tracy, and she shuddered at the thought.

"My Silas," said Ada, "like your Uncle Michael, was a barren tree—or at least he seemed to be at the time. And so, if what was needed was an heir, a Silver to continue the line—if that was the only thing that would ever let him rest—then how could I *not* do what I did?"

"And after it was over," said Tracy. "Are the stories true?"

"Yes," said Ada. Then she stepped back toward the window. "Your great-great-grandfather—my great, great love—he..."

But she couldn't finish the sentence, for she was interrupted by a sob that rose unbidden from the deepest parts of her. And though she struggled to choke it back, that battle was all for naught.

"He was so horrified by what you had done that he killed you," said Tracy, shaking her head. "And he got away with it."

"Yes," said Ada, and it was *that* truth which drove the sadness from the woman's face and replaced it with rage.

Tracy raged with her, so angry at what her own flesh and blood was capable of—no matter how odd and off-putting the circumstances—that she didn't catch Ada pushing the window open until it was too late.

"Yes," said Ada once more, "he got away with it, but his family most certainly will *not*."

"What do you mean?" said Tracy. But even as she asked the question, the cold truth of the matter sent a shiver down her spine. This woman was here to kill her, to kill them all.

But then: why was she headed for the window?

Ada smiled at Tracy, and never before had there been such hate in a set of upturned lips. "You just wait and see," said Ada. Then she leapt from the window and she was gone.

৩৫

TWO DAYS LATER, Ada's first strike against them made the front page of the *Globe*.

"Poor Tony," said Tracy's mothers as the three of them read the paper together that morning, crouched together around the kitchen table.

When her great-great-grandfather finally *did* have kids, he had two. But one of them, Silas' wild stallion of a daughter, had died at the age of 29. And everyone always kinda-sorta forgot that one of the crazy things she got up to before she was gone was getting herself good and knocked up. And though her son had passed on a couple of years ago now, he'd had a son of his own.

That son, Tony, though single, was still ready to mingle. Which got Tracy thinking: maybe the reason Ada went after Tony was the same reason she'd skipped over Michael and Ashley and

Matt and Mom. Ada didn't want to kill anyone she didn't have to. She just wanted to put an end to what she saw as her great love's most poisonous dream.

"The line of Silas Silver," said Tracy, "has to end."

Her mothers asked her what she was talking about, and she explained. But then they asked her a follow-up question that she had no answer for at all.

"But if that's true," they said, "if Ada's trying to kill any Silver who might still have kids, then why didn't she kill you?"

"What?" said Tracy.

"She was in your room, Trace. You could still have kids. So why didn't she kill *you?*"

⚜

YEARS PASSED, as years do. And though Ada didn't kill anyone else after Tony, Tracy couldn't stop wondering why she'd been spared. It was the worst when she got close to someone, of course. So she broke off every relationship she had before there was a chance for it to get serious. Every. Single. One.

Until finally she couldn't, because she was in love—and the dude she was in love with was too stubborn to let her deny it.

"Let her just *try* to come and get us," said the man Tracy would marry. "Let her just *try*."

⚜

THEY WERE RIDING from church to reception, Tracy and the man who'd fallen from the sky to flirt with her, when a pedestrian leapt from the sidewalk and into the path of their limousine.

As the car veered through two lanes of traffic on its way to a collision with the Jersey barrier, Tracy squeezed Kanoa's hand. Kanoa—that was what her man was called. Kanoa. *The free one.*

The freest spirit she'd ever known. Free enough to fall from the heavens. For her.

The limo's front end crunched into the barrier, and their coach smashed apart like the pumpkin it truly was—all of its magic gone.

To be honest, Kanoa had fallen from a coconut tree and not from the sky. He leapt down from the *kumu niu* he'd been climbing to impress the men of a local *hālau*. And impress them he had, climbing higher than any man before him. But then he saw Tracy. And even as the men below him shouted instructions for some final task, he could not help but stare at the *malihini* with the reddened shoulders and the puzzled expression and the map she thumbed at on her too-big phone.

Tracy lit such a fire in him that he could have danced a hula for her right then and there, a performance that might make Pele proud. So, was it really wrong to say that he fell from the sky? Wrong to describe something so epically when what he'd felt was so epic? Tracy's professors had dubbed her the *Hōkū* of Hyperbole. But when you spoke of a man with the mind of da Vinci in the body of Dwayne Johnson, wasn't exaggeration necessary? Or maybe even demanded?

As the car collapsed like an accordion, Tracy locked her gaze on the shoulder just visible through Kanoa's open collar—the shoulder where, a few weeks from now, the top edge of a tribal tattoo would finally be inked onto and into his flesh. It was going to be Tracy's wedding gift to him. She'd saved the money. She'd called the guy. It was all but done.

And she'd been just about to tell him when they'd started making out—when she'd slipped her fingers up into his hair and made him melt into her.

Each night she'd slept in his bed, from the first night until last night, he told her about another shape or pattern he'd imagined for his tattoo. And he told her what each marking would mean, too—mean to him, at least. The Maori spiral, the shark teeth of

Samoa, and the turtles of course! He told her which turtles would be *'aumākua* and which would be merely *honu*, and he delighted as she traced her fingers over the places where she imagined each line and every detail. He delighted in both body *and* soul. He knew from early on that Tracy wasn't some tourist collecting souvenirs to take home to the mainland. The books he read to her, the body he sculpted in the *hālau*, the stories he would one day have inked onto his skin—she cared about it all. She cared about *him*.

She loved him, this beautiful man.

This beautiful man whose skin blanched as they rose into the air.

Tracy held him close, held on as hard as she could for as long as she could—but then gravity won out. His body was torn from her, torn from her arms at the same time a huge chunk of glass tore his head from his shoulders.

When the car, completely upended now, finally skidded to halt, Tracy peered out from the broken window to see if the pedestrian was hurt. And what she saw would forever haunt her: a pale woman wearing an oversized Metallica t-shirt as a dress, with a scrap of bloody fabric tied tight around her neck.

Ada lingered long enough for Tracy to see her shake her head, and then she fled.

෯෴෯

AT THE FUNERAL, Ada was amongst the mourners—but Tracy was too shocked to make a scene. Too worried, too. Though it seemed like everyone else was out of danger, Tracy worried that if she pointed Ada out to her mothers—or any of her other relatives, for that matter—then the vengeful woman might change her mind about sparing them. So Tracy begged everyone to give her a moment to thank this "co-worker of hers," who couldn't come to the gathering back at the house, for her condolences. And it was only once they were all out of earshot that she asked Ada to say her piece.

"I know what you're thinking of doing," said Ada. "I can see it in your eyes, now that you've taken off those ridiculous sunglasses. And I don't blame you," said Ada. "I don't. But I'm telling you now, Tracy: if you bring him back, I *will* kill him again."

"Why not kill me instead?"

"Because I owe you a debt," said Ada. "I couldn't have finished this business of mine without you."

"But I didn't *mean* to bring you back," said Tracy. "It was an accident."

"Nevertheless," said Ada.

"And what if I'm pregnant right now?" said Tracy. "What if the descendant of Silas Silver is growing in my womb right this second."

"Then I'll kill it," said Ada.

"And what if I meet someone new," said Tracy, "and he gets me pregnant?"

"You won't," said Ada.

"I won't?!" said Tracy, and she said it so loud that Uncle Michael took a step back toward her. Then another. Until Tracy waved him off.

"How do you know?" she asked Ada.

"Because you loved him," said Ada, nodding at the casket. "You loved him like you'll never love anyone else."

"Like you loved Silas?" said Tracy.

Ada nodded. "Like I loved Silas," she said, and then she was gone.

☙❧

IN THE WEEKS and months that followed, Tracy took to sitting in her car outside the fertility clinic. She and her husband—because he *was* her husband, even if they'd only been married for twenty minutes before he was taken from her—they had each left a little piece of themselves inside this building.

"Just in case we're really old and we suddenly change our minds about kids," they'd told anyone who offered a quizzical look when they learned that two completely healthy twenty-somethings had put a dozen eggs and half a cup of sperm on ice.

Tracy sat there, outside the building, considering her options. It would be easy enough to go in there, ask them to load up a turkey baster with all that was left of him, and just do the deed already. But did any child deserve the fate that Ada was promising, even if that child's mother could undo fate again and again?

Wouldn't it be better, Tracy wondered, if she just asked them to hand his spunk over to her instead, even if that was a request so ridiculous and so legally precarious that it required pulling every string in existence and greasing every freaking wheel? Because that's all it would take—just a little bit of him added to a potion she could make now with her eyes closed.

Her husband knew what he was getting into, at least. She'd warned him, and he'd stuck with her anyway. And Tracy felt certain that he'd stick with her to the end, if she brought him back—that even death would not shake his resolve. The only real question was whether Tracy could handle the pain of losing him a second time, and a third, and so on. But she'd done it once, and Tracy was pretty sure she could do it again.

And again.

❧ 3 ❧

BELINDA

B elinda first met Ada Coffin on the night that Ada was killed. Belinda was minding the store while Jakob, the old barkeep, went out to collect the recently departed soul. And though Belinda only caught a brief glimpse of Ada at first, as Ada and Jakob rushed through the place on some bit of business or other, it was enough of a gander to set fire to her imagination —and to keep her deep in thought until their return.

Ada was a buxom beauty in a bloody shirtwaist and a torn skirt. Her neck bore the telltale marks of strangulation, but her face remained unspoiled. And though the unkempt state of her hair might have been cause for a kerfuffle in the time from which she'd come, Ada's deconstructed coiffure would've been quite *en vogue* during the age in which Belinda had grown up.

By the time Jakob and Ada had returned, Belinda hungered to know more about where this woman had come from and what made her tick. And so, when Jakob asked Belinda if she minded taking Ada upstairs to find her some clean clothes, Belinda didn't hesitate. She didn't chide her subordinate for asking her to do what any old barmaid could do. No. Belinda simply took Ada by the hand and led her toward the staircase.

She looked shell-shocked, the poor thing, but Belinda didn't ask why—not yet. Instead she led the way in silence, not saying a word until they'd reached the landing on the second floor.

"It's a bit strange up here," warned Belinda, "but you get used to it." Then she pulled on the chain for the overhead lights.

Ada's jaw dropped. "What is this place?" she mumbled, stepping into the cavernous hall.

"The House of Thrones," said Belinda, gesturing at the mass of chairs she'd gathered over the centuries.

"Thrones?" said Ada, running a hand along the arm of a dainty thing made of mahogany and velvet.

"It's a long story," said Belinda, nodding in the direction of a far-off door. "Follow me."

They made their way through the door and into a chamber dominated by an enormous granite table. And though Belinda could sense another question coming from Ada, she didn't feel that the time was right to explain this room either—nor the annual card game she hosted here. Instead, she led the bewildered woman through the space and yet another door. And then, finally, she stopped.

"This is my room," said Belinda. "Now let's see what I can find you to wear."

Belinda threw open the doors of her wardrobe and began to search through it. It was only when she heard a heavy thud behind her that she was broken from her reverie. Then she turned on the spot to see what had happened.

"My belt," said Ada, as she stepped out of her skirt. "It's a heavy, old thing."

"Oh," said Belinda, startled. "But I haven't even found... and I could give you some priva—"

Ada laughed as she unbuttoned the front of her shirtwaist, then she hoisted the thing above her head and dropped it to the floor.

Embarrassed, Belinda turned round and returned to searching her wardrobe.

"Do you have somewhere to wash up?" asked Ada.

Belinda nodded in the direction of her bathroom. Out of the corner of her eye, she spied Ada—now quite naked—sauntering past her. For a moment, she seemed quite comfortable with her new reality—this *un*reality of being *un*dead—but then, just as suddenly as she'd disrobed, Ada was slumping to the floor.

She was a sobbing mess by the time Belinda reached her. Curled up in the fetal position, with her arms clutched around her knees, Ada wept and wept.

Belinda struggled with what to do with the weeping woman, where even to begin, but eventually she settled on taking a seat beside her on the floor. Belinda sat with her legs crisscross applesauce, then set a warm hand atop one of Ada's forearms.

Once Ada had found the strength to sit upright, the first question she asked Belinda was, "Are you dead too?"

Belinda shook her head. "Not quite."

The second thing she asked for was Belinda's name, which of course Belinda gave. And it was that answer which set their friendship on its steady course across the next century.

"Silver?" said Ada, her crying ceasing altogether for the first time. "Your last name is Silver?"

Belinda nodded.

"Well, I'll be damned."

৩১৫৩

IT WAS this first meeting that Belinda thought about as she sat under the graduation tent, waiting for the name "Belinda Michaelson" to be called. It was this revelation of her true name that she found herself thinking about as she made her way to the edge of the dais—just one part of a neat line of smiling twenty-somethings.

It was this memory which was thrown into sharp relief when she spotted Ada in the crowd.

Belinda blanched, a cold sweat breaking out beneath her regalia. She didn't know why Ada was there, but there could be no good reason for it. She'd already killed two people, and though she seemed unlikely to try and hurt anyone in the middle of a crowd of this size, Ada also seemed determined to exact her revenge no matter the cost.

And yet, it wasn't Belinda herself that Ada was focused on. It was someone else, someone seated in the faculty section. And Belinda didn't have to think twice about who the target of Ada's death stare might be. She shuddered to think about it, but it seemed a certainty that Ada was here for Uncle Matt.

As Belinda stepped forward in line, she wondered why. Ada knew that Matt was gay, and that he had no desire for kids of his own. She'd left him alone for four years because of that, because he would be no threat to her plans. So what had changed?

Ada caught Belinda staring and tugged a worn and folded piece of butcher's paper from inside her coat. Then she hid it away again, just as quickly as she'd made it appear in the first place.

Belinda nodded in recognition, stepping forward again—at the edge of the dais now, and about to be called to the stage. Ada's secret document was the family tree Belinda had drawn up and kept in her room, a chart of how the Silver Family had branched out and grown in the reality she'd come from. It had hung over her bed for ages and ages, until the night Ada disappeared, but it had never proven especially useful in predicting how things would turn out in this new version of the universe—and Ada knew that.

"Belinda Michaelson" said the announcer, their voice booming through the tent before it was drowned out by a roar of applause —none of it louder than the clapping coming from Uncle Matt, who still thought he was celebrating a mere student and not the sole surviving member of a family he'd never known he had.

Belinda took the steps of the dais carefully, one at a time, trying to slow the pace of her racing heart. She shook hands with the college's president and took her diploma from him. Then she paused for the flash of a camera, as she'd been instructed to do. But by the time she reached the other side of the platform and was ready to make her descent, she nearly tripped over her own feet and had to reach for the handrail to steady herself. She'd caught sight of Uncle Matt in the crowd on that side of the stage. He was giving her a standing ovation. And though she tried hard to focus on both him and where she was going, it was all too much in the moment.

Because, in the moment of course, she was also thinking about whether this moment might be the last. Once she'd saved herself from the fall, she looked out to see if she could spot Ada, but her old friend had disappeared.

BACK IN THE DAY, back in the bar, Belinda taught Ada how to play cards. That was how they passed the time, the same way Belinda and her mother had done in the years after Dad had moved them to the White Mountains for their safety. And though Belinda found it a struggle to break down the basics of a game she had mastered when she was barely ten years old, Ada was a quick study. She picked up on what Belinda was putting down in fairly short order—and she had the best poker face Belinda had ever seen, a control over her expressions mastered during her years as a brothel worker.

While they played, Belinda regaled Ada with tales of a universe where superheroes had been real—and her father had been one of them. Ada, for her part, told stories of growing up in the Faith of the First Mother—a religious order centered on the worship of a divine feminine energy which flowed from mother to daughter all the way back to "the mother of us all." She spoke too of the potion her mother had taught her to make, an elixir which could unstick a person in time and allow them to confront the ghosts of their past.

"That's come down through the generations, too," said Ada, "though I've never been sure if someone in the Faith invented it, or if it was of Wampanoag design."

Belinda's eyes brightened at the mere mention of the name. She asked if both Ada's parents were native people, or just one.

"My mother," Ada told her. Then she asked Belinda about her own ancestry.

This is where the hand-drawn tree came out, the life's work she'd spent many lifetimes picking away at. As Belinda unfolded that well-worn sheet of butcher's paper, she explained that it wasn't *exactly* the same as the tree she saw playing out in this new version of reality, but that they matched each other in broad strokes.

"Where I come from," said Belinda, "there's still the long, unbroken line of Silases. But there's an extra, a tenth Silas that your reality never got."

Ada scoffed. "And which of the ninth Silas' wives gave the child to him? It wasn't me, was it?"

Belinda shook her head. "He never married you, not where I come from. He married Tamson," said Belinda, pointing at the ornamented line she'd drawn between the two. "Yep," she said, "he married her, and they had Silas X, and that was that."

"Was he any happier for it?" asked Ada, running a hand along the smooth paper, stroking a thumb across Silas IX's name—as if she might smudge it out of existence, though Belinda hadn't noticed that at the time.

"Happier for what?" asked Belinda.

"Marrying his one true love?"

Belinda shook her head. "No," she said. "He was still a right, old bastard."

"Did he live to be a hundred?" asked Ada, turning her attention away from the family tree now and staring off into the middle distance. "Like he did here?"

"No," said Belinda. "Killed himself after his only granddaughter—his favorite grandchild—died of septicemia."

"Septicemia?"

Belinda nodded. "Blood poisoning. She got it from giving herself an abortion, since she had no place else to go."

Ada returned her gaze to the family tree. "Such a different story in some ways—"

"My parents can't get pregnant, for instance."

"—but so similar in others." Ada pointed at the box for Matthew Silver—Uncle Matt—and said "I see he married a man in your time. Will he do the same here, in mine?"

Belinda shrugged. "Hard to say. Though I watched how this whole universe will play out, as I struggled not to drown in the River Without End, my memories of what I saw are foggy at best."

Ada's finger followed the line downward from Uncle Matt and his husband to their child. "This was your cousin, yes?"

Belinda nodded.

"By blood?" asked Ada.

Belinda nodded again.

"And yet: Matthew has no children here, in the here and now."

Belinda shook her head. "No. Like I said, things are different. Sometimes subtly, sometimes not."

And it was here that Ada came to a most important question indeed—and that she finally looked Belinda straight in the eye. "Why?" she asked. "Why do things change?"

Belinda stood and walked to the window, staring out into the dark alley which ran beside the bar. "As near as I can tell," she began, "things change because of a kind of course correction."

"I don't follow," said Ada.

Belinda turned back to face Ada, realizing that she wasn't going to get any more clarity from looking out at the alley and the river than she already had. "You remember how I explained about the reason for reality's reboots?"

Ada nodded. "They happen when a time traveler breaks the cardinal rule that whatever happened happened."

Belinda nodded, sitting on the edge of the windowsill. "So, when reality begins again, things are changed in order to make the cardinal rule true once more. When Emily Henderson traveled backward to make sure that Christ was never cloned, as he was in the version of the universe I came from, reality had to be rewritten to account for the changes she made. All sorts of things had to be updated, including the family she'd been born into: the Silvers."

"It makes me wonder," said Ada.

"What?" asked Belinda. "What does it make you wonder?"

"Who was I, before the universe rewrote my story? Who would I have been, if I'd never met Silas Silver?"

AFTER THE DEGREES had all been handed out, after the president had offered his congratulations to the two-hundred and eleventh graduating class of Kimball College, and after Uncle Matt had hugged his prized student and told her to stay in touch, Belinda hurried out the back side of the tent to see if she could find Ada —to see if she could talk some sense into her.

She found her old friend by the campus chapel, a small nonde-nominational building that was all harsh angles and weathered wood. In front of the chapel stood a small garden, the highlight of which was a tree the ladies of the then-all-girls school had planted in honor of loves lost during World War II. Ada was staring at it, the tree, though she didn't seem particularly affected by the sight. If anything, judging by the foot she tapped against the cobbled stone she stood upon, she seemed impatient. She seemed to be sick of waiting.

"Are you here to kill him?" asked Belinda, getting straight to the point.

"I'd ask if he's seeing anyone, but in today's day and age that doesn't seem to matter. He could simply decide to raise one on his own."

"He has a wife," said Belinda, "though she doesn't have the necessary equipment."

"Excuse me?" said Ada, though she didn't bother to look at Belinda as she spoke.

"Matt's wife is trans," said Belinda. "She can't get pregnant."

"Well," said Ada, still staring at the tree, "thank heaven for small favors."

Belinda strode across the distance that still separated them, then grabbed Ada by the arm to demand her attention. And though there was a venom in Ada's eyes when she finally looked at Belinda, Belinda stood her ground and didn't let go.

"Your family is a plague," spat Ada, "a plague upon this green earth. It's a weed, a vine that will strangle anything it can wrap its slithering tendrils around."

"Then why not kill me too?" Belinda spat back. "Why leave me alive?"

Ada yanked her arm free. "The same reason I haven't killed the other one," she said. "I owe you a debt."

"The other one?" said Belinda, confused. "What debt do you owe Uncle Matt?"

Ada laughed as she stalked away toward Kingsbury Gate. "Not Matthew," she said. "Tracy."

"But you killed her husband!" said Belinda, chasing after her.

With a swipe of her hand, Ada tore a hole in the air in front of her. But before she stepped through the blaze of orange light that was the Veil of the World, she turned and reminded Belinda that while, yes, she *had* killed Tracy's precious Kanoa, she had left Tracy alone.

"So long as she doesn't dare to spoil your well-laid plans, right?"

Ada gave Belinda one last smile, one last wicked smirk, and then disappeared.

After Tracy called Kanoa back to her with the dark magic of Ada's potion, he liked to make her laugh by carrying his smiling head in a cradle made from his interlaced fingers—a pretty basket of pale flesh adorned only by the koa-wood ring she'd carved for him.

Then he got the idea to play *pala'ie* with it and asked Tracy to help. For the string, he took the laces off of the dress shoes he'd died in. For the handle, Tracy collected the midribs of coconut leaves and deboned them. It would have to be much bigger and sturdier, he told her, than what his ancestors would have made; they'd never used a severed head for the ball, after all.

"That you know of," she joked, and he smiled.

Finally, they tied everything together. They secured head to handle with the string he'd made, and he told Tracy to give it a try. She did, but she was no good at it. Kanoa, on the other hand, seemed to have the skill in his bones. Tracy came up with a system for scoring, but not because she had any hope of winning. No desire to, either. No, she started keeping score entirely for the sake of a pun.

Looking up from the paper where she'd scribbled down each point, she told him, "You're ahead of me."

He kept a straight face as he said, "No, I'm a head of myself."

Tracy laughed. "That was good," she said. And then, feeling there was still room for riffing, she decided to set him up for a knee-slapper. She sauntered over to him, swaying her hips as she did, and he stopped to watch her. He quit the game and tucked his head under his arm, as if he were a basketball player during a time out.

Tracy gave him a giggle, then said, "You're so sexy when you're funny."

"Oh yeah?" he said, his head checking her out from its new angle.

"Oh yeah," she said, unbuttoning his shirt. "So sexy."

"How sexy?" he said.

"Makes me want to drop to my knees and give you the best head you ever had."

"Better than this one?" he said. On the head that looked up at her from between his forearm and his ribs, he gave her his best impression of a *haka* face. His tongue spilled from his mouth as his eyes went wide.

"So much better," she said, struggling to keep a straight face as she unbuckled his belt, as she and his pants dropped to the floor.

It was only once she'd been working him for a couple of minutes that he thought to toss his head onto the mat behind her for a better view, a different perspective. She chuckled when she realized what he'd done, although it was an awkward sound with half his dick in her mouth. To save face—to reassure him that she was laughing *with* him and not *at* him—she hiked up her skirt and bounced her butt on her ankles. Not quite a twerk, but the best her silly white ass could manage.

We are so fucking weird, she thought. *Two fucking weirdos in love.*

�&🙙

WHEN THEY BOTHERED to venture out from the crude *hale* he'd built and hidden for them in the valley, Tracy and Kanoa went either to Tunnels Beach (for him to surf) or to a dive bar on the banks of the Wailua (for her to drink). Tracy sewed Kanoa's head back onto his neck, and he wore a tight choker of kukui nuts to keep the questions at bay. It used to be Tracy's, that choker, but no one gave him shit about it. You could tell just by looking at Kanoa that, if you gave him shit, you were going to get something far worse than shit in return.

When they went to the bar, Tracy would order one Midori Sour after another. Once she was drunk enough, she'd ask again about the nature of his renewed existence. Kanoa would sigh as always, telling her that he didn't know much more than she did— that he didn't know *anything* more than the last time she'd asked —and offer the same answer he always gave. The way Ada had phrased it, it turned out, was pretty damned accurate. The people Tracy brought back to this world from the world to come, they were memories made flesh. And, as memories, they were subject to the whims and desires of those who remembered them.

"But that's not entirely accurate," Tracy would say, shaking a finger at him. "Because, if you were subject to my whims and desires, you would tell me what I want to know."

"But," he said, gulping down the last of his own drink, "I know nothing that you don't. I'm *your* memory, after all."

"And, anyway," Tracy said this time, "Ada isn't like that. She has her own desires, the crazy bitch."

"Well," reasoned Kanoa, "she had to come from somewhere."

The waitress set another Midori Sour in front of Tracy, then placed a napkin in front of Kanoa.

"I didn't order—" Kanoa began, but before he could finish she had set a whiskey glass in front of him.

The waitress nodded into the shadows. "It's from her," she said. "A peace offering, apparently."

As the waitress took her leave, Tracy stared into the darkness.

Frighteningly, the darkness stared right back. And Tracy's jaw fell as her eyes adjusted to the light and caught sight of who it was that was sitting back there.

It was Ada.

Kanoa stood and said, "I'll take care of her," but Tracy grabbed hold of him before he could take another step, and she implored him to sit back down.

Ada swept out of the shadows, a trench coat over the ratty t-shirt she'd been wearing since the day Tracy gave it to her. She looked preposterous as she strode across the bar toward them, a bat fluttering through a flock of macaws. In her hand, she carried her own whiskey glass. She raised it and nodded at them as she sat.

"What do you want?" asked Kanoa.

"To share a drink," she said, still holding her glass aloft. "To whom shall we toast?"

When neither Tracy nor Kanoa raised their glass, Ada gave a curt "Hmm" and threw back her whiskey in one swallow. A healthy portion of it soaked through her scarf, so much that it began to trickle down her neck.

"My goodness," she said, plucking a napkin from the table's dispenser. "I'm such a klutz."

"What do you want?" asked Tracy.

Ada smiled as she balled up the napkin and set it on the table. "Don't blow your wig, Tracy."

Kanoa leaned across the table. "What," he said, "do you want?"

Ada's smile passed. She breathed in deep and sat back in her seat. Then she pointed at Tracy. "To watch her take the fall."

"For what?" said Tracy.

And now the smile came back. "For murder," she said.

"I'm not you," said Tracy.

Ada pointed at Kanoa's drink. "Are you going to?" she asked.

When he said nothing, she pulled his drink toward herself.

She downed it in one swallow, just like the last one, then wiped at her lips with her wrist. She paid no attention this time to the drink that dribbled from the gash in her neck.

"The only person I'm going to murder," said Tracy, "is you."

Now Ada laughed. "Oh," she said. "Darling, that is *exactly* my plan." Then she stood abruptly and headed toward the back of the room, toward an emergency exit off to the side of the bar itself.

Tracy ran after her. Kanoa ran after Tracy.

The door, it turned out, led to a back alley littered with broken tables and chairs. On one side, the alley ended at the street out front where they'd parked Tracy's jeep. On the other side, it ended at the river.

"There's a furniture store upstairs," Ada told them, holding a table leg in one hand and tapping it against the other like she was some roughneck enforcer and the table leg was a baseball bat. "It's never open," she added. "But I've seen them load stuff in from that dock over there. All manner of fanciness."

"I'm done with you threatening me," said Tracy. "You ruined my life. *Our* life," she said, waving a finger between Kanoa and herself. "And if it takes killing you to end this, then—"

"In a minute," said Ada, shaking the table leg at Tracy. Then she pointed it at Kanoa. "First, though, we have to get rid of him."

Tracy scoffed. "Ha," she said. "I brought him back once already. You know I can do it again. You know I *will*."

"I do," said Ada, and she stood her ground even as Kanoa marched toward her.

"And when I kill you," said Tracy, "no one will care. It won't be a crime. You've been dead for over a hundred years."

With her free hand, Ada pulled something from her pocket that looked very much like a passport. "Ada Coffin Silver has been dead for that long," she said. "But this woman," she said, shaking the document at them, "the woman I am now—is very much alive."

Kanoa closed the distance in one last stride and yanked the passport from Ada's hand. Tracy watched him examine it, watched as his face fell. "I don't know how she did it, *ku'uipo*, but this is her. You can't kill her. They'll find you. They'll put you away."

As he spoke, Kanoa nodded up at a pair of security cameras looming overhead.

Tracy stared down the alley at Ada. She watched as the woman took a step backward, toward the edge of the river. Tracy knew Ada was planning something, but she had no idea what. Then she saw something dawn on Kanoa's face. He gave her a beautiful shit-eating grin, then turned to face Ada.

"But," he told Ada, throwing the passport at her feet. "That, right there, is a double-edged sword. If Tracy can be charged for killing you, you can be charged for stalking her. They're not going to put *her* away," he said, stepping toward her even as she stepped back from him. "It'll be you instead."

Ada was at the river's bank now, and Kanoa was towering over her. She should have been shaking. Tracy had seen Kanoa when he was angry—not often, and very seldom at her, but often enough to know what he looked like—and she knew that Ada should be terrified right now. But she wasn't. She was *smiling*. She dropped her table leg, her makeshift weapon, but she still seemed in complete control.

"Kanoa," said Tracy. "Be careful."

He looked back at her from over his shoulder and gave her a nod and the shaka sign. But she couldn't hang loose—not right now, not when she had no idea what was about to happen.

And then it happened.

Ada drove a knee into Kanoa's crotch to disorient him. Then, once he'd doubled over and was off balance, she seized his wrist in one hand, took hold of his shoulder with the other, and whipped him toward the river.

Only there was never any splash. As he stumbled toward the

water, the air between here and there shimmered. It *shimmered*, like a veil laced with some precious metal. Sheer—invisible, except where it sparkled with orange light.

Kanoa fell through it, and he was gone.

Tracy screamed as she raced toward Ada, toward the spot where her husband had vanished. And Ada laughed. She laughed as Tracy grabbed at the lapels of her trench coat.

"Where did he go?!" she said, tears in her eyes and a crack in her voice.

"Beyond your reach," said Ada, a satisfied smirk upon her lips.

Tracy howled. Then she shoved Ada backwards, right through the spot where Kanoa had disappeared. But Ada didn't disappear. No. She fell ass-first into the river instead.

She cackled as she stood and brushed herself off, as she cast her drenched coat off of herself and stood in the alley in nothing but the garment Tracy had gifted her so long ago.

"What makes you so different?" asked Tracy, her chest heaving as she struggled to catch her breath and hold together her crumbling heart.

"I came through the door of my own accord," she said. "I didn't break any rules. The door wasn't supposed to be open, but thanks to *you* it was."

"He didn't break any rules either then," said Tracy. "*I* opened the door for him, too. *I* brought him back."

Ada sneered. "And you *loved* him."

"Yes."

The contempt on Ada's face transformed her sneer into a scowl. "What a fragile thing," she said. "Love. It's tenuous, ever unravelling—a cord that snaps under the slightest pressure. And like the coarse and fraying rope that it is, it burns the hands that cling to it. Love burns them until they're willing to let go and settle for its stronger, more comforting cousins: the unbreakable bonds of sentiment and nostalgia."

"Your metaphors are shit," said Tracy. "I have no idea what you're trying to say."

"Love empties!" spat Ada. "Longing fills."

"So," said Tracy, "What? He disappeared because I loved him?"

"Deep down," said Ada, "you'd rather long for him."

Tracy balled up a fist and socked old Ada on the jaw. Ada fell back against the building opposite the bar, but she was smiling as she clutched at her face. Tracy didn't care, though. She jabbed next. Then again. Then threw in a cross for good measure.

Ada staggered.

"Hey," said Tracy. "Hey, you fucking cliché. Now's when you ask me if that's all I've got."

Ada's mouth began to open, blood spilling from her split lip, but Tracy gave her an uppercut before she'd spoken even one syllable aloud.

Tracy watched as the woman fell to her knees. Then she stepped behind her and grabbed hold of both tails of the scarf. In her mind, Tracy heard the voice of the guy from *Mortal Kombat*, the off-screen judge who shouts FINISH HER! near the end of a bout. She remembered the first time Auntie Ashley showed her that game, how she'd been grounded for a week afterward. No video games, no comics, no goddamned internet. But it had been worth it. All the times she'd gotten to rip the spine out of Ashley's ninja chick. All the times Ashley's ninja chick had kissed her blue samurai dude to death.

Tracy clutched one end of Ada's scarf in each hand, and she pulled. She pulled and she pulled, the gash in Ada's neck widening with each second that passed. And it was in those seconds that something awful occurred to Tracy. She was finishing the work her great-great-grandfather had begun over a century before, the work he'd begun when yet another wife had "betrayed" him. For a moment she felt ashamed to be connected in any way to that wretched act—for a moment she felt sorry again for Ada as she had been in 1892. A lovestruck woman just trying to do right by her broken-hearted man.

But it was only a moment. And moments pass.

Flesh rent from muscle, tendons ripped from bone, and yet this *still* wasn't enough for Tracy. She wished the damn scarf was a garrote, a wire so sharp she could finish the thing properly.

When it seemed there was no struggle left in Ada, Tracy leaned in close to check for breath. Her grip slackened as she counted, as she waited. And that was when Ada reached back and scratched at her, drawing blood.

Ada held her breath no longer, gasping for air as Tracy staggered away from her.

"I thought you *wanted* me to kill you," said Tracy as she clutched at her bleeding cheek.

"I want," rasped Ada, "for you to stop—to stop getting in my way. And for that," she said, holding up her bloody fingers, "I need evidence."

Tracy stared at the long fingernails on the woman's hand, imagined the parts of herself that lurked beneath them now. The wounds on her cheek, beneath her now-trembling fingers—defensive wounds. *Defensive.* That's what they'd be called.

Ada laughed at her one last time. Then Tracy crouched and collected Ada's table leg from the ground. She walked slowly toward the woman who had ruined her life. And she stood there. She stood there until her breath was even, until she was sure.

"Finish it," said Ada.

Tracy swung the table leg up over her head, then down. And finish it she did.

But this was no flawless victory, not like the ones Auntie Ashley used to give her by pretending to forget she knew how to play their video game. No, Tracy thought. This was no victory at all.

THE FIRST PIECE of mail she received in prison was a blank notebook from Uncle Michael. On the first page, he'd inscribed a quote from one of their favorite movies. "It's been a long time," he scrawled, "since someone wrote a really good book in jail."

⚜

HER FAVORITE GUARD was an older fella, Kāʻeo, an orator with a yarn for every occasion. His favorites were all to do with his misadventures in a vintage Dodge, a clunker with curves to spare. Just like his old lady, he liked to tell the inmates. *Phyllis*. A fine woman, he told them. They would've liked her.

"We always made it in the cab," Kāʻeo told Tracy one evening. "Never the flat bed."

"A real gentleman," Tracy teased.

"Until it was time for me not to be," he said, and he winked.

One time, he and his Phyllis stopped off the side of the road on a trip back from surfing at Hanalei. They just couldn't wait, Kāʻeo said, until they got home to Poʻipū.

The sun glinted off the chrome of the side-view mirrors, so intense it didn't matter how tightly he closed his eyes. As Phyllis kissed him, the whole world went from black to orange and back again. It all depended on which way she tilted her head. After a while, she noticed how distracted he was and she pushed him onto his back. When she climbed on top of him, he thought she was being frisky and went with it. It wasn't until years later that she told him she hadn't been ready.

Tracy was never sure what to make of that story, and it must've shown on her face the first time he told it.

"I never wanted to hurt her," said Kāʻeo. "But, I guess," he began, then trailed off. "Men," he said with a sigh. "You understand, don't you?"

And she nodded. Because, despite Kanoa, she did understand.

"Is it true?" Kāʻeo asked her, once he'd finally worked up the gumption, "the story you told me the other night? About the ghosts," he added after a moment, as if she didn't know which story he was talking about.

Sensing what he was after, Tracy hesitated.

He nodded, as if this was the response he'd expected. "I'd just love to see her again," he said. Then he gave her a weak smile and resumed his rounds.

Kāʻeo was halfway down the block when she called out for him.

"If she can find her way back," she told him, "if she *wants* to, then she will. But you can't force it. You don't wanna do that."

"That's what you did?" he asked, and she could see in his eyes that he really did believe her. He didn't think she was insane.

"Yes," she said. "But I'll never do it again."

❦ 5 ❦

BELINDA

After graduation, Belinda pitched Matt on becoming his assistant. She wasn't sure about grad school yet, but she thought she might like to teach someday—and she wanted to keep writing besides—so would he mind if she came on board?

When he said yes, she asked if he also might have some place for her to stay in that big house of his. Her landlord was raising the rent. That was the lie that she fed him, that he and his wife bought hook, line, and sinker, and how she ended up renting the basement apartment of their big old house on Kingsbury.

Matt never suspected that she was hanging around to keep him safe. Why would he? And so, they settled into an easy rhythm as master and apprentice.

Even after Tracy seemingly killed Ada way out in Hawai'i, Belinda kept her guard up. Her old friend had come back from the dead once already, after all. What was to stop her from doing it again?

On the November afternoon that things took their next turn, whilst they drove to the airport, Matt regaled Belinda with the most popular—and over-told—story in his repertoire.

"The greatest yarn I ever did hear," he began, "was the one my grandfather spun about our descent from Judas."

Belinda turned her body in the passenger's seat to face him, the shoulder strap of her seatbelt straining to keep her in place.

"We children were seated on Grampy's living room floor, seawater from our wet bottoms seeping into his moth-eaten Persian rug. My sister Veronica held our quivering cousin Ashley in her lap and we all had our eyes glued to the floor. You see, we had lost track of Ashley for a moment outside on the beach, enthralled as we were by the scratching of pencil against thick sketchbook paper."

Belinda smiled. She knew where this was going, knew the story by heart now—from reading Matt's comics, from reading his mind—but she loved to hear him tell it.

"Our cousin Michael had been roughing out a caricature of Grampy's nosy old neighbor, Mrs. Brown, who had fallen asleep four towels down from us. Inspired by the cacophonous racket issuing from the old widow's super-sized schnozzola, Michael had transfigured each nostril in his drawing into a whirring buzzsaw. We were too busy laughing at his efforts to notice that the youngest of our company had disappeared into the surf. And now we were getting an earful in exchange for our negligence."

That was the Eli Silver she'd grown up hearing about—the severe disciplinarian who'd driven his children and grandchildren to great successes and even greater psychotherapy bills, the man who generally seemed nothing at all like the "Grampy" who this reality's Silvers had known and loved.

Belinda was happy they'd gotten the generally nicer version. Grampy 2.0, so to speak.

"As the story went, we Silvers were descended from Judas himself. *The* Judas. Our surname, Grampy told us, was like a flag of shame we'd flown in hopes of redemption ever since. And if we didn't shape up, then we might as well tear up the tickets to heaven for all the Silvers gone by and all the Silvers yet to come.

"This was the first time I heard the story," said Matt, pulling his car into the maze of concrete and pavement that was Boston's Logan Airport. "That was the first time, but it certainly wasn't the last. In fact," he continued, "Grampy dropped it from his repertoire only upon the occasion of my intimation—at the wise old age of thirteen, after a long weekend lost in the pages of Nietzsche—that perhaps our name was less Hester Prynne's scarlet letter and more Harry Fleming's red badge of courage."

Belinda scoffed, an unintentionally derisive noise that transformed into a more honest-to-goodness laugh the more she tried to untangle her uncle's preposterous statement.

"What exactly I meant by it," said Matt, "I could scarcely tell you today. I don't suppose I knew what I was talking about, even then. But, regardless, it was enough cheek to garner as severe a look from Grampy as I ever did see, a look that seemed to suggest I had finally read one too many books for my own good."

The story rattled around Belinda's brain as they parked the car in the central garage and made their way into Terminal E. She so loved hearing about these Silvers, even if they weren't *her* Silvers exactly. It made her feel less lonely here, and helped her to remember what her own life had been like so long ago.

They'd come to the airport to fetch Matt's cousin Michael for Thanksgiving weekend—Michael, who would've been Belinda's dad if he weren't infertile now and if this weren't an entirely new iteration of the universe. And yet, though this should've been a happy occasion, Matt seemed on edge. After a cursory check of the arrivals monitor, he gestured for Belinda to follow him into the newsstand which stood nearby.

The two of them settled in front of a spinning rack of paperbacks that Matt seemed to eye with derision. "The last time I bought a book at an airport was on my honeymoon," he told her, "which was so many moons ago now that I've lost count."

Belinda tried to picture it—Matt and Angelica, back when she was just Angel and still playing the part of the man she most certainly was not—but this was the one area of his life that Matt had always been cagey about.

"We were in San Francisco," he continued, picking up the newest Stephen King from the rack and thumbing through its pages. "It was a layover, our ultimate destination the paradise my dear cousin calls home, and I'd spent so much time doubled over inside the tiny in-flight lavatory that surviving the second leg of the trip without a super-sized bottle of Pepto just wasn't going to be an option.

"As I stood in line, my flask of fluorescent pink salvation clutched tightly to my chest, I scanned the paperbacks on offer and found among them a most unexpected sight: a collection of short fiction. Short stories? At an airport convenience store? Amongst the romances and the ghostwritten memoirs and the paperbacks repackaged with cheap-ass covers borrowed from film adaptations? Would wonders never cease?!"

Belinda laughed.

"And it was not just any collection," he added. "No, it was the selected stories of the bearded old fellow who had made a name for himself writing about and teaching at our very own Kimball College—that institution which had, in its attempt to keep up with the Joneses, Emersons, and Benningtons of the world, recently tenured my sorry funnybook-slinging ass.

"I picked the book up and flipped through its gray pages, trying to remember if I had a copy back home. I'm usually quite good at visualizing what's on my shelves, but I'd moved into my beloved's dilapidated Greek Revival just days before the wedding, and I had yet to unpack my library.

"I tried to think, to puzzle out how I might have come to own it. Perhaps the old man himself had given me a copy during his latter days, maybe on the occasion of my arrival on campus as a student some years prior—me, the much-heralded savior of the languishing department he'd founded an age or two before. Maybe, but I couldn't be sure.

"My brain was addled, and I wondered suddenly if I'd shat a hunk of that overworked organ out of my body, along with everything else. Anyway, I reasoned, I had cash to spare now, so I decided to live a little. When the clerk asked if there was anything else she could help me with, I even splurged on a genuine bottle of Jamestown Ginger Ale to chase away the chalky taste of my medicine."

Matt set the paperback he'd been perusing in the here and now back onto its shelf. Then he picked up another. Suddenly self-conscious that she looked weird standing there without a book in her own hands—and having caught the thoughts of the cashier thinking "What's her deal?"—Belinda picked up a copy of the book Matt had just put down.

Then Matt continued his story.

"Sitting with Angel that afternoon in SFO, and on the plane over the Pacific after that—and probably too often in the coming days for a newlywed lounging in a purported paradise on Earth—I pored over the pages of that book and reacquainted myself with the first author whose stories had rivaled my grandfather's in my esteem.

"It was as I sat on my cousin's lanai, our spouses asleep while Michael doodled sketches of me, that I came across the story of the townies and the murdered girl. I'd forgotten the bit about 'the one college fag' and I said aloud, 'Holy shit, that could have been me.'

"Michael looked up from his sketchbook and arched an eyebrow, the pencil in his right hand still moving.

"'If I'd actually gone to college when I was supposed to,' I explained, 'I could have been the one college fag.'

"Michael shook his head, returning his focus to his drawing as he said to me 'The story was written in the 70s and you were supposed to go to the college in 1989, Matt. By then,' he said, 'there was already a rainbow flag hanging from the rafters of the student center. So, no,' he continued. 'No Homo Solo for you.'"

Belinda laughed. Then she watched as Matt pulled a phone from the back pocket of his entirely too-skinny jeans.

"He's here," Matt said.

When Belinda finally caught sight of Michael strolling out from beneath the archway that on her side was marked DO NOT ENTER, the man was keeping pace with a dashing old dame in a periwinkle pantsuit. It was a strange sight to see him that cozy with someone who wasn't Mom, and even stranger to see him flirting with someone who had twenty years on him at least.

They chatted amiably as they walked, Michael and his silver-haired seductress, smiling and laughing until Michael saw Matt and Belinda in the distance and paused. He took hold of the dame's arm with one hand, pointing in Matt's direction with the other, and the dame offered up her cheek for Michael to kiss.

Which he did, of course, sly dog that he was.

Belinda watched Matt smile and wave at the unlikely pair, watched the old dame give Matt a nod as she took her leave of Michael, and watched as Michael began to fiddle with his phone as he made his way ever closer.

When Michael reached them, he did not at first seem to realize that Matt and Belinda were there together. He turned his back on Belinda and asked Matt, in a poor attempt to keep his query on the down-low, if he thought a hand job counted when applying for membership in the mile-high club.

"That depends," said Belinda, the power of her snark overwhelming the power of her embarrassment in that moment. "Did you reciprocate?"

Michael turned to face Belinda now and raised an eyebrow. He held out a hand for her to shake and said, "I don't believe we've met."

Belinda didn't shake his hand, not at first. Instead, she ribbed him some more. "Before I do that," she said, "I think you should answer the question. Maybe," she continued, "you'll need to wash your hands first."

Matt laughed, then introduced the two of them. Then, finally, Michael answered Belinda's question.

Not verbally, though. Instead, he simply tapped a checkbox on his phone. Then he put it to sleep and tucked into his back pocket.

"Her pantsuit present any problems?" asked Matt.

"Elastic waistband," said Michael as he wrapped his arms around Matt and squeezed him tight.

Belinda watched Matt sniff as the two men hugged, then heard Matt's thoughts in her head. He was wondering if he'd catch a whiff of the old dame's scent on the fingers curled into his shoulder just then.

But it was Matt who was caught, because Michael pulled away and shook his head at him. Then he nodded in the direction of the baggage claim.

As she followed behind the two men, Belinda did her best—at first, at least—to keep herself out of her Michael's head, but eventually the lure was too great. This was the man who would've been her father, if the circumstances of this reality were the same as the one which came before. And he was running around with a list of "things he'd do if he lost his wife"? Belinda had to know how seriously he was taking this. So, she took a peek inside Michael's mind.

The trouble was it was like a mudslide in there, an avalanche of thoughts caked in a brown mess of emotions. There was nothing to hang onto, so Belinda pulled herself out right quick.

As THE YELLOW light atop the baggage carousel began to whirl, the three of them waiting for the machine's siren to announce the arrival of Michael's luggage, Belinda's jet-lagged unfather eyed his silver-haired minx across the way. Then he asked Matt absent-mindedly about the weather.

"It snows and then it rains," said Matt. "Snows and then rains."

"Massachusetts for you," said Michael. Then, with his eyes still set upon the woman across the way, Michael asked Belinda where she was from.

"I grew up here," she told him.

"So you're used to this bullshit weather too, huh?"

Belinda nodded, but Michael didn't notice. He was still too busy staring.

Matt set a hand atop Michael's shoulder. "Careful, cuz" is what he said as he gave the tense muscle a squeeze. "She might get the wrong idea."

Michael scoffed. "And what would she want with a young buck like me?" he asked.

Matt ruffled his cousin's hair then, searching in vain for the grays that were plentiful on his own head by the time he was Michael's age. "You've got some miles on you, too," said Matt. "Don't kid yourself."

The alarm sounded then, and the belt of the carousel began to snake its way along the edge of the gathered crowd. The old dame's valise was the first bag out of the gate, and she collected it with a confident heave. Then she turned to the three Silvers, gave them a wave, and was gone.

When Belinda returned her gaze to Michael, he was wearing a wistful smile. And yet, he wasn't thinking of the dame. No, he was daydreaming about his wife instead. Belinda's unmother: Jenna. Michael was thinking of watching Jenna grow old, of her growing into a wise old broad like the lady he'd just spent a plane ride spilling his guts to—and he was wondering if he'd lost that chance, if he'd lost his wife forever.

Belinda wanted to wrap him up in a hug, the way he had hugged her so many times in the life before this one. She wanted to tell him that everything was going to be alright, the way he always told her: with a whisper in one ear and a kiss on the other. But then it occurred to her that it might not be okay. The last few years had been hell on their family—first Ashley's death, then Tracy's imprisonment, and now this latest trouble—and the last thing Michael needed right now was worthless, baseless consolation.

꧁꧂

It wasn't until they'd made their way back to Matt's car and stowed the luggage in the trunk that Michael asked Matt about the script. The spectacular relaunch of their series *The Children of Judas* was behind schedule. It had been six months since Matt sent Michael the penultimate chapter, and three months since Michael had finished the art for it.

As they stood behind the car—Michael hunched into the ratty black pea coat he only had occasion to wear when he flew back here, home, to the bosom of his family—as they stood there in the cold, in an airport parking garage, talking about the words that Matt owed, Belinda had to stifle a laugh as the line fell out of Matt's skull like a book tumbling from a too-high shelf. The line from *Wonder Boys*—a film all three of them loved. The line. The excuse. The lie.

"It's fine," said Matt, stumbling over his words on purpose, emulating the tentative, stuttering delivery from the film and hoping his performance was convincing. "It's done," he said in a mumble, winking at Belinda once he saw that she got the reference. "Well, basically. I got a little tinkering I've still gotta do."

Matt stared then at a stain on one of the lapels of Michael's coat, a Rorschach of discoloration haloing his middle button. He stared, waiting for Michael to respond and hoping he'd play along. Belinda could tell, having access to both men's thoughts, that Michael had no idea yet that Matt was even making a reference—let alone having any idea what the reference was—but she couldn't exactly tell Matt that, or how she knew.

After a few moments of awkward silence, of Michael not playing along, Matt looked his cousin in the eye again. Michael looked sheepish, behind unkept locks in desperate need of a trim, and he was squinting at Matt now and nibbling on his lower lip.

"What?" said Matt.

"You're quoting something," said Michael, something finally beginning to dawn on him.

Matt gestured with his keys toward the front of the car, but Michael didn't move.

All of a sudden, Michael pulled his right hand from his pocket, snapped, and then waved an accusatory finger at Matt. "Was the silver-hair my Miss Sloviak?" he asked—referring to the mid-flight hookup from the movie in question.

Matt smiled, loving that Michael was finally picking up what he was putting down. "I don't know," said Matt. "You tell me. You're the one who had your hand down her pants."

Michael laughed, and the three of them got into the car—Belinda giving up the shotgun position and climbing into the back instead. Then, once they were buckled, Matt put the car into reverse, threw his right arm back behind Michael's headrest, and looked over his shoulder to make sure he wasn't going to run anyone over. Or any*thing*. It would have been a shame, he thought, if there were a dog back there—a blind bulldog with one hell of a bark—though it might make their plagiaristic evening more complete.

They were at the Sumner Tunnel toll plaza before anyone spoke again, and at that point it was just Michael wondering where all the booth attendants had gone. Matt gestured at the beige transponder glued behind his rearview mirror and explained that everything had gone electronic and automated, Boston's first step toward Skynet. But though that got a chuckle out of everyone, they lapsed back into silence until they were safely out from underneath the harbor.

In the backseat, Belinda smiled a bittersweet smile at the thought she felt taking shape in the car—that *this* Michael Silver was just as freaked out by driving underwater as the one who'd been her father.

"What other parts of the movie are we cribbing?" Michael asked Matt as they pulled up from under the city and out onto the bridge headed out of town. "You sleeping with your boss's wife on the side? Got a hot co-ed lusting after you?"

"Oh, so many," Belinda chimed in, anxious to join in the fun. "But only one of them is consistently clad in red cowboy boots, and he doesn't look anything like Katie Holmes."

Michael laughed. "I suppose," he said, turning in his seat to face her, "there's a brilliant but morose student in his department who I'm going to sleep with by the end of the weekend, much to his dismay."

But before Belinda could say anything, she was taken aback by the thought that entered Matt's head in silent reply to Michael's jokey query—and by him looking at her reflection in the rearview mirror. For five years now, Matt had been struggling to put his finger on who from his sordid past Belinda reminded him of, with her red hair and her dance moves on Friday nights at the Sister—and her ability to whip anyone's ass at any game of cards they could think of—and now he'd finally figured it out.

Tiny Dancer, he said to himself inside his head—the nickname he'd given Michael's wife. *Belinda looks like Jenna*, he thought. *Is Michael going to fall for her without even realizing it?*

The thought was so icky that Belinda shuddered. Her father—or, well, the man who would have been her father—falling for her because she looked like her mother.

"You cold?" Michael asked, but before she could answer he reached over and cranked up the heat anyway.

"Thanks," she said.

"So tell me," he said, facing her again, "is there someone I should be worried about?"

Matt reached over and squeezed Michael's leg. Then he turned for a split second to offer a smile that Michael didn't even see.

"Is that on your list, too?" asked Belinda, a playful jab.

"What?" said Michael. "To fuck a student? No," he said. "I like my job, thank you very much."

And I love my wife, he thought—the first crystal-clear thought he'd had in a good, long while.

৩৵৩

MICHAEL SAT at Matt's desk while Matt and Belinda scoured the office shelves for the two copies of the book Matt had been thinking about all evening. With his feet propped up on his cousin's filing cabinet, Michael leaned back into the thick, scuffed leather of the swivel chair and ran his fingers over the trackpad of the laptop which sat open on the desk.

Matt tried not to pay any attention to the puddle of dirty water pooling beneath Michael's boots that was drifting ever so slightly in the direction of his printer. He tried not to think about what folders Michael might be scrolling through on his hard drive and what he might find there.

Michael asked the other two, "Wouldn't it be under D?"

"They're not sorted alphabetically," said Belinda.

Michael laughed and shook his head.

"What?" said Matt.

"It never ceases to amaze me," said Michael.

"What?" said Matt again.

"Your ability to turn every aspect of your life into a pastiche."

Matt scratched his head in confusion.

"You don't follow?" said Michael, finally removing his feet from the filing cabinet and sitting up straight. "Does the film *High Fidelity* ring any bells?"

Belinda gave him a smile, letting him know that she, at least, knew what he was getting at.

"I must've taken a look at it," said Matt, forgetting if he had or not. "What's your point?"

"How are your books sorted?" said Michael.

"Biographically," said Matt. "They're sorted based on when first bought or read them."

Michael slapped a hand to his forehead and slumped back into the chair. "Oy!" he said. "You do it so much you don't even realize you're doing it anymore."

Matt returned to the shelves, searching between the Grecian columns for a book on wedding planning or Gibran's *The Prophet*, which he and Angel had used in the ceremony. One or the other had to be nearby the copy of the book he'd picked up in San Francisco; he only hoped that one wasn't the copy he loaned to the kid in the cowboy boots at midterm, the copy the kid had promised to return the next time Matt could meet him for office hours.

Finally, after pausing for a few tense minutes to pick at the flaking plaster, Matt found the Gibran. But, alas: to the right of it he found only the book of Hawaiian folklore that Angel bought him on their honeymoon. He pressed his head against the shelf and closed his eyes. And he kept them closed until he heard Michael double-click something on the computer. Then he opened his eyes slowly, waiting for the hammer to fall.

Belinda ceased her own searching and took a gander at what Michael had found. It didn't seem to be anything out of the ordinary, just a plain old Word document with paragraphs that were way too long for the modern reader—as befit Matt's status as a self-professed curmudgeon.

"Holy shit," said Michael.

Matt turned to find his cousin rubbing a hand across his bearded chin as he slouched toward the computer's screen and squinted. Matt asked him "Where are your glasses, you geezer?"

"This isn't just some filler issue," he said, tapping the screen. "Matt, this is a whole new series."

Matt slapped the lid of the laptop closed and took a not insignificant amount of pleasure in the speed and force with which Michael leapt backward. The chair rolled back into the wall as Michael looked up, stunned.

"Drinks?" suggested Belinda.

⚜

THEY ENDED up at the Sister, of course, Matt setting ridiculous expectations as they waited for the first round.

"No matter how many times I've stood out front," said Matt, "waiting for Nadine to hoist her monocle to one eye and check my ID, my body doubled over from the cold of a foul wind whipping off the Merrimack—no matter how many times I've thrown up in the alley out back after too many pints of the swill they keep on tap to please the cheapskates and the hipsters both—this place never ceases to amaze me."

It wasn't until he was drunk on wine coolers and two shots of cinnamon liqueur that Michael interjected himself into Belinda and Matt's circuitous conversation on the nature of evil in the Harryhausen *Clash of the Titans*—a film which Matt had been telling Belinda for years that she only hated because of her age. And what Michael had to say for himself at this point was pure Michael. He waved a finger to get their attention, then informed the others that Professor McGonagall was in that one. "Professor fucking McGonagall," he said.

"Who's Professor McGonagall?" Matt asked him, poking him in the arm as he played the fool, hoping he could get a rise out of his drunk cousin. Suddenly, Matt imagined Michael's face going red and steam coming out of his ears, and he had to put his head down on the table because he was laughing so hard.

"Snob," said Michael, poking Matt in the ear until he sat up again. "The Harry Potter films are cinematic master—"

And now Belinda, drunk herself, grabbed hold of Michael's hand with both of hers—robbing him of speech in the process. She stroked his knuckles for a moment—forgetting who he was to her and seeing only a man in need of comfort—and she said, "He's fucking with you, dude. Totally fucking with you."

Michael looked at her, nodded slowly, then finally and quite unexpectedly, took her hands into his own. Matt looked on, dumbfounded, as Michael brought Belinda's hands to his lips to give them a quick peck.

Belinda, flustered—and suddenly remembering who it was that was kissing her hands—broke away and waved to the waitress for another drink.

۞

AFTER LAST CALL—AND a few glasses of water each—they found themselves standing by the side of the road, staring at Matt's car as they were buffeted by a brisk wind. Matt was twirling the keys around his finger, Belinda was rocking back and forth on her heels, and Michael stood awkwardly between them, jumping up and down every two minutes like clockwork. They were all thinking the same thing: were any of them sober enough to drive? The walk back to campus, while not impossible, would be long and cold.

"You tell Michael your theory about this place?" Belinda asked Matt, all of a sudden.

"Well," said Michael, "I went to school at the college, too. Class of '99. So I might've heard of it."

"Ah," said Belinda, "but this place wasn't here then."

"Where was it?" said Michael, before correcting himself. "I mean, what was it? I mean——"

"No," said Belinda, a mischievous grin on her face that did not at all match the thought in her head that she shouldn't be saying any of this right now. "You had it right the first time."

"It's a ridiculous story," said Matt, as his keys twirled off his finger and into a puddle of gray-brown slush by the curb.

Michael jumped up and down again. Once, twice, three times, as Matt stooped to collect his keys and wipe them off on a pant leg.

"When you get home," said Belinda, "google the name of the bar. It's a trip," she said. "Over the years, there have been at least a dozen bars called the Strumpet's Sister in various places around the world. Maybe even more than that before records were kept and whatnot."

"So," said Michael. "A lot of strumpets had a lot of sisters. What's the big deal?"

"They say," said Matt, "that if you drink enough of that swill they serve, and you follow the right person through the right door, you can jump from one Sister to the next."

"Or to the one that came before," said Belinda, still not sure why she was sharing this much about her place. She wondered if there'd been something in her drink. Had someone down in the brewery changed the recipe somehow? Made it more potent in some way?

Michael's lips curled into a goofy grin, and he looked from one face to the next, then back again. "Are you talking about a——?"

"A time machine!" said Belinda with a squee, a noise of such unbridled and unspoiled exuberance that for once she sounded as young as she looked. "Not quite as cool as a DeLorean," she added, "or a telephone booth, or a police box, but..."

"I'm quite fond of floaty-ball person carriers," Matt interjected.

"But," said Belinda, "imagine where you could go. Imagine *when!*"

Matt looked to Michael and saw what he was imagining, and saw what the effort was costing him—but the thought was gone from Michael's mind before Belinda could listen for it. And yet, in the second before he was jumping up and down again, Belinda saw a tear welling up in the corner of his eye. And suddenly she didn't need her powers at all. She knew who he was thinking about, and she knew it was her fault.

Why had she said what she said? Was she really *that* drunk? Or was some other force at play here? Did she say what she said because she was meant to, because she had no choice? And if that was the case, what did that mean for what was next?

ॐ

BELINDA DROVE them back to Matt's place. She swore she was good to go, and the two men were too busy yawning to argue.

"When would you go?" Belinda asked Matt, as they mounted the bridge over the Merrimack.

He didn't answer at first, since he was entirely unsure of what to say. He thought of his unfinished script—his "whole new series," as Michael put it—and thought of the many brick walls keeping him from his ending. Which of those would he most like to tear down?

"Matt?" said Belinda, trying to keep him from spelunking any further into his pit of despair.

"November 1844," he blurted out, "to meet my great-great-grandfather before he was lost at sea."

"And Michael?" said Belinda.

He didn't hesitate. "Spring Break 1997," he said.

"Ooh," she said, wondering what happened that week to this Michael—and trying to remember if her father had ever said anything about that particular point in time. Then she asked "Why?"

"So I could have more time," said Michael, tapping a fist gently against the dash. "If I'd made a different choice, I could've had more time."

The inside of the car went silent then, save for the heat working its way through the vents. They said nothing to each other as Belinda made the turn off South Main Street and onto Kingsbury. They said nothing as she crept down Kingsbury at a crawl, searching for Matt's house in the dark. No, they said nothing else at all until Belinda pulled them into the driveway, at which point Matt opened the door and offered a goodbye—forgetting for a moment that Belinda was his tenant, that she lived downstairs in his finished basement.

But Michael didn't get out of the car right away. He lingered instead and asked Belinda, "Do you think it works that way? Do you think you can change anything?"

Belinda squeezed his hand, wanting him to know that all hope was not lost—and hoping that she was right about that, that Jenna would forgive him eventually. She told him "If not then, there's always now."

⚜

IN THE MORNING, Belinda woke to the smell of strawberry-scented shampoo wafting across the living room and the sound of a heavy door opening and closing after that.

She was still fully clothed, and though the evening's activities remained a blur in her mind she remained fairly confident that all she and her unfather had done before passing out on their respective couches was talk.

At the breakfast table, Matt was sipping from a Schweppes ginger ale while picking at a bowl of pretzels—his mother's cure for tummy aches since the seventies. It was only when he was well enough to quit staring into the middle distance, only once he'd begun fiddling with Alphabear on his phone, that he heard the padding of bare feet against hard wood.

Unsure who the feet belonged to, and not wanting to risk the exposure of his pathetic high scores to a student who surpassed him in more ways than he was comfortable admitting, he clicked the phone off. And he was lucky that he made that call, as it was none other than Belinda of the Bedhead who fell into the seat opposite him.

"So," she said, yawning and stretching, "how's the misses? I heard her leave for work a few minutes ago."

"She's fine," said Matt. "At least I think so. We haven't seen each other much since the election. Lots of broken hearts to tend to. Lots of broken minds."

Belinda shook her head and sighed. "At least the orange fucker's good for something," she said. "He'll have therapists rolling in the dough for four years."

"Or eight," said Matt, "if we're not careful."

"If *he's* not careful," said Belinda, "it could be two." She mimicked an explosion with her hands, a boom issuing from her lips.

"Or one," said Matt, setting his head down upon the table then rolling it back and forth along the cold lacquer.

"You don't look so hot, Teach," is what Belinda told him then.

"Well," he said, "unlike you, I did not have access to the restorative power of a good lay last night. My prescription, it seems, needs to be refilled."

Belinda's stomach lurched as she imagined the thought of her and Michael... *together*. She reassured Matt that all they'd done, she and Michael, was talk.

Matt lifted his head slowly and squinted at her to see if she was joking. When he found nothing amiss in her countenance, he raised an eyebrow.

"I'm serious," said Belinda with a chuckle, pushing her chair back on two legs as she hung onto the table with her fingertips. "We sat up and talked. He couldn't shut up about his wife. It was sweet."

"Maybe that was on his list," joked Matt. "Take a girl to bed, then bore her with the details of his failed marriage."

"It's not failed," said Belinda, a bit more defensive than she should have been. "Not yet."

Matt nodded, a hint of sadness overtaking the hungover look on his face. He didn't want Michael's marriage to be over either. He liked Jenna. The whole family did. They knew she was the best thing to ever happen to melancholy Mikey.

"Oh," said Belinda, "and the list?" She shook her head, setting her chair back on all fours. "There's nothing on it."

Matt stared at her, dumbfounded, but even before Belinda told him that she'd taken a peek at Michael's phone—a lie to cover up the fact that she'd simply speed-read his mind for a look at the list—even before Matt heard that the list was just a bunch of faux Latin Michael had cribbed from a template he used in his design classes, he understood the truth of the situation.

Michael hadn't been able to bring himself to do it. When Jenna told him, just before she left, to write a list of the things he'd do if he lost his wife, he just couldn't do it—and he'd been going through the motions ever since, performing for anyone who dared to hope he was getting on with the business of living.

Matt knew that Michael missed Jenna, but his cousin had come so close to having affairs so many times during his marriage that Matt had lost count. He'd just figured that Michael would be itching to finally sow those wild oats of his, now that the separation had given him an excuse.

Matt stood too quickly then and had to grab hold of the table for support. "Is he asleep? he asked Belinda, pointing toward the guest room.

"I don't know," she said. "We crashed on the couches in the living room. Last thing I remember is..."

As she trailed off, Matt asked, "What? What's the last thing you remember?"

"He asked me if the Sister served breakfast," said Belinda, feeling sick now.

"And what did you tell him?"

"Yes."

Matt hunched over, hands on his knees as he imagined Michael following some poor, unsuspecting redhead into the alley behind the bar, convinced she was someone else, convinced that the "right door" from Belinda's story the night before would turn up eventually if he followed the stranger for long enough.

"What?" said Belinda, though she had a pretty good idea where Matt's train of thought was heading.

"We need to stop him," said Matt. Then he hurried upstairs to put on some clothes.

৩৵৩

THEY FOUND Michael in a booth near the back, an English muffin laid out on a small plate before him—a small pat of butter melting atop each half of it. He seemed transfixed by the steam rising from his breakfast, and it wasn't until Belinda and Matt had sat down across from him that his reverie was broken. Even then, even after they said his name twice, he seemed intent on keeping himself busy as they spoke. He took a sip of his orange juice, then began to turn the glass round and round in his hands.

Belinda could tell there was something different about him, but she couldn't place it right off the bat. Maybe, she thought, it was the way he was smiling at them—she and Matt—as he took them in. Or maybe it was in the newfound looseness of his shoulders, which he'd been drawing upwards and inwards his entire life, as if the weight of the world really did rest there. Or maybe, just maybe, it was in the twinkle in his eye—the kind of sparkle no one in the family had seen since Jenna left.

"It worked," he told hem, nodding slowly. "I saw her, I followed her, and it worked."

"Saw who?" said Matt, but Belinda already knew who it was Michael had seen. She didn't even have to read his mind to find out. It was written right there on his face, in his smile.

Belinda backhanded Matt's bicep and scoffed at him. "His wife, dummy." That's what she told Matt. Then she asked Michael, "Was it everything you dreamed it would be?"

Michael sighed and closed his eyes, his lips curling into more of a smile with each second of his new reverie.

And it was only then that Belinda noticed what had *really* changed about him. It was only then that Belinda noticed that the crow's feet had dug their way deeper into Michael's flesh. It was only then that Belinda saw, in that head of hair where just last night she could not find a single strand of gray, a streak of silver at each temple.

"Michael," said Matt, "where did you go?"

Michael opened his eyes and looked at his cousin dead on. Then he shook his head and gave them a little laugh. "Man," he said, "have I got a story for you."

6

TRACY

It wasn't long into her sentence that Tracy began to convince herself that she was better off without her husband anyway —to *try* and convince herself anyway. And the thing she focused on the most when she told this lie to herself was the one time that Kanoa had been unfaithful, the one time he had been untrue.

Only he hadn't been, not really, because they'd been on a break.

She remembered all too well the night he dropped her at the airport to fly back home to Massachusetts. It was back when Auntie Ashley was sick, when the cancer was about to kill her, and Tracy didn't know how long she'd be away.

"Maybe we take a break," she said to Kanoa that night, as they held each other by the elbows and stared down at the floor— unable to bear eye contact.

The relationship was young at the time, though even at that early stage, Tracy suspected this might be "the one." Her phone was filled with photos of her handsome Hawaiian man, her mothers had already "met" him via video chat, and she even had the approval of her oldest friends in the world—Tana and Tori—

who had never met a boyfriend nor a hookup of Tracy's that they couldn't find fault with.

But, because it was new, it didn't seem right to Tracy to tie down this hunk of beautiful man for god knew how long. Auntie Ashley might die tomorrow, she thought, or she might be fighting the good fight for six months more.

"What if I don't want a break?" Kanoa asked Tracy, giving her forearms a squeeze to get her to look at him.

She did look at him then, but she couldn't bear the sadness in his eyes. He knew she had to go, but he didn't want her to. He felt it too, that feeling that he'd found something special, and he didn't want to lose it.

He'd tell her all of this later, when he flew to Massachusetts himself to join her at Ashley's funeral, but she could sense a bit of it even then, even in the moment. And yet, she could think of nothing to say to him. She couldn't *un*speak the words she'd spoken, could she?

So they just stood there in silence for a good long while, until there was no time left and she *had* to go through security. They stood there in each other's arms, swaying ever so slightly back and forth—a dance of grief which ended only when Tracy pulled away and left Kanoa standing there unbudged in his tracks.

The other thing Kanoa did when he came to town for the funeral was to come clean right away. Standing on Red River Beach, walking through the surf with their pant legs rolled up, he told her that something had happened while she was away. He told her that he'd been with someone, but that he was too drunk to remember anything about her—anything except for the fact that he couldn't stop thinking of Tracy the whole time.

"And yes," he told her, "I know how much that sounds like bullshit, but it's true."

Tracy didn't say anything to him at first, but she didn't let go of his hand either. Eventually, she broke the silence with a laugh— a laugh that turned into a sob that turned into a laugh again.

"What?" he said, tugging on her hand to stop her from moving on—from trying to run away.

"We were on a break," she said, laughing and crying at the same time—and thinking, all the while, of a TV show her mothers had let her watch too much of when she was too young to fully understand it.

Kanoa smiled, on the verge of laughing himself, but putting on a faux look of concern for the sake of the bit. "Do we have several more seasons of 'will they or won't they' ahead of us then?"

Tracy looked up and down the length of the beach to gauge how alone they were—it was the off-season, after all. Then she looked at her watch to figure out how long it would be until they were missed back at the house. Then, finally, she pulled her boyfriend behind a sand dune and pulled him on top of her.

Now, three years later—sitting in jail with a pen and a pad of paper and a determination to find fault with everything that had ever happened between them—Tracy wondered if that should have been their last hurrah. That sympathy fuck—that release that she needed after months of doing little but watching her aunt die—should that have been the end of it for her and Kanoa? He'd cheated on her, for God's sake. There were no ifs, ands, or buts about it. She'd given him the out of "a break," but he'd refused it. And then he'd gone and slept with someone else anyway.

In her cell, Tracy nodded to herself. Kanoa was just like Uncle Michael. He'd never said 'no' to a pretty girl in his life, and he never would. And if Kanoa was still alive, who was to say that he and Tracy wouldn't end up just like Michael and Jenna? There was only so much trust a woman could put in her man, right? And when the river of his lies flowed hard enough, and for long enough, how could those currents not erode everything in their path?

Tracy stopped scribbling these thoughts down, then looked at that last metaphor. Then she tore the whole page out of the notebook, crumpled it up into a ball, and threw it toward the trash can they'd given her for "good behavior"—missing, as she always did.

She shook her head at herself. Who was she kidding? Who did she think she was fooling? It was all horseshit.

She missed him. She missed him like hell.

৩১১৩

ON THE PHONE that afternoon with Mom, Tracy spilled the beans on what she'd been up to, and she waited for the reprimand she felt certain was coming. But it didn't come. Mom was too busy sobbing. She did that a lot, so much so that nearly every call ended up with her handing the phone over to Desiree to wrap things up.

"Will she ever accept that it's not her fault?" Tracy asked Des.

"Will you ever accept that it's not yours?" said Des.

"Touché."

Desiree wanted to know what Tracy was going to do to keep herself busy, what she was going to do to keep from spiraling down this rabbit hole again. Had Tracy started writing the book Michael had joked with her about when she first got there? Had she checked out the prison library? Had she made any friends?

Tracy laughed. "You hoping I'll go all *Orange is the New Black* and make you proud?"

"Friends, I said. I didn't say—"

"A joke," said Tracy, waving her hands for a truce—as if Des could see them.

"I know you may think them beneath you," said Des.

"I'm not *that* much of a snob."

"But you never know," Des continued. "There might be someone in there who will keep you on your toes."

Tracy got a signal from one of the guards that her time was nearly up.

"Did you hear me?" asked Des.

"Yes," said Tracy. "I'll try."

⚜

AND SHE DID, though the person she ultimately connected with was the intern from U of H who worked in the library. She was a bright blonde called Nancy, an information science major who'd actually heard of Tracy before taking the gig, thanks to Tracy's work on the campus newspaper a few years before. And so, whenever Tracy asked for a new resource, or to borrow a book from some far-off place, Nancy did her best to make it happen. Tracy was a "model prisoner," after all—or so Nancy's supervisors told her—and shouldn't a "correctional" facility do its part to nurture the mind of an inmate who was eager to "better" herself?

"You don't belong in prison" is what Nancy told Tracy on the day they met, "not with a mind like yours."

Tracy told Nancy there were probably a lot of minds like hers locked up in here, only she and Nancy needed to look harder to find them.

She imagined Desiree hearing her say that, a self-satisfied smirk on her face. Like: "See, you *do* listen to me."

Nancy nodded, twirling a lock of her yellow hair around a finger as she and Tracy pored over Hawaiian census records—the U.S. censuses from 1900 on, the kingdom of Hawai'i's records from the 1850s through the 1890s, and the missionary censuses from before that. "I've never felt more aware of my whiteness," said Nancy. "But that's probably a good thing, right?"

Tracy nodded absentmindedly, wanting to say something smart about awareness being just the first step, but she couldn't find the words—and she probably wasn't much further along in the process than Nancy, if she was being honest. Besides, she had found something else while Nancy was speaking, and she was too focused on that to think of anything else at the moment.

It was a record for a set of Kanoa's ancestors, which wasn't all that remarkable in and of itself, but as Tracy ran a finger along the bottom of the row for Nani Kahoa and came to the column for the question "Father's Place of Birth," her jaw fell.

"Massachusetts?!" she said out loud.

"What's in Massachusetts?" asked Nancy, setting her own tablet aside and coming round to the back of Tracy's chair to look over her shoulder.

Tracy pointed to the row she'd been examining. She felt Nancy's weight on the back of the chair as she leaned in to check it out, and she waited a minute for Nance to catch on.

She didn't though. "What am I seeing?" she asked.

Tracy set the tablet down and turned around in her seat to take a good look at Nancy as she spoke. "One of my husband's ancestors," said Tracy, "was from Massachusetts."

"And?" said Nancy, her face screwed up in confusion.

"Massachusetts," repeated Tracy, wondering if Nancy was so bright after all. "Where *I'm* from."

"Oh," said Nancy, her eyes going wide.

"What are the odds?"

"You thought he was 100% Polynesian, I take it?"

Tracy nodded.

"Wouldn't it be funny," Nancy began, laughing to herself before she'd even finished the sentence, "if you were related?"

Tracy thought of everything she'd been through with Ada, of everything she knew about the twisted roots of the Silver family tree, and she sighed.

Nancy went to give Tracy's shoulders a squeeze but stopped at the last second. She probably wasn't allowed physical contact with a prisoner, even an exemplary one for whom the rules were regularly bent—even one who so obviously needed a hug. "I was just joking," said Nancy. "For real, don't freak out. There are lots of people from Massachusetts, and most of them aren't your relatives, right?"

Tracy nodded. That was indeed true, because most of her relatives were dead now. Or dying.

◈

PHONE CALLS with her grandfather had never been a particularly pleasant affair. Robert Silver had never been particularly loquacious. His brother, Great Uncle Albert, was the garrulous one. But over these past few years, as his dementia worsened, Grampa had gotten even more quiet.

"He likes the sound of your voice." That's what Gramma told Tracy, and why she kept calling even though the guards monitoring her calls gave her the evil eye every time, thinking maybe the phone call had ended and she was just dragging out her time outside her cell.

"So, Gramp," Tracy said that night, "want to hear something nuts?"

Silence. One raspy breath, then another.

"Kanoa and I might've been cousins," she told the old man, running her fingernail along the ridges of the phone's cord. Back and forth, back and forth, waiting for him to say something.

More silence.

"Probably freaks you out, huh?" She paused. "It shouldn't, though. Your grandfather was in love with *his* cousin, so it's not unheard of in our family."

One breath. Two breaths. Three breaths. Four.

"And then there were the rumors about him and his sister—"

"Nyyaaaaaaaaaah," Grampa groaned.

Tracy could almost see him waving a dismissive hand in the air. She liked the thought of that. Though she loved the old man, she'd never forgive him—not entirely—for what he'd done to Mom and Uncle Matt.

There was a commotion on the other end of the line, then a few garbled words from a female voice—garbled, probably, by a hand placed strategically over the mouthpiece of the receiver. But somewhere in the middle there, Tracy swore she heard her grandmother asking Grampa what he was all upset about.

"Hi, Gram," said Tracy.

"What did you say to him?" she asked. "He's all riled up."

"I don't know," Tracy lied. She didn't want to upset her grandmother and it was easier to let her chalk it up to Grampa's condition than to explain she was baiting the old man.

Gramma sighed. When she spoke again, it was with a smile slapped onto her voice—that fake cheerfulness she believed it was her obligation to provide, especially when it came to her only granddaughter, and especially under the current circumstances. "So," said Gramma, "how've you been?"

She wanted to make a joke then, say something about eating out a fellow inmate to pay for this extra time on the phone, but she knew the guards would end the call straight away and that she'd get disciplined for her vulgarity.

"Tracy?"

"Okay," is what she finally settled on—because it was the truth and it was only two syllables.

Gramma sighed again. "You're just as talkative as your grandfather," she said. "Do you both just sit here and listen to each other breathe the whole time?"

"Sometimes I tell him dirty jokes."

One of the guards stood up a bit straighter at that moment, as if the mere mention of the concept of dirty jokes meant that one was forthcoming.

"Have you spoken with your mother lately?" asked Gramma.

"Which one?" said Tracy, teasing.

"The one who gave birth to you," said Gramma, and Tracy could almost hear the sound of her eyes rolling from an ocean and a continent away. Almost, because Gramma would've stopped that shit before it started. In her opinion, grandmothers weren't supposed to roll their eyes.

At least not at their grandkids.

"Yeah," said Tracy. "The other night, but she got emotional and I ended up talking to Des instead."

"Any word on appeals?"

Tracy shook her head, then remembered that Gramma couldn't see her. "No," she said. "Sadly."

"But they have the new footage, right? The new angle that shows her pushing someone into the river, the person you were trying to defend?"

Tracy had never told the family about resurrecting Kanoa, so when the grainy footage of a second security camera popped up after the trial—showing someone who looked an awful lot like her supposedly dead husband—she invented a story about a bystander she was trying to protect.

Questions came up: why hadn't she mentioned this at the trial itself? Didn't she realize that if the jury thought she was acting in self-defense she might've been able to plea down to a lesser charge? Isn't that what you did: pled down?

"I did what I did," said Tracy, fingering the latch on the coin return slot. "Do you really think this new thing is going to make any difference?"

"It might," said Gramma. "Don't you give up hope!"

"I won't, Gram" is what she said as they said their goodbyes, as they wished each other a Happy Thanksgiving, but the truth is that she'd already given up hope for herself. What was waiting for her on the outside but another attack from Ada? Sure, Tracy had killed her. She'd watched the life spew out of her as she brought that table leg down upon her head. But Ada had died once before and come back, so what was to stop her from doing it again?

SITTING in her bunk that night with one of a half-dozen legal pads on her lap, Tracy tried to piece together everything she could about Kanoa's Masshole ancestor. The woman he would've married—or knocked up, at the very least—was a native, an indigenous Hawaiian who seemed to have lived her entire life on O'ahu. So she hadn't traveled to hook up with him; he had come to her.

The word *come* made Tracy giggle to herself and she took comfort in that immature part of herself coming out for a second.

While Nancy did her best to try and find a birth record for the product of the Atlantic-Pacific union, which might shed some more light on the subject—but which might take a few days to track down—Tracy decided to scour a print-out of an earlier census, one on which the love child appeared as a child herself.

There was no father present, only the mother, and she was listed as a boarder in the dwelling which she called home—a dwelling which, Tracy noticed, housed only single women. The head of said household? Also a woman.

Tracy wondered. It didn't seem like that much of a leap to imagine what the function of this household was. Then she ran her finger along the left-most column for the address of the place. Sure enough, it was near Pearl Harbor.

It was a moment of elation, putting those pieces together, but it didn't last. Soon enough, Tracy was feeling sick to her stomach. All signs pointed toward the father being a sailor of some sort. And what had been the primary profession of the Silver men since at least the year 1600?

"Are you sniffling down there, Silver?" came a voice from above.

"Sorry," said Tracy. Then, trying to hold back her snark and failing, she added, "I'll try to keep it down."

The voice from above scoffed. "Don't try to make me out to be the bitch," she said. "I was just being fucking polite."

Tracy thought for a second about apologizing, then decided that would probably just make things worse. Instead, she slipped her notepad beneath the others she kept under her covers, blew her nose with a subdued snort, and then turned to face the wall.

It would be gross if it were true, this suspicion she had about herself and her husband, but at least they weren't siblings. At least they weren't first cousins.

And what does it matter, anyway? asked one of the crueler voices in her head. *He's dead.*

Yes, Tracy had to admit, he was dead. But, just like Ada, he had died once before and come back. Who could say what might happen in a world where death wasn't what it used to be?

❧ 7 ❧

BELINDA

In the autumn of 1976, in the small hospital of a small Portlandian suburb, Arthur Worthing's wife was safely delivered of two babies for the price of one.

This was one infant more than the young man had bargained for, and indeed one more daughter than he and his new bride were prepared to name. Had the second child been a boy, he would've been Jade. But Arthur's wife, her head swimming in the green haze swept in by the drugs they'd forced upon her, she swore that was not a girl's name.

Or not *her* girl's name—Arthur couldn't be sure, so slurred were the words of this young woman he barely knew, that he'd knocked up on a night where he'd been slurring just as hard as she was now.

And so: there behind the glass of the nursery window, in neighboring glass bassinets, slept Melancholy Worthing and her unnamed twin.

Around the corner, in the dive bar just opened in the basement of his family's furniture store, sat the babies' father—their *father*, Arthur thought to himself—huddled into a booth with a textbook on abnormal psychology and a tall glass of whatever Cumberland County concoction they had on tap.

"Whatcha reading?" asked a passerby, once Arthur had drained his glass.

Thinking it might be the waiter, and not yet paying heed to the words coming his way, Arthur held up the empty vessel and nodded that yes, he'd like another.

The passerby gave a brief chuckle, and it was only then that Arthur looked up into the older man's face. It was only then that he examined the tweed jacket and sensible spectacles and the neatly trimmed beard.

"I'm sorry, sir," said Arthur. "I thought you were—"

The passerby laughed again, with more bluster this time. "Sir," he said, shaking his head. "I guess I do look old enough to be a sir, don't I?"

"I meant no offense," said Arthur, closing his book and offering up his full attention as a kind of apology. "It's been a long day."

The passerby looked down at the book to gain the answer he'd sought from the beginning. "A long day that ends with abnormal psych must be a long day indeed," he said. "You studying, or is that a sleep aide of some sort?"

Now Arthur laughed, for the first time since they'd put his second baby in his arms and he'd run the numbers in his head about how two college juniors were going to afford two newborns.

The passerby slid into the other side of the booth and looked over toward the bar. Once he'd grabbed the attention of someone over that way, he held up two fingers.

"I'm buying," said the passerby, and Arthur smiled at this kindness.

They talked for a moment about where Arthur was in his studies, about what the stranger did for a living—which was teaching art history at a college in Hawai'i—and wasn't that a coincidence, as Arthur had been born out there during the years his father had been stationed in the Pacific. Then the beers arrived and the stranger asked, "So, what made the day so long?"

Arthur felt himself flush as he sipped at the bitter, skunky brew, as if searching for courage in the foam of its head.

"I don't mean to pry," said the stranger.

"I became a father today," Arthur finally mumbled. "I'm a father now," he said more clearly.

"Congratulations," said the stranger.

"Twins," said Arthur.

"Double the fun," said the stranger, a wide grin playing across his face. "But I'm guessing, by the look on your face, that you weren't expecting—"

"No," said Arthur. "My wife, she suspected something was odd, kept asking me to lay my hands upon her belly and see if I felt two heads, but I never did, so I never gave it much thought."

"Two boys?" said the stranger. "One of each?"

"Two girls," said Arthur. "Only we have just the one name picked out."

"I see," said the stranger, nodding in between sips of his own beer.

"Or," said Arthur, "well, Jane has this other name in mind now, but I just can't stomach it."

"Really?" said the stranger. "Want to run it past me?"

"Guinevere," said Arthur. "She said we should name the second one after me, but when I joked that Arthura was off the table, as was Arthurine, she didn't laugh."

The stranger didn't laugh either, but he did offer a kind smile.

"Then she told me, 'No, a name inspired by yours,' and that's—"

"That's where Guinevere came from," said the stranger. "I get it."

Arthur pinched at the bridge of his nose with thumb and forefinger, then shook his head. He was struck, suddenly, by a vision of his Jane dancing across the lawn of the quad, grass between her toes. He saw her dancing past a cold stone bench where he was studying, saw again the mischief in her eyes as she sauntered by him, felt again the uncomplicated stirring in his loins and in his heart that she'd whipped into him with one simple pirouette, her bare leg peeking out from beneath a flowing skirt. How he longed for those simpler days just now.

"You're not a fan of the ornate?" asked the stranger.

"She's named the first one Melancholy," said Arthur. "And, if there'd been a boy, he would have been Jade."

"Jade?" said the stranger. "With a D?"

"And I understand," said Arthur, "that Plain Jane is no fan of her plain name, that she wants a more unique life for her children, a *special* life, but does she understand what it means to saddle a person with a name like Melancholy? Like Guinevere?"

"She could be a Gwen," said the stranger. "Her sister a…" He searched for a nickname. "A Mellie."

"I was an Arthur," said Arthur. "No matter how many times I tried Art, the kids at school wouldn't let me have it. They saw what the two syllables of my name did to me: the clenched jaw, the furrowed brow."

And this was when the stranger said it, the one thing that made all the difference in the world. "Jennifer," he said. "What about Jennifer?"

"Jennifer?" said Arthur, puzzled, though the music of the name felt pleasant as it moved across his tongue.

"My wife and I," said the stranger, "when we were trying for a kid of our own, we had this book—a dictionary, really—of baby names. And I remember reading that Jennifer derived from Guinevere."

"A compromise," said Arthur, smiling.

Across the table, the stranger finished his beer. Then he added, a ribbon and bow on the gift he'd just given: "If your wife thinks that's too plain, that there are just too many Jennifers in the world today, you might call her Jenna for short."

"Jenna," said Arthur, still smiling. "I love the sound of that. Thank you," he said. "Thanks..." he said, searching his brain for the stranger's name, which he was sure he must've been given by now.

"Michael," said the stranger. "My name's Michael."

⚘

THIS WAS the point in the story where Michael finally stopped for a moment, inhaling an enormous mouthful of now-cold muffin then throwing back a full swallow of his orange juice.

Belinda turned to Matt to see if he was staring too, to see if his jaw had hit the floor as hard as hers had, but he was simply beaming at his cousin.

"Maybe," Matt began, "telling him your name was a bit much. But—"

"But that's what I did," said Michael. "That's what I always did." And then, after another bite, and through that mouthful of muffin, he added, "It's like Harry Potter, the third one."

Belinda shrugged and said she'd never read them, which was true. In the reality she'd come from, Rowling had never written those books.

Matt turned to her and raised an eyebrow. "A kid of your vintage, and you haven't read Potter? Are you from another planet?"

She couldn't tell him that yeah, technically, she kinda was. Instead, she offered up a joke and pop culture reference—the best way to communicate with a Silver in a pinch. Belinda raised an eyebrow, then raised her right hand as well and shaped her fingers into the V of Leonard Nimoy's greeting from *Star Trek*.

Michael went on to explain that he knew what to say to Arthur, and what to do, because he'd already said it—because he'd already done it. It was just like the third Potter, he told Belinda and Matt—"You haven't even watched the movies?" Matt interjected, still flabbergasted—because in that one, Harry, after traveling back through time via a magical necklace belonging to his best friend, conjures a spell that's supposed to be too complicated for a boy his age, "but he has no trouble with it, because he's already seen himself do it."

Incredulous, Belinda reminded him that he wasn't born until a year later, that there was no way he could have seen himself help his future father-in-law name his future wife. She felt her heart race ever faster with each word she uttered aloud. *What if he'd changed something?* she found herself thinking. *He could've ruined EVERYTHING.*

Michael shook his head, a smirk on his face as he mocked Belinda for missing the obvious. "Arthur told me the story before he died," he said. "I knew my lines. I played my part."

As Michael finished his breakfast, Matt grilled him for details. And he seemed happy to oblige. He'd been wallowing in a little hair of the dog when he spotted her in a booth across the way, his Jenna. She was younger than she'd ever been when he'd known her —maybe fourteen or fifteen—and she was doing homework, her head ducked over the books and papers strewn across the tabletop in front of her, but Michael could spot anywhere that mass of Titian curls she'd piled atop her head. She'd been straightening it for a while now, so no one else might have, but he was the one who woke up beside her, the one who bumped into her in the bathroom between shower and flat iron, the one whose fingers tangoing through her tangles could almost convince her to let loose the kid who didn't give a shit—to walk out their door like the little orphan she'd once played on stage, and to hum "It's a Hard Knock Life" all the way to her studio.

When Jenna collected her things and started for the door a few minutes later, Michael followed at a distance—doing his best not to scare her. But as she stepped into the darkened alley out back, he worried over her and was overtaken by the chivalrous desire to offer her his arm.

"But," said Belinda, nervous, "you had to know nothing was going to happen to her, not yet."

Matt glared at her. "There are worse things than death," he said. "Especially lurking in back alleys, especially for the pretty and the innocent."

Yes, Belinda knew that all too well. But she also knew what would've happened if Michael had followed through on his urge, if he'd done something that he wasn't *supposed* to do.

Michael said nothing, letting Matt's objection stand in for his, then continued. "I resisted the urge," he said. "I held back. But a moment later, I wished I hadn't. As I held back beneath the awning, she crossed the narrow expanse of the alley and disappeared into the shadows on the other side."

He rushed to reach her, he told them, to rescue her from whatever foul force had taken her from him, but that's when the truly miraculous thing happened. As he stepped into the shadows himself, it was like the heavy curtains of a proscenium stage parted before him; he was swallowed up then by a whirl of lights strobing from both above and below.

It was like being inside a kaleidoscope, he told them, only the abstract shapes soon resolved into cubist tableaus, which then quickly sharpened into surrealist nonsense, before settling into a series of pop art posters representing critical periods from the whole of Jenna's life. As Michael reached his fingers towards one, the kaleidoscope would slow and the one poster would spread out into a half-dozen smaller ones, each representing an even more specific moment. And as he drew his face close to each one of those, it was as if the moment were a filmstrip in a projector just sputtering to life. When he drew back, trying to take more of this strange sight in, the memories went still once more.

He waded there, in the vast ocean of Jenna's life, for a good, long while—or what felt like a good, long while, at least—before the vision of Arthur leaving the hospital caught his eye. And it was into that current that Michael swam; it was on that wave of emotion and memory that he was finally, ceaselessly, borne into the past. For he wanted to see it all, and so see it all he did.

"In the moments where I had already made my mark," he told Belinda and Matt, "I simply inhabited my younger self. In the other moments, the moments before me—before she met me, that is—I lingered on the periphery. I never really got involved again, after that moment with Arthur."

"And did you learn anything?" asked Matt, searching for the point they were all meant to land on.

"Did you realize," asked Belinda, "that there was nothing you could have done?"

Michael smiled and took hold of one Belinda's hands, and one of Matt's. Then he spoke. "I did everything I could do," he said, "everything I was supposed to."

⁂

WHEN THEY GOT BACK to the house, one of Matt's students was sitting on the front stoop and scraping the scuffed toes of his cowboy boots along the stone of the lowest step. Belinda parked the car, but Matt seemed entirely uninterested in getting out.

"That's Austin," Belinda told Michael. "The hot co-ed that's lusting over your cousin."

Matt groaned at the latest reference to *Wonder Boys*—the movie his whole life seemed to be ripping off this weekend. In his head, he swore he was going to punch the next person who made a joke about it. But when Michael pat Matt on the shoulder and said that the boots looked more maroon than red, Matt didn't even ball up a fist. He just sighed and said, "It's a trick of the light, just a side effect of the jersey he's wearing, which *is* maroon."

This was supposed to mean something to Michael, who was supposed to know that the maroon jersey was a jersey from their high school, but something else caught Michael's eye in that moment, and suddenly he was slapping Matt's shoulder instead of patting it. He pointed at the book the kid was reading and asked Matt if that's what he thought it was.

"Is that a copy of our first trade paperback?"

Matt rolled his eyes, sighed, and told him, "Yep."

"I haven't seen a copy of that yet," he said to the kid as everyone piled out of the car. "It's not supposed to be out until next month. Where'd you get it?"

"Amazon," said Austin, handing the book and a Sharpie to Michael. "Will you sign it?" he asked. "Both of you?"

"Sure," said Michael. "Who am I making this out to?"

"Austin," said Matt, annoyed he had to repeat the name for his forgetful cousin. And yet, the kid lit up at the sound of his name rolling across the professor's lips.

"What was your favorite part?" asked Michael.

"Well," said Austin, "I love the bit where Marcus falls for John at Scout Camp. The writer and the football player," he said, winking at Matt. "Yum."

Belinda saw this and ducked her head, rubbing at the back of her neck. She said to Austin, "You know it's fiction, right?"

"Ha," said Austin, as Michael handed Matt the book and the Sharpie. "This is a roman à clef if ever there was one."

"It's a comic book," said Matt, scribbling a rough approximation of his initials under the elaborate embellishment Michael had made of his own signature.

"Graphic novel," said Austin.

"Well, actually," said Michael, and he started to make some point about how, because it was a collection of issues they'd originally published individually, it was really more of a trade paperback, but he wasn't halfway through the thought before Belinda took his hand and started dragging him up the stairs and into the house.

Matt needed to deal with this himself, she decided, even though she and Michael stood at the door once they'd closed it and eavesdropped.

"How long's *that* been going on?" Austin asked Matt, once they were alone—a misinterpretation of what was happening between Belinda and Michael that Belinda desperately wanted to clear up.

Matt sighed and said, "His whole goddamned life." Then he handed the book back to Austin.

Austin took it and slipped the volume into his knapsack. Matt stared into the maw of the ratty green thing for a second—it had belonged to Austin's great-grandfather, Matt remembered, a souvenir from the war—and again he thought of the movie his life seemed to be plagiarizing. He was soothed that he saw no hint of an ermine jacket inside the bag, no biography of Errol Flynn. And if there was some manuscript in there, Austin had tucked it into some dark corner of his laptop's hard drive where Matt wouldn't have to look at it.

At least not yet.

"Do you like the jersey?" asked Austin.

"It's the wrong number," said Matt.

"Bullshit," said Austin. "He wore this number from the day he started pop warner to the day he retired from the NFL. I've watched his ESPN special like six times now."

Matt shook his head, then jabbed a finger toward Austin's knapsack. "The John in that book is an amalgamation. Carl Jacobson is my *family* for Christ's sake. And not like some distant relation either. He's my first fucking cousin."

"Oh," said Austin, nodding and averting his eyes. "They never mentioned that in the special."

"I've tried to make it clear," said Matt, turning his back on Austin and catching Belinda and Michael peering through the curtained windows on either side of the front door. He groaned and shook his head. "I'm flattered," he told Austin, "but I'm married. And you're my student."

The gravel of the front path crunched beneath Austin's feet as he stood. He mumbled the beginning of a sentence, the beginning of a rebuttal—because with Austin there was *always* a rebuttal—but Matt cut him off almost at once.

"I may be a cliché," he said. "I may be three clichés standing on each other's shoulders in a trench coat, but I'm not *that* cliché. And I never will be."

❧

THAT NIGHT, Belinda couldn't sleep. Stricken with an incredible fear about what Michael might have done, she sat awake in her bed and reached out with her mind to keep an eye on what he was doing. But then Michael fell asleep, exhausted no doubt by his adventures across time, and Belinda found herself spying on Matt instead.

When Angel came home that night and found him in bed with his computer, she paused for a moment in the doorway to observe him, nodded once to herself as she made her diagnosis, then crossed to her dresser. She stopped there just long enough to retrieve the set of mismatched pajamas she favored at the end of long days, then made for the bathroom. By the time she turned back the covers to slip in beside her husband, Matt had finally found what he was looking for.

A few doors down, seeing what he'd found in her mind's eye, Belinda broke out into a cold sweat.

"City directories?" Angel asked Matt, putting on her glasses and glancing at his screen.

"Trying to prove something," said Matt.

Angel grunted as she turned to her nightstand to flip on the light and collect the book she wasn't reading.

"What?" said Matt.

"Prove," said Angel, "or disprove?"

Matt rolled his eyes. Then, before he could even say it out loud, Angel responded.

"I *do* know you so well. And don't you forget it."

Matt turned his attention back to the screen and stared with disbelief at what he'd found. When he didn't say anything in response to Angel's proclamation, she returned her attention to his screen as well.

"That's odd," she said, reading the text of the record Matt had found. "Isn't that the name of the place Belinda's family owns downtown?"

"Yep," said Matt, closing his laptop and setting it aside.

"And where was that one?" asked Angel. "The one you just found."

"Portland, Maine," said Matt, pinching the bridge of his nose as he closed his eyes. "Or, well, it was just over the line in Westbrook. One of the suburbs."

"And you didn't want it to be there?" asked Angel.

"No," said Matt. "No, I did not."

Down the hall, Belinda muttered a "Damn it" to herself.

⚝

She had almost fallen asleep—*ALMOST!*—when, in the dead of night, she picked up on one of Matt's dreams.

He was visited by a vision of the actor Michael Gambon dressed as a flamboyant pirate captain, his tricorn hat held over his chest as he bowed his dreadlocked head. At first, Matt couldn't trace the origins of all the disparate elements his dreaming mind had brought to bear, but when Cap'n Gambon hoisted his leg onto the bed—when he showed Matt the stump where his foot should have been—then Matt put it together.

Belinda sighed. Matt was dreaming about his great-grandfather again, about the sad story of Silas Silver VIII, who was lost at sea in 1844. All that washed ashore of him was his severed foot, clad in a boot and a stocking stitched with his initials. It was a story Belinda knew well and she wished she could have spared her uncle another rerun of it.

At least this version seemed to be weirder, maybe a little more interesting?

In the dream, after staring at the book on his nightstand for a second and trying to find his words in the vision of the weeping angel that was doubled over on the cover—after staring and thinking and staring some more—Matt offered up, in hopes that it was the right line to get thing started, "Who are you?"

"My name is Prior Wal—" the dread pirate Gambon began, but then he stopped. He stopped, turned his head to one side, and lifted a hand to scratch under the lip of his red bandanna.

"You want to make a joke," Matt told him. "But you're confused. We don't have the same name. Like they do in the play," said Matt, pointing at the book.

"Prior to you by some seventeen others," said Gambon, putting his hat back on as he tried to finish the joke he never really started.

"That's actually another Prior's line," Matt reminded the poor, old actor. "The seventeenth, I think."

"You're counting the bastards!" Gambon shouted, smiling, happy for the set-up Matt had given him.

Matt laughed. "You're like a boggart," he said. "And I've confunded you."

"I am no braggart," said Gambon. "I will leave," he said, making to stand despite his missing foot. "I will leave and this will be the day you will always remember as the day you almost caught—"

But he didn't finish, because Matt was laughing so hard.

"Oh, I needed this," said Matt. "I haven't had a good laugh in—"

"Why do you laugh at me, sir?" asked Gambon, thumping the footboard of the bed with his fist. "I bring bad tidings."

"No," said Matt. "You bring the movie I watched to put myself to sleep"—Matt gestured to his laptop and the headphones dangling from it—"the play I'm teaching next semester, and," he said, motioning toward Gambon's missing foot, "the thing I most fear."

"You fear my missing limb?" asked Gambon.

"That," said Matt, "and my tendency to rip off the things that I love."

"Rip off?" said Gambon, holding a hand to his heart. "Are you the one what cleaved me in twain?"

"In twain?" said Matt, shaking his head. "That's cribbed from somewhere too, isn't it?"

Gambon said nothing.

"And that's all I'm going to get," said Matt. "Right? Isn't that your point, Professor Dumbledore?"

"Professor who?" said Gambon, but Matt didn't explain. He was a fucking hallucination, after all. If it were the real Sir Michael, come down with some affliction of the brain and unable to recall his own career, Matt might have called up IMDB on his phone to jog the poor man's memory with a photo or two—beard, robe, wand, and all—but Matt didn't have time for this. In the dream, he stood.

And then, in the real world, he sat bolt upright. He was sick of this dream. He was sick of living a life that was little more than a mash-up of the things he read and watched and listened to. Matt's heart pounded as he tried to chase down the train of thought that was steaming away from him. He knew what he was sick of, what he *didn't* want, but what *did* he want? What did he want more than anything else in the world?

Belinda felt her own chest heaving in time with her uncle's. She was right there with him, in that room a few doors down.

Matt looked at the clock. It was almost morning anyway, so he got up. There was no time like the present, now that he knew what he must do.

No, Belinda thought. *He can't. There's no telling—*

In Matt's room, on the bed, Angel stirred. "Where are you going?" she mumbled.

"The only way I'm ever going to know what he was really like, what any of it was really like," Matt told his wife, "is to see it for myself."

He stopped to kiss her goodbye, grabbed his Moleskine and a pen from his end table's drawer, then made for the door.

Belinda was waiting for him in the hallway. "You forgot to get dressed," she told him.

"How did you—?" he began to ask, but then he got a look at himself and realized that yeah, she was right.

"Get dressed," she told him, "and I'll take you myself."

⚜

THEY DROVE downtown in the early morning light, Belinda behind the wheel again. Matt had all sorts of questions. She could feel them rolling through his mind as if on a conveyor belt, as if being carted up from the deepest, most labyrinthine recesses of his tired mind. But the only one he actually asked aloud was "Did you sleep at all?"

"You think loudly," she said, eyes still on the road. "And dream even louder."

He wanted to ask how she knew that, what she meant by that, but his family had been playing with potions for so many years now that he supposed other kinds of magic had to be possible. So, he didn't ask. He wasn't even sure which words he would have used, and in which order.

"It's a lot," she told him. "You're not going to believe most of it, so I'm going to need my full attention to break it all down. Can the questions wait until we get there?" she asked.

Matt nodded. She caught it out of the corner of her eye, but she felt it in the corner of mind as well. So, okay, that was settled. Now she just needed to get them the rest of the way there.

It was as they made the turn off Main and onto Merrimack Street that Belinda felt the first inkling of something amiss, of something gone awry. It started as a tingle, the hairs on her arm standing up, but soon enough she was shivering. And then she was shaking.

Matt asked her if everything was alright, and she wanted to say that yes, everything was fine. But she knew that it wasn't, knew even before she saw.

Then came the sight of the empty foundation at the edge of the small parking lot, the place where the Strumpet's Sister should have been.

"Holy shit," said Belinda, leaping out of the car almost before she'd thrown it into park. She ran to the place where the bar should have stood and walked amongst the weeds popping up from the cracked concrete.

Behind her, she heard the car's other door open and shut. She listened to Matt's footsteps approaching, then heard him ask a question she knew was coming but dreaded just the same.

"Why'd you drive us out to an empty parking lot?"

Matt had forgotten. He had already forgotten about the bar, about the fact that he'd ever been here—had maybe even forgotten about the research he'd been doing the night before. That's just the way the magic worked sometimes.

"Belinda?" said Matt.

She turned to face him, tears in her eyes and panic in her heart. She didn't know what to say. She didn't know how this could have happened.

"What's wrong?" said Matt.

What she wanted to say was "Everything," but what she said instead was the truth, the simple but absurd truth of what had just happened: "Somebody stole my bar."

❧ II ❧
THE SECOND HAND
UNWINDS
2016, 1971, AND ELSEWHEN

❧ 8 ❧
TRACY

O n the way to the courthouse that morning, as the convoy made the turn off 83 and onto the H-3, the men delivering Tracy Silver to her hearing caught sight of a shabby tavern they'd never seen before. It sat astride a stream that was only really there in the wet months—and there were no roads leading to it, nor any place to park. The bar looked like it had sprouted, fully grown, from the lush greenery surrounding it.

"Where'd that come from?" said one cop to another.

The second cop shook his head, then got on the horn and asked if anyone had heard of a bar called—he paused to check the sign, squinting to decipher it—The Strumpet's Sister.

In the back of the wagon where Tracy was kept, her guard shook his head. "What's a strumpet?" he asked, confused.

"A whore," Tracy told the dimwit—a replacement for her old pal Kāʻeo, who had shuffled off to join his Phyllis in the *im*mortal coil. This new guy was so stupid she couldn't even stand to look at him. Instead, she'd doubled herself over and stared at the floor. In case it might help His Brainlessness understand, she added, "*Wahine hookamakama.*"

"Sounds like a fun place," said the guard. "But only if you like punani," he said in a sing-song voice, referring to a song Tracy had never heard in an off-key falsetto she could only *wish* she'd never heard.

The guard shut up for a second—a blessing, that—but he was yammering again soon enough. "You saying you *don't* like punani, Silver? How'd you stay in that place so long without—?"

"Why were you asking about whores?" Tracy asked, cutting him off. "Making plans for tonight?" she asked. "You don't seem like the type to pay."

"Oh we always paying for it, *wahine*." He laughed. "One way or another."

"Seriously," said Tracy, "what were they asking over the radio?"

"We're about to pass some bar," he said. "No one's ever seen it before. Must be new."

"What's it called?" asked Tracy, not really giving a shit.

"Sister Strumpet's," said the guard, but then he scratched at his nose as if in deep thought. "Nah," he said, shaking his head. "That wasn't it. It was—"

Tracy sat bolt upright, so fast that the guard flinched and fumbled at his belt for something to defend himself. Tracy held up her handcuffed hands and leaned back against the wall, the only apology she could offer. Then she asked if he meant "The Strumpet's Sister."

He snapped and shook a finger at her. "Yep," he said. "That's the one."

"Can't be," she said, though she wasn't sure. She couldn't be sure of anything about that place, not after what she'd seen Ada do there. "Can't be," she said again, as much to convince herself as to convince him. "The Strumpet's Sister is on Kaua'i."

The guard shrugged. "Must be a chain," he said.

She wanted to laugh, to tell him that wasn't possible, that the Sister was a shithole not even the most ironic hipster in the world would see the potential in franchising. But she never had the chance to laugh at him. She didn't get the chance to utter even one more syllable. Because the very next moment, the guard still in mid-shrug, they passed over the stream. And as they passed over it, and past that bar that was the Strumpet's Sister but couldn't be—could *not* be, not at all—the air all around Tracy began to shimmer.

It shimmered as the air behind the bar on Kaua'i had shimmered when Kanoa was taken from her. Then she felt a tug at her sleeve, and though she felt like she could've stayed put if she wanted to, she couldn't help but wonder if the person pulling at her sleeve now was her beloved come to lift her up where she belonged—where the eagles fly, and all that jazz that Jennifer and Joe sang about in that movie where the officer became a gentleman.

Tracy missed her gentleman. She missed him *so* much. And so: she let go.

And she was gone.

৩৯

WHEN SHE CAME TO, it *was* the face of a dead person that smiled down upon her—but it was *not* the face of the man she loved. No. It was the face of *a woman* she'd adored once upon a time, a woman whose poster had adorned the ceiling of Tracy's childhood bedroom. Her mothers had wondered back then, they told her, if her desire to fall asleep staring up into the eyes of Robin Gates was a sign of things to come.

But it wasn't a sign of anything, that poster—not anything romantic, at least. Tracy didn't want to be with Robin (though she understood why seemingly everyone else did—guys, gals, and otherwise). No, she didn't want to be *with* Robin. She wanted to *be* Robin. She wanted to live life the way that Robin did. She didn't want to stop at *saying* "It's better to burn out than to fade away" (in the deep, gravelly voice of The Kurgan, of course, whilst holding a broomstick like a broadsword). She wanted to *live* those words.

And yet: she was Tracy Silver, not Robin Gates. And as much as she longed to burn, she felt too afraid of what came after—or didn't, as the case might be—and so she'd resigned herself to fading.

"You look like you're having a deep interior monologue," said Robin, as she helped Tracy to her feet.

Tracy asked where she was. "I can't see anything," she said, and she couldn't. Not really. Even Robin's face was a blur, now that she wasn't all up in Tracy's business.

"Your eyes'll adjust," said Robin. Then, playfully, she added "Thank god for the moon."

Tracy sighed, understanding that they were now playing the reference game. She racked her addled brain for a moment, then two, but came up empty.

"Maybe it's not the moon at all," sang Robin, and there was a quasi-question mark at the end of the line. Tracy wasn't sure if that was from the song itself, or if it was something Robin added to encourage Tracy to jump in when she was ready.

"I got nothing," Tracy admitted, still squinting and un-squinting her eyes to try and make some sense of where Robin had taken her.

Robin deflated, her shoulders falling at a rate commensurate with the corners of her lips. Now appropriately slouched, given her status as a latter day member of Generation X, she sighed and finished the reference on her own. "I hear," she said, not bothering to sing anymore, "Spike Lee's shooting down the street."

At last the light bulb went on in Tracy's head, its chain swaying and clattering against the insides of her aching skull. "Bah humbug," she said.

But Robin did not smile, even though, yes, that was the line.

"I've always thought *Rent* was overrated," Tracy reminded Robin. "You know that."

"I thought you might finally have developed some taste," said Robin. "In your old age."

Tracy scoffed. "Old?" she said. And then, without thinking—before she could stop herself—she added: "I'm still younger than you were when you—"

"Yep," said Robin, cutting Tracy off. She held a hand to the spot in her gut where the bullets had drilled into her. "Congratulations on that."

Tracy lowered her head in shame, and it was only then that she noticed the blanket of snow at her feet. She snapped back to attention and stared at Robin, waiting.

"We're home" was the answer that Robin gave.

"How?" asked Tracy. "And why?"

A door lurched open in the darkness, a column of dim light spilling out of a bar that looked like—but couldn't be, could *not* be—the Strumpet's Sister. A waitress stepped out toward them, a garbage bag in each hand, and Tracy could not believe her eyes. It was the same woman who'd served them, Tracy and Kanoa, all the time back on Kauaʻi.

Only she was wearing winter boots now.

"Hey, Trace," the waitress called out. She deposited her trash into the cans that lined what Tracy saw clearly now was an alley. Then the waitress came over to Robin and Tracy and gave them each a big smile. "Long time no see," she said.

"What," said Tracy, trying to catch her breath, "is happening?"

Robin and the waitress exchanged a look. The waitress raised an eyebrow.

"I'm getting there," Robin told the waitress.

The waitress frowned and shook her head. "Get there faster," she told Robin, tapping at the place on her wrist where a watch might have been. Then she made her way back to the bar.

Before the door was shut, Tracy used the dim light that spilled from it to give the building a once-over. Sure enough, just like each of the other Sisters, there was a bar on the first floor and some kind of furniture store on the second.

"How many of these have you seen?" asked Robin.

"Three," said Tracy. "One on Kaua'i, one on O'ahu, and now this." She leaned herself against the cold brick wall opposite the Sister. "Where is this one?" she asked. "Massachusetts?"

Robin nodded. "The Cape," she said. "At the mouth of the Red River in Harwich."

But that, Tracy knew, was impossible. She had grown up just around the corner from the mouth of the Red River. She had lived, since the age of eight, in a house that was within spitting distance of that point. Her mothers *still* lived there. And there was no bar there. There never had been. Unless you were talking about a *sand* bar.

"The Sister is wherever she needs to be," said Robin. "If that's what you're wondering."

"But why am *I* here?" asked Tracy. "I'm supposed to be in a courthouse right now," she said. "Or, I don't know, back in prison. I have no idea what time it is."

"You want to go inside?" Robin asked. "I'm buying."

THEY CAUGHT up over Midori Sours—"Michael's drink," Robin reminded her, as if Tracy didn't know—and over plate after plate of mozzarella sticks and marinara. Robin beat around the bush like the tease she'd always been, but Tracy let her. The sound of her voice was like a warm blanket on a winter's day, and it always had been.

In the years since they'd last seen each other, Robin had puttered around Polynesia, toured Thailand, and even gone looking for her mother's family in Manila. She'd grown out her hair and dyed it blonde so that she could start playing shows again, and that had gone great for a while.

"Until the article in the *Enquirer*," said Tracy. "Right?"

Robin nodded, then threw back the rest of her drink. "Last thing I needed," she said, wiping at her mouth with her sleeve. "Can't a dead woman wander the world in peace?"

Tracy smiled, nodded, and then ducked her head.

"I don't hate you," said Robin. "For bringing me back, I mean."

Tracy nodded some more.

"And it's not your fault that Ada hitched a ride," said Robin. "How could you have known?"

Tracy's eyes went wide, her jaw falling.

"Oh shit," said Robin. "You *still* didn't know."

Tracy listened as Robin explained her connection to Ada, and how the magic of the potion had allowed Ada to tag along when someone of her bloodline was brought back to life.

"Ashley never told you any of this?" asked Robin.

"Auntie knew?!" said Tracy, flummoxed. "How? When?"

Robin lowered her head, mumbling something about how she'd told Ash everything. She had expected her to pass along what she knew and couldn't understand why she hadn't.

Tracy sighed. "I didn't tell Auntie the whole truth either," she said. "I never told her about bringing you back, or about Ada. So maybe it's my fault, too."

"Do you regret it?" asked Robin.

"How could I?" said Tracy, looking at Robin again, staring into those eyes that had given her purpose for so long. "You had business to finish. A lot more," she added, "than I even realized."

"And Ada?"

Tracy thought for a moment, then two. When she spoke, it was with great care. "She probably would have found another way out eventually, right? I mean, she's a part of our family's past that we've needed to reckon with for a *long* time."

Now it was Robin who nodded. Now it was Robin who ducked her head.

"What?" said Tracy.

"I want you to do it again," said Robin. "For someone else."

Tracy was shaking her head before she could even get the word "No" out of her mouth.

"I know," said Robin, pressing her hands together in front of her, as if in prayer. "I know what you told me about Kanoa. I know, Tracy. But—"

"No buts!" said Tracy—a little too loudly, it turned out, because the conversations all around them just stopped. And then there was nothing but silence, silence competing with silence until the other patrons finally got back to their own business.

"What about Ashley?" asked Robin. "Would you do it for her?"

⚘

ON THE DAY SHE DIED, Ashley asked if Tracy had anything to compare with the tales she'd been telling. Or, well, Ashley *told* Tracy, whose envy sat like a stack of tottering green bricks in the pit of her quaking stomach, that she *must* have something. "At least one great story," she'd said. They were both Silvers, after all —the children of Judas, according to the old family yarn—so there had to be *something*.

There *were* stories about Kanoa at that point, as adventurous a lover as Tracy had ever had, but the relationship was still young and technically they were "on a break." The whole thing felt *fragile*, like something that needed to be clutched close to the chest.

There was the story of Ada waiting at the foot of her bed on the night they met, but that was creepy. And Tracy felt sure that what Ashley was looking for was something sexy or funny, and certainly not anything creepy.

So she told the story of her first time instead of her second.

She'd lost her virginity—what a dumb fucking phrase, she

paused to tell Ashley, as if someday she might *find* it again, bop it on the nose, and tell it to stay put this time. She'd lost her virginity—and wasn't this hilarious? (no, really; wasn't it?)—on a ratty old couch in the theater her moms had made out of the family's old barn.

"See," said Ashley. "I knew you had something."

"But it doesn't compare," said Tracy. "Not really."

"I've fucked on that couch," Ashley told her. "The leather sticks to your ass something fierce."

Tracy nodded, admitting that was true.

"And there are so many rips," said Ashley, "it's a wonder the dude ever finds his mark."

Tracy feigned a gag, said "Eww!"

"No," said Ashley, laughing. "I'm fucking serious. I'm pretty sure I had to pull a guy out of the exposed foam once upon a time."

Tracy snorted back a laugh, then covered her nose and mouth with both hands.

"Why," said Ashley, "must we always guide them to the promised land? Is there a man alive who could find it for themselves?"

Kanoa had been doing a pretty good job by that point, but Tracy felt certain that the question was rhetorical. So she didn't say anything.

"You know what ruined my first time?" asked Ashley. "Or, not *ruined* it, per se, but *tainted* it I guess."

Tracy shook her head. She didn't know.

"The soundtrack," said Ashley. "He blasted a Sarah McLachlan CD to mask the sounds. Sarah fucking McLachlan. Can you believe it?" she said with a laugh.

"Which album?" Tracy asked, because not all of them were bad. In fact—she did some quick math in her head—almost all of the ones that were out when Ashley lost her virginity were—

"The green one," said Ashley, stepping onto the tracks to stop

Tracy's train of thought. "She's holding her hand to her heart, and—"

"Oh," said Tracy, nodding. "That's *Fumbling*."

"Yeah," said Ashley. "Fumbling. That's a good word to describe that night."

Tracy told her that the arrangements on *The Freedom Sessions* were sexier, and Ashley looked dumbfounded.

"Oh," said Ashley. "You're one of *those* people."

Tracy couldn't tell if her aunt was kidding or not, so she proceeded with her argument just in case. "I swear," she said. "You listen to that one, and you better have a spare set of panties ready to go. Because the floodgates," she said. And then, rather than finish the sentence, she brought her hands together in front of her face, then pushed them apart like she was about to say *voila* —only she said "*Whoosh*" instead.

Ashley laughed and told Tracy that she admired her spunk, that she'd always been jealous of it actually. "If I'd been born thirteen years later," she said, "how much more fun would I have had?"

"It's still hard," Tracy told her. "And we have the internet."

Ashley nodded, sighed.

"A thousand and one hot takes for every little I thing I put into my body, and any little thing that might come out of it."

Ashley raised an eyebrow. "Are the things you put into your body usually little?" she asked. "Cause, *girl*, you *know* you can do better."

⚜

ROBIN HAD BROUGHT Tracy back to Massachusetts for the ashes. Sitting at their table inside the Strumpet's Sister that night, drunk on melon liqueur, Robin explained that she'd gathered everything else Tracy would need. But the ashes were the key ingredient. It was easy enough to find someone behind the veil, Robin explained, if you knew where to look. But if you had no idea where to start, then you needed a piece of the person to call them home.

"I thought you *always* needed a piece of the person," said Tracy.

"The diary you found," said Robin, "Ada's diary? It only tells part of the story. The stuff you've been doing—you're only scratching the surface."

"So," said Tracy, "I could find anyone I wanted, if I looked hard enough."

Robin said nothing for a moment, and it was only then—in that silence—that Tracy noticed how much older Robin looked now. The crow's feet and the laugh lines, the wrinkles and the streaks of silver in her hair—age looked good on her, there was no doubt, but there was more age on her than there should have been. She would've been 41 now, if she'd never died. But she *had* died, and—Tracy tried to do the math in her head, then resorted to her fingers—she'd been dead for four and a half years before she'd been brought back.

Assuming dead people didn't age until they were alive again... Tracy's thoughts trailed off. She was getting a headache, and she wasn't sure how much of that was the liquor's fault—and how much was the sheer complexity of her situation right now.

"It's not just about looking hard enough," said Robin. "It's about looking *long* enough," she said. "And even then..." And now it was Robin who trailed off.

"Who have you been looking for?" asked Tracy.

There were tears in Robin's eyes as she said, "Who do you think?"

And so, here they were, camped out in the family's barn-turned-theater, a pair of binoculars trained on the bedroom window of Tracy's moms. They were supposed to be in bed an hour ago, Tracy told Robin. They had a routine.

Robin took the binoculars from Tracy and held them to her

own eyes. "Oh," she said, "the door's opening now. Here they come."

"Seriously?" said Tracy. "Of all the dumb luck. I finally give up looking and *now* they come. I wanted to see how they were doing." Tracy tapped Robin on the shoulder. "Give 'em back."

But Robin did nothing of the sort. She held the binoculars tight to her face.

"Are you blushing?" Tracy asked her.

"I used to love watching your mother play guitar," said Robin. "She had such a way with her fingers. The things she could do..."

Tracy scoffed. "Yeah," she said. "Desiree always said the same thing."

"I'm sure she did," said Robin, and now she was smiling.

Tracy stepped toward the door. "Am I going in by myself?" she asked. And then, when Robin didn't answer, she asked, "Are you going to be the lookout?"

Robin lowered the binoculars then and turned to Tracy. She looked rattled, but pleasantly so, and she said simply "You don't want to go in there right now."

"They fall asleep quick," Tracy told her. "And once they're asleep—"

Robin shook her head and Tracy quit speaking. "They're not asleep," said Robin, holding the binoculars out for Tracy to take.

Once Robin had stepped out of the way, Tracy held the damn things up to her eyes again and took a look. Her mothers lay naked on the bed, their legs tangled together like a pretzel of flesh. Mom grabbed hold of Desiree's ankles, one in each hand, and then arched her back as she tugged at each leg in turn, grinding her groin against her wife's. Des writhed under Mom's ministrations and let out a yelp that Tracy could hear clear across the yard.

Tracy dropped the binoculars, which were heavier than they looked, straight onto her foot. And it was only then, as she hopped up and down, that Robin finally bust a gut. She just laughed and laughed and laughed.

৩১৫

By the time Tracy crept across the carpet of the house that had once been her home, she felt certain they'd waited long enough. She was sure that her mothers would be asleep, especially given their bedtime exertions.

But, of course, she was wrong.

Mom sat in the shadows and made herself known only once Tracy had reached the mantle. But unlike the overbearing parents in the 80s movies she'd grown up on, Mom didn't pull on the draw string of some old-fashioned lamp. Nope. She just tapped on the screen of the iPad sitting in her lap.

Startled by the blue glow, it took Tracy a moment to see which of her mothers was sitting there.

"She's not in there," said Mom, nodding her chin at the urn Tracy held to her chest.

"What?" said Tracy.

"You know what her last wishes were," said Mom.

"Yeah," said Tracy, "but I also know that you never did it. You were supposed to scatter them, but Desiree convinced you not to."

Mom gave a sympathetic smile. That, and a sigh. "It's a bunch of sand," she said. "From down the beach."

"No," said Tracy. "I needed—"

Mom raised an eyebrow. "You needed your auntie's ashes?"

Tracy set the urn back on the mantle. She breathed in and out, in and out, trying to collect herself.

"What are you up to?" asked Mom. "And how *did* you—"

"I bought a Monopoly card off some old dame for a pack of smokes."

"Which Monopoly card?" asked Mom.

Tracy rolled her eyes at her mother.

"Oh," said Mom. "*Get out of jail free*."

Tracy tapped a finger against her nose. Then she said, "I should go, in case the cops are looking for me."

Mom looked puzzled by this. "Why would the cops be looking for—?"

"I should go," said Tracy again. This time she nodded toward the door.

"Who's waiting in the barn?" asked Mom.

"Huh?" said Tracy.

Mom held up the iPad. "I put a couple of cameras in there after we had some break-ins. That's how I knew you were here."

"Why do you think there's someone else?" asked Tracy. "Did you *see* someone else?"

"Kinda," said Mom, and she bit her thumb in thought. "She looked familiar, but it couldn't have been who I thought it was. Right?"

"Right," said Tracy, nodding.

"Okay," said Mom, nodding herself now. "So, *why* do you need Ashley's ashes again?"

"I really should go," said Tracy, stepping back toward the door.

They stared long and hard at each other, a parent looking at a child she still knew like nobody else did, but who she somehow didn't understand at all anymore—and a child looking at the mother she was *sure* was going to figure everything out if she didn't run right freaking now.

It was a long while before either of them spoke again, or even moved. But then Mom said "Michael. If you need ashes, Michael will still have some."

"But he swore," said Tracy.

Mom's eyebrows lifted ever so slightly. Then she tilted her head to one side, and suddenly Tracy understood.

"Michael," she said with a sigh.

Mom stood then, took Tracy into her arms, and squeezed. And after Tracy was finally inclined to acquiesce and return the gesture, Mom let the hug linger for just two seconds more. Then she broke away and pulled open the door.

"Good luck," she told her daughter.

❦ 9 ❦

BELINDA

I n the midst of her third day without sleep, Belinda
wandered the halls of Matt's vast house clad in nothing but
bunny slippers and a smile.

There was no one home, with Matt out teaching and Angel at
her office on campus, but Belinda wasn't sure if she would've
gotten dressed even if they *were* there. What was the point?
What was the point of *anything* anymore? The calamity was sure
to begin any moment now, the end of the world as they knew it,
as soon as someone somewhere in the time-stream decided to
change what wasn't meant to be changed.

She had failed. All of the work she'd done to keep this world
from falling apart the way her own had—all of the horrible things
she'd done had been all for naught.

Belinda had a vision just then of the day she'd killed her
beloved Nasha's mother, the day that Queen Yona had decided to
defy Belinda's will for a second time. She could see herself
yanking Yona's chair backwards at the end of that year's annual
card game, could see the startled queen tumble to the floor. And
then she could *hear*—she could hear again, right there in the
kitchen of her Uncle Matt's home—the sound of a high heel

driving down into the back of a helpless woman's neck. Belinda could hear the sound of it, the *squelch*.

She sunk to the floor with her hands pressed over her ears, a scream spilling out of her mouth. But the cold linoleum against her backside was the shock to her system that she needed. Presently, she forgot what she was thinking about altogether.

And yet, she knew she had been upset—upset about something big. So she did what her mother had trained her to do when she was a little girl, when the thoughts and the fears came so fast and furious that she felt like a lion cub running for her life in the midst of a stampede. She did what Mom had told her to do all those years ago: she imagined her mind as a silent meadow instead, a field of grass with not even a breeze to disturb its stillness.

By the time Belinda opened her eyes, she could think of nothing but what was right in front of her—exactly as Mom had taught her to do—and what was right in front of her was this: a pair of unshaven legs, a pair of gnarly feet, and the pair of bunny-shaped slippers they had just slipped out of.

"I need a shower," she said to herself. So she took one, and it was a blissfully mindless experience. There were no thoughts in the house to interrupt the feeling of the water pounding against her flesh and washing her clean, no thoughts in her own head and none in anyone else's to find their way in.

As she dressed, Belinda did find herself thinking again though —and what she thought about was this: the person who'd stolen the Sister from her.

It could only be one person, she decided. It had to be her: the pixie who'd been trapped inside the place for years, the girl whose resurrection Ada had used as a way to sneak out into the real world. Robin Gates.

It had been a long time since she'd suspected Robin of collaborating with Ada. They'd had too many conversations over too many cups of tea, Robin flitting in and out of the bar now that she was free of its bonds. And Belinda had seen how concerned Robin was each time she came back empty-handed in her quests across time and space. She had taken to counting the wrinkles on Robin's face, the streaks of gray in her hair. The girl seemed genuinely upset that she had been the cause of Ada's escape.

Could it all be an act?

Belinda pulled on pair of yoga pants and a hoodie, stepped back into her bunny slippers, and ambled back to the kitchen for something to eat.

As she made herself a bowl of oatmeal, she thought of the last conversation she and Robin had. She thought of the topic—Ada's plans to get revenge on the Silvers—and she tried to remember exactly what she'd said, what words she'd spoken to placate the other woman. Probably some version of "whatever will be will be," Belinda admitted to herself—a phrase that must have done little but frustrate Robin. Robin, who seemed determined to make a difference.

"It's my fault that Ada's out there," Robin had said, holding her teacup to her lips but not drinking it. "I've got to stop her, no matter the cost."

"You don't mean that," Belinda told her, sipping at her own drink. "No one really does. Sometimes the cost really is too high."

"Not for me," said Robin, setting her cup down upon its saucer. "I'll keep digging through time to find a way. If I have to go back and change things, I will. I don't care if it kills me."

Belinda remembered how certain Robin had sounded. She remembered wishing she could read the woman's mind to find out *just* how certain she was, but the minds of the dead were off-limits.

A half-hour later, she was still pushing her spoon back and forth through her breakfast— the oatmeal a cold sludge now. When the front door opened, Belinda took one look at her uneaten meal, sighed, and brought the bowl to the sink.

No, she decided, Robin wasn't aiding and abetting Ada—but she might be just as dangerous.

"Hello?" came a voice from the hall, an angel's voice. Angel's voice.

The lady of the house came into the kitchen just as Belinda was rinsing her bowl out in the sink. She set a pocketbook down on the counter and took a seat at the kitchen island, drumming her fingers on the thick wood of the tabletop. It was an absent-minded gesture, as absentminded as Belinda thinking of Angel as "the lady of the house." Had Angel ever thought of herself that way, Belinda wondered. Back before she transitioned, had she been the one to wear the apron and do the laundry and make the bed? It was hard to imagine Uncle Matt doing any of those things. Maybe neither of them did. Who knew?

"I had a break between appointments," said Angel. "I thought I'd come check on you."

"Did Matt say something?" asked Belinda, setting the now-clean bowl into the strainer and beginning to scrub the spoon.

Angel shook her head. "But he didn't have to, did he? Woman's intuition," she said, tapping a finger to her temple and smiling.

"Did you have that before?" asked Belinda. She put the spoon in the strainer to dry alongside the bowl, then tore off three sheets of paper towel to dry her hands.

"What do you think?" asked Angel, not unkindly.

"I..." Belinda stuttered. "I didn't mean to imply..."

"Didn't mean to imply what?"

Belinda tossed the now-moist wad of paper towels into the open maw of the kitchen's trash basket. Then she took a seat across from Angel. Not sure what to say—not sure how to say anything without digging herself a deeper hole—she said nothing. She thought for a moment about reading Angel's thoughts for a little help but decided that would be cheating.

"Do you have questions you'd like to ask me?" asked Angel. Then she began to nod. "It's okay, Belinda. You can ask."

Before she could stop herself, she blurted it out, the question that had been on her mind since the moment she'd realized her Uncle Matt—lover of men—was married to a woman in this universe. A trans-woman, yes, but a woman. "Does he miss it?" said Belinda. "Your—"

Angel laughed. "Does *he* miss it? What about me?"

Belinda blushed. "Do you?" she asked sheepishly.

"Not as much as he does," she said, and there was pain behind the smirk—a sense of rejection, albeit a small one. "Then again, I knew that a part of him would always live in the past. I knew it," she said, nodding, "and I married him anyway."

Belinda wanted to reach out and give Angel's hand a squeeze, but she didn't. She might have lived under the woman's roof for years now, but they hardly knew each other.

This was why she was so shocked when Angel reached out to touch *her* hand. "I gather," she said, once she had Belinda's attention, "that you two had a conversation with Michael the other night, about where each of you would go if you had a time machine."

Belinda smiled and nodded. "Yes," she said. "And Matt was the first to answer."

"He told me," said Angel. "And he told me about the answer he gave."

"November 1844," said Belinda. "To see his great-grandfather before—"

"He was lying," said Angel, and it was as she said this that she got up and went to the refrigerator, plucking a can of Chelmsford Ginger Ale from the crisper.

"How do you know?" asked Belinda, sitting up straighter in her chair. She was taken aback by this. Sure, Matt had hesitated before giving his answer, but he'd seemed so sure of it.

"They all say that," said Angel. "Matt, his sister, their cousins.

They all have this fascination with that part of the family's history, but deep in their hearts they're all more morbidly curious about other dates."

"Do tell."

"Michael," said Angel, "has an overwhelming desire to understand how the death of their grandfather affected him. So, he'd travel to April 1994. For Veronica, it's the day Matt came out—the day that drove her further into the closet. Ashley, when she was alive, couldn't stop talking about the day she and Vern found their grandmother talking to a mirror. And Matt..."

"Yes?"

Angel paused, as if deciding whether or not she was violating some unspoken agreement by sharing her husband's secrets. Her face was screwed up in concentration—her brow furrowed, a frown on her lips. But finally, mercifully, she spoke. "The year he was born," she said. "1971."

"Why?" said Belinda, fearing what the answer might be—fearing what an obsession with one's own birth and conception might be a symptom of.

Angel finally cracked open the soda she'd been carrying around with her as she paced the kitchen. Then she took a seat and leaned in close to Belinda, as if someone might overhear them in the empty house.

"I'm sorry if I'm prying," said Belinda.

"He won't see anyone," said Angel. "He says that's what he has me for, and that it's just a philosophical debate anyway, just a hypothetical argument he likes to have with himself—that it's not actually S.I."

"S.I.?" said Belinda, never as afraid of an acronym as she was now.

Angel took a sip of her soda before she answered. Then she spoke aloud the words Belinda had feared, without knowing exactly what they might be. "Suicidal ideation," said Angel. "He imagines—or *debates*, as he puts it—what life would be like if he went back in time and stopped his father from taking advantage of his mother's youthful adoration."

Jesus, Belinda thought to herself. As much damage as Michael might have done, traipsing about 1976 on the day Jenna was born, what Matt had considered doing would have been so much worse. *Maybe*, she found herself thinking, *it was a good thing the bar disappeared.*

The gentle pressure of Angel's hand atop her own was what it took to break Belinda from this reverie.

"This stays between us," she said. "Understood?"

Belinda nodded.

"I'm telling you because..." She trailed off for a moment, collecting her thoughts. Angel was a woman who tried never to be caught in situation where she couldn't carefully consider each word she spoke. "You need to be careful with him," she said. "I know you're close. I know he confides in you. And I know he looks unbreakable on the outside, but it's a façade. It's all for show, Belinda. Remember that."

Belinda nodded, though she resented the fact that Angel was babying her uncle. It was the people who never confronted these things directly who were the most dangerous, especially when they had access to the potion that these Silvers had access to. Those who used time travel as a form of therapy—those were the people were very likely to doom this universe, just as they'd done the last.

Angel stood and walked herself to a cupboard across the room, a tiny one tucked into an alcove above the Lazy Susan. Then she withdrew a basket from within it and brought it over. When she set it upon the table, Belinda marveled at the contents. It was filled to the brim with corked glass vials.

"These are the empties," Angel told her. "He used to leave Tracy in charge of the stuff, but ever since she went to jail he hasn't been able to stop himself. If you've ever wondered what he's doing when he locks himself up in the office on Saturday mornings 'to write,' wonder no more."

"What was in these?" asked Belinda, playing dumb.

Angel raised an eyebrow. In her mind—Belinda tried to stop herself from reading it, but couldn't—Angel thought *Does she think I'm stupid?*

"What?" said Belinda, keeping on with the lie.

"I'm not going to dignify that question with a response," said Angel, pulling the basket away from Belinda and bringing it back to its shelf in the cabinet. Then she began to make her way out of the room and toward the back hall and its set of stairs.

"Angel," said Belinda, hoping to stop her though entirely unsure what she was going to say if she succeeded in the effort.

Angel stopped at the threshold but didn't bother to turn back and face Belinda.

"I'm sorry," said Belinda, fearing the apology would not be enough—*knowing* it wouldn't be.

"I have no patience for lies," said Angel. "Not in my office, and not in my home."

"Understood," said Belinda.

And then Angel was gone.

&

WHEN SHE FINALLY FOUND SLEEP THAT night, that elusive mistress, Belinda dreamt herself into—of all places—the "gentlemen's club" back on the Avenue of the In-Between, the one just down the street from where The Strumpet's Sister sat when it wasn't hopping from place to place and from time to time. The unimaginatively named Firehouse had been built into, appropriately, an old firehouse—with a catwalk centered around the pole the firefighters had once used to slide from upstairs to down during an emergency. And yet, that wasn't the most striking thing about this place, at least not to Belinda, who had never been inside before now—mostly out of fear of catching her Auntie Ashley taking her clothes off. What was most striking to Belinda was that women of all shapes and sizes graced each stage and pole—and that patrons seemed to be hooting and hollering for all of them, and tipping generously to boot.

How had she ended up in this stripper's utopia? It was almost like...

The word didn't come at first. But then, when Belinda saw the woman strutting down the runway toward her, she said it aloud: "Heaven."

"Hannah, actually," said the dancer, who was the very picture of physical perfection—long legs, tautly muscled arms, a tone stomach, and an ass that looked like she did a thousand squats a day. An idyllic figure, except perhaps for the two scars across her chest where her breasts had once been.

"You."

"Don't have long," said the woman who called herself Hannah but who was in fact this reality's version of Belinda's beloved aunt. Ashley crouched down to get closer to eye level with Belinda. "I don't know how you got here, or how we're able to talk," she said. "I thought the magic was limited to blood relations, but—"

"Go on," said Belinda, not wanting to explain. "You don't have much time."

"They're coming for me soon," said Ashley. "I can feel it. And when they come, they—"

"Who's they?" said Belinda.

Ashley rolled her eyes and sighed. "Shit," she said. "You really aren't prepared for this, are you?"

Belinda bristled and thought to stand up, but she worried there might be a bouncer and didn't want to be seen causing trouble. So, she sat silent and let herself be chastised. It didn't seem like it was going to last long anyway, and she felt certain that she needed whatever information Ashley was going to give her.

"Sorry," said Ashley. "It's just: I don't know you. I don't know why it's *you* I'm seeing right now and not Michael or Matt."

"You think your brother or cousin want to see you like this?" said Belinda, raising an eyebrow.

Now, finally, Ashley smiled. "Good point," she said. "Well, whatever. You're here. Now, listen: my girlfriend, the love of my life, she has this plan to bring me back to life. She wants us to protect my niece, Tracy."

"But Tracy's in jail," said Belinda. "Does she *need* protecting?"

Ashley didn't question how Belinda knew this, but she did stand for a second to stretch out her legs before she brought herself back down into a crouch.

"I'm sorry," said Belinda. "Go on. I'll try to stop interrupting."

"S'okay," said Ashley. "Anyway, she says she wants us to protect Tracy from this crazy Ada bitch, but as far as I can tell Ada is dead and that's why Tracy's in jail. So, I'm worried that Robin's real plans are something way bigger. I think she wants to use this crazy-ass bar we used to hang out in to travel back in time and—"

"Change something," said Belinda, and she felt herself break out into a cold sweat—though whether it was in the dream, or reality, or both, she didn't know.

Ashley nodded. "Tracy's the key, though. I feel it in my bones. So," said Ashley, "if you can convince Trace—"

"But Tracy doesn't know me from Adam," said Belinda. "She might've heard of me, of her Uncle Matt's assistant, but—"

Ashley set a hand gently atop Belinda's panicked head—she would've gone for the shoulders, Belinda suspected, but she might have fallen over—and it was exactly the steadying influence Belinda needed in that moment. This might not be *her* Auntie Ashley, but the effect was the same as it had been when she was a girl and her Auntie had patted her on the head as she, Mom, and Dad fled the city for the mountains.

"I'll recruit Matt to the cause," said Belinda, looking up at

Ashley and beaming at her with a love that the woman could not possibly understand.

"Michael would be better," said Ashley, withdrawing her hand now that she sensed Belinda was okay again. "Trace has always been closer with Michael, though god knows why."

"I can't," said Belinda, standing. "Michael is..." She thought about telling Ashley now who she was, and who Michael was to her, but decided against it. "Michael's too complicated."

Ashley laughed as she rose again to her full height, her knees creaking in protest as she did. "Don't I know it," she said.

"Your knees," said Belinda, pointing. "They couldn't fix that here?"

"In a strip club?" said Ashley, and she raised an eyebrow as she said it.

Now it was Belinda who laughed.

"It's my heaven," said Ashley, lifting her arms to gesture to the whole of the place. "And I want to feel alive, not dead. Pain's a part of that," she said. "And it ain't that bad."

Then she gave Belinda a wink, strutted back down the catwalk toward the pole, and got back to work.

☙❧

WHEN SHE WOKE, Belinda searched her closet for the most seventies-looking thing she could find. She tried to remember the difference between the early 70s—where she was going—and the later 70s, which were the first thing to pop into mind. Did she want bellbottoms, or not? That was the first big question.

Then she realized she didn't *own* any bellbottoms so it was a moot point.

She shook her head at an old joke that came unbidden into her head at that moment, from the show she and her parents had watched far too much of in their seclusion in the White Mountains. Was it really a "moot" point, or was it, as Joey Tribbiani from *Friends* would have put it instead, a "moo" point? A cow's opinion.

As in: it didn't matter. It was "moo."

There was a knock on Belinda's door. Startled, she said "Come in" before she realized she was still only half-dressed.

The door opened and Matt walked in. When he saw the state of her, his assistant clad only in a bra and boy shorts, he turned right around and faced the open doorway as he spoke. "Sorry," he said. "I thought I heard a commotion and thought I should check on you."

"Had a helluva dream," she said, pulling on the first vaguely flowy blouse she could find.

"Sorry to hear it," said Matt.

"Don't be," she said, opening the pants drawer of her dresser and searching for a pair of boot-cut jeans in there. Boot-cut were close enough to bell bottoms, right?

You don't want bell bottoms! a voice in her head tried to tell her, but she ignored it.

"Listen," said Matt. "Sorry if Angel and I are being overly helicopter-like. It's just, you seemed really upset the other day when you said your bar went missing."

"Someone stole it," said Belinda, correcting him as she pulled on the only pair of non-skinny jeans she had.

At the sound of Belinda's zipper zipping up, Matt gave a brief peek over his shoulder to see if the coast was clear. Seeing that it was, he turned around to face her again. Then he asked "How, exactly, does someone steal a bar?"

"She got control of the dice," said Belinda, glancing across the various surfaces of her room to see if there was anything she felt she should bring with her.

"The dice?" said Matt.

Belinda nodded. "Yes," she said. "The dice control where the bar goes next. Only I'm guessing she found a way to rig them. Someone did that once before," she said, nodding to herself as she confirmed that no, she wasn't forgetting anything in the room. Then she finished her thought: "I had that person killed."

Matt laughed nervously. He laughed and laughed, until he noticed that Belinda wasn't laughing. Then he stopped.

"I need your help," she told him. "But first, I need to show you something. Are you in?"

"In?" said Matt.

"This isn't going to be like your potion," she told him. "The way we're traveling, we could do some real damage. So, I need to teach you to be careful first."

"Careful?" said Matt. "Traveling? I'm confused."

Belinda nodded and told him, "I know." Then she ran her hand through the air in the room, looking for a fraying edge—for something to tug on. When she found it, a part of the Veil of the World she could grab hold of, she tore a hole in it.

Orange light spilled into the room as Matt fell backward against the door jamb in shock. He gasped as Belinda slipped both hands into the hole she'd torn in the air, as she pushed it open until it was as wide as her arm-span. Then, when she twisted the orientation of the hole, so that it was taller than it was wide, he said "What the actual fuck?"

"You're going to have to duck," she told him. "This is as big as I can make it."

Matt pointed into the gaping orange hole in the air. He wanted to ask her what it was—she could hear him thinking that —but he couldn't get the words out.

"It's a doorway," she told him, "to a place you've always wanted to go—that you've drunk dozens of ounces of potion to try and reach—and when we get there, I'm going to show you how to change the past."

"What?" said Matt, standing up straighter and taking a step towards the portal Belinda had torn in the air.

"Yes," she told him. "You heard me right. I'm going to show

you how to change it." She held out a hand for him to take. "Then I'm going to show you why you shouldn't."

He wasn't sure. He was intrigued, of course, but he couldn't decide what she meant by any of this. He couldn't decide if what she was proposing was safe, or if he'd be home by dinner—or if he'd ever come home at all, if she taught him how to do what he'd always dreamed of doing.

She felt his uncertainty in the air and in her head, and she was thankful for it. That he was still considering the effect his actions might have beyond satisfying his baser instincts—that was good. But she didn't have time for this, so she took hold of his hand and gave him the gentlest of tugs in her direction.

When he didn't resist, when he took a step toward her, she took that as her cue that he was good to go. Then she yanked him into the hole and they were gone.

❧ 10 ❧

TRACY

U ncle Michael's house sat upon a hill of black lava rock just east of Diamond Head. It was a modest house for the area, but the area in question was a multi-million-dollar neighborhood. "Modest" here wouldn't have been modest anywhere else. The house had four bedrooms, including the one Tracy had slept in throughout her four years studying at U of H, a bespoke art studio over the garage for Michael, and a magnificent lanai out back with a mostly unobstructed view of the Pacific.

In a perfect world, the house would have been empty on the night that Tracy arrived to steal Auntie Ashley's ashes—the final ingredient for the potion she and Robin had been brewing for two weeks now—but Tracy wasn't living in a perfect world. Far from it. When Robin brought the Strumpet's Sister back to Hawaii two weeks ago, the bar had apparently "argued" with her—whatever *that* meant—about *when* it could take them. They'd wanted the Sister to bring them to Hawaii on the same day, or thereabouts, as they'd left Cape Cod. That way, Michael would still be in Mass-achusetts for the holidays. But the bar, having ideas of its own, had deposited them in Honolulu on November 9 instead—bringing Tracy and Robin back in time by *weeks*, back to before

Michael had gotten on his flight and before Robin had sprung Tracy from jail.

The bar brought them back to the day after Election Day.

Was it a cruel joke? Was there something they were supposed to learn by having to live through the immediate aftermath of the presidential election for a second time? Tracy didn't much care. She kept herself locked in a room out back, to make sure nobody spotted her and reported an escaped convict, and she worked on the potion.

Robin, when she wasn't busy serving one downtrodden patron after another, came out back to tell Tracy she was worrying over nothing—that she didn't need to stay hidden. "You haven't escaped yet. You're still in jail, remember?"

Tracy supposed that was true from a certain point of view, but it made her head hurt to think about it. Staying out of sight and focusing on the important work at hand—that was just fine by her.

By the night the potion was ready though, Tracy was itching for some fresh air. And so, she asked Robin if she could be the one to break into Michael's house. She knew the place better, after all. She'd lived there for four years.

"Okay," said Robin. "Just be careful."

And she had been. She had snuck around the side of the house, keeping herself hidden in the trees there until she'd made it to the one side of the lanai that didn't look directly out over the ocean. She was almost there. Michael was already asleep inside, forever a creature of habit, and there was nothing standing between Tracy and Auntie Ashley's urn except for a baby grand piano and ten feet of hardwood floor.

Unless the dog was lurking about.

In the immediate aftermath of Auntie Ashley's death, a grieving Michael and Jenna had purchased a purebred beagle pup who they'd named Chuck. He was a chill dog, never happier than when he was curled up in Michael's lap or at the foot of the bed, but he was also prone to prowling about at night whenever he caught the scent of something interesting. Tracy remembered well the many times Chuck had turned up at her door after she'd spent a night out with Kanoa. She remembered how he'd circle her and sniff before stopping for a scritch behind the ears. She remembered the time she came home after a double date with a bit of the smell of Kanoa's buddy on her, and the smell of that buddy's girlfriend—probably from the hugs goodbye at the end of the night—and how Chuck had tilted his head at her after his inspection, as if asking for an explanation.

Tracy smiled at the memory and sighed at the thought of how amazing a cuddle with Chuck would feel right now, how great it would be to curl up on the couch across the way with a warm doggo to keep her company. And yet, she knew it would cause nothing but problems if the beagle made an appearance. She wrinkled her nose, sniffing herself and smelling nothing. *Please*, she thought, in a silent prayer to Chuck and the universe, *don't smell me*. Then she crept across the floor, stepping as lightly as she could.

The urn sat between a statue of Haumea, the fertility goddess whose presence here Michael had once hoped would help get his wife pregnant, and the mangy old boot of a nineteenth-century ancestor that was supposed to remind him to be true to himself.

What hopes Michael had for the urn, Tracy scarcely knew, but its magic wasn't any more potent than the trinkets bookending it. He was the worst at talismans, Michael—the absolute *worst*. His branch of the family tree was still barren, and he suffered crises of conscience with such regularity that—assuming Shakespeare was right about conscience being "a thousand swords"—Michael could have built an Iron Throne to rival the high seat of Westeros.

And then feel guilty for not making the swords into a thousand plowshares instead.

Tracy sat on the edge of the chaise longue and un-stoppered the urn, a gentle breeze fluttering a set of curtains hanging behind her. She stared into the vessel in deep thought, despite the tickle of linen and cooling sweat on her mostly bare back. But then the unravelling wicker of the aging chaise began to chafe against the backs of her thighs. And so, cursing herself for not sitting on one of the better kept seats, she set the urn in her lap to reshuffle herself.

And that's when it fell.

That's when it fell to the floor and shattered, the breeze scattering the ashes across the lanai and toward the cliff beyond—beginning the work that Michael had long neglected, but with none of the reverence demanded by the enterprise.

Tracy fell to her knees and grabbed for the ashes. From inside the heretofore darkened house came light, the scampering of a barking beagle, and then the hurried footsteps of that dog's weary master.

"Shit," said Tracy, her free hand plumbing the depths of her backpack for a plastic baggie that suddenly didn't want to be found. By the time she had it, her uncle and his dog had arrived. Michael's jaw fell in disbelief at the sight of her, but Chuck didn't seem to care how or why she'd magically returned to their house. He just ran right over, leapt up onto her left leg, set his front paws upon her chest for balance, and began to lick her face.

"Aren't you supposed to be—?" Michael began to ask.

"Yes," said Tracy, cutting him off as she gave Chuck a quick hug and then set him back down upon the floor. He stood obediently at her feet but continued to look up at her. His wagging tail tapped out a frantic rhythm against her shin as she got back to work

"What are you doing here?" asked Michael.

She wrapped one hand around the final fistful of her aunt's remains, while the other fumbled with the ziplock of the baggie.

Michael frowned at her silence. "How long," he asked, "until the police arrive?"

The baggie finally open in her lap, Tracy unclenched her fist over it. Not all the way open, but enough that the dust fell into the bag like sand through an hourglass.

"Tracy," said Michael, a hint of anger and impatience in his voice now, "what are you doing?"

Chuck barked at the shift in Michael's tone, then he nudged Tracy's knee with his nose.

"I broke outta the big house, bro. And orange ain't the new black, kid," she said, affecting the Southie accent they used to use when making fun of their distant relatives back home in Massachusetts. She hammed it up, hoping to keep him distracted from what she was doing. "No matter what they say, guy. Orange don't blend in at all, dude. Doesn't go with shit. Clashes with everything. So, y'know, I had to lay low until I could—"

"*Lie* low," he interrupted, trying to correct her.

"Nah," she said, shaking her head as she zipped up the baggie. "Nope."

"Agree to disagree?" he said. And then he smirked, blinking a tear into oblivion. It was lovely, really, to know that he missed her. And she would've hugged him if she could, but she had to get out of there.

Tracy stood and smiled at him. "I agree, Professor, that you're an idiot."

Chuck circled Tracy's legs, as if asking *Where do you think you're going?* Meanwhile, Michael shook his head and laughed at Tracy's use of 'Professor,' the nickname her mothers had long used to tease him for being an insufferable know-it-all. Then he looked at the floor, and at last remembered what had startled him from his sleep. "What happened?" he asked. But before she could answer, something else seemed to dawn on him. He pointed at the baggie, then stared wide-eyed at Tracy.

The game was afoot.

"Don't try to stop me," she told him, backing toward the edge of the porch, ready to make for the woods if he so much as flinched—ready to jump a cliff or two, if need be. She could be

Lara Croft if she needed to. Like Croft, she had raided a tomb. Kinda-sorta.

Chuck stood his ground and looked back and forth between Michael and Tracy, Tracy and Michael. *Where is she going?* he seemed to ask Michael. *And why aren't we following her?*

Michael shook his head at Tracy. "Don't do it again," he said. "That concoction of yours... you know what it leads to."

"Bullshit," she said, taking another step backwards. "And you know it. It got my mother out of her loveless marriage, it set things straight between you and me, and—"

"And what about what happened to the original enchantress, huh, when she used it on our dear old ancestor?"

Tracy rolled her eyes, the heel of her hiking boot finding the edge of the lanai at last. "I know what I'm doing," she said, careful not to step too much further back without looking. The house was perched on the edge of a precipice, after all. And an unintended splash into the Pacific was sure to test the water resistance of her dollar-store baggie in ways she was not prepared to risk.

"Tracy," he said, stepping forward until he was standing at Chuck's side.

She took a long look at the two of them, the man and his dog. Michael looked tired, with more gray in his beard now than brown. And the half-moons of sallow skin beneath each of his bloodshot eyes betrayed the weight of the baggage he'd carried with him for the three years since his sister's passing.

"I miss her, too," he said, taking another step toward Tracy. "But she's in a better—"

Tracy fumed. "Don't you dare," she spat. *A better place?* He was a fucking atheist, for Christ's sake. He didn't get to say "*a better place*," no matter who he was trying to placate. "Don't you dare finish that sentence, you liar."

Michael took another step in her direction, and Tracy wondered why she hadn't run yet. She loved him, it was true, but he was a weak man—a man whose weaknesses weakened her—and she didn't have time for that.

But those hazel eyes of his, those eyes boring holes in her soul at this very second—you could find any color in them that you wanted, and any answer. "It's true," he was saying, when Tracy came back to herself—but she couldn't remember *what* was true. Or what truth was, after all. "Tracy," he said, drawing nearer still, "we both know it's true."

It was the "we" that did it, that finally unstuck Tracy from the spot. She turned tail and ran, ignoring Chuck's barking as she stumbled over the fallen fruit of their coconut tree. She rolled her ankle once and then again, coming up lame. Tracy hopped on one foot for a second, grasping at the hurt to try and pull it out of herself. But she couldn't linger. She could hear them coming, Michael and Chuck both. And so, hurt though she was, Tracy ran as hard as she ever had. There would be nothing to stop her this time.

Nothing, and no one.

☙❧

WHILE TRACY BURGLED Michael's house, Robin kept watch over the cauldron. They'd AirBnBed the nearest and most affordable place they could find for the night and set up shop there, sick of hanging out in the Sister and listening to drunk patrons sob about the president-elect—and "done" with the bar now anyway, according to Robin. But even the short distance from Michael's house to their rental was too much for Tracy's rolled ankle. When she crossed the threshold, she could barely stand.

Robin lingered at the cauldron's edge as Tracy sat on the floor and made the final preparations. She sprinkled the ashes she'd stolen from Michael's house into a Solo cup they'd found in the rental's cupboards, which they could throw away afterwards. Then she ladled the cauldron's brew into the cup with a plastic spoon, hoping that the quality of the vessel and the utensil didn't really matter. They didn't want to leave even a scrap of potion behind for someone else to use, and they didn't want to risk tainting any of the house's cups or cutlery with their magic.

"Your ankle," said Robin.

But Tracy paid Robin no more mind than she paid her injury (now that she was sitting, at least). There was no time. She couldn't be sure that Michael hadn't followed her. And if Michael found them, she had no idea what would happen.

So Tracy said nothing. Instead, she stirred. Seven times to the left, seven to the right. Then she pocketed the spoon and spoke the incantation. "Leaves of magic," she chanted, "leaves of must—do not break our sacred trust."

The draught went still in the cup. Then, after a moment long enough for Tracy to lose her breath—and a bit of her faith—it began to turn again, to whirl in the opposite direction.

Tracy brought the cup to her lips and swallowed its contents in one giant gulp.

She leaned back against the couch and closed her eyes, not opening them again until Robin told her "It's happening."

Tracy looked to the window, which is where Robin was pointing. Outside, where night had fallen fully during her escape, there was a blinding light. It was if the noonday sun was in the sky again.

"She died on one of the brightest days of the year," Tracy told Robin, as the light grew ever more blinding. The two of them held their arms up over their eyes, but even that seemed like not enough. It felt as if they were *swallowed* by the light.

And then, just as suddenly as it had come, it was gone. The light was gone from the window and the whole room was dark. All of it.

All of it, except for a sliver spilling from under the lip of the bathroom door.

Tracy made to get up, wincing as she did, but Robin held out a hand to tell her to stay put. So "stay put" is just what she did. Tracy watched the other woman cross to the door, then held her breath as Robin knocked.

"It's open," spoke a voice from beyond the door.

Robin turned the knob and pulled it open.

Standing before the mirror, naked as the day she was born, was Tracy's Auntie Ashley. Her breasts were still gone, her head still bald but for the stubble that had sprung up in the days since she quit the chemo (and quit shaving because of the chemo). She was still too thin and too tan—her dying wish having been to lay out under the sun one last time. But she was as beautiful as Tracy had ever seen her, and she seemed to know it too. Because Ashley, standing at the mirror that night, was smiling. Smiling as she hadn't smiled at her reflection for years.

"I haven't seen you look so happy in front of a mirror since..." said Tracy, trailing off. "You seeing something that you've never seen before?"

Ashley turned to face Tracy and gave her a sad smile. Tears were rolling down her cheeks.

"What?" said Tracy. "What do you see?"

"Nothing," said Ashley. "I don't see anything at all."

꧁꧂

IN THE GETAWAY car that night, Robin explained that, yeah, the people who Tracy brought back to life—they couldn't see their own reflections.

"Something to do with the light," Robin explained. "And with the state of us, y'know? We're here, but we're not here."

Tracy, torn between watching the road to see where Robin was taking them and watching Ashley in the backseat, nodded along with Robin's explanation.

"You can see us," said Robin, "but we can't see ourselves."

"Because you know the truth," Tracy told Robin. "You know

the truth that we can't accept: that you're not supposed to be here."

"Well," Robin stuttered. "Um..."

"Kanoa never mentioned that," said Tracy. "Not that we were around a lot of mirrors out there in the forest."

As the clock struck eleven on that Saturday night, she tried to get her bearings. She knew they'd turned onto the H1 at some point, but she hadn't paid much attention to whether they were headed to the windward or the leeward side of the island. Aside from the fact that they weren't on the interstate anymore, Tracy wasn't sure *where* they were.

Then, almost without warning, there was the ocean on the left. Without thinking twice about it, Tracy rolled down her window to see if she could catch a whiff of the sea.

Robin, seeing what Tracy was doing, followed suit. When Ashley saw that the other two were forgoing the AC in favor of fresh air, she got in on the act. Soon enough, each of the women had an arm out one side of the car or the other and Tracy, feeling like a kid again, made waves with her hand, imagining the wind was water.

In the distance, the smokestacks of the power plant at Electric Beach pierced the dark veil of the night sky and Tracy smiled. She smiled at the memory of snorkeling there with Kanoa on one of their first dates. She remembered how he'd taken hold of her hand as they waded out into the break waves, how he taught her not to judge the place by the cloudiness of the water near the shore, and how he assured her the pipes coming out of the plant were outflowing clean water and not the kind of toxic waste that you'd get at the beginning of a superhero origin story. But mostly she remembered the fish: so. many. fish.

The warm water flowing out of the plant's cooling pipes was like the milkshake in that Kelis song: it brought all the fish to the yard. Kanoa would tell her the names of each species later—the surgeon fish, the trigger, the butterfly, the *damsel*—but when they were underwater and could not communicate except through their smiles, she delighted in trying to name each one before they disappeared. This led to derivative names of course, to fish named after the seven dwarves and the knights of the round table, but there was at least one Aloysius and two Cleopatras.

And then there were the sea turtles congregating around the coral, the spinner dolphins taking their afternoon naps, and, of course, the pod of mermaids resting on the beach.

Tracy remembered them best of all, the gaggle of little girls with their zip-on tails basking in the sun. She remembered how they'd asked her if her boyfriend was The Rock, and how he'd tried to raise one eyebrow up high like The Rock did—and failed miserably, much to the delight of the pint-sized sirens all around them.

By the time she slipped out of this daydream, they had long since passed the attraction which had inspired it. And yet, she was still basking in the afterglow of the memory as she asked "Where are we headed?"

From the backseat came a grumble. Ashley asked Robin why she hadn't told Tracy the whole plan.

"How do you know," Robin began, a flirty lilt to her voice "that *you* know the whole plan?"

"Quit it," said Ashley, obviously not in the mood.

"It's okay," said Tracy, trying to make peace. "I didn't mean to start a—"

"You didn't," said Ashley, giving Tracy's shoulder a squeeze.

They drove in silence through the towns of Nanakuli and Maili and were on the outskirts of Wai'anae before Robin said something. Tracy had spent that whole leg of the drive sneaking peeks at the expression on Robin's face. Whenever an oncoming car illuminated it for long enough, Trace tried to guess at what was going on behind the stoic, focused look their driver wore on her poker face, but she got nothing. Robin was a closed book for once, never once letting on whether Ashley's "quit it" had bothered her or not.

When she wasn't looking at Robin and trying to figure out what was what, Tracy played with the buckles of the knapsack sitting on her lap. She squeezed it around the middle now and then, as well, trying to guess what was inside. A change of clothes, she imagined. But what else?

When Robin finally spoke, it was simply to let Tracy know they were headed toward a harbor. Then she went silent once more, as if daring Ashley to find fault with the few words she'd uttered.

Ashley, with considerably less aggravation in her voice than before, asked "Is the Sister parked there on one of the streams?"

Robin nodded. "The Kawiwi," she said. "I'll give the signal when we pass by."

"Signal?" said Tracy, hoisting the knapsack into her lap—in case maybe she was supposed to be ready to disappear again, to be transported somewhere else.

Robin nodded again. "A signal," she said. "Yes. Like I told you, we don't need the Sister anymore. I'm going to let the girl we left in charge know she can bring it back to the owner now."

"There's an owner?" said Tracy, though she felt foolish even as she asked the question.

There was another grumble from the back seat, but Robin didn't address this one at all.

"You'll meet her someday," said Robin. "If we're lucky."

As they passed the town's Jack in the Box, Tracy felt a rumble in her stomach that reminded her how long it had been since she'd eaten. She supposed that skipping meals was one of the perils of hanging out with the undead. They could eat—she knew this from those blissful days with Kanoa 2.0—but they didn't have to.

And yet, the feeling of hunger quickly turned to a feeling of unease when, to distract herself, Tracy looked to the other side of the street and spotted the town's police station.

Ashley must've seen it too, for at that moment she began to massage Tracy's shoulders from her spot in the back.

"How was it inside?" Ashley asked her. "Everything Netflix made it out to be?"

Tracy laughed. "And more," she joked.

"But she didn't hook up with anyone," teased Robin, giving Tracy a playful jab in the thigh.

Ashley gave Tracy's shoulders a squeeze. "Why not?" she said. "Surely Kanoa will give you a pass."

Tracy ducked her head and sniffled back a couple of tears. "He's dead, Auntie" is what she told Ashley. "I've got to accept that. I can't keep bringing him—"

"But what if you could?" said Robin. "What if you were *meant* to?"

Tracy turned in her seat so that she could get at least half a look at each of the women she was riding with. Was this the plan all along, she wanted to know? To bring Kanoa back again, to risk Ada's wrath one more time?

She asked each of these questions in turn, but she received an answer to exactly none of them. What she got instead was an exchange of looks between Robin and Ashley that was heavy with meaning, practically *dripping* with it. But whatever it was that they knew, they weren't ready to share it with Tracy.

She was being treated like a child, and she wanted to scream about it—but she knew that would just prove that she *was* the kid they took her to be. So Tracy mustered her composure and sat there in her seat, waiting for one of the others to be the first to break.

As they drove over the bridge which crossed the Kawiwi, the Strumpet's Sister looming large to their left, Robin brought two fingers to her temple and then flicked them quickly away from her face. A moment later, the Sister disappeared in a flash of orange light and Tracy gasped as two dozen drinkers stumbled away from where the bar had once been and back to their cars—none of them paying any attention to what just happened.

"You deserve to be happy," said Robin, out of nowhere—as if what had just happened outside her window was commonplace and entirely un-miraculous.

"Yes," said Ashley, leaving it at that.

"But Ada," said Tracy, and she felt herself shiver as she spoke the name aloud. "She won't stop."

"You leave that to us," said Robin, flipping on her directional to signal their turn into the parking lot for the harbor.

"Yes," said Ashley again, and Tracy wondered when she'd suddenly gotten so agreeable—and if the word 'Yes' was the only one left in the usually loquacious woman's vocabulary.

Tracy sniffled, thinking of Kanoa kissing her in front of the little mermaids back in the day—thinking of the delight he took in fulfilling their request that The Rock kiss the princess. "I want to trust you," she told Ashley and Robin. "I want him back so much," she said. "But—"

"No buts," said Robin. "We've got a plan," she said.

And then Ashley added, proving that she could say more than yes—and that maybe, just maybe, she still believed in whatever plans Robin had in store—"We have a plan, and we're sticking to it."

BELINDA

Belinda knew well the story of how Matt's parents met. Though Matt and Michael had embellished a great deal of their family's history in their comic book, *The Children of Judas*, Matt admitted that most of the material surrounding his conception and birth was lifted straight from real life. Michael had used photographs from the period to design the background, Matt had written real snippets of conversation into the dialogue —or, well, they were real enough, though he supposed nuances might have been lost in translation as the stories were passed down over the years—and the names of the real life people had been barely obscured by the veil of fiction. Silvers became Golds, and so on.

And so, it was no surprise to Belinda that, when she and Matt walked into the Christmas Party at Andre Francisco's place in December 1970, it was more like walking into a memory than any other trek through time she'd ever taken. It was Matt whose jaw had to be picked up off the floor. He'd always imagined that he gotten *most* of the story right, but he'd never imagined just how many of the particulars he'd positively nailed.

There were the stereotypical details of the early 70s that

would have been hard to fuck up—ash trays everywhere, plenty of polyester, and bell bottoms galore—but then there were the specifics about this particular party: the trio of buzz-cut dads at the poker table, struggling to find common ground with their long-haired sons; the De Rosa sisters, flirting with any and everyone who came their way—and especially hard with anyone rocking a mustache; and, of course, Old Man Andre, who was kicking the ass of anyone who dared to challenge his ping-pong supremacy.

It was that sight, of Andre tapping his ping-pong paddle against his thigh as he waited for the next challenger—it was *that* sight which most captivated Matt and Belinda's attention. And for good reason. This man was the closest Matt had ever had to a second grandfather, though he was actually Matt's *mother's* grand-father—and only then by marriage. The sight of him still in good health, health that would be in decline by nine months from now, was remarkable.

Trouble was, Matt stared too long. And he got a ping-pong ball thrown at his head to pay for it. Luckily, the reflexes that had served him so well as a shortstop once upon a time were still sharp. It took very little effort at all for him to tilt his head to one side and snatch the hurtling ball out of the air.

"Nicely done," said Andre. Then he waved his paddle at Matt and told him to drag his sorry behind over to the table.

Matt did as he was told, Belinda following close behind. When he reached the table, he gave the old man a smile and picked up the paddle.

Andre nodded at Belinda and said, "You look a little young for him."

"Oh," she said, blushing—both at what Andre said and at what he was thinking, the lascivious nature of the picture of her that went running in slow motion now through his mind—"we're not..." she stuttered, distracted by the thoughts she was picking up from all over the room now that she'd opened her mind, thoughts about her in her too-tight pants that were coming in from all directions.

Andre laughed as he picked up a stogie from the ash tray he'd left on the corner of the table. "I'm just kidding," he told her. "Don't sweat it." Then, as he took a puff and the pungent smell of the thing wafted in the direction of Matt and Belinda, he asked, "You all from around town?"

"No, sir," said Matt, and Belinda wasn't sure why he was lying. More importantly, she wasn't sure how convincing his lie was going to be.

"You're not from Billerica, are you? Lowell?"

"Haverhill," said Matt, offering up the city where he'd moved to as an adult. So, it wasn't a lie after all, Belinda realized. At least he wasn't trying to overdo it.

Andre deposited his cigar back into the ash tray. "How'd you end up at my party then?"

"Customer," said Matt, "of ol' Eli Silver." Then he began to bounce the ping-pong ball off the table—back and forth between the palm of his hand and the surface that Old Andre saw as his kingdom.

Andre nodded. "Good guy that Eli," he said. "That family's been through a lot. His oldest boy's just back from the war."

"Oh," said Matt, still bouncing the ball. Belinda noticed how steady he was with it, how precise. "I didn't know that," said Matt. "He here tonight?"

Andre pointed his paddle off to the other side of the room. "Sure is," he said. "Over there, keeping the eldest of my grand-daughters company."

Matt turned to take in the moment, and Belinda could feel the conflict in him swelling. He didn't know what he was going to do when he spotted his parents flirting with each other—his twenty-year-old father getting ready to take advantage of his lovestruck seventeen-year-old mother. Was he going to run over there and try to stop it, as he'd long imagined? Or was he going to chicken out, the vision of himself blinking out of existence too much to bear?

When he finally caught sight of them, it was something of a disappointment. They were just two kids standing in a corner and making small talk. Robert Silver hadn't made his move yet, whatever move it might be. If anything, young Lydia De Rosa seemed to be paying Rob more attention than he was paying her.

Matt sighed. It was supposed to be more awful than this. And yeah, maybe it would get there before the night was over—maybe his father would prove himself to be every bit the rapey asshole Matt had long imagined him to be. But for now, there didn't seem to be anything to stop. So he turned back to Andre, bounced the ball across the table to him, and made ready to get his ass kicked.

"You gonna move the ash tray?" he asked Andre, pointing his paddle at it.

"Tell you what," said Andre, a twinkle in his eye, "ten bucks says you don't get one anywhere *near* it."

"You're on," said Matt.

❧

AFTER MATT LOST two out of three to Andre, he and Belinda excused themselves to get some refreshments—but not before Andre handed over a crisp new Hamilton to make good on their bet. He was still laughing as they left, positively in stitches about the faceful of ash he'd gotten for doubting his guest's abilities.

"At least he can laugh at himself," said Belinda to Matt.

"He'd cry his eyes out if he couldn't," said Matt, cribbing a line from an old Indigo Girls record that they both adored.

Matt's grandmother Carlene was holding court in the kitchen, ever the hostess—even back then. The only difference in the seventies was the attention she was getting from the town's eligible bachelors, who were lining the walls for a chance at the foxy thirty-four-year-old's attention.

As Matt and Belinda made their way toward the punch bowl, Belinda asked him if he was ready.

"For what?" he said, as he first filled her cup and then his own.

Belinda nodded back toward the living room, toward the couch where Matt's parents were now sitting next to each other—Lydia's hand on Rob's knee as she regaled him with some story or other, completely oblivious to the boredom in his eyes.

"What do you want me to do?" asked Matt, as they took up spots on either side of the doorway and tried to look inconspicuous.

"I want you to go over there and try to interrupt them," she said.

"How?" asked Matt.

"It doesn't matter," she said, shaking her head. "You won't get that far. I just want you to start heading in that direction."

Matt looked at her like she had two heads, like he wanted to ask how she could be so certain of his imminent defeat. But then he gave her a nod and got himself underway. And sure enough, he'd barely made it halfway across the room when a long-haired kid with walrus-looking mustache got all up in his business.

"I seen you looking at Lydia," said the kid—who looked familiar to Matt, but who Matt couldn't place for the life of him. "I seen you looking, and I'm telling you to buzz off. You catch my drift?"

"Listen," said Matt, looking down at the kid and admiring his spunk. "I was just going to see if she was alright. That guy she's with looks a little old for her."

"He is," said the kid, who looked like he'd been giving the matter a lot of thought. It suddenly occurred to Matt that maybe this kid was after his mother too, and that he'd been beaten to the punch. So to speak.

"You know him?" asked Matt. "He a friend of yours?"

"He's my brother," said the kid, looking more annoyed than ever.

Matt tried not to let his jaw droop even the slightest bit as he finally recognized the fifteen-year-old version of his Uncle Albert standing before him. Back by the door, Belinda did her best not to run over and give the man who might've been her grandfather a hug.

"You're not going to get her away from him," said Albert, glancing over his shoulder at the scene as he said it. Then, looking Matt in the eye again—looking up at this tall stranger and trying to figure out what his deal was—Albert said, "but you're welcome to try." Then, finally, he stepped aside.

Matt gave Albert a nod and started again toward the couch where his parents-to-be were getting cozier and cozier with each passing minute. But just as he was passing the TV, that old wooden thing he remembered from Grammy Carlene's house that was probably brand new right now—just as he got within spitting distance of disrupting the past—he was surrounded by a whirlwind of butterflies.

It was the strangest damn thing. No one else seemed to see them, no one seemed to take note of anything amiss until Matt stumbled backward to get away from the maelstrom of many-colored wings. And even then, they got back to their drinks and their conversations quick enough—so quick Matt realized this couldn't have been the first freakout they'd seen that night, and that it probably wouldn't be the last.

He made his way back toward Belinda, only daring to ask "What the hell was that?!" once he could whisper it into her ear.

"The Butterfly Effect," she said, smiling. "Never let it be said that God doesn't have a great sense of humor."

THEY STEPPED OUTSIDE for what Belinda had planned next. It was one thing for the crowd at the party to see Matt bugging out about the butterflies. That was something they could chalk up to a bad trip or a bit too much punch. But what she was about to show him now—if they saw how he reacted to this, there'd be no explaining that.

She led him around the back, into the small patch of trees that divided the yard of the Franciscos and De Rosas from that of the neighbors. Matt was pointing up at a darkened window on the second floor of the house as Belinda made ready for her next revelation.

"That's my mother's bedroom," he said, jabbing a finger in that direction. "That's where it's about to happen," he said, and then he wheeled around and was all up in Belinda's business in the blink of an eye.

"What?" she said.

"Why couldn't I stop it?" he asked. "What the fuck was with the butterflies?"

"The butterflies are what happen when you get too close," she told him, taking a step back and trying to get some breathing room. He was upset, understandably so, and though she liked to think she knew what he was capable of, the truth hit her harder now than usual: this was not *her* Uncle Matt. He was close, but he wasn't the real thing. Truth was, if she was being honest, she had no idea what he might do next.

"Too close to what?" asked Matt, trying to catch his breath and to calm his temper.

"To changing something," she told him. "We live in a world where whatever happened happened," she said. "Every trip you've ever taken, every trip your sister has taken, your cousins, your niece—those were all supposed to happen. That's the way the universe works," she said. "Until it doesn't."

"What are you talking about?" he asked her.

She held out a hand and asked him to let her show him. It would be easier that way.

He hesitated for just long enough for Belinda to doubt herself. She'd read millions of minds since arriving here in this new reality —billions, really, and maybe even *trillions*—but she'd only ever shared her own thoughts with a handful of people over the years. Would it work the same as it had the last time?

Matt took her hand and squeezed, and together they found out. They tangoed through time, through Belinda's long, long life, with Belinda always in the lead. And when Matt threw out a pop culture reference to make himself more comfortable with the insanity of it all—when he told her "it's hard to do this backwards" in the whiny voice of Mark from *Rent*—she spoke exactly the reply he was waiting for:

"You should try it in heels."

When the dance was done and they were standing again in a darkened corner of Old Andre Francisco's yard, Matt was crying. In his head, he wanted to ask her if she'd really lived through everything he'd just seen—through kings and queens and guillotines. But then, as that phrase came into his head and he realized he was ripping it off from somewhere—Aerosmith, he suddenly remembered, the *Draw the Line* album—it dawned on him that Belinda could see everything he was thinking, could hear it. That was one of the things he'd just found out—just one of many, but it was the hardest to understand.

"How?" That was the only word he could get out of his mouth. The thought of her knowing *everything* was overwhelming. She knew every secret he'd ever kept, every lie he'd ever told—to his family, to Angel, even to himself. And he couldn't stop her from knowing, even if he tried.

Matt bent over and vomited a stomachful of punch onto the freshly fallen snow.

"When my world ended," she told him, "I ended up in the river—that never-ending river that seems to circle the whole universe. And then, before I knew it, I was watching a new world being born. Thrashing about as the river pulled me along, I watched creation restart itself. I watched as the history I knew was rewritten, often in the subtlest of ways."

"And then you saw your parents," said Matt, still doubled over and now crying again. "At the fertility clinic."

Belinda nodded. "That's when I started to pull myself to shore," she said. "I was *so* angry at first, but as I swam closer and closer to land, I got to see more of their lives play out. I got to see them happy, and the *world* happy—happier than it had been when I was growing up, that's for sure. And by the time I crawled up onto the beach, I wasn't angry anymore. Just exhausted," she said. "And determined."

Matt started, tentatively, to stand up straight again—to try and rise to his full height—but then he stopped when he was eye-level with the girl who would have been his niece if fate was less cruel. "Everything you did," he began, and he was thinking about the people he'd seen her kill—the old queen most of all, her lover's mother—"everything you did, you did to protect them. Them, and their new happiness."

Belinda nodded and reached out a hand to see if he needed some help getting fully upright again. But he shooed it away just as soon as she'd offered it. And then, with a grunt, he finished standing up. He closed his eyes to try and calm his churning stomach, waited for a moment, and then swallowed back the last of the sick trying to slosh its way up his gullet.

"Was it worth it?" he asked her, and there were so many emotions and thoughts running through his head that Belinda couldn't tell *what* he was feeling or thinking anymore. She'd actually been trying to stop reading him altogether, but his brain was being so damn loud now that was impossible

"I don't know," she said, and it choked her up to admit that. "But I do know," she said, with a touch more confidence, "that one person's selfishness, one person's desire to have the world that *they* want, shouldn't end a world for everyone else."

"But isn't that what *you're* doing?" spat Matt, and now she could see clearly that he was pissed off. She didn't need to read his mind to figure that out, not with the way he loomed over her now.

"I don't want this world!" she spat back, poking him in the chest so hard that he backed off. "But I don't get to decide," she said. "That's my point. I don't get to decide, and *you* don't get to decide. We all decide together."

Over Matt's shoulder, Belinda spotted a light blink on in Lydia De Rosa's room. This was the moment of truth. *This* was the moment they'd come for. And so, she pointed. She pointed and she told Matt to turn around. She wasn't going to trick him into missing it, into missing his chance to do what he'd long dreamed of doing. She was going to let him have his moment, see what he decided to do, and then react accordingly.

Matt turned on the spot and watched the two silhouettes on the drawn curtain come closer together—closer and closer, until they became one. Then he watched the shadow monster of his imagination begin to shed clothes from itself.

"This is your chance," Belinda told him. "Barge back in there, ask someone if they've seen Lydia, and it'll all be over."

Snow began to fall again. Belinda watched Matt gritting his teeth, watched him balling and unballing his fists. Then she saw, through his mind's eye, a butterfly fluttering by and dodging snowflakes. One butterfly, then two—then two dozen. But still Matt did not move—not physically, at least. Inside his head the gears were turning and he was considering whether Belinda would try to stop him, and how hard she would try.

The thing that finally gave him pause, that finally made him unclench and give up his "what if?" dream, was the same image that had been stopping him in his tracks ever since he'd first started having his fantasies of interrupting his parents' first night together. It was a vision of his sister, Veronica, her wife Desiree, and their daughter Tracy.

The picture was of the three of them together, when Trace was still young. They wore matching overalls, and Tracy was getting a piggyback ride from Desiree as Veronica looked on beaming. Michael had taken the picture, then painted a portrait of it for Des and Vern's first Christmas as an official couple. It was adorable—so precious, in fact, that it almost made Matt want kids of his own.

If I'm never born, Matt thought, *then Vern will never be born. And if Vern...*

Matt turned round to face Belinda again, and he had tears in his eyes. He could see in her face, in the heartbroken expression she wore too, that she'd been reading his mind the whole time.

"Fine," he said.

Behind him, the light in Lydia De Rosa's window went out and history proceeded as it was meant to.

❧ 12 ❧

TRACY

Bobbing about in the dinghy they'd stolen, Tracy held the knapsack tight to her chest and did her best to keep from hurling. And yet, between the steady roll of the waves and the googly eyes that Ashley and Robin were making at each other, keeping dinner down in her stomach—down where it *belonged*—was proving to be quite the challenge.

It wasn't that Ashley and Robin getting back together bothered her. No. Their lusting after one another was certainly better than the bickering and tension they'd seemingly left behind in the car. But the idea of two ghosts having sex with each other—that was giving Tracy pause.

How would it work? They seemed corporeal enough to her now, but what happened when things started getting hot and heavy? Could they hold themselves together for long enough to get the job done?

Tracy set the knapsack aside. Then she doubled over and rested her head between her knees. Closing her eyes, she asked how much longer they were going to be waiting.

"It's not an exact science," said Robin, "but they should be here any moment."

What they were waiting for—the reason they were drifting further and further out into the Pacific right now—was a ghost ship. *More fucking ghosts*, Tracy thought to herself. *Great*. It was the best way to get where they were going, Robin claimed, if they didn't want Ada following them.

"Why?" Tracy had asked.

"Because," Robin had said, "it's nigh impossible to catch a ride with these guys. So almost nobody even tries."

The name of the ship, Tracy knew from asking, was The Antagonist—not that she should expect, she was told, for those words to be tattooed on the side of the thing. It was a pirate ship, after all, and had once been meant for an entirely different purpose—before it was stolen that is.

Who had stolen it? Tracy knew that now, too. They'd been out in the dinghy for a good long while now and she'd learned more about the boat that was coming to rescue them than she needed to know. It was a naval cutter, whatever that meant—did Robin even know what it meant, Tracy had asked, but she had never gotten an answer—and it was one of fastest sailing ships the world had ever known. Before it disappeared in the Bermuda Triangle in 1742, the ship and its crew were infamous all along America's eastern seaboard—feared whether they were flying their bloody red flag or not.

When Tracy asked Robin why they, the three of them in the dinghy, shouldn't fear these ghost pirates themselves, it was Ashley who answered. This was the one thing she knew, apparently—and the only reason she'd allowed Robin to put Tracy's life in danger.

"The captains of the ship," said Ashley, "were our ancestors: Silas and Bethiah Silver."

Tracy had asked which Silas they were talking about, because the sea sickness was keeping her from thinking straight. Hadn't they all died on land, all of them until Silas VIII?

It was Silas IV, Ashley told Tracy, and yes, he had died on land.

Somehow, he'd escaped the fate of his wife and the rest of their crew and made it back to shore. He didn't die for another thirty years, until the Red River Massacre—the day that two dozen Redcoats stormed the beach near the Silvers' home on Cape Cod and slaughtered three generations of Silver men all at once.

And so, Ashley and Robin posited, when The Antagonist overtook their dinghy and brought them aboard, there was no way that Cap'n Silver—Captain *Bethiah* Silver, that is—was going to make her descendants walk the plank.

Tracy told them she was pretty sure that 'walking the plank' was a myth, but they paid her no mind. They just went back to making fuck-me eyes at each other.

And so, here they were—*still*, an hour later—being tossed about by an increasingly angry sea, waiting for their piratical rescuers to come.

"I'd say 'get a room'," said Tracy, "but I suppose those'll be in short supply."

"Sure," said Robin, "but 'get a hammock' doesn't have the same ring to it."

All three of them laughed at that, in varying degrees of amusement. Then they went silent again, in part because there was nothing else to say—no great way to continue the joke—but in part because it looked like Robin had heard something.

Presently, she pointed toward the horizon—toward a thick fog gathering there and headed in their direction. "Look," she said, and Ashley and Tracy did as they were bid.

Just peeking out from the highest reaches of the fog was a mast rigged with massive white sails. And in the crow's nest atop that imposing sight was a figure with longish hair that blew chaotically in the breeze—a figure pointing at their dinghy and presumably shouting information at their crew mates below.

"Here she comes," said Robin, and she took hold of Ashley's hands as she said it. Tracy thought she looked positively giddy, as if she'd been waiting for this moment her whole life.

And maybe she *had* been waiting a lifetime to get here, Tracy remembered. She had no idea how long Robin had been wandering the afterlife in search of Ashley. Time worked differently inside the Strumpet's Sister. Sure, only a few years might've passed out here in the real world since the day Tracy had brought Robin back to life, but who knew how many years Robin had spent inside the Sister in the years since?

The bow of The Antagonist cut through the fog that had just a second before been surrounding it, and in no time at all, the vessel had outrun the meteorological menace from whence it came. It seemed like it was mere seconds later that Tracy could make out the faces of the mariners working the decks, and only moments after that when the three ladies in the dinghy were being brought aboard at gunpoint.

The guns being straight out of a *Pirates of the Caribbean* flick, Tracy soon realized, or from that show *Black Sails* that Kanoa used to watch on Starz. Blunderbuss pistols, she believed they were called—or *Dragons*, of all things—not that she'd ever expected to see one of them in person, let alone a half-dozen of them. They had short barrels and flared muzzles and a rather elaborate looking mechanism on top that she supposed was for igniting the gunpowder. Honestly, taking one look at these guns, Tracy thought their heavy wooden handles looked like the more practical weapon. She could imagine herself braining someone over the head with one but couldn't understand how you were meant to fire the thing at all.

While most of the crew stood around them to keep the ladies in place, one ran over to the helm to relieve the sole woman of their company—a short and svelte figure who Tracy took to be her ancestor Bethiah.

Bethiah strode over to them, looking like Mom when she was on a mission. Her sun-bleached hair was lighter than Veronica's, and her features were softer and less angular, but she had the death stare down pat.

"Who are you?" asked Bethiah, stopping in her tracks once she was an arm's length away and then raising her weapon right up into Tracy's face.

"Hold on," said Robin, holding up two hands in panic and trying to de-escalate the situation.

"Get that gun out of her face," said Ashley, seething, not caring about calming things down at all as she said, "Lower the gun, or I'm going to shove it up your ass."

Tracy stared down the gold-plated barrel and try not to flinch. But flinch she must have, because Bethiah narrowed her eyes as her finger itched the trigger. "Nervous?" said Bethiah. "Got something to hide?"

"We are the Children of Judas," said Robin with confidence, as if that was supposed to mean something—as if that nickname for their family weren't something Tracy's great-grandfather had invented to put the fear of God into his grandchildren.

And yet, judging by the softening look on Bethiah's face as she took in Robin's words, it looked like being the Children of Judas *did* mean something to *her*. At last, she lowered her weapon. Then each of the men lowered theirs as well.

"Silvers?" asked Bethiah, giving her new passengers a once-over.

Ashley and Tracy nodded. Robin shook her head and said that no, she was a Gates.

"Gates?" said one of the crew, a man with a thick mane of black curls spilling from beneath the reddened leather of his hat. "Who was your father, girl? Not Leonard Gates, was he?"

"No," said Robin. "But Leonard was my..." She trailed off and looked to Tracy for help, knowing that Tracy had looked all this up for a biography of Robin she'd written.

"Her three-times great-grandfather," said Tracy.

"He was a Child of Judas as well?" said the pirate in the red hat, and he looked crestfallen as he asked the question—as if he feared how Robin might answer.

Robin nodded. "His father was Silas VIII."

"Bad form," said the pirate in the red hat, shaking his head as he stalked away from the group for a moment. "Bad form, bad form, bad form," he said, throwing a fist into the wood of the mast when he reached it.

"James!" shouted Bethiah to her stricken compatriot.

James, the pirate in the red hat, nodded at his captain and returned to the group.

"What the fuck was that all about?" asked Ashley. Then, seeing the state of James' knuckles, she added, "Dude! You're bleeding."

"Apologies, my lady," he said to Ashley, doffing his hat and holding it to his chest.

"Apologies?" said Ashley, confused. "Dude, go get that shit wrapped up! You're going to get an infection."

"Her mother was a doctor," said Robin.

"Is," said Tracy.

Bethiah nodded at James to let him know it was okay to go below decks to take care of himself, and James did as he was bid.

"Why was he so upset?" asked Tracy.

"Your friend's ancestor," said Bethiah, nodding at Robin, "after he stumbled into the wrong century and crossed the wrong man, he was put to the sword. On James' orders." Bethiah sighed. "If James had known what blood flowed through Mr. Gates' veins—"

Robin sighed. "*He* didn't know," she said. "He was adopted."

Bethiah raised an eyebrow. "Then how did you come to discover—?"

"Ada," said Robin. "Ada told me."

Again, Tracy waited for the pirates to ask for some kind of explanation—for them to admit they had no idea who Ada was—but again, Tracy watched as a look of terrible recognition dawned on Bethiah Silver's face.

"The scourge of the Silvers," she said with a nod.

"Captain," said one of the sailors, pointing toward the rear of the ship. "It's gaining on us."

Everyone—the whole lot of them—turned toward the ship's stern. The fog which The Antagonist had outrun in their determination to overtake the wayward dinghy—it had nearly caught them again.

"To your stations!" shouted Bethiah, her crew springing to action before she'd even finished the sentence. Then she turned to her trio of passengers. "Below decks," she told them, pointing at a hatch to the side of the helm. "If you please."

Ashley gave Robin the briefest of looks, then Tracy felt her aunt grab hold of her hand and yank her forward. Robin followed close behind, the two older women sandwiching Tracy as if they could keep her safe from whatever it was that was inside the fog.

Bethiah threw open the hatch for them, then stepped back behind the helm.

They tumbled down the steep stairs into what must've been the captain's quarters. They had enough time see a single bed in there, and the cluttered desk Bethiah had crammed between the two sets of stairs which led above deck—just enough time to note that the bed was big enough for two but was unmade on only one side—and then the hatch they'd entered through was slammed shut, plunging them into darkness.

"You two better not be making out over there," said Tracy, trying to lighten up the situation as she reached out with both arms to find a wall or something else to hold onto.

What she found, eventually, was the soft flesh of someone's breasts—Robin's she realized quite suddenly, remembering that Ashley's were gone—and she recoiled in horror and embarrassment, crashing backward into what felt like a chair. Only the cushion of her knapsack helped to soften the blow.

"Ouch," said Robin, though she laughed as she said it.

"Does anyone have a phone on them?" asked Tracy, feeling her way into the chair she'd bumped into.

In the darkness, she heard the sudden creak of a bed frame as someone plopped down onto Bethiah's mattress. Then she heard the sound again.

"Seriously?" said Tracy. "No one?"

"We're ghosts," said Ashley. "And you just broke out of jail."

"Best to just sit tight," said Robin, the bed creaking as she said it—her voice creaking too, as if she were adjusting herself and her position over there. Or maybe adjusting someone else.

"Sit tight and do what?" said Tracy, turning in her seat to run her hands along the surface of the desk.

There was no answer, not that she needed one. Tracy knew all too well what was going on across the room. She wanted to ask them if they'd thought about why only one side of the bed was unmade, if they'd even considered that Bethiah was keeping her lost husband's side of the bed neat and tidy for the day he eventually found his way back to her.

She wanted to ask, but she didn't.

Instead, she kept her hands busy and kept on exploring Bethiah's desktop. There was a spyglass rolling back and forth inside a vast wooden tray of some sort. Beside that, there was a wide piece of parchment—a map maybe?—that lay unfurled, an unlit candelabrum holding it in place on each side. And off to the other side of that was an ink pot and quill, a thick book which she imagined to be the captain's log, and a pair of compasses—the pencil at the end of one arm sharpened into point that was *so* sharp Tracy imagined, in the dark, that it wasn't a pencil at all. Instead, she daydreamed it into the needle on a spinning wheel—a magical relic from her favorite fairy tale. God, how she wanted to be Aurora the Sleeping Beauty at this point—how she wished she could prick her finger on a sharp point right now and just fall dead asleep. She wished she was the one on the bed, and that she had some foolproof way to conquer the racing thoughts she was sure would be waiting when she finally lay down.

"We're not making out," said Robin, out of nowhere. "In case you're wondering. We're just cuddling."

"If you want to sleep," said Ashley, "we'll get up."

Tracy shook her head. Then, realizing they couldn't see her, she said "No, that's alright."

From above deck, though the sound was muffled by the wood between them, the ladies in the captain's cabin heard the captain herself shout "Hard to starboard!"

A moment later, the ship lurched to one side and Tracy fell out of her chair with a thud. A moment after that, there was a knock at the door—a door they hadn't seen, but which they should've known was there.

"All right in there, ladies?" asked the voice of James o' the Red Hat.

Robin played at a sniffle. "Oh, but we're so frightened," she said. "Good sir, won't you come in and offer us your protection?"

Tracy rolled her eyes as she picked herself up off the floor and retook her seat.

"Strictly speaking," said James, from beyond the door, "that wouldn't be proper."

"Oh," said Ashley, "but don't you want to make it up to her? The slight against her family, that is?"

There was silence for a moment as, on the other side of the door, James considered this. Then the door creaked open and the light from James' lantern spilled into the room.

Tracy looked at James for a moment and took in the look of confusion on his face—the look of conflict—but then she turned her attention to the bed. Robin and Ashley were both sitting up, but their limbs were a tangle of flesh and their bodies were clothed in naught but their undergarments. Tracy sighed. They might have just been "cuddling," sure, but they definitely had other things in mind.

"I'm charged with keeping an eye on you," said James.

Ashley waggled a come-hither finger at him as she said, "You can see us better from over here."

"But my hand," said James, holding it up.

Tracy stood. Then she took James by the arm and dragged him into the room. "It's useless to resist them," she said. Then, looking over James' shoulder at the two women on the bed, she said "I'll go find a place to sleep."

"But..." James protested, as Ashley grabbed hold of his belt and dragged him toward the bed. "I'm to look after all three of you!"

Tracy gave him a smile as she stepped out into the crew's quarters. "I can take care of myself," she said, and then she closed the door behind her.

❦

MOONLIGHT SPILLED down into the hold from the grates overhead—not a lot of it, mind you, but enough that Tracy could at least see where she was going now.

She'd emerged from the captain's quarters into a small galley with a round table for four off to one side. Beyond that, in the center of the ship, a wide aisle of empty space cut between stacks of barrels on either side. And beyond that, at the far end of the ship, hung the crew's hammocks—two levels of them, one hung on top of the other from the rafters.

It was on one of the lower beds that Tracy caught sight of a figure she'd fully expected to still be above deck: the captain. She didn't appear to be sleeping, though she was lying down. In fact, given that she had her head tilted in Tracy's general direction, Captain Bethiah seemed like she was just biding her time.

Tracy took a seat on the hammock opposite and shrugged her knapsack off. Meanwhile, Bethiah swung her legs over the side of her own hammock and sat up. Then she eyed her descendant for a good, long while.

"A disappointment?" said Tracy. "Softer than you'd like?"

A hint of moonlight glinted off Bethiah's off-white teeth as she smiled in the darkness. "Taller than I expected," she said, "given my own stature."

"I've seen some things," said Tracy, trying to win Bethiah's respect—but also unsure why she cared. "It may not look like it, but I have."

"I don't doubt it," said Bethiah. Then she reached into the depths of her hammock and produced a bottle of rum. She took a healthy swig, then passed it to Tracy.

Tracy eyed it suspiciously, having always been a bit of a lightweight when it came to alcohol. This was going to be far less fruity than she was used to, but if she wanted to win this woman's respect...

"Careful," said Bethiah with a laugh, as Tracy drank too deeply from the bottle and came up for air with a wicked cough.

Tracy passed the bottle back to her forebear. Then she asked where they were headed.

"We're bound for the same port we've been chasing for years beyond counting," said Bethiah. Then she took a healthy pull from the rum. "We'll never get there," she said. "That's our curse. But we keep trying."

"Where is it?" asked Tracy, taking the bottle back for her turn with it. "The port you've been trying to get to?"

"Harwich," said Bethiah. "1776."

Tracy nodded, understanding. Bethiah had somehow found out what was destined to happen to her husband and his family, and she was determined to stop it. The fog that was chasing them, she decided suddenly, must be time itself—or fate, or whatever—trying to make sure they failed.

"O'course," said Bethiah, taking the rum back from Tracy when she saw the girl wasn't going to drink any more of it, "we'll need to make a detour to wherever it is you're headed."

"Why?" said Tracy. "Not that I'm refusing your offer, of course. I just don't understand."

"You're the Children of Judas," said Bethiah, drinking deeply from the bottle once more. Then she added, with just the slightest crack of sadness in her voice, "And you're my children, too."

They sat in silence for a moment, acknowledging the depth of the emotion that had just passed between them—and acknowledging too, perhaps, that they were both a bit drunk now. Then Tracy gestured for Bethiah to give the bottle back.

"You're three sheets to the wind," said Tracy, and her eyes had adjusted enough to the dark to see that Bethiah found the phrase amusing. "And yet," said Tracy, "I'm only two." Then, after throwing back another healthy swallow, she added, "Let's balance the scales."

BELINDA

Rather than dash about the space-time continuum like a pair of chickens with their heads cut off, Belinda and Matt rented a room at the old hotel in the center of Chelmsford. They'd decided to stay in one place for a while, while they worked things out.

The abandoned train tracks of the Framingham and Lowell railroad ran right by their new apartment, and once spring came the pair of them took to walking the tracks deep into the woods —where they wouldn't be disturbed as they tried to suss out what Robin Gates' plan might be, to figure out exactly what moment in history she might be set on rewriting.

A decade from now, during Matt's childhood, he would lead his sister and his young cousins on expeditions through their back yard and onto these same overgrown tracks and crumbling bridges. He would spin yarns for them about a ghost train that sped by at night to steal children from their beds, and they would believe every word.

A couple of decades after that, in the time from whence Matt and Belinda had come, these same tracks would be converted into a paved "rail trail" for walking and cycling.

But now, fewer than fifteen years since they'd been in active use, the tracks felt truly dangerous—as if a locomotive might rumble through at any moment. There were weeds growing up from the gravel now—nature trying to take back what was hers—but if you didn't look too close you'd be forgiven for daydreaming about the train scene from the movie *Stand by Me*. You'd be forgiven for wondering whether or not you were about to have a life-or-death experience on the level of the kids in that film—whether you were about to have to run for your life and leap off to the side in just the nick of time.

Which was exactly what Matt was thinking about, Belinda realized. She tried to dig deeper into the thought, to determine whether Matt saw himself as Wil Wheaton's sullen Gordy or Jerry O'Connell's gullible Vern, but she didn't get far before Matt noticed what she was doing—before he could see it in her eyes and in the way she screwed up her face in concentration—and asked her to stop.

"Sorry," she said.

"You gotta stop doing that" is what he said as they kept walking, his tone a mix of annoyance and understanding. Slowly but surely, he was stepping into the role of "uncle." That meant giving her a little more leeway than he would someone else who kept violating his privacy, but just a *little*. Not a lot. And Belinda sensed she was running out of chances to fuck up and be forgiven.

"Anyway," he said, keen to change the subject, "Let's get back to it."

The ideas they kept coming back to, whenever they considered where Robin would go and what she would do, were twofold. They thought she would either travel to Cambridge in 2006 to stop her own murder, or that she would march on Cape Cod in 1892 to try and stop Old Silas from killing Ada.

It didn't seem to matter who started the conversation and who ended up playing devil's advocate—they arrived at the same conclusions each time. Stopping her own murder felt too self-centered, even for Robin. And yet, stopping Ada's murder seemed too complicated—and too laden with the possibility of disaster. If you stopped Ada from being killed before she got pregnant by the ghost, then Robin's family line would be cut off at the source. But if you tried to stop it *after* the impregnation and just before Old Silas wrapped his hands around Ada's throat, you weren't leaving yourself much wiggle room. No more than a few minutes, really.

"And even if you succeed," the devil's advocate would say, "you've altered history to the point where Robin and Ashley might never meet. And would Robin want to risk that?"

They crossed the bridge over the small stream which snaked through the woods, a leftover of the massive canal which had run through here once upon a time—in the decades before the railroad came. Matt spent the whole crossing looking down through the cracks between the now-rotting boards. Their decline had just begun really, but he knew it wouldn't take long in the grand scheme of things for their disintegration to begin in earnest.

Just like his own.

"You aren't *that* old," Belinda said aloud, blushing once she remembered that she'd promised to stop reading his mind.

Matt shook his head at her, then cast his glance off to the left. Through the trees just beginning to go green again after a hard winter—through yards and yards of pricker bushes—he spied the back yard of his grandfather's house. There was a backhoe off to one side of it now, the side where they were clearing land for a second house—the house Baby Matt would be brought home to in a few months, where he would spend the first eleven years of his life.

He was feeling nostalgic—Belinda had quit her attempts to stay out of his mind now, because his thoughts were just too loud—and he was wondering why Robin Gates thought she had the right to take all of this away from him. The good, the bad, the ugly—gradually, he was coming to realize that all of it had brought him to where he was.

He hoped he could convince her, Robin, that the same was true for her. But she was dead, and he supposed if it was *he* who was dead then he'd be acting exactly as she was.

"Maybe she's going to try and change something small," Belinda suggested. "Maybe she's got some crackpot theory about how changing one small thing will—"

"Or maybe she's going to try and sink the Mayflower at sea," said Matt, interrupting.

"To save Ada's family?" asked Belinda. "You think she really believes that sinking one ship would stop the Europeans forever?"

"I don't know!" shouted Matt, exasperated. "I was making a fucking joke."

They passed by the swamp and the stone wall which marked the end of the Silver family's property and continued on. They usually walked the tracks until they reached the High Street crossing at the bottom of Robin Hill, and it didn't seem like there was any reason to break the routine. This was their only real exercise, after all—both of them spent most of their free time writing —and occasionally they did stumble across a new idea to add to their list of places to explore.

Occasionally they stumbled across other folks out in the woods, too. The path wasn't nearly as populated as it would be decades later—once it was paved over for use by cyclists and pedestrians—but Matt and Belinda were far from the only people out there. It was a favorite spot of the delinquent sons and daughters of High Street's doctors and lawyers—those teenaged ne'er-do-wells who needed a place to smoke pot and make out—and of the slightly poorer kids from Littleton Road, on the other side of the tracks.

In fact, it was a pair of these kids who Matt and Belinda nearly walked right into on that fateful afternoon. Both of them were familiar, but for different reasons. One was the son of the woman who ran their hotel, a sixteen-year-old called Phil. The other was a mustachioed fifteen-year-old: Albert Silver, whose whiskers and mane were growing more gloriously long by the day.

Just before they bumped into Matt and Belinda, the two boys were passing a joint back and forth. The moment they realized there was someone out there in the woods with them, however, they hid their contraband behind their back. It wasn't until Albert recognized who they'd bumped into that he seemed to breathe again. Then he nodded at Matt and told Phil that they, Matt and Belinda, were cool.

"You sure?" asked Phil, still holding the joint behind his back. "They're staying at my mom's hotel down the center."

"We're cool," Matt insisted. "Well, I am," he said. Then he shook a thumb at Belinda. "Her, I'm not so sure about."

Phil nodded, then brought his arm out from behind his back. He held out the still-smoking joint for either Matt or Belinda to take, but each of them shook their heads.

"You guys enjoy it," said Matt, smiling. Then he looked at Belinda and nodded in the direction they'd been walking, indicating she should take the lead and get them back on their way.

As the two of them made their way around the boys, Albert called out to them—fresh off a toke—and asked how they were liking their stays at the Gates Motel.

He was laughing his ass off as Matt and Belinda turned around to face the boys again. Phil, on the other hand, didn't look all that amused.

"Get it," said Albert, laughing at his own joke. "Gates Motel? Like the *Bates* Motel from *Psycho?* Get it?"

"You're Phil Gates?" asked Matt.

Phil nodded. "You're not going to tell my mother," he said, holding up the joint. "Are you?"

Belinda shook her head and grabbed hold of Matt's arm to keep him from doing anything rash. She didn't have time to search his mind and see what he might be thinking about doing.

"Why you so tense, man?" Phil asked Matt.

Belinda looked at Matt and saw that he was, indeed, scowling. And yet, the look was gone a moment later—a blink later, really.

"He's tired," said Belinda. "Neither of us got much sleep last night."

"Ain't he a little old for you?" asked Albert, grabbing the joint from Phil and taking another hit.

"We're writers," said Belinda. "We're working on a big story."

"About Chelmsford?" said Phil, and he was laughing before he could finish saying the name of their boring little town.

Belinda tugged at Matt's arm and started to turn them away from Phil and Albert. "We gotta get going guys, okay?"

Phil and Albert nodded, then turned around themselves to boogie on down the road.

⚜

IN THE HOTEL room that night, Matt laid on his bed and stared at the popcorn ceiling. Meanwhile, Belinda tried to find patterns in the wood-paneled walls that she hadn't seen yet. Each panel was like a Rorschach test, and so far she'd found screaming ghosts, scampering dogs, and a combination of faux knots in one panel which she swore was a perfect replica of a vulva—its labia parted in order to expose an enormous clitoris, and a vagina the size of the Lost River Gorge.

When Matt tired of staring at the ceiling, he turned his attention to the lamp which sat atop room's single nightstand and took to flicking the light on and off. The bulb, which sprang from the head of a plaster fisherman, went off and on. Off and on.

Belinda thought about asking him to quit it, but in his mind Matt was devising even better ways to annoy her if she so much as flinched at what he was doing now—let alone if she said something aloud in protest.

Instead, she took to scrutinizing the pattern of their gold and brown bed linens. They reminded her of Escher's "Sky and

Water," a print of which had hung in her father's office once upon a time. How many days had she stared at that thing, waiting for Dad to finish work, and trying to decide if she could count more fish than Dad said there were in the painting—or more birds. How she'd stared at it, trying to add details to the painting that weren't there.

Or were they?

Belinda sat up and looked around the room. She decided it was no wonder that orange was her father's favorite color. This was the decade when he would be brought into the world, and there wasn't an ounce of blue in sight. Everything was gold or brown, rust or honey, marmalade or ginger.

Out of nowhere, Matt said "We gotta interrogate the kid."

Belinda turned to face him and swung her legs over the side of her bed. He was still staring up into space, but his speaking felt like an invitation.

"He knows something we don't know," said Matt. "I've got a feeling."

"He's sixteen," said Belinda. She didn't want to discourage him, but she hadn't met a lot of brilliant sixteen-year-olds in her many millennia of existence. She knew that she certainly hadn't been one.

"He might've heard something," said Matt, ceasing his flicking and staring at the ceiling again. "An old family story, something he's going to share with his daughter a decade or so from now."

"From what I understand," said Belinda, "Robin knew precious little about her family's history before Ada dropped the ancestry bomb on her in 2003."

Matt turned his head to face Belinda. "Why are you harshing my mellow?" he said.

Belinda gave him a smirk. "I'm just trying to be realistic," she said.

Matt returned his attention to the ceiling once more. "I think I found Ursa Major," he said.

THEY FOUND Phil on the porch of the hotel the next day. He was sitting in one of the chairs there, looking out at the five-way intersection that was the town's most famous landmark—a snarl of pavement that would come to be known as Chicken Corner in later years, thanks to the feeling it gave drivers of taking their lives into their own hands. In the kid's lap was a worn leather baseball glove, and in one hand or the other at any given moment was the ball he was using to play catch with himself.

It was a Saturday morning, and it was time for their morning walk. Belinda nudged Matt in the direction of the train tracks, trying silently to steer him away from what she knew would be a fruitless conversation, but Matt didn't budge. Instead, he waited until Phil had acknowledged them. Then, just as Phil got back to tossing his ball into the air, Matt snatched the thing and started down the steps.

"Hey," said Phil.

"Let's have a catch," said Matt, nodding in the direction of the hotel's mostly empty parking lot—using a version of the expression that no one in town would use until 1989, after they'd seen *Field of Dreams*.

"*Have* a catch?" said Phil, following after Matt.

Belinda rolled her eyes and took Phil's seat. She hoped this wouldn't take long, and that Matt wouldn't embarrass himself any further.

The two boys—for that's what Matt became in this moment: a boy, just like Phil—stood about twenty feet apart. Then Matt wound up and threw a fastball at Phil, the likes of which the kid had probably never seen. Phil got his glove up just in time to save himself from a trip to the ER, but he was smiling by the time he lowered it.

Matt motioned for Phil to toss it back to him.

"You don't got a glove," he said.

"I'm good," said Matt, repeating the gesture.

"You're 'good'?" said Phil, confused.

"I've got this," said Matt, thinking that expression would do the trick.

"Nah," said Phil, teasing. He held up the ball. "*I've* got this."

Matt smirked. "Just toss it back," he said.

Phil did as he was bid, tossing it back to Matt—but with slightly less velocity, keeping in mind that Matt would be bare-handing it.

"Your dad around?" asked Matt, rolling the ball between his hands.

"Dick?" said Phil. And then, seeing Matt's eyebrows go up at the sound of the word, he added, "Dick's my old man."

Belinda could feel Matt trying to restrain laughter, even from several yards away. "Dick... *Gates?*" he said, trying not to chuckle.

Phil smirked. Then he pounded his fist into his glove and made ready to receive Matt's throw.

Matt nodded and threw it normal this time, like two fielders practicing instead of an idiot forty-something trying to relive the glories of his youth.

"He *is* a bit of a pussy," said Phil, tossing the ball back to Matt. Then, remembering Belinda was just behind him, he turned to face her and said, "Pardon my French, ma'am."

Belinda gave him a smile to let him know it was okay.

"But he's not around?" said Matt.

"He's around somewhere," said Phil.

They threw it back and forth a few times in silence before Phil spoke up again.

"Kinda runs in the family," he volunteered. "Not being there for your kids. My pop's pop was a real winner, too."

"And his pop?" asked Matt. The only restraint left in him, it seemed, was the restraint it took to not turn to Belinda in mid-throw and shout "I told you so!"

"Don't know much about him," said Phil, "but I take it he was out at sea a lot. You know that old saying 'a girl in every port'?"

Matt nodded.

"Yeah," said Phil. "That was him." Then he hurled one at Matt with all he had in him, as if the very idea of his great-grandfather was too much to stomach.

Up on the porch, Belinda sat up straighter in the chair. Could Matt really be onto something here? And what exactly was it that he was onto if he was?

"Damn," said Matt—not going directly for the question, which is what Belinda had expected him to do. Instead, he shook his hand in pain—as if Phil's latest throw had been too much for him. Whether he was exaggerating or not was unclear.

"The old man had a thing with a black woman down the Cape," said Phil. "And a Cubana from Havana, too," he added, counting off on his fingers. "And o'course we can't forget his Pearl Harbor prostitute, the one my gramma called the Hawaiian Whore."

Belinda couldn't believe it. They were close to something. She could feel it.

But just as they were about to uncover whatever dirty laundry Matt had been sifting through the hamper of the Gates' family's past to find, the door behind Belinda opened and Phil's mother stepped out of the hotel.

"Phillip!" she shouted. "You've got chores to do." Then she turned to Belinda and apologized on behalf of her son. "I hope he wasn't bothering you and your fella."

Belinda shook her head as she watched Phil race up the steps with his head hung in shame.

Matt called out from the foot of the stairs. "Hey, kid," he said, "you forgot your ball." Then he gave it a toss in Phil's direction— but it was Phil's mother who caught it instead.

"Wow," said Matt, "that was some catch, Mrs. G."

Belinda watched their landlady nod but watched the expression on her face too. She was annoyed by Matt's tone of surprise. There was something more that Mrs. G wanted to say. And yet, she had more important things to do than to defend herself. So she nodded at the pair of them, Matt and Belinda, and she followed Phil inside.

Matt climbed the steps and stood before Belinda with a grin on his face. "I told you so," he said.

Belinda rolled her eyes at him. "Sure," she said, "but what exactly did we learn?"

"Everything!" said Matt, with almost a laugh in his voice—as if he couldn't believe that Belinda had missed that. "I know exactly where Robin's going now. *Exactly*."

❧ 14 ❧

TRACY

When Tracy woke the next morning, it was to the sound of Ashley calling her name. She sat up slowly, bracing herself for the hangover she felt certain was waiting for her, but she needn't have worried. She felt pleasantly rested and that was all. Tracy turned to thank the captain for the evening of good drink and even better company, but the hammock beside hers was empty now.

"C'mon, kid," said Ashley. "You gotta see this."

Tracy nodded and followed Ashley up a rope ladder which led, through a nearby hatch, to the main deck of the ship. She tightened up her eyelids, again bracing for something awful—the bright light of the sun, in this case—but again she was pleasantly surprised by what was waiting for her. The sky was overcast and easy on the eyes.

Robin was standing right there, at the top of the ladder, waving at the two of them to hurry up and saying, "We're going so fast you're going to miss it."

Together, the three of them ran to the ship's rail. But though what they were supposed to be looking at was right there, it took Tracy a moment to understand what she was seeing.

Right there, not a hundred yards off the port bow, an enormous snow globe stood upon a rocky island. Inside the thing, surrounded by a starry sky which seemed bound by the glass, stood a small cluster of buildings—including a courthouse which looked frighteningly familiar to Tracy.

"Is that—?" she began, but before she could finish the question Robin was filling her in.

"The Court of Memory," said Robin. "The place where you put Michael on trial."

"But I made that shit up," said Tracy, trying to take the place in as The Antagonist raced past it—the menacing fog still nipping at their heels. Or their stern, as the case might be.

"It was a hallucination," said Tracy.

Robin slapped her on the arm. "Was *I* a hallucination?" she asked. "Besides, look what else is there," said Robin, pointing at a structure which looked like the entrance to a subway station.

"What?" said Tracy. "It's a subway station."

Robin looked at Tracy with a dumbfounded expression on her face—jaw agape, eyebrows raised, head tilted to one side. She didn't want to spell it out for Tracy, but she would if she had to. But did she have to? That's what the look on her face seemed to be asking.

Ashley gave Tracy's arm a gentle squeeze. "Where did your mom's fucked-up dream begin?" she asked, trying to jog Tracy's memory. "The one that changed her life?"

Tracy set two hands upon the railing to keep herself from falling down. The Strumpet's Sister had been one thing, a real place that others had seen, but Tracy had been *so* sure that everything she and her mother and Michael had gone through had been all in their heads.

"It was real?" said Tracy aloud.

"That," said the captain, who had crept up behind them during their conversation. "And so much more."

THEY WOULD SEE the Skerry of Souvenirs twice more before they were through, the captain told them.

"And what, exactly, is a skerry?" Ashley asked the captain.

"It's Scottish," said Tracy, chiming in now—even as she squinted to watch the Skerry until it was gone. "It's their word for a small, rocky island."

"Oh," said Ashley. "I knew that."

"Once we've passed it twice more," said the captain, picking up where she'd left off, "we'll cut back through the Veil of the World and into the Pacific."

Tracy shook her head at the sound of all these weird names. Then, finally, she turned her attention away from the water and back to the conversation at hand. "The Skerry of Souvenirs?" she said, scoffing. "The Veil of the World? Where are we now?" she asked, with a derisive snort. "The Ocean of Oblivion?"

"Why, child," said Bethiah, "this here is The River Without End."

"A river?" asked Tracy, raising an eyebrow—her curiosity outmatching her snark, for the moment at least. "A river," she said, "and not an ocean?"

"It flows like a river," said Bethiah, pointing over the rail at the current they were currently fighting against. "And it's bounded on both sides—"

"By what?" said Tracy, staring off the starboard side of the ship at a vast spread of water that extended all the way out to the horizon.

"Over yonder," said Bethiah, pointing, "is the world as you know it." Then she spun Tracy around to face the port side of the ship. "That way... well," she said, taking Tracy by the shoulder and guiding her across the deck, "that way lies Eden."

Tracy snickered. "Eden?" she said.

"Aye," said Bethiah. "Beyond the great desert."

"You're shitting me," said Tracy.

Bethiah held up a finger for Tracy to wait just a moment, then dashed toward the helm. After a brief hello to James o' the Red Hat, who was just then minding the wheel, Bethiah opened the doors of a cabinet which stood between the helm and the ship's mast. When she returned, she had a spyglass in her hand.

Tracy watched as Bethiah extended the contraption and searched off the port bow for whatever it was she was looking for. Then, with a grunt that seemed to indicate she'd found her target, she handed the spyglass to Tracy to take a look.

"We're passing by the Bay of Beauty right now," said Bethiah.

Tracy wanted to laugh at that name too, but then she took a look through the spyglass and was astounded instead. It was one of the most stunning vistas she'd ever laid eyes upon, a magnificent river splitting a vast desert in twain. On either side of the river, a small but lush flood plain played home to a quaint village that looked like something straight out of a storybook. She looked closer at the cobbled streets and alleys which ran between the little Medieval hamlet, searching for any sign of the people who lived there, but found no sign of life.

"How do you get cobblestones in the desert?" she asked, still staring through the spyglass.

"It's a magical place," said Bethiah, as if that answer were good enough—as if *any* of her answers about this strange land they found themselves in were even *adequate*, let alone comprehensive.

Tracy lowered the spyglass and turned to Bethiah, ready to ask a question about where all the people were, but Bethiah answered the query before it ever made its way out of Tracy's mouth. "Abandoned," said Bethiah. "Except for when God gets angry and decides to start over."

"Has he done that a lot?" asked Tracy.

Bethiah looked somber as she considered how best to answer the question. Then she gestured for the three women—Tracy, Robin, and Ashley—to follow her.

She walked them toward the ship's stern, nodding at James as they passed the helm and ascended the three steps to the poop deck. Once they'd reached the absolute back of the ship, she pointed toward the fog that was chasing them and handed the spyglass back to Tracy. "Take a look," she said.

Tracy raised the instrument to her eye once more and trained it on the fog. She saw nothing at first, but then she caught sight of vague ship-like shapes in the mist—hundreds of them. Twisting the end of the spyglass—she'd seen someone do that in the movies once, right? —she tried to get a better look. And sure enough, one of the ships came into greater focus. But when Tracy saw what that ship looked like, the spyglass dropped from her hands and tumbled onto the deck.

She took a step back and turned toward Bethiah once more. "That ship..." she stuttered. "Are they all...?"

Bethiah nodded as Robin picked up the spyglass to take a look herself. When Robin said "Holy shit," Ashley grabbed the thing and took a glance too. It didn't take her long to turn away and return her attention to Bethiah, Robin, and Tracy.

"Some things change when God begins anew," said Bethiah. "And some don't. But one thing that has always been certain is this: The Antagonist will always make a name for itself, and then The Antagonist will always fall."

"All of the ships out there," said Ashley, pointing. "They're all copies of *this* ship?!"

Bethiah nodded.

Robin looked stricken. "How many times has God started over?"

Bethiah shrugged. "No one knows for certain. And no one knows exactly why—no one on board my ship, that is."

Robin blanched. Tracy could tell she was trying to keep it together and could tell that she was struggling at the effort involved. It occurred to her that Robin *did* know, and that what she knew might be tied into her plans somehow—but that she was only now realizing the potential consequences of what she'd set out to do.

"I need to go lie down," Robin mumbled to Ashley, leaning into her for support.

Ashley nodded, then the two of them headed toward the port-side hatch.

"Have her rest in my cabin again," said Bethiah to Ashley. "I'll be up here for some time yet."

Ashley gave a thumbs up with the hand she wasn't using to help keep Robin upright. Then she threw open the hatch and helped her girlfriend down the stairs.

Tracy stood with Bethiah, not sure what to say next. There were so many questions brewing in her brain—about the nature of the so-called Eden off to their left, about the storm of ships that was hot on their tail, and so much more—but the questions were a maelstrom of their own in her head, a thousand words whipped into a frenzy, everything moving so fast she couldn't grab hold of anything at all.

Bethiah, perhaps sensing the tension in the air, invented an excuse to get them out of it. "I need to relieve James," she told Tracy, nodding at the helm.

"Yes," said Tracy in return. "And I should go check on my aunt and my friend."

They gave each other a polite nod and went their separate ways.

❧

BELOW DECK, Tracy found Robin curled up in Ashley's arms. They were sitting on the captain's bed, backs against the wall, daylight streaming in through the row of windows above them. And though it looked like the crying was done, there were signs that crying had been a thing fairly recently: streaks of mascara, a pile of tissues, and the ungodly sound of Robin sniffling back her sadness.

It occurred to Tracy in that moment to wonder where Robin had been keeping her makeup, and when she'd had time to apply it, and why she'd bothered. But she didn't ask.

Instead, she grabbed a seat on the edge of the bed and gave Robin's foot a squeeze. "You want to talk about it?" she asked.

Ashley looked over the top of Robin's head at Tracy and began to shake her own head in a silent "no," but then Robin began to speak.

"I had no idea," said Robin, still sniffling. "I really didn't," she continued. "I..."

Tracy picked up Robin's foot and cradled it in her lap. Then she began to massage the cold flesh, trying to decide if it was cold because of poor circulation or because Robin was more like a ghost than she looked.

"It's okay," said Ashley, running a hand through Robin's hair.

"No," said Robin, "it's not. I'm putting all of you in danger. The whole world, for that matter. The fucking universe, even! And what if I'm wrong? What if God decides that I—"

"You really think 'god' decides?" asked Ashley, a note of derision in her voice. "You really think it's not some more malevolent—"

"I'm taking the captain's word for it," said Robin, sitting up now and straining her neck to look behind her and look Ashley in the eye.

The three of them rearranged themselves on the bed, each taking a corner now. Once they were settled, Robin flexed her foot in Tracy's direction as a signal to keep rubbing.

"So," said Tracy, doing as she was told and continuing the massage, "what you've planned, you think it might be audacious enough that God—or whoever," she added quickly, to pacify Ashley, "that they'll wipe the slate clean."

Robin didn't answer for a moment. She lowered her head and

stared at the bed instead. Then, as she began picking at a loose thread in the coverlet, she said, "Maybe. I don't know."

"Maybe?" said Tracy with a snort. "You don't think maybe you should be sure? You're going to play God based on a hunch? A gut feeling?"

"Why don't you just tell her?" said Ashley to Robin. "Why are you keeping it a secret?"

Robin looked up from the thread she was picking at. She looked up and gave Ashley a kind of death stare. And it looked to Tracy like Robin was hoping the look would suffice, that words wouldn't be necessary—but then Robin spoke anyway.

"How did *you* react when I told you?" said Robin.

"I ran away," said Ashley.

This was news to Tracy, and it was disconcerting. When Robin told Tracy that she'd "lost" Ashley in the halls of the Strumpet's Sister, she'd taken Robin at her word. Tracy frowned at herself. She should've known better. She knew who Robin was. She'd written the book on her for Christ's sake—literally written the book: *Anything Goes (Except That): The Life and Death of Robin Gates.*

"I want to know," said Tracy, and now she finally stopped rubbing Robin's foot. "What's the plan? I think I've waited long enough. All you've told me is that it involves me seeing Kanoa again. But how? Because if me seeing my husband again ends with the world blowing up, then I think I can be a little less selfish and just deal with my grief."

Robin pointed to the floor of the room, to the spot where Tracy's knapsack had fallen during their descent the night before. "Bring me the notebook," she said.

Tracy scooted herself off the bed and crossed to the side of the room where the knapsack lay on the floor. Just at that moment, the ship lurched to the left and Tracy stumbled against the desk— hitting her head in the process.

"What the hell was that?" said Ashley.

"Doesn't matter," said Robin. "I'm sure they're figuring it out up there. Kid," she said to Tracy, "Now."

Tracy, rubbing at her head, pulled a spiral-bound notebook from the knapsack.

"A pen, too," said Robin, before Tracy had left the knapsack behind altogether.

Tracy grabbed a pen from the front pouch of the bag and crossed back to the bed. Plopping back down on her corner, she handed pen and paper to Robin.

Robin opened the notebook up and began flipping, searching. Tracy was about to ask what she was looking for, but then Robin stopped leafing through the pages and said, "Ah. Here we go." She turned the notebook around for Tracy to see.

The page was filled, from top to bottom and side to side, with a crudely drawn chart of Kanoa's family tree. All the information matched the research Tracy had been doing back in prison, and she found herself nodding along as she glanced over each name—happy that their research matched up. But then it occurred to her that Robin had never expressed very much interest in genealogy before, least of all the genealogy of the dead husband of her girlfriend's niece. So why had she done all this research, research that it had taken Tracy years to compile herself?

Tracy was about to ask when Robin tapped a finger on the page, pointing at a box with three question marks inside of it—the dead end in their research, the identity of Kanoa's great-great-grandfather.

Tracy felt a shiver down her spine as she considered what Robin was about to say. It could be just that Robin had found some information in her travels through time that Tracy could never have dreamt of having access to. But it could also be that... Tracy shuddered as she waited for Robin to speak.

Instead of speaking, Robin wrote. She crossed out the three question marks, then started to replace them with a name. And though the first name—Leonard—was not one Tracy was familiar with, the last name began with exactly the letter she'd feared.

G-A-T-E-S.

"Kanoa's ancestor," said Robin, setting the pen down upon the notebook, "is my ancestor, too."

"And," said Ashley, "if he and Robin are related, that means that you and Kanoa are—"

"Distantly," Robin hastened to add.

Tracy began to cry. She wasn't sure why. She could already— even in her shock—begin to understand what Robin's plan was, and it wasn't a bad plan after all. It might even work, except for...

"Hey," said Ashley, squeezing Tracy's knee as she misunderstood the cause of the girl's tears. "We've had first cousins marry in our family. You guys are, what, *fourth* cousins? It's no big deal."

Tracy gave Ashley's hand a squeeze, then offered up a weak smile. "That's not what I'm worried about, Auntie. It's Ada I'm worried about, and Robin's plan."

"You don't think she'll believe us?" said Robin, and now she looked panic-stricken herself.

"Wait," said Ashley, "I'm confused. What's the plan?"

"We bring Kanoa back," said Tracy, eyeballing Robin to make sure she was getting it right. "Then we tell Ada, when she inevitably shows up to kill him again, that Kanoa is her own blood —that he and any children he has are one final shot at Ada fulfilling her mother's dying wish that their bloodline continue." Tracy turned her head to fully face Robin then. "Did I get that right?"

"Yes," she said, though she couldn't look anyone in the eye as she said it.

Tracy was about to demand that Robin quit it with the lies and omissions when Robin spoke again.

"There's one part I haven't told you about, though," she said. "In order to—"

But she didn't get to finish her sentence, for just at that

moment there was an enormous BOOM overhead. Then another.

And another.

"Was that," Ashley began to say, before she was interrupted by another BOOM, "a cannon?"

The three of them raced to the two hatches which led to the decks above—Robin and Ashley to one side, and Tracy to the other—and they, perhaps stupidly, ignored the calls to go back below decks. Once they had a peek at what was going on up there, they couldn't believe their eyes—and they needed to see more to understand just what was going on. And so, the three of them climbed the stairs up to the main deck.

Off their ship's starboard stood another vessel, a massive ship flying a British flag—the familiar Union Jack tucked up into the corner on a field of red. On the deck of said ship were a detachment of Redcoats. And yet, neither ship nor soldiers were the strangest sight of the morning. No. The strangest sight of that morning was the familiar coast of Cape Cod in the distance, and a most unfamiliar house standing in the middle of the yard where Tracy had grown up.

"Bethiah!" Tracy shouted out to the captain, struggling to make her voice heard over the sounds of battle. "Are we here?" she asked, as she dashed to within earshot. "Are we where you've been trying to get? *When*, I mean?"

Bethiah nodded. "James," she said, pointing at the lifeless corpse slumped over the half-destroyed helm. "I don't know how, I don't know why, but..." She trailed off. "I'm so sorry, Tracy. I didn't mean to break my promise. I really did mean to get the three of you where you're bound, and without delay. But..." She gestured to the scene which surrounded them.

"It's okay," said Tracy, patting her ancestor on the back. "Are we in time?"

Bethiah looked white as a ghost as she said, "I don't know." But then the look on her face went fierce, one hand on her blunderbuss and the other on her sword. "But we're about to find out."

❧ III ❧
OBJECTS IN THE
REARVIEW MIRROR
1915, 1776, AND 33 AD

❧ 15 ❧

BELINDA

Belinda and Matt stayed in 1971 just long enough for Matt to watch his parents bring the newborn version of himself home from the hospital. They crept from the train tracks, through the woods, and to the edge of the Silvers' property, then trained a pair of binoculars on the gravel driveway of the new house that'd been built for the new family.

Belinda had spent the intervening months collecting period-appropriate clothes for their next jaunt across time and she was preoccupied with thoughts about where they were going next. Still, it warmed her heart to see Matt coming to terms with his own existence. Even as distracted as she was, she could feel a sense of relief wafting off of him as his parents' car pulled in. And soon enough he was crying—positively weeping at the sight of his father scooting around the old Fairlane to open the passenger door for his mother.

By the time the pair of them were walking up the path to their new house—with newborn Matt in his father's arms and not his mother's, a part of the story he had never heard before—Matt had to hand the binoculars over to Belinda.

"It's all going to go so wrong," he said to Belinda, sniffling back what snot and tears he could and then wiping the rest off with his sleeve. "How is this going to go so wrong?"

Belinda gave his shoulder a squeeze, warned him that what she was about to say would sound trite, but then said it anyway: "It all works out in the end. You're here," she added. "You're proof of that."

⚜

BACK IN THEIR hotel room they dressed for 1915. Matt donned a tweed newsboy's cap, a plaid driving coat, and a bow tie. Belinda wore her hair up and dressed more simply than Matt was used to, wearing a long-sleeved button-up blouse and an ankle-length blue skirt.

"Are you sure this is the right look?" Matt asked her. "You sure you shouldn't be dolled up like Daisy in *The Great Gatsby*? I think you could pull off the glitzy flapper look quite nicely."

"You're about seven years off," Belinda told him, offering a kind smile as she corrected him. "And besides: we're traveling to downtown Boston on a Tuesday, not some Long Island mansion on a Saturday night."

Matt nodded, fiddling with his bow tie as he looked himself over in the mirror.

"You left the rent money?" asked Belinda, looking around the room to make sure they hadn't forgotten anything.

Matt pointed at the envelope he'd slipped halfway beneath the feet of the fisherman lamp. "We're all set," he said.

"Alright then," said Belinda, feeling around in the air for a seam. "Let's go."

⚜

NIGHT HAD FALLEN on Boston Common on the day they arrived in 1915. It was chillier than Matt had expected, but he was taking comfort in the fact that at least there wasn't any snow on the ground. Belinda guided them toward the Brewer Fountain at the corner of Park and Tremont, and they grabbed a spot on a bench there.

Matt pointed at one of the bronze figures which sat at the fountain's base and asked, impatience in his voice, if they were here to admire Amphitrite's tits.

Belinda said "No," adding that the goddess's husband, jealous old Poseidon, wouldn't take too well to that. "You remember the story of the minotaur, don't you?"

Matt rolled his eyes at her and asked what they were doing there, what they were waiting for.

"I've shown you what stands in your way if you try to change the past," Belinda told him. "We're here so that you can feel what it's like when someone succeeds. Or, well," she said, "since witnessing an actual success would be followed up by the end of the goddamned world, I'm here to show you what it feels like when someone *almost* succeeds. It's the best I can do."

Matt nodded, then leaned back into the bench. Then, when the two seconds of silence was too much for him to bear, he shook a thumb at the church which stood behind them on Park Street. "My great-grandfather, Old Silas, married his first wife in that church back there."

"I know," said Belinda. "Maybe that's why this is the place Emily is going to turn up in just a minute."

"The first wife's name was Tamson," said Matt. "She was his first cousin."

Belinda nodded. "Tamson Emily O'Rourke," she said. "Emily was her middle name. At least where I come from. And the Tamson we're about to meet, she comes from where I come from."

Matt's mouth fell open. "You aren't the only one?" he said. "You aren't the only survivor?"

Belinda shook her head. "No," she said. "I survived by accident, but Emily—and everyone else who has ever bent the river—they're cursed to see how each new reality plays out."

"Bend the river?" said Matt, an eyebrow arching as he spoke.

"Change the past," said Belinda, putting it more plainly. She was about to continue, to explain about The River Without End, but it was at that moment that she felt the hairs on the back of her neck prickle in anticipation.

"What?" said Matt, sensing something was happening but not quite sure what it was.

"Here she comes," said Belinda, pointing past the fountain to a rather odd sight: an elderly woman—old, but spry—being chased up the hill by a redheaded girl, no more than twenty years old, who looked to be about nine months pregnant.

"What the hell?" said Matt. He made to get up, but then a butterfly flitted across his field of vision and he thought better of it.

Belinda pointed out who was who. "The older woman," she began, "is Emily. *Tamson*," she corrected herself, trying to make things easier for Matt.

"And the pregnant girl?" asked Matt.

"Your great-grandmother," said Belinda. "Annie O'Reilly Silver, pregnant now with her second child."

"Should she be running like that?" said Matt, as the two of them watched the chase wind its way up Beacon Hill toward the State House and its golden dome.

"No," said Belinda. "But she'll be alright," she said. "Until she's not," she added ominously.

"Is this the night she dies in the delivery room?" asked Matt.

"In an alley," said Belinda. "She'll never make it to the delivery room, though that's what your great-grandfather will tell your grandfather and your great aunt as they're growing up. He was a hard man, yes, but he did *try* to spare his children pain when he could."

Matt grunted, not sure he believed that.

Belinda wasn't sure she believed it either, but it was the best explanation she had for why Old Silas Silver had lied to his children about the untimely demise of their mother.

"So what are we supposed to do?" said Matt. "Just sit here and wait?"

Belinda nodded. "Tamson is trying to stop things right now," she told him. "When she gets close to succeeding," said Belinda, "we'll feel it."

"Even though we're here?" said Matt. "And she'll be wherever she's going?"

Belinda nodded again. "But if you want," she said, "I can follow them with my mind and show you what happens."

Matt nodded.

Carefully, Belinda lowered her hand onto Matt's thigh and closed her eyes. Then she reached out into the darkness, found Annie Silver's mind, and let the story unfold from there.

๛

THE CRONE FLED across the Common, and Annie followed. It was a struggle for her, with a belly fit to burst any day now. Nevertheless, she persisted. She might be nine months along, but Annie felt confident she would overtake the old woman in time. She'd been pregnant more often than not in the years since she first set her cap for a man, and it'd been a long time since her condition had stopped her from doing *anything*.

The chase wound up the slope of Beacon Hill and past the gilded dome of the State House, then down the other side and through the streets and alleys of the West End. By the time they reached the river, Annie was all of a dither. The crone was making for a bar of some sort, a hive of scum and villainy if ever Annie had seen one—and she had seen more than her share. If she lost the crone there, amidst that crowd, all might be lost.

So she shouted at the top of her lungs to "Stop that vagrant," waving her arms to draw the attention of the patrons milling about the stoop. "Stop her! She's stolen my purse."

They did nothing. Some of them cast a glance at the crone, yes—out of sheer morbid curiosity, Annie supposed—but not one lifted a finger to aid Annie's cause.

The truth was that the crone had stolen nothing from Annie, nothing save an overlong glance from across the way. But that look, the look in the old woman's eyes as she leered at Annie from the other side of the enormous fountain—there was something there that Annie had never seen before. It'd been a fierce look, yes, but that ferocity had been tinged by an intense affection— and maybe, if Annie was right, even a sense of pride. It was as if the crone knew Annie in some way. But how?

Before she'd had a chance to ask, the old woman had run.

And now, making her way through the huddled mass of ne'er-do-wells ogling her as she passed, each of them focused on some other fine thing she carried on her person, Annie had indeed lost her quarry. She stood on tiptoe to peer over the heads of the throng, once and then again. But there was nothing doing. The crone was gone.

"You're after the old woman?" asked someone from behind her.

It was a hooded figure, one of six crowded around a small table. They looked like something straight out of the book of fairy tales she read each night to her precious Elijah—the first of her children not born a bastard, the first she'd been allowed to keep. This was a coven of witches, perhaps—or perhaps a secret guild of huntsmen come to clear the king's woods after the death of his daughter. But there had been few witches in these parts since the people of Salem had taken to burning them alive, and there were no woods in Boston to speak of, at least not anymore. No, these traveling cloaks were as anachronistic an affectation as she had ever seen, and they were so tightly pulled around the figures' slim bodies that Annie could not make out any other detail. She wondered for a moment if they might not be characters from a fairy tale at all, if they mightn't be from Mister Wells' novel instead. Might their time machine be tucked into an alleyway out back? It was an enticing thought, a thread she might follow at any other time, but she was burdened with glorious purpose here and could not afford further digression.

"Yes," she told the strangers. "Did you see which way she went?"

One of them pointed a gloved hand at a door to the right of the bar, near the very back of the place. "You best hurry," they said.

And so she did, turning her belly this way and that to avoid elbows or worse, sweating so much it was as if tarnation itself were steaming up from between the floorboards. The door was a relief once she made it there, the draft that whipped across the threshold and between her jellied legs so refreshing that Annie might have stopped to rest her head against the jamb if not for the urgency of her undertaking.

Instead, she threw the thing open and stormed out into an alley way that was lit by an eerie orange glow. Annie searched for its source and was startled to find that the effulgence emanated from a what looked to be a tear in the very air. Or, now that she squinted at it, less a tear than the parting of two great curtains. Presently the light went out altogether. And then, from the darkness, Annie finally heard her quarry speak.

"Oh," said the crone. "Oh shit."

Annie doubled over, panting, clutching at a stitch on one side and the raging kicks of her baby on the other. "Who," she began, in between harried breaths, "are you? And what," she asked, pointing at the spot where the glow had been, "was that?"

"You don't want to ask me these questions," said the crone. "Annie, trust me: you really don't."

Annie stood bolt upright at the shock of hearing the stranger speak her name. Her jaw went slack and her voice deserted her.

"We can change things," said the crone. "I've done it before."

"Change what?" said Annie, raising an eyebrow in confusion. "Done what?"

"I..." the crone stuttered. "I've... I have visions sometimes. Visions of terrible things. And if I'm careful, I can stop them."

Annie watched the crone carefully. She was hiding something. The way she paused between words—it was like she was making this up on the spot, or at least part of it. But Annie could swear there was a sliver of truth in there somewhere as well, some small morsel. So, once again, she persisted.

"How do you know me?" asked Annie.

"You don't want to ask me that," said the crone. "You want to stop asking me questions altogether. That's the only way this will work."

Annie scoffed. "You don't know me at all," she said. "I'm the most quizzical person you'll ever meet." She puffed up her chest with pride. "Quizzical to a fault, according to my dear Silas."

The crone sighed and shook her head, then cast her gaze down at the ground.

"I'm sorry I exasperate you so," said Annie. "But I will have my answers."

"Quizzical to a fault," repeated the crone. "Did he really say that?"

"Yes, indeed," said Annie. "He's a man of a certain age, my Silas, and he cannot be—"

"He's a curmudgeon, you mean to say."

Annie looked down her nose at the stooped old woman and shook her head. "Each man on God's green earth is born with a certain ration of patience. My Silas can't be faulted for having spent his long before he met me."

"Sure he can," said the crone, a smirk playing across her lips. "And he never had much patience to begin with, to tell you the truth."

"You knew my Silas?"

The crone laughed, then nodded. "You might say I was the first to *know* him."

"Who are you?" asked Annie.

The question sobered the crone straight away. She blanched, her pale, wrinkled flesh drained of what little color it had left. Under other circumstances, this transformation might have been enough to make Annie give up and give in. But the crone was spry for her age—their chase had proven that. She could take a bit more heat before Annie let her out of the kitchen.

"Who are you?" Annie asked again.

"There are too many answers to that question," said the crone.

Annie stepped forward and took hold of the lapels of the crone's moth-eaten topcoat. "Enough riddles!" she said. "Answer me."

The crone lay her hands upon Annie's belly then and began to cry, and Annie wasn't sure whether it was the touch or the tears that made her recoil so quickly and with such force. Both women stumbled backward away from each other, nearly falling to the ground before righting themselves.

"Annie," said the crone, through sobs that threatened to choke the voice right out of her, "this is it. This is your last chance. I've already said too much. And I am begging you: please don't make me say more."

Annie set her own hands upon her belly then, searching for movement, frightened. It had been the slightest of touches, the gentlest, but still she feared that this strange woman might have done something to her baby or might have meant to. After all: she'd seen the woman stitch together a tear in the air with nary a word or a gesture. Who knew what conjurations she was capable of? One of Silas' wives had been an enchantress of some sort, and she'd tried to snuff the life right out of him. That's what Silas had told Annie: Ada Coffin had tried to kill him dead with her witchcraft. Who was to say that the forces of evil had ceased their machinations against his family that day?

"Turn around," said the crone, wiping the tears away with her tattered sleeves, trying desperately to collect herself. "Turn around and go home, Annie. I'm begging you."

But Annie stood her ground and asked one last time, "Who are you?"

The crone sighed. Then she began, saying: "I've had many names."

"No more riddles!" spat Annie, tired of the tricks, sick of the stalling.

"My name is Emily Henderson," said the crone. "Or, well, that's what it's been since I married Ernest some years ago. Before that, I was Emily Gold. But of course that was to keep my parents from finding me, or my husband's. It should have been Emily Silver, really."

"Silver?" said Annie. "But that's my—"

"Silas and I—for a moment, we thought that me using my middle name would be enough to keep me hidden. But in the end, we decided it was too risky."

Annie's heart was all aflutter and she pressed a clammy hand to her chest to help steady the panicked organ. Was she hearing what she thought she was hearing? Could this be–? But she was dead, wasn't she? That's what her dear Silas had told her, that this woman had died during the war. Long, long ago. "Your husband's name was Silas, too?" she stuttered. "Si–Silas Silver?"

The crone cackled. "Not 'too,' dear girl. My Silas is your Silas now."

And with that, Annie swooned as she had never swooned before.

⚶

BACK ON THE other side of the hill, Belinda began to feel the tell-tale signs of a riverbend. She could tell, through the connection they still shared to eavesdrop on the now-unconscious Annie, that

Matt felt something too. But she also knew that he would just pass it off as an upset stomach if she didn't say something.

"It's happening," said Belinda.

"What?" said Matt.

"That feeling in your stomach, and throughout your body— that feeling of you folding in on yourself—that's the first sign."

"And then what?" said Matt, standing up suddenly to look around—as if the next sign might come from the night sky. But then, just as suddenly as he'd stood up, he was sitting down again —and holding his head as he did so.

"Déjà vu?" said Belinda.

Matt nodded. Then he closed his eyes. "What's happening?" he said. "It's like someone's holding a flashlight up to my face." He opened his eyes to look at her. "Were you just holding a flashlight..." he began, then trailed off. "No," he said. "It's like the whole world is tinting toward sepia."

Belinda nodded as the light began to fade. "If she'd succeeded, the light would get even brighter: a big orange flash. And then the storms would come."

Matt doubled over, resting his head on his knees as he tried to get his bearings. "Does everyone feel this?"

"Yes," she said. "But most folks forget about it the next second, except for maybe the déjà vu. It's just too much for the brain to process. You're only going to remember it because I made you focus on it."

Matt sat up straight again, slowly but surely. Then, taking his hat off for a moment and running his fingers through his hair, he sighed. "Let's get back to it," he said, holding out a hand for her to take so she could bring the both of them back into Annie's mind.

WHEN ANNIE CAME to her senses, she was supine on the cold concrete of the alley floor. Above her, the first stars were peeking through the veil of dusk. And she would have lain there for a good while longer, her purpose here forgotten, if the crone hadn't stooped into view to adjust the traveling cloak that she'd taken off of herself and repurposed as a blanket for Annie.

"Oh," said the crone. "You're awake."

"How long was I–?"

The crone smiled. She wasn't missing nearly as many teeth as Annie had suspected she might be. "Long enough," said the crone, "to give an old woman palpitations."

Annie studied the crone's face as the old woman dabbed a damp cloth across her forehead. And she saw, for the first time since the fountain, that glint of affection she'd been searching for an answer for.

"Have you read any of Mister Baum's Oz books?" asked the crone.

Annie nodded. Gently, of course, for her head felt like it had been torn apart by a cyclone straight out of those novels.

"I imagine you feel quite like Dorothy," said the crone. "I only hope you don't think me the wicked witch."

The conversation was coming back to her now, the words that had swept Annie off her feet. It was said—never by Silas himself, for he was too good a man to compare any woman to another—that Annie was the spitting image of his first love, that that was why he was so taken with her. So Annie searched the crone's face for the resemblance, trying to imagine away the wrinkles and pockmarks and sagging skin and to see the Tamson O'Rourke that she'd heard so much about.

Tamson, she thought. The first wife's name was Tamson, not Emily.

"What?" said the crone, her gray eyebrows raised, her face screwed up as she tried, presumably, to tease out why Annie's own countenance had just gone sour.

"His first wife was Tamson," said Annie. "Tamson, not Emily."

"I told you," said the crone, wiping the cloth across Annie's brow once more, "we used my middle name to hide me from my parents. From Silas' parents, too. I haven't gone by the name Tamson since all before you were born."

"But," said Annie, "you died during the war. That's what Silas told me."

A painful smile played across the crone's thin lips. "Oh, I died a little," she said, "every time I thought of my love bleeding out on some battlefield. But I'm not dead, not yet."

"Then why would Silas—?"

The crone held a finger to Annie's lips and begged the girl's patience while she explained. Then she spun a yarn for Annie that was so colorful—and preposterous—that neither Mister Baum nor Mister Wells, for all their skill, for all their notoriety, could have pressed the public to believe it possible.

"I don't believe a word of that," said Annie.

"Do you think I could invent it?" asked the crone.

"Tamson O'Rourke was as much a student of Shakespeare as my dear Silas," said Annie. "If you are her—and I still have my doubts—then I'm sure you could invent just about any story you wanted. But you will not pull the wool over my eyes, ma'am. No, you will not."

The crone shook her head. "All you need believe is the bit about my abduction—that I came to this bar, The Strumpet's Sister, in a moment of weakness and that I was stolen away from my Silas and from my dear..."

Annie stared at the crone as she trailed off, as she held a hand to her mouth, rolled her eyes in disgust with someone—with herself, Annie guessed—and sighed.

"Your dear who?" asked Annie. "There was someone else as dear to you as our dear Silas?"

The crone held a cold hand to one side of Annie's face, thumb stroking cheek. The other hand played with Annie's hair as the crone leaned in close and spoke. "I've said too much, Annie. But we can still stop this. Let me walk away, and we can—"

"Let you walk away?" said Annie, shrugging off the crone's hands and sitting up at last. "I've fainted in an alley way, with a baby fit to burst my belly at any moment, and you want to walk away?"

The crone stood and hurried back toward the spot where Annie had seen her tear a hole in the air. Then the crone began to wave her hands about that spot again, as if searching for something. No, not searching. Conjuring!

"Answer me!" Annie shouted, trying to stand and then thinking better of it.

The crone found the edge of something there in the air, her fingers disappearing for a moment, and then she prized apart the curtains that Annie had glimpsed before. Behind the curtains, the sun was rising. It was the sun back there, Annie realized. But how? How?

"Who was as dear to you as Silas?" asked Annie.

The crone's head fell forward, pointed chin pressed against heaving chest. Then she let the curtains of darkness fall back into place, the orange light behind them blinking out of existence once again.

"Who?" Annie asked.

The crone faced Annie with tears in her eyes. "My daughter," she said.

The words would not sink in, as hard as Annie tried to make them. Her Silas, who had married again and again in his efforts to start the family he had long dreamed of—trying, yet never succeeding until Annie had given him their Elijah—her Silas had another child, a child he'd never known?

"I left her that night," said the crone, "in the ramshackle room that we called home. I'd been out of work for months, since before the birth, since the moment I'd begun to show really. We'd been living off the kindness of friends, performers I'd worked

with at the theaters around town in the months after Silas' depar-
ture. But I was tired of their charity, felt unworthy of it, so I took
this weary, worn-out body of mine to a place where it might be of
some profitable use to my baby and me—to *this* place," she said,
gesturing to the brick wall of the bar. "I was sure I could find
someone here who would pay for an hour of my company. I was
sure the baby wouldn't even notice I was gone. I thought I'd be
back before she woke," said the crone. "But I wasn't. I never made
it home."

"And what happened to her?" asked Annie. "To the baby?"

"An orphanage," said the crone. "The neighbors woke to the
sound of my daughter's wailing, and they called the authorities."
She sniffled back tears, straightened herself up, and added, "But
she wasn't there for long, dear. A good Irish couple adopted her,
got her out of this city of misfortune, and brought her with them
to Cape Cod."

"And how do you know this?" asked Annie. "Did you come
back for her?"

"I couldn't. As I said, I was abducted and taken far away from
this place. But in the years since I earned my freedom," said the
crone, "I've watched my daughter from afar. Watched as she grew
and prospered, married herself a fine man, had herself many children, and even took in a few who weren't her own."

"Orphans?" said Annie.

"Orphans?" said the crone. "No. Bastards," she said. "She took
in the bastard children of her own young daughter and said they
were hers instead."

Annie smiled, thinking of her own mother's charity. The
crone's daughter sounded so much like Annie's mother as to be
laughable. It was only when her mother's hair began to grow more
silver than a storm cloud, when she could no longer take credit for
the children that a promiscuous young Annie continued to deliver
unto their doorstep, that Annie's parents had sought a husband
for her.

"Sound like anyone you know?" asked the crone.

"As a matter of fact, your daughter and my mother sound an awful lot alike," said Annie. It wasn't until she'd finished the sentence that she felt her stomach churn. "Wait," she said. "What are you saying?" asked Annie.

"You know what I'm saying," said the crone, lowering her head —unable to look Annie in the eye.

"But," said Annie, "if you're my mother's mother..."

"Then Silas is your mother's father," said the crone.

"And," said Annie, her stomach now thrashing like the seas that stole her dear husband's father from him so long ago, "that makes Silas my... my..."

The crone ran to Annie then, as the color drained from her face. "Yes," she said, "but they're all just words, Annie. He is your husband. That's all that matters."

Annie fell backwards, her head bouncing off the alley floor. But her body would not let her slip away into unconsciousness this time. *No rest for the wicked*, Annie thought. And that's most certainly what she was. Wicked. *Wicked, wicked, wicked.* "Not just husband," she stuttered. "Also... also..."

And it was then that her water broke, a trickle beneath her skirts at first, and then a gush that puddled at her ankles on the cold, dirty ground.

"Why did you tell me?" said Annie. "I asked, but you needn't have answered. You could have kept running. Your exit was right there in front of you. Why did you tell me?"

"It's what I do," said the crone, clutching one of Annie's hands between both of her own. "It's what I've always done. It is, I guess, what I will always do."

ON THE OTHER side of Beacon Hill, still seated on the bench, Matt and Belinda sat now in silence—a *stunned* silence for Matt.

"That," said Belinda, "is the fate which awaits all riverbenders. They get the new world that they fought for, that they changed the past to win—but then they have to live through it. They have to watch as new miseries play out to make possible the change they gave the life of their universe to have. In the version of the universe that Emily and I came from, Annie never married Silas. There was no fate so awful and gross as that waiting for her. In my universe, Annie never even *met* the old man. But when Emily decided to travel through time and mess with things, the universe rewrote itself to make the reality Emily wanted possible. And that meant millions of revisions, including the downright revolting one you just saw."

Matt nodded. Then he stared at the ground.

"That's the fate that awaits Tracy and Robin if they succeed in their endeavor."

Matt nodded some more. A single tear fell from his cheek toward the cold ground. But then, before he could wallow in his pit of despair for even a moment longer, a gunshot rang out in the distance.

He sprang to his feet but couldn't decide if he wanted to run toward the sound or away from it. The thought plagued him. Why would he want to run *toward* the sound of gunfire? He was no superhero. He *wrote* comic books; he was not the star of them.

"You want to run toward it," said Belinda, rising to stand next to him, "because that's what we do."

Matt looked at her to make sure she was serious, but he didn't even wait for a nod before he was running up Beacon Hill and into whatever fray awaited them there.

Belinda chased after him, not sure where this was going to lead—and hoping to hell it didn't end with a bullet in one or both of their brains.

It wasn't long before they reached a sight that stopped them in their tracks. A body lay face down on the path which led from the State House to where they'd been sitting, a bullet hole in the back of a silver haired head that looked all too familiar. Belinda wanted to tell Matt to leave the corpse alone—for that's all it was now, the husk of a soul that had already fled this earth—but she knew in her gut that he wouldn't listen, that he'd have to see it for himself.

Matt crouched to lift the head ever so slightly off the ground, then stumbled backward when he found there the shocked face of Old Emily.

Belinda looked around to see if she could spot a gunman, not sure what she'd do if she did, but all she saw was another old woman wandering off in the distance. She was a peculiar thing, clad in a long cowboy's duster, but she didn't look capable of hurting a fly. Maybe when she was younger, but... Belinda shook her head. Then, just to pacify the curious part of herself, she reached out with her mind.

Inside the old woman's head, beyond a thick veil of pain which seemed to be coming from her shoulder, two phrases were repeating themselves: "It's done" and "Clean shot."

"Holy shit," said Belinda aloud, pointing at the old woman. "Matt, that's her. That's the killer."

Matt sprang to his feet and started running. Belinda, once again, gave chase.

It didn't take long to overtake the old woman, even once she heard them coming and broke out into a run of her own. But once they'd cornered her, the iron fence which ringed the Common at her back, she dropped the rifle at their feet.

Unfortunately for them, in the split second they were distracted by her apparent surrender, the old woman pulled a pair of revolvers from inside the dark recesses of her coat.

"Let me be," she told them, cocking both pistols at the same time.

"You killed a woman in cold blood," said Matt.

"Not the first time," said the old woman. Then she gave the

faintest nod toward Belinda, all while still keeping her eyes on the both of them. "I'd like it to be the last, though."

"Why'd you kill her?" asked Matt, not giving any ground.

"None of your concern," said the old woman.

While Matt had her distracted, Belinda reached into the woman's mind to see what she could find. She pushed past the pain in the shoulder and the calculations the old woman was making and remaking about which of them—Matt or Belinda—she would shoot first. Underneath all that, Belinda found the pieces of a broken heart.

"You loved her," said Belinda to the woman. "Tamson," she said, using the name the woman knew Emily by. "You loved her, didn't you?"

The old woman didn't flinch, but she did turn her attention to Belinda. In her mind, she decided she would shoot Matt first—if he so much as flinched himself. The girl, on the other hand—Belinda —the old woman wasn't sure about. Was it intuition that made her ask what she'd just asked? Or did she have some of the same kind of magic about her as the voices that visited in the night.

"Who are the voices?" asked Belinda.

"The ones that hired me," admitted the old woman. "The ones that told me Tamson had to go in order for my..." She stopped herself from saying what she was going to say next.

"Your brother," said Belinda, pulling the rest of the sentence from the old woman's mind. "You're Sarah Silver," she said. "Your brother is Silas."

The old woman nodded. "The voices told me that Tamson had to go in order for my brother's wives to stop dying."

"The voices," said Matt, sounding like he was about to ask a question.

The old woman raised the gun pointed at Matt ever so slightly, trying to warn him to be careful with what he said next, but she winced as she made the move.

That must've been the shoulder, Belinda now realized, that Sarah had injured while firing the rifle.

Matt putting his hands up to let Sarah know he wasn't going to do anything, that she was in control. "Was one of them called Ada?" he asked. "Was one of the voices one of your brother's dead wives?"

The name was what did it, that name and that connection. Sarah lowered both her guns now, too bewildered to continue the way she had been.

"Yes," she said. Then she added, "All of the voices were his wives, once upon a time."

❧ 16 ❧
TRACY

J ust before the British ship opened fire on the Silver family's old saltbox-style home—the second of many houses which would stand upon that swampy, undersized plot of land— Tracy watched as the women and children dashed from the place. That would be Thankful, Tracy realized, and her daughter-in-law Mehitable—the wives of Silas V and VI respectively—and in between them Mehitable's twin daughters, just barely old enough to walk. Following close behind them, stumbling along with the aid of what looked at first to be a walking stick, was an ancient old man who Tracy realized with great pride must be the aging Silas III.

A second after Tracy gave him a smile from her far-off position on the deck of The Antagonist, Silas III raised what had heretofore appeared to be his walking stick and what now was plainly a rifle. Then he took aim at someone in the boat that was ferrying the Redcoats to shore and fired.

Tracy watched as one of the officers—Bethiah had pointed them out—fell overboard and into the waters where she had swum so often as a girl. A moment later, another soldier slumped to one side—a splash of blood exploding from his forehead as a second musket ball found its mark. And the moment after that, another fell into the churning waters of Nantucket Sound.

Tracy didn't know much about eighteenth-century guns, but she wasn't sure that *anyone* could get off three shots that fast—not with any musket she had ever seen, not during a Fourth of July parade, not during a reenactment on Lexington Green, and not even during a Hollywood movie. She scanned the coast and saw that two more Silvers had taken up positions beside their aging patriarch. The younger of the two was a severe-looking chap who was reloading muskets at a speed which would have made Hermes swoon. The older man wore a wild mane of silver hair beneath his tricorn hat, and the kind of beard that the hipsters of 2016 could only dream of.

"That's my Silas," said Bethiah, pointing at the wild-haired man who had just taken aim and taken out another Redcoat.

Tracy was about to tell Bethiah that she figured it was him, but just at that moment came the call of a British voice crying out "FIRE!"

Every cannon on the starboard side of the British vessel fired upon the Silvers' home, a show of force entirely unnecessary given the already dilapidated state of the house. And yet, as Tracy understood it, there was a great desire for vengeance amongst the men in command of the British ship—and burning the Silvers' home to the ground would only go so far in sating them. They were so blinded by their desire for revenge, in fact, that they had completely given up on defending themselves from The Antagonist. All of their gun crew was on the other side, readying for the next volley that was headed landward.

"FIRE!" Bethiah shouted to her own crew, and the guns of The Antagonist laid into the hull of the British ship.

But still the British paid The Antagonist no mind. The cutter and its dinky four-pounders were a nuisance only. The British captain smirked at Bethiah, then returned his attention to the task at hand: destroying the Silvers on that beach.

As the story went, the Red River Massacre was an unsanctioned retaliation by a British vessel gone rogue. The ship was crewed exclusively by men who had survived an encounter with a Colonial ship crewed by, among others, the dashing young Silas Silver VI. And the British ship's captain? He was out for revenge, too. During his boyhood, the old salt had been the sole survivor of an ambush by The Antagonist. He thirsted now for the blood of the Silvers who'd commanded that dastardly bark—and the blood of their kin, as well.

The second volley from the British ship knocked what was left of the Silver's saltbox to the ground—but by the time the first boat they'd launched reached shore, there were naught but a handful of Redcoats still breathing. And by the time those handful had reached the position of the trio of Silver men on the beach, only one of them was alive.

He was dead a moment later, three musket balls piercing his flesh all at once—one through the neck, one through the heart, and the last through his unmentionables.

And yet, his slaughter was distraction enough for the second boat of Redcoats to get far closer to shore than the first had. They all died too, but it took a lot more out of the Silvers to do that deed. And so, they were winded by the time the third boat was in the water.

"There's none of them left aboard," shouted a voice from above—the voice of the lad in the crow's nest of The Antagonist.

"Has anyone got a shot on that boat?" Bethiah cried out, trying to maneuver her ship into position to provide support for the men on the beach—*her* man among them.

The next moment, two of Bethiah's crew were standing behind the two railside swivel guns which sat nearest the bow. The moment after that, they'd blown a hole in the bottom of the rowboat and blown the head clean off the captain.

Satisfied by the actions of her crew, Bethiah raced toward the rail of the ship. Then, a split-second later, she was diving overboard.

"Where are you going?!" Tracy began to say, but just then, out of the corner of her eye, she saw the fog closing in off the stern—and two copies of The Antagonist racing out of it, as if to join the fray.

Robin and Ashley ran to Tracy's side then and saw what she was seeing, each of them gasping as they tried to understand what was going to happen next. The logical thing would be for those other Antagonists to join them in defending the beach, but none of them were sure that logic would win the day here.

The sound of fresh musket fire filled the air. Someone in the British rowboat had taken aim at the swimming Bethiah and missed. The Silvers on the beach had taken aim at the dinghy in retaliation and found their marks. Three more Redcoats were dead. Only a half-dozen remained. But they were about to make landfall.

Bethiah got there just ahead of them, trudging out of the water and stealing a pistol off the first dead body she saw. Only now did her aging husband begin to realize exactly which ship had come to their rescue out there on the water—and exactly which captain had just swum to shore to aid their cause.

"Bethiah?!" shouted Silas, standing up as he spoke and forgetting himself at the sight of the woman he'd thought dead for thirty-four years.

A musket ball whizzed by his head, nicking his ear as it sped past. With a howl, he raised a blunderbuss and fired wildly at the man who'd shot at him—entirely missing his mark.

Bethiah's aim, however, was true. She shot the man who'd taken aim at her husband and got him right in the gut—in just the right place to make sure he'd suffer before the Lord took him.

It was too late, however, because the five remaining Redcoats had finally found the time to line up in their deadly formation. They had finally found the time to make ready, to take aim at the three Silvers they had come for—the father, grandfather, and *great*-grandfather of the seaman who'd caused them such pain and misfortune—and to fire.

The five British muskets laid low the eldest of the Silver men first, old Silas III, who was running off to check on the women and children—though of course the Redcoats couldn't have known that, and perhaps suspected he was racing off to gather reinforcements. Poor old Silas, Tracy thought. He had lived long enough to see his country declare its independence from the colonial powers he so despised, but now died mere months later.

Bethiah, from her position at the Redcoats' flank, took out another of them as they made ready for their next volley. Her son, older now than she appeared to be, killed one more. But that left three, because Bethiah's love—the aging Silas IV—missed his mark. And three, three would be enough.

Their next volley felled the two remaining men, Bethiah howling as her husband and her son dropped to the ground.

On the ship, Tracy howled too. Ashley, more angry than sad—and more present than any of the rest—gave the order for The Antagonist's crew to fire at will upon the now empty British vessel, to send it to "Davy Jones' locker."

Whether they knew what she was talking about or not, they followed her command. And it was at that moment that the two Antagonists which had come racing out of the fog arrived as well. They added their own cannons to the mix—their own howling Bethiahs giving their own commands to their own crews.

A few minutes later, a cannon ball found the powder magazine and the British ship blew sky high. But it was too little too late for the Silvers on the beach. And it was at that second that the two extra Antagonists faded back into the fog from whence they came—and that the fog disappeared altogether.

Tracy, Robin, and Ashley leapt into their ship's rowboat and sped themselves to shore—to find Bethiah and collect her from the carnage there.

When the trio of modern-day women disembarked, Bethiah was cradling her lost love in her arms. She had turned herself away from her son's body—unable, Tracy presumed, to bear the sight of it—and she was staring at the shoreline instead. A few yards away, the eldest of the Silver men—Silas III—lay with his arm outstretched toward his long lost daughter-in-law, but Bethiah was paying no heed to his corpse either. The only thing on her mind seemed to be the man in her arms, and how close she'd come to saving him this time.

As Ashley and Robin knelt to console Bethiah, Tracy caught sight of the women and children who'd been hiding. They were peeking out from the doorway of the neighbor's house, still unsure whether it was safe to come out or not, but not wanting to wait much longer to see what had become of their men.

Tracy told Ashley and Robin that they didn't have much time. She knelt and told Bethiah, "We need to go. There's no way we can explain." She tried to remember if she'd heard any strange stories passed down through the family about this day and came up with nothing. "Even if we could explain," she told Bethiah, gently taking hold of her chin to make her listen—to make her see—"even if we could, we didn't. We never did."

A note of anger raced across Bethiah's weary face, as if she wanted to scream at Tracy right now for trying to make sense in the midst of a predicament which made no sense at all. But just as quickly as the look overtook Bethiah's face, it was gone.

She kissed her lover goodbye, set his body back to rest on the sand, and ran for the rowboat with the others.

THE ANTAGONIST SPED toward the horizon, fleeing into the east as the sun set behind them. When the time was right—and Tracy couldn't tell at all what made that moment the right one, and not any of the others before it—Bethiah spun what was left of the helmsman's wheel and took them hard to starboard. A moment later, they passed through a veil of orange light and arrived back on the waterway that Bethiah had called The River Without End. There, once again, was the rocky island that she had called The Skerry of Souvenirs, an enormous snow globe sitting atop it.

"I was about to ask you," said Robin to Bethiah, "if we were headed for the second star to the right, and straight on till morning."

Bethiah gave Robin a sidelong glance that seemed to suggest she had never heard of a heading so preposterous in all her life.

"It's from a movie," said Ashley by way of explanation. She wrapped her arms around Robin's waist and rested her chin on the woman's shoulder.

"And what, pray tell, is a movie?" asked Bethiah.

WHEN IT CAME time to lay ol' James o' the Red Hat to rest, Bethiah's crew wrapped him in linens and chains and then hoisted him over the rail. They had been spared of any other casualties, and they thanked the maker for that blessing in between the memories they shared of old James.

"He had an eye for me," said Bethiah, once everyone else had a chance to say their piece. "And he would've made a fine lover," she said, "if only I'd ever gotten over my first."

She wore his hat after that, in honor of his memory—just the same as she now wore her Silas' coat. It was an odd pairing, the plain and unadorned fabric of her husband's old jacket and her bosun's brash headpiece, but Bethiah was an odd woman. This was the one thing about her that Tracy knew now for certain: that it was hard to know *anything* about her for certain.

THAT NIGHT IN HER HAMMOCK, Tracy dreamed a dream that was two things at once. *At least* two. The first was her brain trying to remember the plot of the movie *About Time*, and the second was a fantasy about what she'd do to Kanoa once he was resurrected and she could take him to bed again.

Somehow in this fantasy, Kanoa became Rachel McAdams and Tracy became Domhnall Gleeson—at least in terms of their roles in the scene. Kanoa was the unsuspecting partner whose lover kept getting better and better at satisfying him each time they stepped into a closet to regroup. Meanwhile, Tracy was the cross-time Casanova. She'd rock his world once, take mental notes, step into the closet that let her rewind the clock, and then satisfy him even more efficiently the next time around. By the end of the dream—by the final time she stepped out of the closet to seduce him—Tracy made Kanoa come with just a look, and the promise of pleasure that came with it.

She woke when she tumbled out of the hammock and onto the floor, her right hand down the front of her pants. She was entirely unsure whether she'd been asleep for the whole of the fantasy, or if she'd woken up somewhere in the middle and sleepily convinced herself to stick with it. All she *was* sure of was that she'd hit her head really hard.

"Trace," whispered Ashley, stirring in her own hammock, "are you alright?"

"Fine," she said, standing up and deciding to walk it off. Some fresh air, she decided, would do her good.

Up on deck, Bethiah was still manning the helm. Tracy meandered that way, taking her time to breathe in the air before she asked Bethiah if she'd had any sleep.

"Got to get you where you're going," she said, "and nobody can steer this ship like I can."

Tracy nodded and sat down on the edge of the poop deck. The black of the night sky was fading into a deep purple up ahead of them. Tracy asked Bethiah how far they had left to go.

"We're about halfway," said Bethiah. Then she jerked a thumb over her shoulder. "At least we don't have the fog to outrun anymore. One less thing to worry ourselves over."

"True that," said Tracy.

Bethiah smirked at the expression, perhaps admiring the economy of it. Tracy wondered if she'd find a way to incorporate it into her lexicon.

"Had myself a helluva dream," said Tracy, making small talk. "Fell out of the damned hammock."

"A dream of your beau?" asked Bethiah.

"How'd you know?" said Tracy, blushing.

Bethiah smirked. "You were as pink as you are now when you first came above deck. Positively flushed," she said.

"I've tried so hard *not* to think about him," she said, forgetting for a moment who she was speaking to and what this woman had just been through.

Bethiah seemed to sense Tracy's unease. "Pay me no mind," she said and she offered a weary smile as her signal for Tracy to finish her story.

"Seeing you with Silas today," said Tracy. "Knowing that you'd do anything to bring him back... now I'm thinking what right do I have to do anything less, especially when the chance is within my grasp?"

"No right," said Bethiah plainly. "You're right," she said. "If I had the power, I would bring my Silas back right this instant. And so," she continued, "if you want to repay me for what I'm doing for you—if you truly want to settle your debt to me and the crew of this ship—you will bring that man of yours back to life, and you won't let anyone take him away from you again."

Up ahead, the deep purple of the before-dawn was breaking and the yellow light of the morning sun was rising to take its place.

"I'll try" was what Tracy said in that moment, stunned by the beauty they were speeding towards, by the beauty they would soon pass by—that would soon pass *them* by. What hope did she have against time, against fate, and against whatever else was ready to stand in her way?

What hope did she have against Ada if Ada came back?

"Yes, try," said Bethiah, giving the helmsman's wheel a gentle turn to the left. "That's all any of us can do, child. But try your damnedest," she said. "Do that for me?"

Tracy looked up at her ancestor, who was looking back at her in that moment. She looked at Bethiah and she gave her a nod. It seemed like such an insignificant gesture, but it was all she had.

And yet, judging by how quickly Bethiah returned to the task at hand, it was all the captain needed.

❧ 17 ❧

BELINDA

O nce they were sure she wasn't going to shoot them, Belinda and Matt bade farewell to Sarah Silver and started back up Beacon Hill. Rounding the State House, Belinda wondered if she could distract Matt by asking for an anecdote about the gold dome—a distraction that might stop him from freaking out about the fact that the ghosts of his great-grandfather's dead wives had just ordered a hit on someone. And on an elderly Emily Henderson, for God's sake—someone they should've seen as one of their own. Someone who *was*, in a previous version of the universe, one of their own.

"A previous version of the universe?!" said Matt, screaming out loud at the increasing preposterousness of his situation.

"Know any good stories about the dome?" Belinda asked him.

Matt side-eyed her and gave her half a roll of his eyes before telling her the story of "the three domes." The first, he told her, was the shingled one that architect Charles Bullfinch designed. The second was copper, installed by the company of Paul Revere to make watertight the original leaky design. And the third? The third was the gold leaf which stood up there today, laid down in 1872.

"And the whole thing," he said, as they started their descent down the other side of the hill, "the whole building was built on a foundation of shit."

Belinda laughed.

"No," said Matt, laughing along with her. "I'm serious. The state house was built where John Hancock's cow pasture used to be. Fitting, I think, for a seat of government."

They hurried their way through the West End toward the river, Belinda remembering all too well where the Sister had been on this day. It was on a patch of grass along the Charles, just past Mass General Hospital. Years from now, the land would be home to a baseball field named after a young Red Sox fan. But now, now it was the perfect out-of-the-way spot for a dive bar and a furniture warehouse.

When the Sister finally came into view, Belinda lit up inside. She had never been happier to see the place. Never happier—until, that is, she caught sight of a row of hooded figures standing just beneath the awning. There they were: the ghosts of Silas Silver's wives, just looming ominously.

"Shit," she said aloud, breaking out into a run.

"What?!" said Matt, sprinting after her.

The hooded figures hurried inside the building once they'd caught sight of Belinda and Matt running their way.

"NO!" said Belinda, trying to find more speed within herself. Trying, and failing.

Matt overtook her and poured it on, racing toward the building with everything he had—which was still, even at forty-five, quite a bit.

And yet, it still wasn't enough. By the time he was within arm's reach of the Sister's front door, the building blinked out of existence in a flash of orange light.

Belinda stumbled over her own feet and landed face-first on the grass. Frustrated by both the fall and her inability to see this turn of events coming, she pounded on the ground with both fists

—one after the other after the other, until she was so mad that she was slamming both arms into the ground at the same time. And she screamed all the while. She had never, not since the calamity which had stolen her parents and her universe from her, had so little control over the situation at hand. Was this the universe's way of getting back at her, after a lifetime of playing God?

"Fuck! You!" she said to the earth, yelling at it as she continued to pummel it with her fists.

When Matt came back to help her up, his hand extended as he said, "C'mon," she did not relent at first. Instead, she went still, closed her eyes, and pressed her forehead into the dirt.

"You gonna give her a head-butt?" asked Matt.

With her eyes still closed, Belinda asked, "Who?"

"Mother Earth," said Matt.

Belinda opened her eyes and scoffed. "If she were ever real," she said, sitting up now, "the woman's dead by now. We've surely killed her at this point. Climate change, and all that."

"Fair point," said Matt. Then he gave Belinda's shoulder a squeeze. "It's going to be okay," he said. "You're a smart kid. You'll figure it out. You always do."

⚜

SITTING on the banks of the Charles River that night, waiting for an idea to come to her, Belinda took comfort in Matt's arm around her shoulders and in the scent of his ocean-breeze deodorant—the only modern-day product he couldn't time-travel without. Her head resting against her uncle's chest, she closed her eyes and breathed in a deodorant-maker's rough approximation of what the sea might smell like.

It was certainly sweeter than the smell of the Charles in 1915, a river in the years *after* the Industrial Revolution but *before* any attempts to clean it up.

"We could just go straight where they're going," said Matt. "Right? I mean, what's stopping us? You can open a door to whenever you want to go, right?"

"I can open a door to wherever my blood has been," said Belinda.

"But aren't both Tracy *and* Robin our blood?" asked Matt.

"They haven't been where we're going," she said. "Not yet. And we want to get there before them. The Sister would've helped us do that."

"Isn't Kanoa our blood too?" asked Matt. "Technically?"

Belinda sat up and turned to face him. Aside from wanting him to know what a riverbend would feel like, the reason they'd come to 1915 was because they still disagreed on exactly where Robin was planning to take Tracy.

They agreed that Robin planned to bring Kanoa back to life, and to use her newfound knowledge about his ancestry to persuade Ada to stop murdering him once and for all. Where they disagreed, Belinda and Matt, was on where this resurrection was going to take place.

Matt's notion—and it was a romantic one, yes, and Belinda *wanted* to believe it—was that Robin was going to bring Tracy back to Hawai'i in 2013, to the time when Tracy and Kanoa were on a break, all in the hope that Future Tracy would be the heretofore anonymous girl that heartbroken Kanoa would cheat with while his Tracy, 2013 Tracy, was away for her Auntie Ashley's funeral. They'd time it so they arrived when Tracy was ovulating, then she'd get pregnant, and they'd use the blood connection between the fetus and its father to bring the father—Kanoa—back to life.

Matt always forgot to factor Ada into the equation, but Belinda forgave him that. It was a beautiful dream of a story, the fairy tale ending that Tracy deserved.

And yet.

Belinda maintained that Robin's ego would get in the way, that she wouldn't settle for any plan in which she wasn't the hero. Belinda believed that they—Robin and the rest—would steal Kanoa's semen from the sperm bank where he and Tracy had made their "just in case" deposits years before, and that they'd use *that* to bring him back. Then Robin would use her own blood connection to Ada to bring *her* back for the ultimate intervention. Robin would believe that Ada would see this as an olive branch, and that she wouldn't just move straight in for the kill on Kanoa. But she'd be wrong, and disaster would strike.

On the banks of the Charles River in 1915, Belinda and Matt sat beside each other and tried to break through this impasse once again. By staring at each other and saying absolutely nothing.

Hawai'i was the only thing their theories had in common. She could take them there, to the home of her would-be parents, and have them hang out until the time was right. But she hated the imprecision of that plan. If she had the Sister at her disposal, she could take it wherever they needed to go in an instant—if she were willing to rig the dice as Robin had, which now, of course, she was. Once they were inside, they'd have all the time in the world to figure out what to do next.

"Your bar is not the be-all and end-all of everything," said Matt, getting pretty good at reading her mind for someone with no psychic powers to speak of.

Belinda laughed and played it off as a 'you're right' kind of chuckle. In reality, Matt was dead-wrong. The Strumpet's Sister *was* the be-all and end-all of everything. It was the last refuge of the living each time the world came to an end, and it was the first building built each time the universe was remade. Belinda had never understood why, had never found anyone who could give her an answer, but—

"Jakob," she said aloud, her jaw falling as she spoke the two syllables.

"Who?" said Matt.

Belinda stood up and held out a hand to help Matt to his feet. "Steady," she said, "don't fall in the river. You have *no* idea what's in there."

Once Matt was standing too, Belinda reached into the air above the river and felt for a seam. It wouldn't be that hard, given that The Veil of the World was at its thinnest near bodies of running water, and sure enough it was only a moment later that she was pulling the fabric of reality apart.

Orange light spilled out onto the grass of the riverbank and Belinda once again implored Matt to step forward into the unknown, to trust her.

"Who's Jakob?" he wanted to know. He was standing still and seemed intent on staying put until he got some answers.

Belinda smiled and told him. "Jakob," she said, "is the star of the greatest yarn you ever did hear."

⚜

THEY ARRIVED on the banks of the River Jordan on a Friday afternoon in April of the year 33 AD. Still clad in the clothes they'd worn in 1915, they needed to keep their distance so as not to arouse suspicion. Belinda wasn't interested in watching the gore up close anyway. She brought them to a moment after their ancestor—their *blood*—had already left the city, to a moment he'd repeated several hundred times now across several hundred different iterations of reality: the march back to the river, and to the strange pub from whence he came.

"Jakob," said Belinda, as they stepped out of the orange light of the veil and into the late afternoon of Judea in the first century.

Jakob, who seemed only mildly surprised by the sudden arrival of two anachronistically dressed strangers, said, "Well, this is new."

Matt tilted his head in confusion and turned to Belinda for clarification. "Shouldn't he be speaking Aramaic or something?"

"I've been living on a loop for longer than you can possibly imagine," said Jakob, not bothering to stop for them. "I've picked up some things."

Belinda nodded at Matt, as if to say, "Trust me," and the two of them dashed to catch up with their quarry.

Matt was casting glances all around the whole time though, and nearly tripping over his own feet as a result. He couldn't believe his eyes, though he'd seen plenty of depictions of the scene over the course of his life. Atop the rocky knoll of Golgotha, there were three crucifixes, just as he'd expected. He couldn't make out faces or signs above heads or any of the other things that might've signaled to him which of the victims was *the* guy, but he imagined it was the one in the middle. Then he wondered if he was missing the point, if maybe the point was that you couldn't tell who was who—if that's what *the* guy would want. Then Matt tripped and fell flat on his face.

"Shit!" shouted Belinda, stopping in her tracks to help him up. "Are you alright?"

With Belinda's help, Matt stood and brushed himself off. There was a tear in one knee of his slacks, and a laceration on that knee to boot. Matt prodded at it gently to see just how bad it was, and he was satisfied when the palpation didn't make him wince.

"Jakob!" shouted Belinda, waving at the man who was still wandering away from them, "will you please stop?"

Finally, mercifully, Jakob did stop. And yet, he didn't turn around to face them. He simply waited there for them, not making a move except to wipe the sweat from his brow with the back of one forearm and then the other.

Once they'd made it to the spot where he stood still, Jakob asked them what they wanted.

"Have you met me yet?" asked Belinda.

"That's an odd quest—" Matt began to say, but then Belinda held a finger to her lips to shush him.

"I have not," said Jakob. "I always start there," he said, shaking a thumb back at the holy city. "Are you the new Gamemaster?"

Belinda nodded. "But the Gamemaster isn't me," she said. "Not yet."

Jakob nodded like he understood this. Matt scratched his head.

"We're just going to make our way into one of the back rooms," said Belinda, "and bide our time."

Jakob gave a curt nod, an even curter grunt, and got back to walking.

Belinda and Matt followed suit, and they walked in silence for a bit. Matt took off his coat and loosened his tie. Belinda unbuttoned the top button of her blouse. Then, after looking around to make sure no one was watching—she didn't want to be stoned to death for public indecency, after all—she unbuttoned the button below that.

"So, where are some of the places you've been?" Matt asked Jakob, making small-talk. "Or *when*, I guess? "

"Who said I was a time traveler?" asked Jakob.

"But aren't you?" asked Matt. "I thought that's how people changed things," he said. "By traveling through time."

Jakob turned to Matt and offered him a cold smirk. "Not me. I did something I wasn't supposed to, yes. But I did it in the moment I was in."

"What did you do?" asked Matt.

For the final time that afternoon, Jakob pointed back at the hill they were running away from. "I brought *him* back to life."

18

TRACY

They were on their one-hundred and sixteenth trip around the lost continent of Eden when the storm rolled in ahead of them. It shouldn't have been there, Bethiah told Tracy. It wasn't on any of her charts.

"You have charts for when you're going to encounter storms?" asked Ashley, incredulous, as she and Robin cuddled closer together under the blanket they'd brought from below deck.

"Aye," said Bethiah. "I've traveled this river for years beyond counting. Between James and myself, we've kept a record of every gale. And this one," she said, nodding to Tracy to take the wheel, "isn't supposed to be here."

Tracy stood behind the helmsman's wheel and held it steady. She'd guessed without being told that *that* was what she was supposed to do. If anything more complicated were expected, she was pretty sure Bethiah would've called a crew member over.

Then again, Tracy realized, Bethiah was distracted. And panicked. She was searching the cabinet just in front of them for her logbook, but she was trying to keep a weather eye on the horizon at the same time.

Presently, she produced a logbook from the cabinet and began to page through it—pausing every four or five flips to look up into the sky.

"What?" said Ashley. "What are you seeing?"

"Aye," said Bethiah, handing the open logbook to Ashley and retaking the wheel from Tracy. "Middle of that page. See that description," she said, pointing.

Tracy shuffled over to look over Ashley's shoulder, and sure enough there was a description on the open page of the logbook which matched the storm perfectly—down to the number of thunderheads and the frequency of the lightning.

"Note the date," said Bethiah.

Tracy looked and read aloud, "November 1844."

Ashley groaned. "I thought you said we were in the 1890s already."

"We are," said Bethiah. "We passed that storm forty-eight revolutions ago. Skirted right past it, as we always do. And yet, here it is again."

Tracy dragged a hand across the top of her head and through her windswept locks, trying to understand what this might mean. She knew that November 1844 was the month that her ancestor, Silas Silver VIII, was lost at sea. She and Bethiah had had a long conversation about it as they passed the storm the first time. But why would it be appearing again in the 1890s?

The answer came to Tracy in a flash, and she felt her stomach and her spirits sink. "What year are we passing now?" she asked Bethiah. "What year exactly?"

Bethiah looked at Tracy and blanched. They had shared a lot of stories over a lot of rum these past few weeks, but one story had come up more frequently than the rest—and it involved the year they were about to pass.

"It's 1892," said Tracy. "Isn't it?"

Bethiah nodded. Then she bellowed to her crew to "batten down the hatches."

1892 was the year that Ada Coffin summoned Silas Silver

VIII, her husband's late father, back to life. She'd used the same potion that Tracy and Robin used to resurrect Ashley, and she encountered the same side effects. Just as the potion had brought the sunny weather of Ashley's dying day along with her, so too would Ada's concoction bring a portion of the day Silas died back with him. And he had died in the middle of a November gale in 1844.

Tracy turned to Ashley and Robin then and told them they should hurry below deck.

Ashley nodded and began to rise straight away, seeing the seriousness on Tracy's face. Robin, on the other hand, grumbled at being displaced from her resting spot upon Ashley's shoulder. "There's no storm she hasn't gotten us through yet," said Robin as she stood up. "Why should this one be any different?"

"This is the night your branch of the family begins," said Tracy.

Robin's eyes went wide. "Holy shit," she said, recalling the story Ada had told her of that night all too well. "C'mon," she said to Ashley, grabbing her by the arm as she threw open the hatch, "let's go."

🐛

TRACY STAYED ABOVE DECK, not just because she had no one to cuddle with below, but because she wanted to see it for herself. If this were to be the end of The Antagonist—maybe even the end of everyone on board—then she wanted to witness it all with her own two eyes. To only *hear* it—the sounds of disaster, and nothing else—would be far worse. That's what she decided, and she was sticking to it.

She wished she could stick to the deck, though. What she wouldn't have given just then to be Peter Parker or Miles Morales or that alternate reality version of Gwen Stacy—or any of the various comic book Spider-People, really. As it was, she was holding onto a rope that she prayed wasn't supposed to be holding something else in place.

Bethiah, meanwhile, looked like a madwoman. She reminded Tracy in this moment of Lieutenant Dan from *Forrest Gump*, screaming up at God as he and Forrest tried to outlast a hurricane. "Is that all you've got?!" is what Tracy imagined Bethiah was shouting, but the truth was she couldn't hear a word of what Bethiah was saying—not over winds howling like dogs in heat, or in battle, or maybe both.

When the rogue wave came, looming over them like a skyscraper sprung from the sea, Bethiah threw an arm up and gestured to her crew. Tracy wasn't sure what the gesture meant, but the crew must've understood it as "hard to port!" because at the next moment Bethiah spun the wheel and Tracy tumbled to the deck.

As she struggled to keep hold of the rope that was her only real tether to the ship, Tracy saw Bethiah shouting something in her general direction. If she was reading her ancestor's lips correctly, the question was something along the lines of "Are you alright?" And rather than second guess herself, Tracy threw up a thumb to say that yes, she would survive.

It occurred to her suddenly to wonder exactly how old the thumbs up was as a gesture, and if Bethiah would even understand what she'd meant.

The ship banked hard to the left and Tracy watched as Bethiah tried to hold the wheel steady. She watched muscles strain in the woman's arms that she'd never noticed before. And then, mercifully, they had turned themselves about and Bethiah was able to let go.

Tracy turned around and looked up at the massive wave behind them, hoping she wouldn't see the telltale line of white at the top that signaled the thing was about to crest. Alas, there it was. It was all about to come crashing down.

She turned in a flash to tell Bethiah what she surely already knew, only to find that the crew were maneuvering sails like the experts they were and doing their damnedest to pick up speed. *Will it be enough?* Tracy wondered to herself, unable to decide if she should look forward or back.

And then it happened. The stern of the boat began to rise, slowly but steadily, and the incline took Tracy's feet right out from under her. She slipped and slid down along the deck toward the bow, the rope burning her hands as she struggled to keep hold of it. As the ship went vertical, looking back became looking up. Presently, all light disappeared as the wave loomed large overhead.

It hurt so much to hold on. Tracy felt the skin on her palms burning. She looked around to see if she could see who was still at their stations—if anyone—but the only person she found was Bethiah, still holding onto the ship's wheel for dear life. Bethiah found her too, and the two women looked each other in the eye.

They each wanted to say they were sorry. For a hundred things each, they were sorry. But the cacophony of the storm was too loud for words, so the look they shared would have to suffice.

Bethiah lost her grip first, plummeting into the sea below, and Tracy gave up only after that—deciding that it was doing her no good to hold on any longer. The storm would decide what to do with her now.

The storm. Or fate. Or God. Whoever it was that was in charge.

If anyone was.

❧

WHEN SHE WOKE, it was to a mouthful of sand and to rain pouring down upon her back. Tracy coughed and tried to push herself up from off of her stomach, but she ached so much that she decided to stay put for a second. And so, instead of getting up, she turned her head to one side to see what she could see.

Night had fallen and the storm still loomed overhead, but the moon was doing its best to shine through the gloom.

There to the left, once again, was the stretch of beach which had been her playground from the age of eight. And off in the distance, standing on the lot where her own childhood home would eventually be built, was the grandiose Victorian that Tracy had only ever seen in old black and white photos—curled and coffee-stained squares smaller than Polaroids. It was in far better condition now than it would be by the time it was photographed. In this moment, after all, it was barely two years old.

Tracy closed her eyes and buried her face in the sand. She would've buried her whole head, but she didn't have the energy.

Shit, she thought to herself. *We're really here.*

Suddenly, she felt someone shaking her shoulders. "Tracy?" said Auntie Ashley, who just then decided to flip Tracy over to make sure she was still breathing, "Trace?!"

Tracy blinked to let her aunt know she was alive. That's all she had in her. She was too weighed down by the reality of what had just happened, and by the sopping wet clothes she was wearing.

"Is she okay?" asked Robin from some distance away, her voice trembling.

Ashley told Robin that yes, Tracy was fine, but she didn't leave Tracy's side to go and care for her lover. Tracy detected a hint of anger in Ashley's voice.

"I'm okay," said Tracy, sitting up now. Maybe by letting them both *see* that she was okay, maybe then she could stop whatever lover's quarrel was brewing right there in its tracks.

Way to mix your metaphors, said one part of Tracy to the other.

"Bethiah?" she asked, looking around the beach for the captain or any of her crew but finding no hint of them nor any hint of wreckage from The Antagonist.

Ashley shook her head. "Just us," she said.

"And what a sorry sight you are," spoke an unfamiliar voice.

The three women turned about in the dark and in the rain to

see where the voice had come from. Tracy caught sight of Ashley reaching for some weapon or other, but anything they might have been carrying while aboard The Antagonist appeared to be gone.

From the road just beyond the dunes emerged a shortish figure with a weak lantern. As Tracy's eyes adjusted to the light, she guessed the brown-skinned person with the glorious beard was a man, but she didn't want to assume.

Robin, on the other hand, appeared to have no such qualms. "You're him!" she shouted, pointing. Then she turned to Ashley and said, "He's the bartender I met when I was a kid, the one my mother worked for that February when I found my obituary."

"Your obituary?" said the person with the beard, a smirk playing across their lips. "I shall look forward to seeing how that story plays out."

"Right," said Robin, nodding as she tried to wrap her head around their situation. "You haven't met me yet."

"I have now," said the bearded person. "And no," he said, turning to Tracy, "before you ask, she hasn't misgendered me."

"Did you just read her mind?" asked Ashley, standing up and moving between the bearded man and her niece.

The bearded man shook his head. "No," he said. "I've just been around the block enough times to guess what that look on your friend's face was all about." He paused for a second, assessing the situation. "I mean you no harm," he told Ashley. "None of you. I'm here to help. My name is Jakob," he said. "And I am indeed a barkeep." He shook his thumb toward the nearby river. "You're welcome to a room in my pub for the night, if you'd like."

"The Strumpet's Sister?" asked Robin, as she and Ashley each took hold of one of Tracy's arms and helped her to her feet.

"Indeed," said Jakob. Then he waved his arm in the general direction they were headed and said, "Shall we?"

WHEN JAKOB PUSHED OPEN the door, the spirits of the waterlogged women were buoyed by the sight of the hearth and the roaring fire within it. They nearly tripped over each other to grab a spot in front of that beautiful fireplace and Tracy delighted in the sound of Jakob's boisterous laugh as she sprinted across the room. He had seemed like a rather serious fellow, so the realization that he had at least some mirth within him was a pleasant surprise.

"I'll see which rooms are open," said Jakob. "In the meantime, I'll have someone bring you over something hot to eat and something stiff to drink."

A few minutes later, one of the barmaids brought a tray of soups and ales to the table nearest the fire. Robin and Ashley abandoned the blaze straight away and grabbed seats at the table, asking Tracy if she had any preferences before grabbing a bowl and a mug a piece. Tracy, meanwhile, turned so that she could see her companions and warm her wet backside at the same time.

But though it comforted Tracy to see Robin and Ashley safe under this roof and filling their empty bellies, her thoughts soon turned to poor Bethiah and the crew of The Antagonist. Had they survived? Were they still sailing The River Without End somewhere out there at the edge of the universe?

Tracy thought to ask Robin and Ashley, but she didn't want to burden them with her melancholy and she felt fairly certain that they would just try and comfort her with empty words anyway. She didn't need to be told that everything would be alright right now, that everything had happened for a reason. *I mean, seriously*, she thought to herself, rubbing her hands across the seat of her pants to try and help the fire do the work of drying her off, *what is the point of being able to travel through time if you can't change things?*

"You haven't eaten yet," said Jakob when he returned. He smiled at Tracy, a small, sympathetic upturn of the corners of his lips. "The fire's good," he admitted, "but the food's better."

"Did you find us a room?" asked Ashley, slurping up the last of her soup without any sense of modesty or decorum—just one long *slurrrrrrrrrrrp*.

Jakob nodded. "I have something ready for the two of you," he said to Ashley and Robin. "Still working on something for your friend by the fire," he said. "Though she might want to finally sit down and eat. It might be a while yet."

Tracy did as she was bid and took a seat at the table, just in time to watch Ashley and Robin rise and follow Jakob down a long hallway. She saw Robin reach out for Ashley's hand and Ash only grudgingly accept it, holding on with only the lightest touch —and that made Tracy sigh. God how she'd hoped, if only for a few minutes, that the trouble between them would be resolved by soup and ale.

There was a hearty-looking roll on the tray that she hadn't noticed until now, probably one of three, and she felt glad they'd left it for her. Tracy dunked it absentmindedly into her bowl of tomato soup but didn't eat any of it, not at first. She was too distracted. One moment she was thinking about Bethiah searching the waves for all eternity, trying to find them again; the next she was trying to stop the image of Ashley and Robin kissing and making up from devolving into a far more explicit vision; and the moment after that, she was thinking about Kanoa and what it would be like to see him again. Each daydream ended with a powerful need to banish it from her mind, which then brought up the next fantasy, and the next.

"You look like you've had as rough a day as I have," spoke a familiar voice—a voice that sent a shiver down Tracy's spine, a shiver she did her best to stifle.

Tracy lifted her gaze from the now soggy roll she'd been stirring through her soup and found herself staring at, of all people, Ada Coffin.

Ada offered Tracy a kind smile, clearly having no idea who Tracy was at this point. She was wearing an anachronistic tavern wench's get-up: a brown corset with golden laces, a ruffled white bodice, a dark green apron, and a skirt of brown and beige stripes. The top bared both her shoulders and the bruises on her otherwise beautiful neck—a neck Tracy had strangled herself once, and wanted now to strangle again.

"Ada," said Jakob, returning now from the pub's back rooms. He pulled her aside, taking her by the arm with a bit more force than Tracy thought was strictly necessary. The momentary concern for Ada's well-being revolted her, and yet the observation about Jakob felt important somehow.

Tracy watched Jakob let go of Ada almost immediately, and that put an end to the uncomfortable urge to stand up and come to the defense of the woman she hated more than anyone in the world. But as she watched Jakob point at Ada's neck and tell her to cover it up if she intended to work down here, Tracy again felt unsettled. What was Jakob playing at? Sure, maybe Ada's bruises would make the customers feel uneasy. But if he felt that strongly about it, shouldn't he have just had her rest in a room out back until they'd healed.

Suddenly, Tracy remembered Ashley's still-missing breasts and the gunshot wound in Robin's abdomen which never healed. Suddenly, she remembered that the only reason she'd been able to strangle Ada to death all those years ago—or all those years from now, depending on your perspective—was because she was just finishing the job her great-great-grandfather had started.

Ada nodded at Jakob and hurried upstairs. Then Jakob returned to the table and apologized to Tracy.

"You were a bit rough with her," said Tracy, nodding toward the stairs. But even as she said it, she felt ridiculous. She was going to kill that woman one day. *Kill* her. Part of her wanted to kill her right now, before she had the chance to do any of the horrible things she was apparently "destined" to do, but she knew she couldn't do that without risking the wrath of the universe— because that's not what was "supposed" to happen. And so, why was she being so kind here? Why did she care?

Because this Ada isn't the Ada who's going to hurt you, she thought to herself. *Not yet.*

Jakob blushed and nodded as he conceded the fact that Tracy was right about his treatment of Ada. "Indeed," he said. "I was rougher than I should've been. A bad habit I'm working on breaking."

"Keep working," said Tracy.

"I shall," he said. "I have that room ready for you now," he said, gesturing toward the hall he'd taken Ashley and Robin down.

Tracy nodded, stood, and followed him. It was only as she entered the hallway that she realized how long it was. She couldn't even see the end of it, and she wondered if that was a trick of the dim light or the result of some magic she'd yet to encounter. Every fifteen feet or so, there seemed to be a new hall branching off the main one. How big was this place?

She was about to ask Jakob that very question when one of the doors just in front of them opened up. All of a sudden, another familiar figure came stumbling out into the hall—a tall, muscular figure who was obviously wasted.

"I'll go ask Jakob for some more," said Uncle Matt, speaking to someone he'd left behind in the room he'd just emerged from. Then he turned and caught sight of Jakob and said, affecting a horrible British accent, "Jakob, my fine chap! Speak of the devil. We should very much like another bottle of—"

It was in the middle of the sentence that he finally noticed Tracy standing there, and that he pulled her into a bear hug.

"I'm so glad to see you," said Uncle Matt, pulling himself away from her to look her over, tears welling up even as he smiled at her. Then a stern but absolutely silly look overtook his face.

"What?" said Tracy.

"You, young lady, are grounded."

✣ 19 ✣

BELINDA

A s they continued on their way toward the first century's version of The Strumpet's Sister, Jakob regaled Belinda and Matt with a recitation of "The Tragedy of Yesh and Jude."

"Jude?" said Matt, still reeling from the revelations of the past few minutes and trying now to regain some level of comfort by way of a joke. "I thought your name was Jakob?"

"It is," said Jakob with a smile. "I haven't been Jude in a long time."

Matt shook his head, confused. "How can you change your name and not bring about the apocalypse in the process?" he asked, ignoring the finger Belinda raised to her lips to shush him. "Judas is a pretty essential character in the narrative of the world. Are you saying you didn't see the fucking butterflies when you decided to call yourself something else?"

Now Jakob shook *his* head. "I was Judas six hundred and sixty-eight lifetimes ago," he said. "There have been more than six hundred Judases since, including," he said, jerking a thumb towards Jerusalem, "including the one back there who just betrayed the six hundred and sixty-somethingth edition of Jesus."

Matt stood still and silent for a long moment, then nodded. "You're him, though?" he said. "You're Judas? Or, well, you *were?*"

"I was," said Jakob. "Now," he said, "can I tell my damned story?"

༄

ONCE UPON A TIME, there was a closeted gay Jew. No, not the first. And not the last. Just one of many. And all that kept this unhappily married man from drowning himself in the River Jordan was news of a charismatic traveling rabbi. "Jude," the men in his village told him, "you must hear this Yeshua speak."

One man, who knew why Jude was unhappy in his marriage, added, "Yes, Jude; he must be seen to be believed."

On the morning of the rabbi's sermon, Jude—surrounded on all sides by his devout neighbors—was struck first by the rabbi's divine handsomeness, and only second by the man's teachings. And yet, he was enamored enough with what this Yeshua from Nazareth was saying that he followed the man out of the village the next day—leaving his wife and children behind in the process.

There were many times over the years they spent together that Jude confessed to Yesh a love beyond the love the other disciples bore him. But each time Jude made his proclamation, Yesh rebuked him. Never out of disapproval. Never with an ounce of disdain or disgust, but always with a certainty that the romance Jude so desperately wanted could never happen.

As time wore on and the momentum of Yesh's ministry built, Jude worried that everything was happening too fast. As Yesh and his disciples neared the holy city, Jude worried that Yesh's desire to openly proclaim himself the messiah would provoke both the Roman tyrants occupying their country *and* the religious establishment already in place—and that innocent Judeans would suffer the consequences.

And beyond that, Jude feared that the Romans would kill the man he loved.

Jude begged Yesh to reconsider, but Yesh was resolved and would not be swayed. He told Jude, "I will do what I must, as will you."

Before the last supper that they would ever eat together, Jude left Yesh's side and went to the chief priests of the holy city. He agreed to turn over Yesh that evening—and though he attempted to refuse it, they paid him 30 pieces of silver for his help.

Maybe a night in jail will cool him down, Jude thought. The crowds in the city for Passover would disperse. The extra soldiers would leave. And Yesh could make his proclamation in a way that wouldn't cause all hell to break loose all at once.

And I know what you're thinking: how could Jude not consider that Yesh would face death once he was arrested? How could Jude be so stupid? The answer is: he—*I*—was blinded by love, made dumb by it. He couldn't think of any other way to stop what seemed like it was inevitable. Maybe the Romans *wouldn't* kill Yesh if he was reasonable upon apprehension. Maybe some deal could be struck: a banishment or something. There had to be a way, Jude told himself. And this, the betrayal, felt like it might be it.

That evening, at the appointed time, Jude moved through the throng toward his beloved Yesh—bent, of course, on identifying him to the soldiers. But though he had planned simply to point out his great love with a finger, Jude was implored by Yesh to betray him in another way.

"You may have your kiss now," said Yesh.

Heartbroken and hurt, Jude did not kiss the lips he'd finally been offered. He kissed Yesh on the cheek instead. Days later, the Roman governor allowed one criminal to be spared. When the assembled crowd chose to spare a murderer instead of the rabble-rousing Yesh, Jude's heart broke for a second time.

After Yesh was crucified and laid to rest, Jude waited by the tomb to see if his love would bring himself back from death—a miracle Yesh had worked on others in the past. But Jude's heart broke a third time when an angel of death, the Ferryman, stepped out of the shadows, moved aside the boulder sealing Yesh's tomb, and made to carry the corpse toward the River Jordan.

The Ferryman, having laid the body of Yesh in its boat, began to punt out into an early morning fog. But Jude, angrier than he had ever been in his life, swam out to grab hold of the skiff before it was gone. And despite the best efforts of the Ferryman to stop him—despite the best efforts of the river itself and the butterflies which swarmed about him from out of nowhere—Jude over-turned the boat, grabbed Yesh's body, and pulled it toward shore.

The waters of the river, infused now with the magic of the celestial river the Ferryman had been pushing his boat towards—the same magic Yesh had used to perform his miracles—these waters revived the fallen rabbi. Together, Yesh and Jude swam for the shore. Then, exhausted by the effort, they finally lay in each other's arms.

But before Jude could ask for forgiveness from the man he had betrayed, before he could ask dear Yeshua what would happen next, wind blew in from all sides of existence—swallowing them in a sandstorm the likes of which the universe had never seen—and the world they knew came to an end.

WHEN JAKOB WAS DONE with the story, Belinda tried to tease out what he was thinking from the look on his face. And yet, all that she saw in his eyes was confusion.

"It's not there," he said, as they reached the top of what was meant to be the last rise between them and their destination. He laughed. "Well, that's new. Good to know the universe can still surprise me on occasion."

Belinda stared down the hill at the small strip of grassland which straddled the river. This was where, Belinda imagined, The Sister was meant to be. And yet the promised land was empty, save for an anachronistic-looking tent and a smoldering campfire.

"Is that where it's supposed to be?" said Matt, frowning as he pointed toward the Jordan.

But before Jakob could answer, there was a sudden commotion a few feet ahead of them. A smallish figure popped up from under a well-concealed hiding place in the sand and brandished a staff twice their size.

Matt screeched and tumbled backwards onto his ass. Belinda and Jakob closed ranks around him.

The smallish figure, who looked to Belinda to be a cloaked little boy—maybe eight or nine years old—stepped forward and pointed the end of his staff at the fallen Matt. He asked through a snarl, "Who goes there?"

Belinda felt a single obsessive thought swelling to fill the whole of the boy's mind: *Protect Mom.*

Chancing the fact that her insight might set the boy off, Belinda tried to diffuse the situation. Holding up both hands to show that she held no weapons and posed no threat, Belinda told him, "We're not here to hurt you... or your mom."

The boy growled at the mention of his mother, and the runes carved into his staff began to glow. An orange light pulsed from each of them in turn, beginning with the glyphs closest to the boy's hand and spiraling upwards.

"She can read minds," said Matt to the kid, still now but for the moving of his loose lips. "That's how she knew about your mum. Please turn that thing off!" he said, pointing at the now-glowing staff. "We're not here to hurt you."

The light pulsing from the staff's runes dimmed ever so slightly, as if Matt's explanation had done at least a little good.

"That looks elvish," said Jakob, nodding at the staff.

"Elvish?" said Matt. "Are we in Palestine here, or Haradwaith?"

"Mom won it," said the boy, "in a card game with an Elind Knight."

Matt rolled his eyes, probably hoping the boy wouldn't notice. But this boy seemed to notice everything, and once again the runes on his staff began to pulse a threatening orange.

"He's not calling you a liar," said Belinda. "He's—"

But whatever words she was about to speak disappeared from Belinda's lips as the boy swung his staff in her direction now.

So he knew how to use it, Belinda realized, backing up. It wasn't just a tool of his mother's he'd stolen while she was away or asleep.

And yeah, where *was* she? Belinda thought that "asleep in the tent" was the most likely answer, but surely she would've heard the commotion by now. Surely she would have—

As if on cue, the flaps of the tent's front door flew apart and a woman burst out onto the grass yelling "Arty!"

It was as the woman looked about, a hand held to her brow to shield her eyes from the sun, that Belinda got a good look at her. The woman was short, curvy, and solid. Belinda understood the boy's worry over his mother now to be a son's natural desire to protect and nothing else. His mother didn't *need* protecting, even if there were several streaks of white in the mop of auburn curls atop her head.

"Arty!" the woman yelled, finally catching sight of the scene playing out on the hill and running toward them.

Before she could reach them, though—her son and the trio he held hostage with his staff—the woman stopped dead in her tracks and stared at Matt.

Matt stared right back. And though it took a moment for recognition to dawn on him, Matt was all smiles once he realized who it was—or who he thought it was, at the very least.

"Tiny Dancer?!" he said.

It was only then, as Matt spoke aloud his nickname for his cousin Michael's wife, that recognition dawned on Belinda as well.

How had she not seen who it was straight away? How had she not put two and two together until right now, as Arty's mother set a hand on the boy's shoulder to let him know that all was well and that he could stand down—*how* had Belinda not recognized the woman who would've been her own mother, in another life, until this very moment?

"Jenna Silver," said Jenna, extending a hand for Belinda to shake. "You're Belinda, right? Matty's assistant?"

Belinda nodded and shook her would-be mother's hand, trying not to cry.

The moment was over mercifully quickly though, for it meant far less to Jenna than it did to Belinda—and there was still Jakob to meet as well.

Jenna and Jakob shook hands now, with Jakob offering up nothing but a curt nod before asking Jenna if she knew when the bar would be back.

But Matt, it seemed, was less ready to get down to business. "Hold up," he said. Then he pointed at the still-hooded and still armed Arty. "We've got one more introduction to make."

Arty handed the staff to his mother, then reached up with both hands to draw his hood back from his face—with a sense of drama befitting the hero of an epic fantasy. And yet, the thick mop of flaming red curls which sprung outward and upward once the hood was gone—that changed the genre of this cinematic moment entirely. Suddenly, it felt like a quirky children's film where the heretofore tough guy is brought down a peg by his obnoxiously silly coiffure.

Matt didn't laugh, though. As Belinda studied his face, trying to puzzle out what he was thinking without resorting to reading his mind, she saw her uncle tear up. Then Matt stiffened his upper lip like the good little soldier he was—the weary veteran of the wars of toxic masculinity—and he held out a hand for Arty to shake.

"Matthew Silver," said Matt, giving Arty the curt nod that

Grampy would have given in this situation—good and truly taking on the role of the family's elder statesman for the first time in his life. He gave his outstretched hand a little wiggle, his way of imploring the kid to take it.

"Silver?" said Arty, twisting his head back and forth to look at his mother and then Matt. Matt, and then his mother.

Jenna set her hands atop Arty's shoulders and the boy focused entirely on Matt again. "Art," said Jenna, "this is your Uncle Matt. The one I've been telling you about."

Belinda felt a flash of her would-be mother's thoughts in that moment, a maelstrom of memories of the nine years—from Jenna's perspective—that she'd spent hiding out in various corners of the time stream. She had given birth in Athens in the third century BC, under the care of the legendary midwife Agnodice. She had raised Arty in aboriginal Australia for a time, and in pre-Cabraline Brazil after that. They—Belinda couldn't get a clear picture of who "they" were yet—had hidden the aging Jenna and a growing Arty in South Africa and Samoa, on Okinawa and in Aotearoa. Basically, they'd brought her wherever they knew Ada Coffin couldn't get to or wouldn't think to look. And now they were here, camping out in the Holy Land—passing time by playing cards and perfecting their pirouettes.

Belinda smiled at the thought of Jenna teaching Arty the same things her own mother—her own Jenna—had taught her. This world's Jenna and Michael had lived for so long believing they couldn't have children, had lived for so long without the life that Belinda's Jenna and Michael had with her. It was beautiful that the universe had finally seen fit to grant them this gift.

Except, Belinda now realized with a frown, Michael had no idea. Michael had never met his son. Michael thought his wife had abandoned him. Belinda turned her attention toward her would-be little brother, toward Arty, and she wanted to cry. She wanted to cry for him and for Michael, and for all that had been stolen from them because of Ada's rage.

Arty's lower lip was trembling as he considered Uncle Matt. His thoughts grew so loud that they overtook Jenna's in Belinda's mind. Arty didn't want a handshake. He wanted a hug. He wanted a hug from the closest thing he had to a father right now.

And yet, Matt didn't seem to realize. He was still standing there like an idiot with his hand outstretched, ready for the handshake.

Belinda reached towards Matt, touched the bare skin of his arm and sent the thought his way.

A moment later, Matt was on one knee with both arms outstretched instead of just one. A moment after that, Arty ran into the arms of his uncle, wrapped his arms around him, and promised himself he would never let go.

Inside Matt's head, Belinda heard her uncle make himself the same promise.

❧

THEY DID LET GO of each other eventually, but only once Arty had made Matt promise to help him fish for supper. And it was as the two of them walked the banks of the river looking for "the perfect spot," that Jenna, Belinda, and Jakob sat on the grass outside Jenna's tent and answered each other's questions.

The Strumpet's Sister, Jenna explained, should be back any time now. She and Arty were nearly out of supplies, and the person who'd sent them here was concerned for their safety above all else.

"The person who sent you here?" asked Belinda, who had gone back to keeping her brain out of other people's brains now that the situation had calmed down.

"A ghost," said Jenna, "of my husband's ex-girlfriend."

"Robin," said Belinda, putting the pieces together.

Jenna nodded. "I know it sounds crazy."

Belinda shook her head. "I can read minds," she said. "So

I *know* crazy, and one ghost ain't it." She offered her would-be mother a kind smile. "Two maybe, but one? Nah."

Jenna smiled, and Belinda wanted to stare at that glorious sight for the rest of her life. But she was aware of how weird that would seem, especially since Jenna couldn't read *her* mind and still had no idea who Belinda was—aside from Matt's assistant, of course.

"When the bar arrives," said Jakob, sounding weary and looking wearier still, "we'll need to account for the fact that a version of Ms. Michaelson here will already be inside." He nodded at Belinda, in case Jenna didn't know the girl's last name.

But Jenna still looked confused. "A version of her?"

"I've been around for a while," said Belinda, hoping she could leave it at that.

"You're a ghost too?" asked Jenna. "Like Robin?"

Belinda shook her head and smiled. "Not exactly."

Jenna shrugged and shook her own head now. "Gotcha," she said, though she obviously didn't 'get' half of what was going on here. "To be honest, I gave up trying to understand what was happening the moment my husband's dead ex showed up on my lanai to protect me from an undead witch."

Jakob wanted to know what their plan was, but Belinda ignored him and pressed on with the question that was most pressing in her mind. "Is that why you left Michael?"

Jenna lowered her head, averting her eyes before anyone had the chance to see her cry—a move that Belinda knew well from her own childhood—from watching her own Jenna so closely back in the day, and from reliving those memories so many times since. When Jenna looked up at Belinda again, it was with a mix of sadness and whimsy—only a single tear managing to have wet the corner of a single eye.

"Does he miss me?" she asked, a hopeful smirk playing at the corners of her lips.

"More than you could ever imagine," said Belinda.

Jenna laughed. "I don't know," she said, "I can imagine a lot." Then, after a pause—a moment of reflection where she ducked her head again—she snapped her head up and returned her attention to Belinda. "Did he write the list?" she asked. "The list of things he'd do if he lost his wife?"

"Ladies," said Jakob, interrupting again, "we need a plan. The tavern could be here any—"

"He tried," said Belinda. "Wrote the title at the top of a piece of paper," she said, "but that was it."

Jakob stood with a grunt and stalked off toward where Matt and Arty were now fishing.

And that was the moment when, in a blinding flash of orange light, The Strumpet's Sister appeared atop the small patch of grassy floodplain stretching between where Jakob was and where a startled Matt yelped, without remembering his nephew was standing right next to him, "What the actual fuck?!"

A moment later, a woman in a Lycra mini-dress stumbled out of the front door and retched onto Jakob's sandal-clad feet. Her stomach emptied, she looked at Jakob with her sad, pale face and begged forgiveness with her eyes.

Then she stepped past him, her heels sinking into the soft ground with each step, and scanned the horizon. "Where are we?" she said, in a posh British accent. "This doesn't look like Dubai." She squinted, looking for a skyline where there was none to be found. "Where's the Burj?"

Jakob rolled his eyes and put a gentle hand on the poor woman's shoulder—assuming his role as Barkeep already, even though he hadn't yet been hired. Then he guided her back inside.

❧

WHILE JENNA BEGAN TEARING down the tent, Belinda hurried around the side of the building to collect Matt and Arty. While she made her way toward them, she couldn't help but cast glances up at the Sister's upper floor—hoping against hope that she wouldn't see herself staring through one of the windows.

Had she seen herself? She racked her brain, but she couldn't remember. Then she looked around to make sure she didn't see any butterflies, to make sure she wasn't doing anything she wasn't supposed to.

Matt and Arty met her halfway, but Arty kept running right past her and towards his mother—ever the helpful son.

As Matt and Belinda turned and followed the boy, Matt marveled at how much the kid was like Michael. "But better," said Matt. "All the best parts of both of them," he said. "Jenna and Michael, I mean."

"I thought they were infertile," said Belinda, speaking aloud the inconsistency which had been troubling her ever since she realized who Arty was, and who his parents were.

Matt shrugged. Then, in his best approximation of Jeff Goldblum from *Jurassic Park*, he said dramatically, "Life... finds a way."

۞

ONCE INSIDE THE Strumpet's Sister, Belinda led them towards the back hall. She led them through the labyrinthine passages, making one turn after another until she'd found a door she liked.

Belinda ran her hand along the surface, waiting for the wood to tell her its story. Then, when she was satisfied, she turned the knob and held the door open for the others.

"This room won't get us there straight away," she said, "but it's the best option we've got."

Jenna nodded and nudged Arty inside, the boy plopping down upon the first flat surface he saw—an ornate couch with the scene of a fox hunt stitched into the fabric.

He was asleep almost before his head hit the golden yellow cushion.

Belinda asked Matt to go to the bar and grab them something

to eat and drink. He nodded and took off, forgetting to ask for directions.

"Is he going to get lost?" asked Jenna, setting down her back-pack and camping gear on the floor of a room which looked straight out of a film about people in powdered wigs.

"Maybe," said Belinda. "But not for long," she added, taking a seat on a settee that was even more ritzy-looking than the sofa. "Not for long," she said. "We're almost there."

❦ 20 ❦

TRACY

It was a few days and many rounds later that Tracy bumped into Matt in the hallway, but it was only moments after that —after their awkward hug and Matt's proclamation that she was grounded—that Tracy was ushered into her uncle's room and found herself surrounded by a confounding collection of faces.

Besides Matt, there was his assistant Belinda. Aunt Jenna was there too, who had split from Uncle Michael a couple of years ago now and hadn't been seen since. And, as if Jenna's sudden reappearance wasn't enough, she held in her lap a boy who looked like —though he couldn't have been, just could *not*—the spitting image of a young Michael.

Except for the mop of flaming red hair, that is.

Tracy fell into the cushions of an altogether ancient settee and tried to collect herself. What, exactly, was she seeing? *Who?*

"He's your cousin," said Belinda. "*Second* cousin, actually, but..." She trailed off and cast her gaze down upon the floor as if feeling guilty about something.

About what, Tracy couldn't tell—but she didn't care. She wanted to know how it was possible, how her infertile uncle had gotten his wife pregnant—and why said wife had run away instead of sharing the blissful news.

Then the answer came to her, and she spoke it aloud: "Ada."

Tracy looked into the eyes of the boy in Jenna's lap and asked him for his name, this boy who wouldn't have lived if Jenna hadn't done what she'd done.

"Arty," said the boy.

Tracy extended a hand for him to shake and said, "I'm Tracy."

Arty looked up at his mother with a curious expression upon his face. "I thought you said they were huggers," he said.

Tracy laughed and extended both arms now, telling her little cousin, "Bring it in, kid."

OUT IN THE tavern's main hall, over the course of the next few days, Tracy listened to arguments over what should be done next. When she wasn't marveling over how the decor of the place seemed to advance twenty or so years after each night they emerged from their accommodations, Tracy felt rather like the judge she'd pretended to be when she put Michael on trial for his "crimes against femininity."

"When we get to 2013," Robin argued over dinner one night, "she's got a destiny to fulfill."

Belinda shook her head. "You have no idea what that destiny might be," she said, tearing a piece of warm bread in half. "You've been gallivanting around time—"

"And what have you been doing exactly?" asked Ashley, rather matter-of-factly, as she sipped at her beer.

Tracy appreciated that Auntie Ash still had no patience for bullshit, but that she'd learned to modulate her reaction to it.

"I wouldn't call it gallivanting," said Uncle Matt, trying to chime in. But when Ashley turned to him and offered her cousin a deadpan stare, he shut up right quick and turned his attention to the plate of mozzarella sticks he'd ordered in lieu of a real meal.

"I know what I'm doing," said Belinda.

"Playing God?" asked Ashley, still just as calm and just as measured.

"No," said Belinda, pointing at Robin. "That's what your girl-friend's been doing. I've built a life around *stopping* people from playing God. The universe has a will of its own, and defying it—"

"Have you guys seen any butterflies along the way?" asked Matt, seemingly out of nowhere. And yet, before he could elaborate and before Tracy could ask what the hell he meant, Robin lost her cool and started yelling.

"You think I don't know that?!" she spat at Belinda. "I was twelve when I found a copy of my own obituary. *Twelve!* I know all about predestination. But if you think that means I'm gonna stop trying to change things, then you're out of your fucking mind."

৩১৩

THE NEXT DAY, Tracy stumbled out of bed early—unable to sleep after an innocent enough dream of Kanoa had taken a turn toward the naughty. Out in the main hall, as she waited for Jakob to pour her a coffee, she caught sight of Robin sitting by the fire-place and staring into the flames.

"What's up?" asked Tracy, grabbing a seat at Robin's table.

The sound of Tracy's voice broke Robin's reverie. But though she did turn to offer Tracy a somber smile, Robin had no imme-diate answer for the inquiry.

A clink of cup and saucer broke the silence instead, as Jakob set Tracy's drink upon the table.

"I missed it," said Robin as Tracy took a first tentative sip from her steaming cup.

Her mouth full, Tracy raised an eyebrow in lieu of asking aloud for Robin to go on.

"The day I found my obituary," said Robin. "We skipped right past it. It's 1991 out there right now," she said, pointing toward the front window. "At least that's what Jakob says."

Tracy turned her attention to the window, which rattled now from the force of some fierce wind or another. There was snow piling up on the sill outside, and it reminded her of the story her mothers told about 1991—about the last day of that year and how a trio of guys had crashed their girls-only New Year's Eve party. A trio including the glorified sperm donor who still had the audacity, on Christmas and birthday cards he sent to the prison, to call himself Tracy's father.

Tracy returned her attention to Robin and asked if Jakob mentioned where the Sister was parked today.

Now it was Robin who raised an eyebrow. "Why do you want to know?" she asked. "Feeling self-destructive?"

Tracy smirked, then took another sip of her coffee.

"Do you think the redhead's right?" asked Robin

Tracy laughed. "Which redhead?" she asked. She figured Robin was talking about Belinda, but there were three gingers in their company now, after all—and every one of them more opinionated than the last, even young Arty, who was more precocious than Tracy had been at his age.

Which was saying something.

"She might," said Tracy. "Have a point, that is."

"Does that change things?" asked Robin. "Our plan, I mean."

Tracy shook her head.

AT LUNCH THAT DAY, when Ashley finally joined them to work out their final plans for the evening, things were eerily quiet. It wasn't until they were fifteen minutes into their discussion of how to ensure they wouldn't skip right past their destination that Tracy realized what was wrong.

She looked around the bar for any sign of the others—Matt or Belinda, Jenna or Arty—and found none. They must've been back in their rooms. When she drew Robin and Ashley's attention to this fact, Robin said not to worry.

"They'll do what they think they have to do," she said. "But we're more determined, we're more prepared, and—most importantly—we're *right*."

⚜

THAT NIGHT INSIDE THE SISTER, Ashley and Robin alternated between standing guard over Tracy and sitting in the bar to wait for it to reach Hawaii in 2013. They couldn't be too careful, they reasoned, because Ada could turn up at any minute—their Ada, the murderous one. And it was in the middle of that fitful night of sleep that Tracy heard the door to the hallway creak open. She sat up in bed as the dim light reached into her room to fill the darkness, then she waited for the figure in the doorway to tell her what was what.

"Trace," said Auntie Ashley. "You're not going to believe it, but he's here. In the bar. Right now."

Tracy shot out of bed and crossed to the room's dressing table, cringing when she saw the state of her hair in the mirror there, then cringing again when she caught sight of the dark circles beneath her eyes, and again when she turned to the side and let her belly hang loose for a moment.

Ashley laughed, but the sound was more sympathetic than anything. "Sit," she said, and she grabbed a hairbrush off the table.

Tracy did as she was bid and sat on the edge of the bed, turning her back to her aunt to let the older woman try and work some magic.

"You are *not* allowed to stare at the mirror," said Ashley, tapping her niece on the shoulder with the back side of the brush. "Keep turning."

As Ashley ran the brush through her hair, Tracy thought about what she might wear. That pink party dress that drove him nuts every time? The high-waisted jeans which made her legs look impossibly long and her ass impossibly firm? And could she fit the leather jacket in there somewhere, the one she'd been wearing when he picked her up for their first date? She was halfway through the closet in her mind before she remembered the closet existed *only* in her mind these days. All she had to wear was the outfit she had on—the t-shirt and shorts Robin had provided after the jailbreak.

Ashley, perhaps sensing the panic setting in, tapped Tracy again with the backside of the brush. "It's not going to matter, Trace. He's three sheets to the wind already."

Tracy nodded and the two of them made their way out into the hall, but she was so focused on smoothing out the wrinkles in her top that she ran into something almost immediately.

She looked up and found herself face-to-face, not with Ashley —who had been right in front of her a second before—but with Matt, who must've been waiting by his door to intercede this whole time.

"Butterflies," he told her.

"What?" she said.

"If you see butterflies," he continued, "you stop. Promise me."

Ashley gave Matt a punch in the arm and told him to get out of the way.

"Promise," said Matt to Tracy. "I'll keep the others at bay, but you have to promise me that."

Ashley shoved him now, checked him into the wall like they were on the ice at the Boston Garden. Then she grabbed Tracy by the arm and pulled her past her shocked uncle, who was massaging his arm and looking quite affronted indeed.

Not so affronted, of course, that he couldn't shout "Butter-flies!" down the hall one last time.

※

ONCE THEY'D MADE it through the labyrinth of the Sister's backrooms and into the bar, it took only a second for Tracy to spot Kanoa. He was sitting alone at a high-top, a half-empty pint of something in front of him, and he looked miserable. She wanted to run over there and wrap her arms around him—it had been *so* long and she missed him *so much*—but she knew that wasn't what had happened. They wouldn't see each other again for months, not until she came home after Ashley's funeral. The only way this was going to work was if Tracy played the part of the other woman.

She prayed that this was what had always happened, that what she was about to try and do was what the universe wanted. She didn't want to cause a paradox or something. She didn't want to see "butterflies," whatever that meant. Tracy wanted to be the other woman, the one Kanoa had slept with while they were on their "break." She didn't want to take that other woman's place, the one she'd imagined for years (however much she'd tried not to). She wanted to *be* that woman.

But was he truly drunk enough to not recognize her?

And is he sober enough to give consent? asked a voice inside her head, a voice that part of her wanted to shush but she knew in her core she could not silence. She would have to reckon with that dilemma before this day was over.

Tracy felt Ashley's hand on her shoulder, felt a sympathetic squeeze as Ashley told her to make her move.

Ashley gave her aunt a nod, then made her way over to the bar. Surrounded by girls in tighter dresses than even the ones she'd dreamed of wearing a few minutes before, it took a while for the new bartender to pay her any mind—the short-haired woman who'd taken over for Jakob sometime in the early aughts, or so Tracy had been told. But when the barkeep had finished serving and flirting with the other ladies, she still had a smile for Tracy as well—and Tracy was ready with her order.

"A Creamsicle Delight?" repeated the bartender, with a question mark to match her raised eyebrow.

"Two parts orange soda," Tracy explained, "two parts ginger ale, a part and a half of vanilla vodka, and whipped cream on top."

The bartender nodded, beginning her work. "Anything else?"

"An orange slice and a cherry," said Tracy, "if you don't mind."

"For the fella over there?" asked the bartender, nodding in Kanoa's direction.

Tracy smiled. "Was I staring?"

The bartender laughed. "Just a bit." Then she asked, "You drinking this, or is he?"

"I'm a Diet Coke girl myself," said Tracy. "But I've always liked the way he tastes after he's had one of these. When we kiss, I mean."

The bartender shook the can of Reddi-Wip as she nodded. "You know each other?" she asked Tracy.

Tracy blushed, ashamed she'd just given away part of her secret, and tried to figure out how to explain. Then she remembered where she was, and how time worked in here, and she realized this couldn't possibly be the strangest story this bartender had ever heard.

"You want me to make you something too?" asked the bartender.

Tracy shook her head as she laid her money down on the countertop.

"And are you taking this over yourself?" asked the bartender, setting the cherry *just so* atop the whipped cream. "Or am I having someone bring it over for you?"

Tracy pondered the question for a moment. She'd imagined having a server bring it over and pointing to her at the bar. She imagined the wave she'd give, the way she'd lean against the bar, and even the angle of her hip. But did any of that make sense? She had to have the same conversation with him either way—the chat about how she could *possibly* know what his favorite drink was and how she looked suspiciously like his girlfriend, who was supposed to be back home in Massachusetts.

The bartender offered a *hem-hem* to break Tracy from her thoughts.

Tracy smiled and took hold of the drink, deciding to abandon at least one level of artifice. Then she made her way across the room.

When she reached him the first words out of her mouth were "This seat taken?" and Tracy felt pretty damn stupid. Inside her head she asked herself, *That was the best you could do?*

Kanoa looked up at her with a mixture of sadness and curiosity. Then he tilted his head to one side to get a look at her from a different angle.

"Do I have something in my teeth?" asked Tracy, a laugh and a lilt in her voice.

For a moment, Kanoa turned his attention to his half-empty mug. Then he asked aloud, "How many of these have I had?"

Tracy—deciding the man was too drunk to ask her to sit—set her drink on the table and sat in the chair opposite him.

"Is that a—?" Kanoa began to ask, pointing at Tracy's cocktail.

"Yes," said Tracy, cutting him off. Then she smiled and kicked a foot absentmindedly in his direction, the edge of her sneaker *just* brushing against the edge of his shin. She had the sudden urge to keep it there, to run her foot up and down the length of his muscled leg, but she decided that would be a little too forward for him. Since she was supposed to be a stranger, and all.

Kanoa laughed. "You look just like her," he said, shaking his head. "Sound like her, too."

"Girlfriend?" said Tracy. "Ex?"

Kanoa frowned, then sighed. "Bit of both," he said.

The sadness in his voice was almost too much to bear, and the sadness she was there to cause him—sadness she wouldn't ever be able to explain or apologize for, unless he miraculously came back to life for a second time—*that* was too much to bear, too. Tracy thought for a second about excusing herself and leaving him alone, about abandoning this whole idea.

But then she saw a butterfly dancing fluttering around her once and future husband's drunken head. It was a white monarch, Kanoa's favorite—a species native to O'ahu, surprisingly, given its name, and not one brought to the islands by colonizers.

Uncle Matt's words of warning echoed in Tracy's head. If she saw a butterfly, she was supposed to stop. But if she'd been about to stop and *then* she saw the butterfly, what was she supposed to do? Stop stopping?

Tracy took a healthy gulp of the Creamsicle Delight. If ever there was a moment for a drink, this was it. Then again, the drink tasted like him—like his tongue—and so was it such a good idea after all?

Kanoa laughed. At what, Tracy didn't know. But then he asked, "That good, huh?" and she knew that some aspect of her countenance must've betrayed her naughty thoughts.

"Want to see for yourself?" she asked him, sliding the drink across the table.

Kanoa pushed his empty mug out of the way and took hold of Tracy's drink instead. "Can I tell you a secret?" he asked before he took his first sip. Then, without waiting for her to speak, he added, "Mixed drinks have always been my favorite."

"So why you fronting, dude?" asked Tracy with a laugh, pointing at the unfinished mug he'd pushed aside.

Kanoa blushed, then took another sip of the Creamsicle Delight. "Well," he said, "some ladies—"

"*Your* lady?" asked Tracy, interrupting.

He averted his eyes and sipped some more.

"Oh," said Tracy, glancing around the bar. "You're trying to pick up a different kind of girl tonight," she said. "One who'll take your mind off her?"

Kanoa looked at her again. From over the lip of the drink, with the tiniest bit of an orange-cream mustache, he looked like a kid who'd been caught with his hand inside auntie's cookie jar.

Tracy reached across the table and took one of his hands into both of her own. Then she gave him a squeeze. "It doesn't make you an asshole," she said.

Kanoa sat up straight, pulled his hand free of Tracy's, and pushed the drink back towards her. He looked truly ashamed of himself now, but with the way he screwed up his face he also looked a little pissed off. He wiped his hands across his shorts, along the length of his thighs—a nervous gesture she knew all too well, a sign that he was eager to get himself out of whatever situation he'd just gotten himself into.

"What?" said Tracy.

"Doesn't make me an asshole," he said. "Just makes me a *guy*, right?" Then he pulled his wallet out of his back pocket and dug a pair of twenties out of it.

"That's not what I meant," said Tracy, praying he would calm down and hoping against hope that she hadn't just fucked everything up. But then that fucking butterfly fluttered past his head again. And then there was another one. And another.

Kanoa slapped the twenties on the table, gave Tracy a quick nod, and stood.

"Mahalo for the drink," he said. Then he pointed over Tracy's shoulder to the corner where Ashley stood. "And my apologies to your wing-woman. Tell her I just can't," he said, then he made his way toward the door.

The butterflies stayed, though. And for the few moments that Tracy sat there in stunned silence, the trio of monarchs took turns fluttering past her head. Each of them seemed determined to annoy her into action.

But it was only when Ashley called out from behind her that Tracy so much as flinched. *Ashley had spoken to Kanoa?!* That was so dangerous! What if he'd recognized her? Tracy wondered if she—younger her, that is—had shown Kanoa a picture of Ashley yet. *Jesus*, what was Ash thinking?

"Trace!" shouted Ashley. "What the fuck are you waiting for?!"

Tracy looked over her shoulder, a butterfly narrowly avoiding a collision with her nose, and she gave her aunt a concerned look. *We're going to need to talk later* is what she wanted to say, but she wasn't Belinda. She couldn't communicate with a thought.

Tracy ran for the door, chasing after Kanoa. As she stumbled out onto the beach, the light of the sun nearly blinded her. It glinted off the stream the Sister had landed alongside, and off of the nearby Pacific Ocean as well. But though it took longer than she would have liked for her eyes to adjust—precious moments during which she was losing ground on Kanoa—it wasn't long before she caught sight of him strolling along the water's edge, the ocean's tides covering and uncovering his sandy feet.

He held his sandals in one hand and the back of his neck in the other, and he was staring at the sand as if in deep thought. As Tracy made her approach, she could tell by the way he clenched and unclenched his eyelids that he was trying not to cry.

This was never going to work, she decided, if she wasn't honest. So she cried out his name—"Kanoa!"—and ran towards him.

He stopped dead in his tracks and he looked at her with longing in his eyes.

When they met at the edge of the beach, Tracy looked up into his eyes and told him, "It's me." She reached up to touch his face, to wipe away the tears he couldn't hold back any longer. When he didn't stop her, she brought her other hand up to the other side of his face and she held him still as she said again, "It's me. It's Tracy."

"I know," he said, taking hold of both her forearms to steady himself. "Your aunt told me. The one who's supposed to be dying right now. Or is dead. Or something, I don't know."

Tracy laughed uncomfortably. That couldn't be true. Talking to him was one thing, but Ashley wouldn't have risked revealing *that* much, would she? Tracy shook her head at Kanoa and said, "You're drunk."

He shook his head in return. "Maybe a tiny bit buzzed from the bit of your Creamsicle Delight I sipped, but I was downing Diet Cokes before that." He smiled at her. "Ashley told me not to get drunk. 'Consent and all that,' is what she said. So, I ordered the first non-alcoholic thing I could think of. I guess I miss the way you taste when we kiss," he said.

"She told you," said Tracy, pushing her hands up into his hair now and stroking his scalp with her fingers. "She told you and you believed her?"

Kanoa set his strong hands upon Tracy's hips, obviously feeling a bit steadier on his feet now. "She didn't tell me *all* of it," he said, "because she said it would blow my mind. But she told me enough. And Trace, you've told me about the potion already. This isn't that much weirder. I don't know why you didn't just tell me," he said, and a bit of the anger and confusion which had driven him from the bar was there again in his voice.

Tracy frowned. "Me traveling through time to hook up with the younger version of my—" She stopped herself *just* before she said 'husband' and said 'boyfriend' instead. "That's not weird?"

Kanoa shrugged and smirked. "You're a weird chick, *ku'uipo*," he said.

Then something dawned on Tracy, and she pulled one hand out of his hair to give him a gentle slap on the cheek. "You told me, or, well, you're *going* to tell me that you slept with someone else while I was—or *am*, I guess—away."

Kanoa arched an eyebrow and gave her a bit of the old smolder. "Are we *not* going to sleep together?" he asked.

She took the other hand out of his hair and slapped his other cheek. "Why even tell me?" she asked. "Why not keep it a secret?"

"Maybe," he said, his thumbs hooking through a pair of the loops at her shorts' waistband, "I can't lie to you." He smiled, then hastened to add, because he knew that he *was* going to tell a lie of omission when it came down to it, "at least not completely." He wouldn't lie to her about sleeping with someone else. He just wouldn't tell her who that someone else was.

Tracy smirked at him now, rolled her eyes, and shook her head, all the while unable to let go of his face—the beautiful face of this beautiful man that she missed *so* much. She loved the feel of his stubble against the palms of her hands, so she kept them there on his cheeks—though a thumb seemed to be venturing of its own accord toward his lips, lips that puckered now, ever so slightly, to kiss that thumb.

All of a sudden, her lips were jealous of her fingers. Such a silly feeling, that, but it was true! So, she pulled his face to her own and kissed him hard, so hard that she threw him off balance and they tumbled backwards into the sand.

After a laugh, they were kissing again there on the beach. When he opened his lips to let her determined tongue explore his hungry mouth, she could taste the orange soda all over—the sweet tang of citrus more intoxicating than any drink they could have concocted for her back inside the bar.

She paused for a moment, looking around for butterflies, but they were gone. They were nowhere to be found. *Okay then*, she thought, and she pressed on.

"Here?" he said, looking up at her as she straddled him and fumbled with the button of his shorts. "In the daylight? In the sand?" Then he laughed. "Don't you remember the Dybek story? From that lit class last fall?"

Tracy laughed now, too. She *did* remember that story. Her hands moved from Kanoa's waistband to his chest, though she slid them up under his shirt because the hell with even the flimsiest of fabric standing between her hands and his pecs.

"Sand in the condom," said Kanoa, as if he was unsure that she remembered which part of the story he was talking about. "Sand *everywhere*."

"And a dead body washing ashore," said Tracy, nodding. "I remember," she said, the memory of the story triggering a darker memory, one drawn from life: Ada pushing Kanoa into the river behind the Strumpet's Sister.

Off in the distance, a group of teenagers shouted "Get a room!" at them, laughing as they strolled down the beach. It was a group of guys *and* girls, and they were smiling, so Tracy took the callout to be good-natured, but the kids and Kanoa did have a point.

"You park near here?" asked Tracy. She dismounted him and stood, extending a hand to pull him to his feet.

"You don't want to get a room back inside?" he suggested, jerking a thumb over his shoulder at the Sister. "The back seat of my car is a bit cramped."

Tracy gave it a thought but frowned at the idea almost immediately. Yes, she could tell Belinda and Matt that the butterflies had gone away and that she knew was she was doing. Yes, she could tell them that she was a grown-ass woman capable of making her own decisions and they should leave her alone. But would they listen? And did she want to go back into that building with Kanoa anyway, that building where she'd lost him the last time?

"Okay," he said, taking the look on her face for an answer, "the car it is."

As CRAMPED as it was in the backseat of his old yellow Jeep, they made it work. He'd put the soft top on because it was supposed to rain later, and that afforded them all the privacy they needed. And though Tracy supposed she should have gotten on with it, gotten on with the important business at hand, she opted to take her time instead. This might very well be the last time she'd ever get to spend in this man's arms, so they cuddled for a good long while that morning before any clothing came off. In fact, Tracy caught herself drifting off to sleep at one point—and Kanoa along with her.

"Is the me that you know this boring?" Tracy asked sheepishly, running a finger along the collar of Kanoa's shirt.

"Boring?" he said, giving her a gentle squeeze with those massive arms of his. "I love cuddling." Then he teased, "Do you know me at all?"

Tracy laughed as she looked up at him, but things went quiet as they studied each other's faces—as they looked deeply into each other's eyes. *We might never see each other again*—that's what the look was meant to say, Tracy's look at least. Before she could cry at the thought, she leaned in to kiss him.

And then, in the backseat of Kanoa's car, Tracy made love with her man like it was the last time. *Because it might be*, she thought, before she stopped thinking altogether and turned her body over to instinct and feeling. *It might be.*

❧ 21 ❧

BELINDA

Out of the dozens of lovers she'd taken over the centuries, Nasha was Belinda's favorite. Despite everything that would come between them eventually, the early days had been wonderful. The dancing in Ibiza, the gambling in Monte Carlo, the sketching in the Louvre, and all the sex they had along the way. Yes, the sex. But Belinda had enjoyed the cuddling, most of all. She had relished how safe she felt in Nasha's arms. So now, in the middle of the ordeal she found herself in with Tracy and the rest of her almost family, Belinda dreamt herself back into Nasha's bedroom.

She imagined the two of them dancing in their altogether, a breeze slipping in through the window to raise gooseflesh across their naked, glistening bodies. She saw, once again—and *felt* once more—Nasha's muscled arms around her waist, her own arms around Nasha's neck, her fingers in the blonde hair they kept cropped short atop their head.

She imagined their breasts pressed together again, and how that had felt different after years of being crushed against the hardened chests of the guys she used to go for. She remembered looking up into the gold and blue of Nasha's eyes and seeing vulnerability there for the first time, and how it felt to know that Nasha trusted her enough to let down their defenses. And then Belinda remembered the day that Nasha finally answered her persistent question about the scar which ran from their jaw to their hairline—and about why it branched out in two directions after it reached beyond the eyebrow.

"Where did that one come from?" she had asked, expecting a war story of one kind or another. "Where did that one come from?" she asked again in the dream she was having right now.

But just as Nasha was about to tell her once more, to reveal that the battle where they'd earned the scar had been with their sister's cat—*just* as Nasha's lips began to move—a horde of butterflies swarmed between the two of them and swept Belinda back into the waking world.

She sat bolt upright in her bed, slick with sweat and gasping for breath. The butterflies had never visited her while she was asleep, had never pulled her out of a dream before, but here they were fluttering about and trying to rouse her to action. Frantically, she looked around to see what was happening, but nothing seemed to be amiss at all. Jenna and Arty were still asleep across the room. And though Matt was gone, that wasn't anything out of the ordinary. Belinda was used to waking up to the sight of his tangled bedsheets by now.

Belinda got up and got dressed, and as she did the butterflies fluttered and faded away. With her head still buzzing from what she'd seen, she made for the door. An English muffin and a cup of coffee seemed like an excellent idea indeed—especially if all the butterflies had wanted her to do was to get out of bed.

And yet, when she went to turn the knob, it wouldn't budge.

"Hello," she said. "Is there somebody out there?"

"Best you stay in there," said Matt, from the other side of the door. "Strange things are afoot."

"Strange things?" said Belinda, trying the knob again to no avail. "What are you talking about?"

Matt opened the door just a crack, just enough for Belinda to see in his eyes that he was up to no good, and then he said, "I'll keep watch."

But before he could close the door again, Belinda snuck her sneakered foot into the crack to stop him. Then she reached into his mind to see what he was up to. She knew she was breaking her promise to him, but *he* was the one trapping her inside

When she found the memory of Matt telling Tracy that he'd "keep the others at bay," Belinda nearly screamed. Then she remembered her almost-mother and almost-brother were still asleep in the room behind her. So, she didn't say a word.

She did, however, yank the door open with all her might.

Stomping out into the hall, she scared Matt so much that he stumbled back against opposite wall. And yet, she waited until she'd closed the door behind her before she laid into him. Arty didn't need to hear this, and Jenna would over-complicate things if she got involved.

"How do you know she'll stop if she sees the butterflies?!" Belinda asked Matt. "This is the love of her life we're talking about here. This is *exactly* the kind of situation that leads to calamities."

"I..." Matt stuttered. "I... I had to let her try."

"No," said Belinda, striding off toward the Sister's main hall, "you didn't."

On her way toward the front door, Belinda passed Ashley and Robin having a row over lunch. But though the volume of both their voices and their thoughts reached out to distract her, she pressed on. They would sort out their lovers' quarrel, like they always had before, or they wouldn't. It didn't matter anymore.

If she didn't stop Tracy, *nothing* would matter.

"Belinda!" shouted Matt from behind her. "Wait!"

She heard the scraping of chairs against floorboards now, as well. *Shit*, she thought. Ashley and Robin were joining the chase.

Belinda broke out into a run and burst through the door a

moment later, stumbling on the Sister's front steps as the daylight blinded her.

By the time she'd made it onto the lawn and her eyes had time to adjust, Belinda was being spun around by one of her pursuers—Matt, it turned out—and being laid into with a barrage of words and thoughts that were enough to drive her to her knees.

They stopped once she'd fallen to the ground, going mercifully quiet for a minute. And yet, it was the briefest of respites. Belinda felt their next words coming before she heard them.

"I didn't feel anything," said Matt, cutting the others off and speaking first. "None of the signs you taught me to watch out for. And she's been gone a while now."

"And what makes *you* the boss of the future anyway?" said Robin, enough venom in her voice to match the care and concern in Matt's. "Do you think you're some kind of god?"

Belinda thought it would be funny in that moment to say that yes, she *did* think of herself that way—or that she *had* when she'd been a bit younger and a bit more dramatic. "The One True Goddess"—that's what she'd told them to call her up in the Sister's game room, back when she was freshly separated from her parents and the world she'd known, back when she was drunk on the power of her ability to read minds.

And it *would* have been funny, and the others might've even gotten a kick out of it—all of them having been melodramatic teenagers themselves once upon a time—but Belinda lost her chance to share the story with them when she sensed someone making their way toward her from behind, a fresh bundle of emotions and thoughts. But not a new one.

Belinda looked over her shoulder, out onto the lawn, and saw Tracy making her way toward the Sister. And she was about to sigh in relief, to admit that maybe the others had been right, that there was nothing to worry about after all.

Ashley started toward Tracy, a big smile on her face, and asked, "Soooooooo?" while she raised her eyebrows in anticipation.

Robin waved a hand in Tracy's general direction and side-eyed Belinda in a silent "Told you so." And Matt? He smiled, though he couldn't look Belinda in the eye. He didn't want to gloat, she supposed.

Or knew, rather, because she'd slipped back into her bad habit of reading his mind without his permission.

Belinda was about to touch Matt's hand, get his attention, and apologize for her intrusion, but then she spotted something that nearly made her heart stop.

"Belinda," said Matt, raising an arm and pointing.

"What is that?" said Robin, but she blanched as she asked the question, as if she already knew.

A few feet behind Tracy, someone had torn a hole in The Veil of the World. Orange light spilled out onto the grass as the gap widened to let that someone step through—a mangled figure with a revolver in their hand.

"Ada," said Belinda, disgusted by the taste of the two syllables in her mouth and disgusted too by the inevitability of it all. Of course, this was how it was going to end. *Of course* it was.

The woman looked like a true monster now. Muscle and sinew were visible through the tears in her neck and one side of her skull was caved in from where Tracy had beaten her with the leg of a broken table. Even the way she walked, the way she *trudged*, betrayed how little humanity was left in her. Ada had died twice now and it was only hate which drove her in this third shot at life.

She raised her pistol before anyone had time to react, but she didn't take aim at Tracy. Instead, she gunned down Ashley first. One shot between the eyes. Then, as Robin screamed in horror, Ada shot her too—a bullet straight through the singer's throat to shut her up for good.

Tracy stumbled forward with hands over her ringing ears, falling to the ground even as Belinda pushed herself up off of it. But before Belinda could try herself to disarm Ada, Matt pushed her aside and rushed at the old witch with a scream that might as well have been a war cry.

A cloud of butterflies appeared out of nowhere to follow him, but he waved an arm to shoo them away. He didn't care anymore, not one damn bit.

Belinda's eyes widened in horror at the sight of that swarm, and she suddenly understood. She was supposed to get there first, she realized—the whole world tinting toward sepia as this dawned on her. *She* was the one who was supposed to stand between Ada and Tracy. Not Matt.

It's supposed to be me, thought Belinda, doubled over by the feeling in her gut now—the feeling that her body was folding in on itself. And yet, she couldn't give in to that feeling. She couldn't give up, not now. So she got to her feet and rushed toward the fray to try and make things right.

"I have no quarrel with you," Ada told Matt as he stood between the murderous witch and her quarry. "I have no quarrel with a sodomite who's going to let his family line die out anyway."

"Yeah," he said, "but what about my niece? Huh? And what about my cousin's wife and their son?"

Belinda reached for Matt's arm, to give it a squeeze and stop him from saying what he'd just said, but she was too late.

Ada stumbled backward in shock at Matt's news, that a new Silver had been born despite all her best efforts, but she kept her footing. She kept herself from falling down. She kept her pistol steady and then she shot Matt in the chest.

"No!" shouted Belinda, as she watched Matt fall to his knees and then slump over onto his side. "No," she said, as Ada stepped around her and around a still stunned Tracy on the way toward the Sister's front door.

"No!" shouted Belinda. *But I already said that,* she thought. *No, I already said... I already said No.*

Fuck, she thought. *Déjà vu.* The third sign.

"Ada!" shouted Tracy, struggling to get to her feet. "Don't! I have something to tell you." But Ada wasn't listening. Even if she had been *trying to*, she wouldn't have heard Tracy anyway. Because just at that moment, lightning flashed and thunder filled the air. Then the sky, which had been clear just seconds before, let loose a downpour the likes of which none of them had ever seen.

None but Belinda. And she knew what was next, knew it even before gale force winds began to blow, knew it even before the Ka'a'awa and the Pacific began to flood.

This was the beginning of a calamity. This was the end of the world.

IV

ONE ROLL OF THE DICE

2013-2017

❧ 22 ❧
TRACY

Tracy stood in stunned silence as rain poured down in torrents from above, and from the side—and even, at times, from below. She knew what she needed to say, knew what the plan was for this moment, but she couldn't stop staring at the bodies of the women who'd conceived said plan— and the body of the uncle who'd warned her what disaster might be unleashed if she did what she'd been planning to do with Kanoa.

What she'd done.

Uncle Matt's body was the most painful to look at, his death far more unexpected and therefore far harder to comprehend. Ashley and Robin—they'd been dead already. Somewhere inside herself, Tracy had known they wouldn't be back to life forever. And yet, staring too long at their fallen forms was still unnerving —as unnerving as it had been to look down upon Ada's corpse the day she'd strangled and beaten her to death (or *back* to death, as it were). Tracy had fully expected Ada's body to disappear, like it would have in a movie. And she'd expected the same thing here and now, with Ashley and Robin. Ghosts weren't supposed to leave corpses behind—not the second time around, at least. But there they were.

Tracy shook her head, trying to free herself from the clutches of overthinking and bring herself back to the moment at hand—a moment which found her standing there, doing nothing, while Ada pistol-whipped poor Belinda.

There was a split second where Tracy thought of her womb and what might be happening in there, but she pushed the thought aside. Would she be able to look her child in the eye— assuming there was a child, and assuming she lived long enough to give birth to it—if she stood aside and let Ada kill someone else?

Tracy charged at Ada with her shoulder down, with the form her football-playing grandfather had drilled into her when she was a girl. Though the ground grew muddier with every step, she still had decent enough footing to spear her undead antagonist off her feet.

Ada's six-shooter tumbled off toward the water's edge—an edge which was drawing nearer and nearer to Ashley and Robin's bodies now, now that the swelling Kaʻaʻawa was less a stream than a minor river. Ada growled at the fact of her disarmament, throwing a punch as Tracy tried to pin her to the ground.

Tracy dodged one swing after another as she wrestled for control of Ada's arms—and she tried too to dodge the thought that, if she could just reach the pistol, this could be over in an instant. Because that wasn't the answer—it *wasn't*. Ada would keep coming back, unless she learned the truth.

But even then, spoke a pessimistic piece of Tracy's mind, *what's to say she'll stop?*

But Tracy knew that she had to try, knew that despite her desire for vengeance in this particular moment—a hunger made even more insatiable by the fallen bodies all around her, bodies which were about to be swallowed up and carried away by a river that was growing angrier and angrier by the moment—Tracy *knew* that she had to try.

So, with all of the strength in her body, she took hold of Ada's wrists and slammed the woman's arms down into the mud. "Listen!" she spat in Ada's face as the woman continued to struggle. "Listen. To. Me."

Ada shook her body one last time, trying to dislodge Tracy, but she soon realized it was no use. Then she stared up at the woman who sat astride her chest and waited for her to go on.

Tracy breathed in deep, not sure where to start now that she'd finally been given the opportunity. Out of the corner of her eye, she watched the river's current tugging at Robin's corpse—and she noticed something she hadn't before. In her last moments, Robin had reached out to take hold of Ashley's hand. If the river was going to take Robin, it would take Ashley too.

It was enough to make Tracy cry. It was enough to make her abandon the plan and beat the life out of Ada one more time. But she didn't. She held back the tears and the grief, the scream and the rage, and she returned her attention to the task at hand—the task of healing, of reconciliation.

"Your son," she told Ada, "was a mariner. Like all of the Silvers before him, and like almost none of them since. And he was a cliché."

Ada snarled.

"He had a girl in every port, as the saying goes. The wife at home in Chelmsford, which you knew about; the one on Cape Cod, which you suspected; and at least one more."

Ada's eyes widened, even as she tried to blink the falling rain out of them.

"The one he kept on this island," said Tracy. "The one who gave him a child you never knew about."

Ada roared, the strength of her anger giving her a second wind. She used her knees to push Tracy off of her, then made a run for the gun. And yet, she stopped short and screamed when she saw the pistol was sitting in a puddle now, a puddle amidst a new stream, a stream that was soon to be a tributary of the newly mighty Ka'a'awa.

Tracy saw all this too, saw that the gun was wet and useless now, but that Ada had picked it up anyway. The old witch held the weapon in one hand while she made elaborate gestures over its barrel and body with the other. Did she have a magic spell for this? *Probably*. That would be Tracy's luck. So, she got to her feet and stumbled through the mud toward Ada. The pistol was useless now, but it might not be in a minute.

As she slogged through the mud toward Ada, Tracy caught sight of the river sweeping Ashley and Robin's bodies off toward the Pacific. But while sadness tried to take hold of her in that moment, Tracy pressed on. If she succumbed to it, to the thought that this was all a lost cause— that there was just too much rage left in Ada, too much rage for any measure of truth to counteract —then what would have been the point of this whole journey? Tracy knew she couldn't just fall to her knees, into the mud, and wait for fate to have its way with her. Not today, and not any day going forward—if there *were* any days after this one.

A warm amber light surrounded Ada's pistol as she wheeled around to take aim at the approaching Tracy. The spell was done then, Tracy figured, as she watched Ada consider returning her attention to the unconscious Belinda. And yet, Ada's pondering lasted but a moment, just a fleeting moment in which Tracy could only grasp at straws for an idea about what to do next. Presently, Ada pointed the gun at Tracy and held her finger against the trigger.

Tracy held her hands in front of her, at just about chest height, but she stood her ground. Ada hadn't fired yet. If she got close enough and still hadn't pulled the trigger, Tracy might be able to get an audible word in above the roar of the storm.

As Ada drew closer, one plodding step at a time, Tracy searched for something to say—but all she could think about was having something to hold onto when the bullet came, some memory or feeling or *something*. And the moment she arrived at, the memory she grabbed with both hands, was the day that Kanoa fell out of the tree to flirt with her. There had never been a moment in her life more rife with possibility, and if she had to move on to whatever was next, whatever was after this life—if she *had* to—then that's how she wanted to go out. She wanted to die feeling like anything was possible, because maybe anything was.

And that was the moment when, near the river's edge, a hand shot up out of the water. A hand and then an arm, another arm and then—

"Kanoa!" Tracy shouted, watching her husband pull himself up and out of the water—still dressed as he'd been the day Ada pushed him into the river all those years ago. His shirt was plastered to his chest and his cargo shorts were drenched, but at least he hadn't lost the kukui-nut choker that—together with Tracy's shitty sewing job—was keeping his head on his shoulders. When he shouted at Ada in the next moment, the sound of his voice was deep and guttural—a kind of growl Tracy had never heard come out of his mouth. And the language he chose to issue his command to the old witch, a language she wouldn't know, seemed picked on purpose to further disarm and frighten her.

"*Kū kupuna!*" said Kanoa, bellowing through the maelstrom.

All the color drained out of Ada then, as she realized she was surrounded: Tracy on one side and Kanoa on the other.

"Put the gun down," said Tracy. She held her hands above her head to signal Ada that she meant no further harm, all the while trying to think through what further harm she herself could inflict to stop this chaos. Out of the corner of her eye, she looked to see if Uncle Matt's body had been swept away yet, but he was still there.

What would Matt do? That's what Tracy thought as she watched Ada's attention turn, panicked, between the potential assailants on either side of her.

What would Matt do? That's what Tracy was trying to figure out as another figure came racing out of the Sister's front door—a small boy carrying a big stick.

"You leave them alone!" shouted young Arty, pointing his mother's "magic" staff at Ada like he meant to use it.

Startled, Ada turned the gun on him. And without a moment's hesitation she pulled the trigger.

23

BELINDA

The crack of the gunshot brought Belinda back from the brink. Head quaking, lip and brow bleeding, she pushed herself up out of the mud and fought to get her bearings. The first thing she saw, as her vision unblurred, was Tracy tackle Ada to the ground, the two of them landing in a puddle so big and so deep that one of them might drown the other beneath its murky surface.

Then she saw the hulking figure of Kanoa, Tracy's undead husband, run toward the fray to try and separate the two women wrestling in the muck.

And finally, her attention drawn there by a yelp of anger and pain, Belinda turned toward The Strumpet's Sister. There, under the awning of the tavern's front porch, Arty held the two halves of his shattered staff.

"You broke it!" shouted Arty, throwing the remnants of his prized possession at the floor. Then, screaming the unhinged battle cry of an irate eight-year-old, he stomped down the stairs— intent on entering the fray and earning his revenge.

Belinda wanted to shout at him to turn around and go back inside, but she didn't have any voice to speak of yet and she had just barely managed to sit up. She didn't seem to be as bloody or as sore as she'd expected to be, but the wind Ada had knocked out of her during the pistol-whipping had not yet returned. Luckily, however, someone else came running out of the Sister at that moment to rescue brave-but-foolish Arthur Silver.

His panic-stricken mother.

Jenna raced toward the mud wrestling match her young son had inserted himself into. She knelt in the muck, dodged flailing arms and legs, and wrapped her arms around Arty's waist to get him out of there. When she was finally able to pull him away from the fight, dragging the struggling boy back toward the bar, he had a fist full of someone's muddy hair in his hand. But even as Belinda watched Jenna take care of the situation, even as she watched the two of them disappear back up the stairs and into the safety of the bar, she didn't find it any easier to breathe. It wasn't really "safety" that was waiting for them inside. It was *relative* safety. After all, the river was still flooding, the wind was still gusting in from every direction, and the rain showed no signs of letting up. Eventually, even The Strumpet's Sister would succumb to the now-unfolding calamity. It would either sink into the swelling river or be carried off by the raging winds. And when that happened, would Jenna and Arty be among the lucky ones who survived the ordeal unscathed?

Am I lucky? Belinda asked herself, considering her own survival of a calamity. *Lucky? Is that what I am?*

Belinda turned to Matt's corpse. Ada's gunshot to Matt's chest had started this whole mess, so she supposed the only way out of it was to figure out what he was meant to do. She'd been meant to stop him and maybe even get shot *instead* of him, or at least that's how she interpreted the appearance of the butterflies just before all hell broke loose. So, if she could take his place now, then maybe the universe, or God, or fate—whoever or *what*ever was in charge—would relent. Maybe, if Belinda could do now what Matt was meant to do, they would all be allowed to live on and fight another day.

Or would she have to do something darker to rebalance things, something more tragic? Belinda turned to Tracy, eyeing her midsection as Kanoa pulled her off of Ada. She imagined for a moment the new life that might even now be taking root in her almost-cousin's womb. Was *that* where the trouble had truly begun? With a baby that was not meant to be?

Ada, gasping for breath, reached again for her gun—which was glowing for some reason, maybe because of a spell Ada had cast to dry the thing out. But Kanoa, even as he struggled to restrain his raging wife, had the presence of mind to kick the six-shooter away.

And right toward Belinda.

Belinda picked up the glowing gun, questioning whether it was going to do anything or if it was still too darn wet, and she picked herself up off the ground in the process. Then she held the pistol aloft and fired it into the air—into a sky which suddenly went still. No more rain, no more wind, and no more clouds.

Everyone stared at her now, having fallen away from each other at the crack of the gunshot. They were a muddy mess, the lot of them, but at least they'd stopped fighting.

Belinda tried to think of what Matt would say, knowing that she had only bought them time and hadn't yet stopped the calamity altogether. Then the words came to her and she did what Matt would have done: she just said them. She spoke without thinking.

"I'm sure He's fine," she said, nodding up toward the heavens. "Probably just a flesh wound. But it did the trick, right?"

"What magic is this?" asked Ada, who stood now and took a step toward Belinda. "You stopped everything—all that was happening—with a single bullet?"

Belinda lowered the gun and pointed it at Ada. "I did it by being an asshole," she said. "I did it by wasting a shot to get everyone's attention when I could've just shot you and been done with it."

Ada raised her hands and nodded, stepping backward.

Then Belinda nodded at Matt's body, still resting on the sodden ground. She noted that the waters of the river had begun to recede, that the "river" was quickly becoming a stream again.

"He wasn't supposed to die," said Ada.

"No," said Tracy through clenched teeth. And though she looked like she was ready to go another round with Ada right that very second, she sat in the mud and leaned back against the chest of her husband.

Ada's attention shifted from Belinda to the body and back again. "You did what he would have done," she said. "I was supposed to shoot you and *he* was supposed to be the one who shot the gun into the air."

"Yes," said Belinda.

Ada took a step toward Matt's body and then knelt beside it.

"Don't you touch him!" shouted Tracy, struggling to break free from Kanoa's grip now.

Ada brushed a lock of Matt's wet hair away from his face. She stared into his still open eyes for a moment. And then, finally, she stood and turned to face Tracy.

"We need a pint of Sister's Swill," Ada told Tracy. "It's not as potent as the potion, but it will do."

"What?" said Tracy. "You think if you help me bring him back to life, all is forgiven?"

Ada shook her head. "And I'm not going to help until I've seen if what you said about my son having descendants I didn't know about is true. You're going to go into the bar and get the pint while I search your husband's blood for answers."

"My blood?" said Kanoa, confused. "What does my blood have to do with anything?"

Tracy turned around to face him, then held his face in her hands as she said, "Your blood is her blood."

Kanoa blanched. "But she killed me," he said. "Twice."

"I didn't know," said Ada. "And I still don't know for sure. That's why I'm going to conduct my investigation. And if I'm not satisfied with what I find," she said, directing her next words at Tracy, "I'll kick your uncle's body into the river—where you'll *never* find him again."

Tracy shook free from Kanoa at last, then made her way to Ada. "I'm not lying," she told the old witch, over-annunciating each word—as if trying to make spittle fly into the face of the woman she hated more than anyone else in the world. "I have proof," she said, and now she held a hand over her abdomen. "Because how did you come back from death this time around if not for the child that's growing in my womb right this second?"

"Child?" said Kanoa, a squeak in his voice as he spoke the word.

Ada's eyebrows twitched tentatively upward, but then she caught herself and put her poker face back on. "Robin was right over there," she said, pointing. "It could just as easily have been Robin's blood that allowed me to come back."

"But you came back right behind *me*," said Tracy. "You appeared closer to *this* descendant," she said, patting her belly, "than that one," she added, pointing to the place where Robin's body had lain before it was swept away.

Then Tracy turned on the spot and marched into the bar.

Ada stood still and silent for a moment before nodding at Kanoa and saying, "Come to me, child, and we'll see if you are who your wife says you are."

Kanoa stepped tentatively towards Ada, asking her, "How are you going to tell?"

Ada gestured towards Belinda. "We'll perform a ritual that Belinda once taught me. The Dance of Dreams," she said. And then she pointed at the Sister's porch, at the discarded halves of Arty's staff. "Belinda, would you mind grabbing me one of those?"

Belinda nodded and did as she was bid.

"What do we need a broken staff for?" asked Kanoa, stopping in his tracks.

Ada returned her attention to Kanoa. "Belinda can perform the dance with but a touch," she said, "because of certain abilities of hers, but the two of us, boy, need blood."

Belinda returned and handed each of them one half of the broken staff. Kanoa hesitated, perhaps unsure if he even *could* bleed now.

"Hmm," said Ada, either *a*mused or *be*mused—or maybe a bit of both. Then she dragged the sharpest edge she could find across her palm, dropped her half of the broken staff to the ground, and held out her bleeding hand for Kanoa to take.

Kanoa dragged the sharp edge of his own piece of staff across his own hand, wincing as he did—betraying the fact that he had no experience with his ancestor's arcane traditions. Then he dropped the broken staff to the sodden ground, where it hit with a distracting *squelch*, and held his hand out, palm up, waiting for Ada to make the next move.

Belinda looked to Ada and nodded, confident her old friend remembered the intricacies of the ritual—and that she was prepared for the ordeal. Then Ada stepped toward Kanoa and pressed her bloody palm against his.

It was strange for Belinda to watch the dance as a mere observer, and stranger still to watch it in quiet. She tried to count in her head the number of times she'd been alone with dead people and no one else—a mind reader with no minds that she could read. Any thoughts drifting through the heads of the people in front of her—any thoughts at all—were off limits. It was a pleasant feeling, but disconcerting. When was the last time she'd felt it without isolating herself in some fortress of solitude or another? Had she *ever* been in this situation before?

She would never know if she could see their spirits dance because she had performed the ritual before herself, or if any passerby could have seen what was happening if they looked closely enough—and if they knew what movements to look for.

It began with the fluttering of their eyelids, which flickered open and closed in time with a rhythm which the universe had been drumming since the dawn of, well, *time*. But when you looked closer, you could see so much more. If you *dared* to look closer, if you weren't frightened away by the odd sight of two people standing still as statues with their palms pressed together, you could see ghostly muscles twitching out of fleshy cages. You could see souls departing bodies to dance across a plane of existence just out of sight, just beyond the comprehension of a distracted, unobservant, and uncaring populace.

Ada and Kanoa's spirits moved away from each other at first, pulling as far apart as the blood which tethered them together would allow. Once they'd stretched taut the crimson cord which bound them to one another, once they were as far away from each other as they could get, each began to dance a solo of sorts.

Kanoa danced a haka to show her who he was and where he was from. I am born of the shimmering air of a hot summer's day, he seemed to say, the movements of his hands, his arms, and his legs a symphony of sorts.

Ada countered with an Eastern Blanket Dance. It was a tradition she'd learned from her mother—but a tradition which seemed strange, to Belinda at least, for Ada to be performing in these circumstances. As Ada began the dance, with the blanket enveloping her, Belinda thought of where the ritual was meant to end up: with the girl—Ada, in this case—laying the blanket at the feet of the man who she wished to marry. *What was Ada playing at?* Belinda wondered.

The answer came when Ada danced her way back to Kanoa and set the blanket before him. But when Kanoa, obviously moved by this gesture, though not entirely sure what it meant, went to pick it up, Ada kicked the blanket away and into oblivion.

What happened next was as modern a dance as any Belinda

had seen before. Ada ran away from Kanoa until the cord binding them stretched taut once again and then she fell to the ground.

She looked back at Kanoa with a pleading look in her eyes, then began to pull herself toward him with the cord. With each few steps, as she began to rise off her knees and dared to stand once again, Ada feigned being struck across the face and knocked back down. When she finally rose to stare her supposed descendant in the eye, with naught but an inch between them, she stood there for but a moment before pushing herself away from him again. She mimed the movement of an expanding belly, of a womb filling with life, and let that be the thing which separated the two of them.

Then she plucked the imagined child from her imagined womb and presented it to Kanoa, just as she'd presented the idea of the child to Silas Silver all those years ago. Belinda knew what was coming next, but she couldn't take her eyes off of Ada.

The old witch mimed being hit again, mimed the child being knocked off into the darkness, and then she wrapped her hands around her own throat. Ada swayed and spun, tripped and twirled, all whilst choking herself, making a mess of her death throes. Then she collapsed onto the ground.

Belinda watched her lie there for a beat, then two, then jumped backward at the sight of Ada jerking upright again—as terrifying a resurrection to watch as it must've been to go through.

Ada finished the dance by running about the space looking for her baby, looking to and fro with no luck until she stood in front of Kanoa again with a seething anger on her face and sweat dripping from her brow.

Kanoa, for his part, stood silent and took this all in. He stood there for a full minute, letting Ada's anger wash over him, unflinching. Then he reached out to her with his free hand, the one not bound to her by the tether of their blood, and he held it tentatively over her cheek, not touching her but giving her the choice to accept what he was offering or to deny it.

Belinda waited to see what Ada would do with bated breath. She waited a moment, then two, and sighed. Ada stood as still as Kanoa had, but with a look in her eyes that was entirely unmoved and unyielding.

Kanoa withdrew his hand and nodded. Then he stepped back and away from Ada and began a new dance, one which Belinda did not expect at all.

He danced a hula, but he danced it without any of the bombast or athleticism that Belinda equated with the male version of the dance. Instead, he kept it graceful and soft—as if trying to invoke someone other than himself.

And that was how, for the first time since Ada and Kanoa had begun, they were truly transported through time. As Kanoa continued his dance, bringing himself and Ada—and, perhaps by accident, Belinda—further and further into the past, one decade after another, he became less and less himself and more and more the woman whose story he was trying to tell.

Suddenly, they were in the hallway of a Pearl Harbor brothel in 1922. On one side of a doorway, Kanoa had become Leilani, his great-great-grandmother. On the other side, a startled Ada stood above a bundled baby—*her* bundled baby, who she'd thought forever lost, and who was growing into a man before her very eyes. Then, as the man she'd given birth to made ready to knock upon the door, Ada was drawn into him. In a way, she *became* him.

And then she—*he*, Mr. Leonard Gates—knocked.

Leilani opened the door in a silk kimono, leaning against the jamb with a puzzled look upon her face. And though Leonard seemed to be waiting for her to speak, she seemed equally determined that *he* should say the first word.

"Well," said Leonard, "this is awkward."

Leilani nodded, but otherwise stayed still.

"How long you been doing this?" asked Leonard.

"Since you left," she said.

Leonard blushed. "Can I see her?" he asked.

Leilani did nothing for a second. She didn't speak and she certainly didn't move. What she seemed to be doing instead was sizing Leonard up. Once she'd seen the first bead of sweat upon his brow, she nodded and she stepped back into her room.

Leonard lingered in the doorway as Leilani disappeared into a room that came slowly now into focus. And though the space looked spartan at best, save for the lavishly dressed bed, it looked far less austere than Leilani's old apartment. She'd been making a decent living for herself, making the best of a bad situation, and he respected her for that. But the thing which brightened up the room more than anything else, Leonard decided, was the bassinet that Leilani had tucked between bed and dresser. Or, more to the point, it was the *occupant* of said bassinet which brightened things.

Leilani plucked her child—*their* child, hers and Leonard's—from the wicker cradle and held the sleepy babe to her chest. Then she strode back across the room to the doorway and presented Leonard with his daughter.

In that moment, Belinda could see Ada's spirit glow inside of Leonard's body. When the baby reached out to stroke her father's cheek the light which came over Ada's soul was blinding.

Belinda closed her eyes.

"She's your fourth?" asked Leilani, as Belinda reopened her eyes.

"That I know of," said Leonard, staring now at the finger his daughter had wrapped her tiny fist around. "Hell of a grip," he said, looking into the baby's eyes for a moment. And then, because the pain of looking was too much for him—the pain of knowing this might be the only time he'd ever see her—Leonard handed the child back to her mother.

As Leilani brought the baby back to her bassinet, Leonard fished inside his jacket for something. As he looked for whatever it was he was looking for, he made small talk. "How do you handle things," he asked Leilani, "when you're working?"

"Are you asking," said Leilani, returning to the door with a mischievous smile on her face, "if I see customers while she's in the room?"

Leonard rolled his eyes, but gave her a smirk as he did so.

"I trade rooms with one of the other girls," said Leilani. "She watches Nani while I work, and I give her a cut of whatever I make."

Leonard nodded, finally producing from his coat that which he'd been looking for: an off-white envelope stuffed with cash. He handed it to Leilani as he said, "It's not much, but—"

"You've got three other mouths to feed," said Leilani, accepting the envelope then setting it on a table inside her room.

"That I know of," said Leonard, and he stared at his shoes when he said it this time.

"Okay," said Leilani, "it was good to see you."

"Yes," said Leonard. "And if I'm back this way again," he began, but then trailed off.

Leilani nodded, then shut the door to send him on his way.

Belinda watched as Leonard, still with the spirit of his mother inside of him, walked down the hall. She watched as the scene of Leilani's brothel faded away, the bodies that Ada and Kanoa had occupied fading with it, and she watched as the soggy front lawn of The Strumpet's Sister came back into focus.

The blood bond between Ada and Kanoa snapped them back toward each other, until they were standing palm to palm once again. Then the two of them opened their eyes, returned at last from the journey they'd taken. They stared deeply at one another. Ada held a hand to each of Kanoa's cheeks then, her blood still flowing freely from the hand she'd cut. Then her legs wobbled. Then they buckled out from under her. And then finally, falling to her knees at Kanoa's feet, the old witch wept. She held onto his legs with all her might, and she sobbed.

24

TRACY

When Tracy stepped out of the Sister again, a bottle of the bar's house-made Swill in her hand, she froze in disbelief at what she saw. There, amidst the muck and the mire of the tavern's front lawn, her husband had fallen to his knees to take their nemesis into his arms.

"What the actual fuck?!" shouted Tracy, but neither Kanoa nor Ada paid her any mind. The only person who seemed to have noticed her return at all was Belinda, who rushed up the stairs to take the bottle of Swill from Tracy's hands.

"I'll handle Matt," she said. Then she nodded toward the bewildering sight of Kanoa and Ada's intergenerational embrace. Belinda told Tracy, "You go talk to them."

Tracy nodded, as if she had any idea what to do next. What had happened while she was inside? And *what*, exactly, was she supposed to talk to them about? Where was she even supposed to begin with unpacking this unexpected denouement? Tracy had no idea. So, when Belinda rushed off to revive Uncle Matt's corpse, she watched her. She just stood there and watched.

Belinda knelt beside Matt's body, plucked a hair from his head, and dropped it down the neck of the bottle Tracy had brought from inside. Then Belinda did her best to recite the incantation Ada had taught her years before.

Tracy hoped she hadn't messed it up. Sure, there were more bottles of Swill inside, but she was tired and she wanted this all to be over with as soon as humanly possible. Or *in*-humanly possible, as the case might be.

Stressed out now by both scenes playing out in front of her, Tracy returned her attention to whatever it was that was happening between Kanoa and Ada. She walked gingerly down the front steps and then across the sodden lawn, the squelch of her boots signaling to Kanoa and Ada that someone was coming. They each turned to face her.

Kanoa freed an arm up to wave at Tracy, to invite her to turn the hug into a group affair, but she shook her head.

"*Fuck* no," she said. "I'm dirty enough already. And," she said, "I have no idea what's happening here, so how about you explain before we go any further?"

It was Ada who stood first, and as she walked toward Tracy she held her arms wide with her palms out—doing her best to show that she meant no harm, though the blood on one hand ruined the intended effect.

"Whose is that?" said Tracy, taking a step back.

Kanoa stood now too. "A bit of both," he said, holding up his own bloody palm.

Ada was within arm's length now, and she gestured at Tracy's abdomen. "May I?" she asked.

Tracy thought of all she had been through these past few years, and of how many of those ordeals had been the work of this woman who stood before her now. Then she did her best to imagine what *Ada* had been through, and she sighed. Tracy saw herself then as the blindfolded Lady Justice, with a sword in one hand and a set of scales in the other—as if only she could decide if the universe was in balance now.

It wasn't the first time she'd seen herself this way. Tracy

thought back to the "trial" she'd given Uncle Michael for his "crimes against femininity," and she blushed with shame. Though that incident had strengthened their relationship in the long run, how much had she hurt her uncle by deciding that she was above him—that she, all-knowing Tracy, had the right to pass judgment?

Ada withdrew her hand, interpreting Tracy's hesitation as a silent "No." But then, without thinking any further on the subject, Tracy took hold of Ada's hand with both of her own and stepped toward her.

The old witch's flesh was cold—her touch made colder still by Tracy's drenched t-shirt—but Tracy held Ada's hand anyway. She held it firmly in place on her abdomen, both to connect her child with its past and to connect Ada with its future. And perhaps it was this—her determination that a bond would be formed right here and now—perhaps it was this which led to the fluttering in Tracy's womb. She knew it was too early—far, far too early—but there it was. And given all the strange things she'd seen and lived through, who was she to deny it?

Ada certainly wasn't. She sunk to her knees in this moment and pressed both lips and hands to the spot where, deep inside, new life had taken root. Then the witch sang a soft incantation into the flesh of Tracy's belly, and though Tracy thought for a moment to shove Ada away—fearing these words of hers were a curse and not a blessing—she instead set her hands atop Ada's head and held the woman steady.

Which was good, because the old woman was shaking now. Suddenly she wasn't just old in theory—she'd begun to *look* old, too. Beneath Tracy's fingers, Ada's brown hair went white. The skin of the hands pressed against Tracy's body, skin which had remained supple even through two deaths, wrinkled now and turned sallow.

"Ada," said Tracy, pushing the woman's face away from her to see what was happening. "What've you done?"

Ada stood now, holding onto Tracy as she strained under the

effort of rising to her full height—a height which was significantly shorter than it had been just minutes before, owing to the stooped shoulders and hunched back she'd obtained as a part of whatever spell she'd just cast, whatever bargain she'd just struck.

"Ada?" said Tracy, looking into the withering face of the old woman—staring into eyes watery with age and with sadness, but also with joy.

Kanoa came forward to try and keep Ada upright, but even his strength was not enough and soon all three of them—Ada, Kanoa, and Tracy—had sunk back down to the ground.

"*Kupuna,*" said Kanoa, as Ada continued to fade—as her whole body began to go translucent.

"No harm," said Ada, and she winced as she spoke—as if every syllable were a struggle. "Blessed life," she said. "My gift. My apology."

And then—in a flash of orange light which swept over Tracy with a warmth she had never felt before outside of her husband's or her mothers' arms—Ada was gone.

☙❧

TRACY AND KANOA held each other close for a few minutes then, bewildered by what they'd just seen. When Belinda asked, "Are you're ready?" Tracy was not, not at all. She wanted to linger there in her husband's embrace, to relish the relief she felt alongside her bewilderment. And yet, she knew there was something else that needed doing—the resurrection of the uncle who was never supposed to die in the first place. So, she sighed and nodded.

Tracy and Kanoa rose to their feet and walked hand-in-hand toward Belinda. Tracy studied the weary face of her almost-cousin and wanted to say something, wanted to comfort this woman who had been through an ordeal all her own over these past few months. But Tracy had no idea what to say, and wouldn't have had enough strength to speak the words, even if she could think them.

Belinda handed the bottled potion to Tracy and said, "I'm not exactly sure what will happen. This is the first time I've tried this with someone whose body is still right here."

Tracy nodded as she looked down at Uncle Matt's corpse. Her experience had been the same. The last time she'd done this, it was to bring back Ashley—and Ash had been dead for three years by that point. She'd just appeared out of nowhere. Would Matt have to disappear in order to reappear, or would the husk in front of them spring back to life as if they were living through the last act of a horror movie?

After thinking about it for a second and deciding she didn't much care what happened, so long as it happened quickly, Tracy brought the potion to her lips and got ready to chug it. But then Kanoa snatched it away from her before she had the chance.

"You can't," he said. "You're pregnant."

"The potion works better when the drinker is someone who's blood-related," she told him, reaching for the bottle which Kanoa held out of arm's reach.

"Didn't we just discover that I *am* blood-related," said Kanoa. "Distantly, of course?"

"I don't know what'll happen if a dead person tries to bring back another dead person," said Tracy, holding out a hand for him to give it back to her. "Just give it to me. It won't hurt the baby. It's been transformed by the incantation. I'm sure of it."

"Belinda," said Kanoa with a tilt of his head. "Does the incantation burn off the alcohol?"

Belinda didn't know. She didn't know if the potion would work when drunk by the undead either. She supposed that she could try to drink it, given that she *had* been Matt's relative in another timeline, but who knew what effect that might have?

Kanoa shook his head, impatient, and chugged the potion. "If it doesn't work," he said when he was done, "we'll just make it again, right?"

For a moment, nothing happened—nothing at all but Kanoa,

Belinda, and Tracy staring at each other as they stood over Matt's corpse. Then a fine mist overtook them, and Tracy knew things were underway. Mist became drizzle, then drizzle became rain.

"Not this again," said Kanoa with a frown.

Tracy took one of his hands back into one of her own, then gave it a squeeze. "This is how it works. We return, however briefly, to the moment he died. And then—" A bolt of lightning cleaved the sky in twain, thunder pealed through the air above them, and the downpour became a raging torrent.

Except that this time it lasted all of a minute and ended with Matt springing to his feet instead of dropping to his knees.

The rest of them leapt back in shock. Though they nearly fell onto their asses, Matt reached with both hands to steady them.

Once everyone stood still and steady again, and once the rain had stopped, the four of them stood in stunned silence and surveyed the aftermath of their astonishing afternoon.

"Did we win?" asked Matt.

Tracy stared at the bullet hole in her uncle's chest, then glanced over at the place where Ashley and Robin's bodies had been before the river washed them away. "We certainly lost," she said. Then she held a hand to her stomach, to the place where she imagined she felt her baby growing even now. "Whether we won remains to be seen."

❦

INSIDE HER ROOM in The Strumpet's Sister that night, wrapped up tight in her sleeping husband's arms, Tracy considered her knapsack. It sat on a chair in the corner, and the sleeve of her prison jumpsuit was hanging out of it. Somewhere inside that same sack, probably buried at the bottom and tucked into some corner where they would take forever to find, was the pair of handcuffs she'd been wearing on the day Robin plucked her out of the prison convoy. The day she knew now for certain that she must return to in the morning.

There was no other way, Tracy decided. As much as she might want to run off with Kanoa and live life on the lam—and *God*, she wanted to right now, with his body pressed against hers and the smell of their lovemaking in her nose—as *much* as she might want that, there was a baby to consider now.

And then there were all the people who had a right to love that baby, Tracy's two mothers chief among them. All it took for Tracy to know what needed to be done was to imagine Veronica and Desiree curled up on their couch on Cape Cod, passing the bundled child back and forth as they debated who would be the first to see a smile. Seeing in her mind's eye the goofy faces her mothers would make, faces they'd stopped making for her so many years before—*so* many years—Tracy knew she couldn't deprive them of their grandbaby, the only one they might ever have.

So Tracy extricated herself from Kanoa's embrace, kissing his hand as he tried to pull her back into bed, then she made her way toward the Sister's showers with her knapsack in hand.

⚜

ONCE SHE'D SHOWERED and dressed and had pulled her hair back into an approximation of the ponytail she'd been wearing on the day in question, Tracy searched for Belinda. There was no time like the present, she decided, to make her return to the past.

And yet, her almost-cousin proved elusive. Belinda wasn't in her room. She wasn't in the pub's main hall. And she wasn't out front to survey the Sister's new location either, a side street inside a walled city of some sort—a place that felt both medieval and modern, and which smelled perpetually of oranges.

"There's a grove over yonder," Belinda had said when they arrived, pointing toward the city center and a second set of walls

—towering things which surrounded a castle and looked straight out of a storybook.

Tracy desperately wanted to know where they were—and *when* —but Belinda told her she wouldn't believe her if she told the truth.

But that didn't matter now, Tracy told herself. What mattered now was finding Belinda and getting done what needed doing. She snuck around the side of the building and into the alley. It was the last place she could think of to find her, but it turned out that it was the first place she should have looked.

Alas, Belinda wasn't alone.

She stood a few steps away from a muscled figure in blue and gold armor who was paying more attention to the pocket watch they were holding than to Belinda. They snapped the lid open and shut as Belinda spoke, and Tracy decided that this person, whoever they were, could not bear to look Belinda in the eye. But Belinda wasn't having that. No, sir. She reached for the figure's comparably massive forearm and said, "Nasha, please."

So this was Nasha, Tracy realized. *This* was Belinda's great love, the one who had to pretend to be a woman because of the rights of inheritance in their far-off homeland. This was the person Belinda had most wronged in her single-minded pursuit to keep reality intact, and who she'd been trying to apologize to for years now.

"I'm sorry," said Belinda, squeezing Nasha's forearm. "What I did, I did to—"

And yet, whatever words she'd been about to speak, they never made it past her lips. Before Belinda could finish, Nasha backhanded her with enough force to knock her back against the brick wall of the Sister.

"Hey!" said Tracy, shouting in defense of her almost-cousin.

Startled, Nasha wheeled around to face the stranger. In one fluid movement, they unholstered the pistol hanging on their right hip and unsheathed the sword hanging from their left.

Tracy held her hands high above her head to show that she was no threat.

"It's okay," said Belinda to the others, massaging her cheek as she spoke. "I deserved that."

"Who are you?" asked Nasha. They holstered the gun, then slipped the sword back into its sheath.

Slowly, carefully, Tracy lowered her arms. Then she nodded to Belinda as she said, "Her cousin."

Nasha stared at Tracy for a moment, as if struggling to comprehend the words she'd just spoken. Then Nasha looked at Belinda—Belinda and then Tracy, Tracy then Belinda.

"She wears the sacred color," said Nasha to Belinda. "Is this blasphemy another—?"

"The sacred color?" Tracy interjected.

"Orange," said Belinda to Tracy. Then she refocused on Nasha. "It's not meant to be another insult," said Belinda. "It's the color that prisoners wear where she's from."

"Where're *they* from?" asked Tracy, bewildered. "They don't have Netflix?"

Nasha raised an eyebrow at the word 'Netflix' and Tracy's head hurt at the thought.

"*Orange is the New Black*?" said Tracy. "It's a TV show," she said. "Set in prison?"

Nasha returned their attention to Belinda. "Why should it surprise me you're related to a criminal?" they said, then they stalked away—past Belinda, past Tracy, and then out of the alleyway altogether.

Tracy watched as Nasha took the path which led up the hill and toward the castle. Then she turned to face Belinda again and asked, "Is *this* where they come from? Is that why we're here?"

Belinda didn't answer the question. Instead, she asked a question of her own. "Are you ready?" she said.

Tracy nodded—except she *wasn't* ready, not anymore. Given

the scene she'd just stumbled into, she felt compelled—nay, *oblig-ated*—to dispense some wisdom before she took off.

"I don't need advice," said Belinda, having read Tracy's mind once again. "I know what I need to do."

"Do me a favor," said Tracy, handing Belinda the knapsack she'd carried for so long now. "Stop with the telepathy for a sec, and just listen."

Belinda nodded, clutching Tracy's backpack to her chest as if it were a teddy bear or some other talisman meant to ward off evil spirits and dark thoughts.

"You're a good person," said Tracy. "Everything you do comes from a good place."

Belinda's eyes watered at the thought.

"But you're like your father," said Tracy. "At least, you're like the version of your father that I know. He's a good person too. But his lies, even his lies of omission, eat away at the beautiful things he's built. His art, his relationships, *everything*. Like rats in the cellar, his falsehoods breed further falsehoods, until they've overrun the place—from the foundation to the highest beam."

"Your point?" said Belinda.

"Be like Uncle Matt instead," said Tracy. "Or Auntie Ashley. Our parents—your father and my mother—they could've learned a lot from their siblings about radical honesty. But since they didn't, we have to."

Belinda pointed down the alleyway in the direction where Nasha had gone. "I tried honesty," she said. "I *keep* trying."

Tracy wondered for a moment whether Belinda was ready to hear what she had to say next.

Then Belinda said, "I'm ready."

"Maybe Nasha's not the one for you," said Tracy. "Sometimes the universe gets us close," she said, "and we focus so much on how close we are that we come to believe we're already there."

Belinda raised an eyebrow. "I can read minds," she said, "and even I don't know what you mean by that."

"Your dad thought Robin was the one for him," said Tracy. "But his sister, Ashley, was the one for Robin. Robin was just a way for Michael to figure out what he wanted," said Tracy. "And what he didn't."

Belinda looked longingly off into the distance, and Tracy thought to turn and see what Belinda was seeing. She didn't have to, though. She knew all too well, from all the times she'd lost Kanoa, what that look in Belinda's eye meant.

Tracy walked the few steps it took to close the distance between herself and her cousin and she gave Belinda's forearm a squeeze. "And maybe I'm wrong," said Tracy. "Maybe Nasha *is* the one, and maybe it's just that now is not the time."

Belinda nodded. "Maybe I need practice," she said, as she searched the air for the place where she could tear open a portal for Tracy. "With the honesty, I mean."

Tracy nodded now, as well. "Start with your parents," she said. "Don't think of them as *almost* parents anymore. They'd be happy to have you."

"They'll have Arty now," said Belinda, tearing The Veil of the World asunder and making ready to send Tracy back to the prison van on the day that she escaped.

"Think of Arty then," said Tracy, staring into the glowing orange hole in front of her. "You know he'd love a big sister."

Belinda nodded, tearing up as she did. Then she asked Tracy, nodding at the tear in the Veil as she did, "You sure about this?"

Tracy smiled and sighed. "It's the honest thing to do," she said, then she leapt through the hole and back to where she belonged.

✿ 25 ✿

BELINDA

S tanding in the alley behind the Sister, Belinda watched The Veil of the World stitch itself back together. As the last flickers of orange light disappeared, she dreamt for a moment of where she'd run off to—and *when*—if only she didn't have people to bring home again, and things to set right, and promises to keep.

If only she, like her cousin, wasn't so obsessed with honesty right now. If only she hadn't decided to come clean, once and for all.

Disney World, she decided—a carefully crafted kingdom of make-believe. She'd dreamed of going since she was a child, hiding out from the apocalypse with her parents in the White Mountains. But though she'd been around for centuries now, since reality rebooted—millennia, really—she'd never gone.

Maybe she could take Arty. Maybe she and her almost-brother and her almost-parents could all go. Together. Maybe they could walk hand-in-hand, right down the middle of Main Street, U.S.A. And maybe there'd be a ragtime band playing as they strolled down that lane, toward the castle which had been dropped anachronistically at the end of the road. Maybe they'd get hot dogs from the corner shop—the one her friends swore she had to visit. And maybe they'd have their picture taken together, just the four of them, just like the family Belinda wished she'd always had.

Belinda sighed at the thought of "maybe." Yeah, *maybe* she would get to do all of those things, to have all of those moments. But first she'd have to be brave enough to tell them who she was, and she felt way too tired to be brave right now.

She looked at the door which led back inside the Sister and decided she was also too tired to be social. She was too tired to do anything but be alone. So, Belinda found a relatively clean spot in the alley, leaned herself against the cold brick wall, and slid down until she was sitting on the grime-covered pavement. Then she drew her legs up close to her body, slouched forward, and rest her weary head upon her knees.

※

WHEN BELINDA WOKE, it was to the sounds of the Sister's side door swinging open, a parade of footsteps, and a mixture of groans and laughter which could mean only one thing: Uncle Matt had just told a joke. Belinda lifted her head up to find four people looking around for someone—her, as it turned out—but looking everywhere except down. She *heh-hemmed* to get their attention, then accepted a hand to help herself up.

"Were you sleeping out here?" asked Jenna.

"You coulda had my bed," said Arty, who was bouncing up and down on the balls of his feet. "I was too excited to sleep anyway."

"You been out here since Tracy left?" asked Kanoa.

"Tracy left?!" said Matt, exasperated. He threw up his arms. "I thought she was meeting us out here. Like, what the fuck?" he said, back-handing one of Kanoa's massive pecs. "She left you, dude?"

Belinda interjected and told Matt that Tracy believed it was the honest thing to do.

"Leaving her husband?!" said Matt, shaking his head as he paced back and forth.

"Going back to prison," said Kanoa. "So that she can get out of prison, so that we can live a normal life after that."

Matt tutted in disapproval. "What's normal about time-traveling to get pregnant and then shacking up with your undead husband?"

Arty looked up at Kanoa and raised his eyebrow. "Undead?" he said. "Are you a zombie?"

Kanoa shook his head. "More like a ghost," he said.

"I can't see through you, though."

Kanoa laughed. "But I can't be a zombie if I don't want to eat your brains, right?"

Arty thought about this for a second, stroking his chin with thumb and forefinger as he did—and looking very much like his overly contemplative and extremely clichéd father in the process.

"Do you have a craving for blood?" asked Arty.

"I'm not a vampire," said Kanoa.

"Are you a wizard who dabbled too deeply into necromancy?"

Kanoa laughed again. "You know what a lich is?"

Jenna took hold of Arty's shoulders then, perhaps trying to get him to cease his interrogation, and said, "We've had a lot of time to kill. We played some D&D."

Kanoa crouched down until he was at eye-level with Arty. Then he looked deep into the boy's eyes and said, with the utmost seriousness, "The only thing I hunger for these days is family. And if I don't scare you too much, kiddo, I'd love to be part of yours."

Arty smiled. "It's decided then. You're a love vampire. And that's good. They're the best kind."

Kanoa nodded, rose again to his full height, and mussed Arty's hair with affection. Then he turned to Belinda and asked, "Where you will send me?"

Belinda shrugged. "With the others," she said, "it's obvious. With you, I'm not sure. You could stay with me until Tracy gets out," she said. "We could try to get you guys set up in a house on O'ahu in the meantime, assuming she's not able to leave the state while on parole."

Kanoa nodded, the look on his face one of sad resignation. Meanwhile, Matt paced the alley while shaking his head.

It killed Belinda that she couldn't read his mind anymore, now that he'd died and come back. She wished she knew what to say to him to make him understand Tracy's decision. On the other hand, he was a grown-ass man who should be able to figure out shit like this on his own. For god's sake, Tracy's own husband was taking this better than Matt was.

"Matt," said Jenna, "you're going to give yourself a heart attack."

Matt stopped and wheeled about to stare at the rest of them. "Can I even *have* a heart attack anymore?"

"Yes," said Belinda soberly, as she thought of undead Ashley and Robin being shot by Ada—each of them killed for a second time.

"We're supposed to pretend nothing happened?" said Matt. Then he slapped at the spot in his chest where his shirt hid the bullet wound which had killed him. "I'm supposed to go home to my wife and... and tell her what?!"

"I thought you were gay," said Arty.

Jenna gave Arty's shoulders a squeeze. Then she leaned over to tell her son that Uncle Matt thought his wife was a boy when they first met.

"She thought she was a boy, too," said Matt—who seemed calmed by Arty's question.

"Well," said Arty, "it's really cool that you didn't break up with her when you realized she was a girl, even though you like boys."

Belinda felt herself tear up at Arty's candor, and at the sweetness of his very good point. Then she saw Matt tear up as well.

"That *is* really cool," said Matt. "Isn't it?"

"Now," said Arty, turning around to find Belinda. "Can I go meet my dad?"

He was bouncing up and down again as he said it, and looking up at her with his great green eyes, and how could she say no to that?

Belinda looked to Jenna then and asked her, "You're settled on where and when you want to arrive?"

Jenna nodded and gave Arty's shoulders a squeeze. "We're likely to knock him off his feet no matter when we show up," she said, "so yeah."

Belinda nodded and began to search the air for a seam in the Veil. But before she could properly get started, she noticed Matt trying to get her attention. And though this was another instance where being able to read his mind would have saved Belinda a lot of time, she felt pretty sure that she knew what he was trying to say, the point he was trying to get across without words.

He wanted her to tell Jenna and Arty, to tell them right now, but she wasn't ready—not by a long shot. So Belinda tore the veil apart in front of her and she sent her almost-family on their way before Matt could give anything away. Once Jenna and Arty were gone, Belinda turned to Matt and said, "You next."

Matt's jaw fell as he slouched forward and threw his arms wide. "How could you let her leave without telling her?!"

Kanoa looked confused. "Without telling her what?" he asked.

Matt stood up straight again and pointed at Belinda. "Consider the red hair, the freckles, the green eyes which look like they're casting a spell on you every time you look at her."

Kanoa looked hard at Belinda for a good, long moment. Then his jaw fell and he pointed his forefinger back and forth between Belinda and the place where Jenna and Arty had just disappeared.

"Yes," said Belinda. "She was my mother, but only in another life. Here," she said, "here, she's a stranger."

"But she's not," said Kanoa. "She's family. She is the very definition of *ohana*. Did you not see the way she looked at you? The way *the boy* looked at you?"

Belinda said nothing. She tore open a new hole in the Veil and gestured for Matt to step inside.

Matt walked toward the portal, looking somber as he did. But just before he stepped into it, he asked Belinda, "What was this all for? If you're going to be dishonest now, why did we do everything we just did?"

And then he was gone.

KANOA DECIDED that he would stick with her for a while, so they stepped into the next portal together and stepped out onto the corner of Punchbowl and Pohukaina under cover of darkness. It was 2016, Belinda told Kanoa, though he searched the street corner for a newspaper box just to be sure.

"It's 2016," said Belinda again. "Do you really think there are any newspaper boxes left?"

Kanoa nodded and returned to her. Then he shook his chin in the direction of the circuit courthouse across the street, that Brutalist monolith of cold concrete. "She in there now?" he asked Belinda.

"A couple hours from now," she said. "After the sun comes up."

"So this is the day Robin plucked her out of the prison van?" said Kanoa. "This is the day she came back to?"

Belinda nodded.

"And we're just going to hang out?"

"Up to you," said Belinda. "This is the closest I could get us without rousing suspicion. Most people aren't used to portals of orange light appearing out of thin air, y'know, so I try to keep it on the down-low."

Kanoa stared across the street at the courthouse, at the bars of concrete which ran up and down between each window. Then he sighed and said, "You go in there and it's like you're in prison already."

Belinda nodded again.

"I can't stand to think of her in there," said Kanoa, "let alone in the prison. And now with our baby inside her!" He pushed his hands back through his hair until they rest on the nape of his neck. Then he closed his eyes.

Belinda sighed. She didn't need her powers to read this guy's mind. She knew all too well what the feeling of powerlessness looked like. And in this man—with his massive arms, and the way his hands clutched at the back of his neck just then—it looked like he was going to snap his head right off his shoulders. Or at least pop a few of the stitches that held the two parts of his undead body together.

"There's nothing I can do," said Kanoa, opening his eyes as he let his arms fall down to his sides. "I'm sorry I dragged you here."

"It's okay," said Belinda, trying to reassure him.

Kanoa turned to her and with sadness in his eyes asked, "Can we go kill some time?"

Belinda laughed at the turn of phrase, laughed at that particular combination of words coming out of Kanoa's mouth after everything they'd just been through, but Kanoa looked wounded by her guffaw.

"What's funny?" he said.

"Time," she told him. "You want to kill time? I mean, I don't blame you. After all this," she said, holding her arms wide, "maybe time deserves it. But..." She trailed off and raised an eyebrow, hoping she'd said enough for him to understand.

Kanoa blushed and laughed. "Yeah, okay, I get it now," he said. Then, walking away from her as he shook his head, he added, "Let's go."

THEY WALKED in the direction of the nearest river they could think of—a stream, really, which split Chinatown in half. It was a longshot, but Belinda thought it couldn't hurt to search for the Strumpet's Sister there—the most modern version of it, which had been lost to her since Robin stole it right from under her back in Haverhill.

While they would've walked down by the harbor during the day, to soak in the scent of the sea and bask in the sun glinting off of it, in the night they chose to head northeast on Punchbowl and hang a left on South King. That allowed Belinda to catch glimpses of Iolani Palace and the statue of King Kamehameha as they passed by. They paused for a moment so they could each pay their respects to the old monarch, resplendent in gold on his tall white plinth.

"Do you know what his crown is called?" asked Belinda. "There's a word for it, right? And it's nothing so pedestrian as 'crown,' as I recall."

Kanoa smiled. "It's a feathered helmet," he said. "A *mahiole*." Then he pointed to the other parts of the king's regalia. "The cloak is called *'ahu'ula*, which signifies he's a chief. And the sash is *ka 'ei kapu o Liloa*, a symbol of his supreme authority."

"Impressive," said Belinda, smiling as she nodded. "You're a fountain of information."

Kanoa blushed and chuckled. Then he pointed at the plaque on the statue. "It's all on the sign," he said.

Belinda gave him a playful punch in the arm but Kanoa laughed it off. "I used to come down here on Friday afternoons," he said. "After class, I'd get high on some edibles and just stare at it."

❦

WHEN THEY REACHED the Waolani Stream, the Strumpet's Sister was indeed right there. Belinda breathed a sigh of relief at the sight of it. At least Robin, with all her faults, had been listening all those times Belinda explained the importance of the annual card game. At least she understood that the Sister needed to be back in Belinda's possession before then, so that all hell didn't break loose.

And yet, she was about to run off with the bar again in just a couple of hours. Robin was probably already making preparations to move the Sister to the northeast part of the island, where she would rescue Tracy from the prison van. And so, the smile that Belinda might have smiled at the sight of her tavern gave way to a frown—a frown which only grew frownier when she caught sight of Robin stepping out of the front door.

"Didn't she just die?" said Kanoa, confused.

"This Robin," said Belinda, pointing, "has only died the one time so far. The death you witnessed is still in the future for this one. So, best you don't mention it."

"Is it over?" said Robin, once Belinda and Kanoa were within earshot.

Belinda and Kanoa stopped once they'd gotten close enough, keeping a healthy distance between themselves and Robin.

"You're wondering," said Robin, "how I know you're not the version of you that I just stole this bar from."

Belinda nodded.

Now Robin nodded too. "Fair question. I guess I'm just assuming the Belinda I stole the bar from would be a lot angrier. Oh," she said, "and you have a strapping Hawaiian stud standing next to you instead of a bitter forty-five-year-old white man, so there's that too."

Kanoa stepped forward and extended a hand. "I love your stuff," he told Robin.

Robin smiled as they shook hands. "Good thing," she said. "I imagine Tracy played it all the time."

"She did indeed," said Kanoa with a smile, as they ended their greeting.

Robin turned once again to face Belinda. "So," she said, "is it over?"

Belinda nodded.

"And did it work?" asked Robin, her face looking hopeful.

Belinda searched the air around her for butterflies, not sure what she was supposed to say. But when she didn't immediately spot one, the word "Yes" came straight out of her mouth.

Robin smiled. Then she turned and led them inside the Sister. "I'm about to move it," she said, "though I suppose you already know that."

"We do," said Belinda, as she and Kanoa followed Robin through the door.

The main room was empty, so Robin waved a hand around and told them to take a seat wherever they wanted. Then she stepped behind the bar, filled three mugs to the brim with Sister's Swill, and made her way to the high-top the others had chosen.

After she'd set the drinks down upon the table, Robin hopped up into a chair of her own. Belinda could tell that she was getting ready to make a proposition, but Kanoa interrupted before Robin could even begin.

"How did you know where to find us?" he asked.

Robin took a deep breath, then smiled. "It was a lucky guess. I assumed that if everything worked out, you would end up here to meet Tracy after the hearing."

Kanoa raised an eyebrow and leaned forward over his drink, as if he had to whisper conspiratorially here—even though the bar was empty. "A *lot* of things would have had to go *exactly* to plan for us to..." He trailed off. "It strains credulity. How did you *know*?"

Robin shrugged. Then she picked up her mug of ale. "That's what I do," she said, and Belinda knew which line from pop culture Robin was about to borrow even before she said it—even before she said, "I drink, and I know things."

Belinda rolled her eyes and took a pull from her own beverage.

Then she got to the point. "What's your proposition?" she asked Robin.

"I know the card game is in three days," said Robin. "I need the Sister for two."

"Go on," said Belinda.

"This morning, I grab Tracy when her transport crosses a stream between the prison and the courthouse."

Belinda nodded.

"By tonight, I'll get her to Cape Cod to gather some materials we need." And here Robin paused. "That may or may not go as planned. If it doesn't, I might need to improvise."

"You'll need an extra day?" asked Belinda.

Robin shook her head. "No," she said. "I've built in time for fuck-ups. At any rate, by the time we get to the second night, it's go time and I'm returning the bar to you one way or another."

Belinda considered this. She'd have just one day to pull the game together. If anything went wrong and she had to call the whole thing off, the negotiations she'd made with the players would be null and void. And then what would happen?

She supposed that was the question she'd been pondering all along. What was going to happen next? As terrifying as that question was, she'd always felt in control of the situation before. She'd always felt confident that she'd figure it out. But if these last few days had taught her anything it was that she was as guilty of hubris as she'd once accused Nasha's mother of being. Did she *really* have any control over anything? And given how poorly things had gone under her watch lately, *should* she be in control?

Robin waved a hand in front of Belinda's face to get her attention. "Hello!" she said. "Earth to Belinda."

"We have an accord," said Belinda. Then she pushed her chair back and stood up from the table.

"Where are you going?" said Robin. "You can stay right here. I'll hand you the keys as soon as I'm done."

"I need a nap," said Belinda, shaking a thumb toward the Sister's back rooms.

Kanoa turned to her with a look of concern on his face. "You want me to stick around?" he asked.

Belinda patted his forearm and said, "I'll be fine. I'm home now."

"So I should go back to the courthouse and wait for Tracy?" asked Kanoa. "Like Robin said?"

Belinda threw up her hands and shrugged. "It's a mystery," she said. "This is my first time through this particular moment. So your guess is as good as mine. Just watch out for butterflies," she said.

"And the signs of a riverbend," he said with a nod, "and all the other weird shit you guys've been telling me about over the past few days."

Belinda nodded. "Yep," she said with a smile and a laugh. "*All* the weird shit." Then she strode down the hall in search of the first empty bed she could find, not even having the energy to climb the stairs to her bedroom on the second floor.

☙❧

WHEN SHE WOKE, Belinda wasn't sure if she'd been out for two hours or two days. It had been a dreamless sleep, but not a particularly restful one. She was groggy and sore as she sat up, a myriad of muscles registering their complaints as she pressed them into service once again.

Her discarded clothes rested in a pungent pile atop the room's dressing table, and Belinda wanted to throw them into the garbage right that very second. She never wanted to touch it again, that acrid ensemble, and she had half a mind to walk out of the room wearing absolutely nothing. It wouldn't take that long to run upstairs to her rooms there, to the wardrobe full of splendid garments she'd collected over the years—and who was going to yell at her? The Sister was *her* place after all. She was in charge.

She was Inda of the Mount, The One True Goddess, for fuck's sake.

But was she anymore? Was she *really?* And did she even want to be? Hadn't the events of these past few weeks proven that she couldn't control this unruly universe and its unruly people, even though she wanted to? Hadn't her cousin and her cousin's allies shown her that no matter how hard she worked to save this reality from the fate of her own, she'd never be able to save these people from themselves?

It took everything in Belinda's power not to fall back onto the bed and curl up under the covers once more. Then a knock at the door pulled her out of the pits of her despair. "Yes," she said.

"Goddess," asked a familiar voice—familiar but cold. "Might I come in?"

It was Nasha outside the door, beautiful Nasha who hated Belinda right now—who had hated her for a very long time, if Belinda was being honest, and with good reason.

"Belinda?" said Nasha from the other side of the door, using for the very first time the name that Belinda had been begging them to use since the day they met.

"Just a second," said Belinda, considering her options. She looked over at her pile of dirty clothes and gagged at the sight, but she considered also her nakedness and how telling Nasha to come in while she was nude might be seen as some kind of prank or manipulation. And so, Belinda got beneath the covers of her bed and drew the sheets up to her chest. Then she said, "Come in."

Nasha opened the door slowly and stepped inside with their arms laden with clean clothes and a bathrobe. "I was told," they began, "that you might be in need." Then they set their burden down on the end of the dressing table furthest away from Belinda's dirty laundry.

"Thank you," said Belinda. "Would you take the dirty things," she said, nodding at the malodorous mound, "and throw them out?"

Nasha nodded, collected the things, and made their way back toward the door.

"Nasha?" said Belinda, just before they were gone.

"Yes," said Nasha, stopping in the doorway but not turning to face her.

There was so much she wanted to say, so many things she'd wanted to say since their confrontation a few days before—a few months ago for Nasha. But Belinda wasn't sure the apologies or the promises that she'd changed were going to go over any better than they had before, so she decided to say something else instead —something she'd been thinking about for a while now, in the back of her head, but had been too terrified to say out loud until this very moment.

"Goddess?"

"The game is tonight?" said Belinda, wanting to confirm that before she said what she said next.

"Yes," said Nasha.

"I'll be playing for the house," said Belinda. "You, my friend, will play for your own kingdom."

This, finally, made Nasha turn around. Their jaw, always so strong and steady, had fallen.

"Will that be a problem?"

"Onterey hasn't had a seat at the table since you killed... since my mother's passing."

Belinda looked into the eyes of the person she wished could love her the way she loved them, the eyes of the person who *might* have loved her if she'd made different choices—so many different choices. Then she said, "You've earned it."

Nasha reset their jaw, their whole countenance, and nodded. Then, ever pragmatic, they asked Belinda whose seat Onterey would take at the table.

"Your choice," said Belinda. "Now hurry off so I can wash this filth off of me and get dressed."

BELINDA STRODE into the game room that evening resplendent in a sea-green dress which made her feel, for the first time in many months, like the goddess she had long ago proclaimed herself to be. Around the stone circle of the room's table sat representatives from the seven governments which Nasha, on Belinda's behalf, had selected to play cards and determine the fate of the universe. Belinda smiled at the sight of them, imagining what Arty would say if he saw this collection of characters all together in one place, or if he'd be able to say anything at all before his little head exploded.

There was Nasha, of course, who was human but not an Earthling. Nasha wouldn't have surprised the boy at all, not even with their pronouns. Such was the splendidly evolved state of kids, these days. Then there was the horned and red-skinned shapeshifter, Srima, stoic in her kimono as always. She sat next to winged Roway, the crowned jester, who flirted playfully each year with tiny Merama, a pretty halfling who smeared her face before each game with the war paints of her ancestors. And beside that adorable pair sat Nergard the dwarf, a brooding old codger whose wild tangle of red hair was streaked with silver now.

On the other side of the empty seat which Belinda now stepped up to sat the elf called Achado, a challenging fellow who'd been a regular presence since the year after they'd lost two players in one game—one of them Nasha's mother. Beside Achado sat Gentleman Tyon, who would have been invisible to the human eye, he said, were it not for the bandages he wrapped around himself.

It was not lost on Belinda that Nasha had gathered the same folks who'd been there the day their mother died, all but the fool who'd lost that day along with Queen Yona and been banished for the slight of not folding. Belinda sighed in resignation, realizing once and for all that there were some wounds which could never be healed, not even once she was done what she planned on doing this day.

As she strode round the room to collect the deck from the cabinet, Belinda reminded the players of the rules. The game was five-card draw, the house would not fold, and those who folded before the showdown could leave with the seats of power they'd carried in.

Then she reached into the cabinet, past the stack of decks Ada had enchanted for her in years gone by, past the stash of completely mundane decks she'd procured from the Dollar Tree, and pulled from that cupboard a deck that, in her younger days, she'd sworn she'd never use.

It wasn't wrapped in cellophane like the others because this deck was handmade, with illustrations that were the work of Belinda's father—a gift he'd made one year for his poker-loving wife. Belinda held the deck close to her chest and closed her eyes, wondering if she was ready to do this, to do what she'd decided should be done. She might have stood there, pondering forever, if the players hadn't begun fidgeting in their seats.

She opened her eyes and strode back around the table, heading for her seat.

In her seat, as she shuffled the cards, Belinda marveled once again at how well they'd survived her long ordeal in The River Without End. This one memento she had of the world she'd come from, how had the water not destroyed it? How had the churning rapids not plucked it from her hands?

No one in that room understood what these cards meant to her and this realization almost made her lose count as she dealt out each player's hand. The only person who *had* understood was Ada, and the only reason Belinda told her was because knowledge was the price Ada demanded for the curse she put on the deck.

"Why am I cursing *this* one?" Ada wanted to know.

And so, Belinda told her. She told her how it had been a gift from her father to her mother. She told her how Mom had refused to open it for years, until that fateful day—just before the rains of a calamity came—when Mom finally said "What the hell?"

"The cards were in my hand," Belinda told Ada, way back when. "Mom had asked me to get them. And Dad was smiling ear-to-ear that we were finally going to enjoy the fruits of his labors. That was the last time I ever saw them. The next thing I knew, I was swept away, swallowed by The River Without End."

Ada had looked moved by this, a pained smile upon her face as she asked, "Then why am I cursing them, if they mean so much to you?"

"Because," Belinda told her, "on the day I finally decide to use this pack—if I *ever* do—I'll need the memory of my parents to remind me to do the right thing."

And so, Ada performed the spell. And now, more than a century later, the moment had come. It was time for Belinda to lose.

With the cards dealt, the usual business began. Nergard was stewing as he surveyed the hand he'd been dealt, one hand already tangled up in the snarl of red and silver locks upon his head. Srima sat stoically, staring at her own hand, which still lay face down upon the table. Merama and Roway had each folded already, turned to each other, and begun to flirt.

On Belinda's other side, Tyon had selected one card to discard and was deciding whether to get rid of another. Achado held his cards close to his face, overthinking things as always—or so Belinda presumed from past experience, because this time she was keeping herself out of his head. Meanwhile, Nasha was alternating glances between the cards they'd been dealt and the face of Belinda, who they could tell was up to something.

Belinda picked up her cards and examined them. Sure enough,

just as Ada had promised, she who had dealt the cards had no hand to speak of. No pairs, no high card, and nothing to build a straight or a flush off of.

Belinda deferred, allowing Tyon to begin the draw. As Belinda dealt cards to each of the remaining players, she considered her gambit. The curse on the deck was guaranteed to give her a losing hand, and to provide the other players with fantastic hands to start with, but it had no control over what the players *did* with those hands. Given how risky messing with Belinda had been in the past, would any of them dare to stick around through the showdown? What could she do to guarantee one of them did? And what, if anything, could she do to guarantee that someone was Nasha?

Belinda sighed at herself—realizing that even now, as she was getting ready to give up control, she was still trying to control who she gave it up to. But the truth was that, out of all the people at the table, only Nasha could be counted on to run the House of Thrones as a just and benevolent gamemaster.

At last, it was time for Belinda to discard. In that moment, she opted to follow her gut. She gave up a trio of her highest numbered cards, announced to the table that the dealer was taking three, then picked up what she was owed. She restrained a laugh as she took a look at her new hand: the same set of numbers, just in different suits than before. And yet, as reserved as she tried to be, some measure of her amusement must've found its way into the look on her face, for the remaining players all sighed or groaned in reaction. All except Nasha, whose poker face remained.

Without thinking about it, Belinda reached into Nasha's mind to see what they were thinking. The thought they found there both frightened and reassured them.

No matter what she does, Nasha thought, *I'm sticking to the end. And if she wants to do me dirty like she did to my mother, so be it, but I won't be half as easy to kill.*

Tyon and Achado folded, Nasha checked, Srima folded, and Nergard continued to stew.

Belinda turned her to attention to Nergard, who had never before pondered this long, but who had never looked this old before either. It was strange. For all his bluster, the dwarf knew what was what in this room and always folded when he was supposed to. He'd been here the day Belinda killed Nasha's mother for her insolence. Was he finally weary enough—or *bitter* enough—to risk forfeiting his throne, and maybe even his life?

No, it seemed. A moment later, as Belinda slipped into a panic about what she'd do if Nergard stayed in the game, the dwarf tossed his cards onto the table in disgust. Then he grabbed tight hold of his beard with one hand and began to twist it so hard that Belinda thought he might be aiming to yank the hair straight off of his chin.

Belinda turned her attention back to Nasha and nodded for them to lay down their cards, which Nasha then did. One by one, Nasha laid down their clubs—the eight, the seven, the six, the five, and the four. Then they stared across the table and dared Belinda to do better.

The thoughts of the seven players bombarded Belinda all at once. They knew what hand she'd need to beat Nasha and they knew how unlikely it was that she had it, but they'd also seen the dealer in this House of Thrones win in preposterous ways before. They were thinking *What if we joined together? If she cheats again, could we unseat her with a united front?*

Belinda looked down at her cards, then across the table at Nasha, then back to the cards. This was it. She was going to lose, just as she'd planned. The deuce and the four, the six and the eight and the ten, they couldn't save her now. The only thing she could do now was to invent some new rule, some archaic thing she'd have to travel in time to insert into the handbook before this game started. The only thing she could do now, if she wanted to win, was cheat.

But Belinda was sick of cheating. And, to be honest, she was sick of winning—of hollow wins, at the very least. She fanned out her cards upon the table and said to Nasha, "Congratulations. The House is yours."

The sound was deafening—great rounds of applause mixed with peals of Roway's infectious laughter and the boisterous bellows of Nergard's war cries.

Only Nasha was silent—quiet as a mouse even as they were clapped on the back by each of the other players in turn, even their mind a blank slate as they struggled to comprehend what had just happened.

Belinda pushed her seat back from the table—Nasha's seat now—and stood, looking to make her exit while the others were preoccupied. But she could feel their protests coming in her mind even before the words left their mouths.

"Wait!" shouted Nergard. "What is your penalty for losing?" he asked, and his mind was filled with the image of the murder of Nasha's mother.

"She has given up her power," said Nasha, speaking up for the first time as the new Gamemaster. Their word was law now inside the four walls of the House. "That is enough," they added.

Belinda nodded at Nasha in thanks, then turned to make her exit. She hoped someday she'd be able to return, to continue her apology to the person she'd come to love. For now though, it was time to leave. For now, it was time to move on.

With tears in her eyes, one for each of the dozens of conflicting emotions she was feeling in that moment, Belinda climbed down the stairs, leaving behind the house which had been hers for years beyond counting. And yet, she was not sad—not really. No, because she was bound for a dwelling which might be a *new* home—the home, perhaps, that she was always meant to have.

If her almost-family would have her.

❧ 26 ❧

TRACY

When Tracy reappeared inside the prison van on the morning of her hearing, it was as if no time had passed at all. The guard was still in mid-shrug, having just said that the Strumpet's Sister they were passing must be part of a chain; Tracy was back in her handcuffs and ankle chains; and the convoy was making its way down the H-3 like nothing had happened. They just kept on trucking, as if their prisoner hadn't been on the run for weeks now.

Tracy remembered that she'd been ready to laugh at the guard, to shake her head at the notion that the Sister might be part of some chain. She remembered thinking that no one in the world, not even the most ironic hipster in existence, would have seen the potential in franchising that place. And yet, her heart had softened. The Sister, dive though it was, had saved her life on more than one occasion now.

"I guess it could be," she said to the guard.

He raised an eyebrow. "What could be what?"

"The bar," she said. "I guess it could be a chain."

"What bar?" asked the guard, having already forgotten it—a

side effect of the Sister's magic that Belinda had warned her about, but which was disconcerting nevertheless.

"Never mind," said Tracy.

৩৯৩

IN THE COURTROOM THAT DAY, listening to arguments over the new security footage which had been found—footage which her attorney argued was evidence of self-defense—Tracy had a hard time concentrating on anything other than the fluttering in her womb, that feeling that was far too early but was far too persistent to ignore. Whatever was decided in the courtroom that day, the only thing Tracy cared about now was where she'd be in nine months.

Would she be giving birth while shackled to a hospital bed, kept company only by an armed guard? Or would she be at Uncle Michael's house on parole, bringing new life into the world while surrounded by family, her inexplicably resurrected husband among them? Tracy was lost in thought, considering both options, when the judge asked her to stand. Her lawyer had to give her sleeve a tug to bring her back to reality.

Many words were spoken—many, *many* words—but the only words which didn't sound like an out-of-tune trumpet, like the infamous sound of the adults in a Charlie Brown cartoon, were the words. "Ten months with good behavior."

Ten more months, thought Tracy, as she nodded that she understood. Not nine. Ten. *Shit.*

৩৯৩

A MONTH LATER, sitting outside the warden's office, Tracy pondered the pregnancy test they'd finally allowed her to take and the whirlwind of questions which followed the positive result. "Who's the father?" was the query at the heart of every question, but the questions varied widely in tone depending on who was asking them. Some wanted to know which guard had raped her. Others wanted to know which of them she had seduced.

Sitting across from her, her attorney was paging through notes in a manila folder with Tracy's name on it. He was trying to hide it, but he had a shit-eating grin on his face. If all went well, he'd told Tracy, she'd be out of here early.

When the door to the warden's office opened, a guard walked out with his head down. It was the man who'd been with her in the back of the wagon on the day of her hearing, and he looked like a puppy who'd just had his nose pushed into a pile of his own shit. As he trudged past Tracy, he cast her a sidelong glance with what looked like tears in his eyes.

Shit, she thought to herself. *They're blaming him?* The guy was an ass, but he wasn't an ass*hole*. He had a girlfriend—and he was looking to adopt her kids as his own, for Christ's sake. Tracy hoped this accusation wouldn't follow him home.

Inside the warden's office, debate raged about what was going to happen next. And yet, Tracy didn't take part in it. She sat silently in the corner instead. For one of the first times in her life, she didn't know what to say. Though she'd told her lawyer that the father wasn't any of the guards, she hadn't had an answer for him when he followed up to ask who it *was* then. What was she supposed to say? And so, they'd settled uncomfortably on her saying nothing. He would do the talking, he would make the implications, and he would argue for early release in exchange for not suing the prison. All Tracy had to do was not say a word.

But as the warden and the lawyer debated the merits of Tracy's case against the prison, Tracy couldn't help thinking about the guard who'd just been sent home on unpaid leave. What would happen to him, and to his girlfriend, and to the little family of his own he was trying to start?

"It wasn't him," said Tracy.

The two men turned to her, her lawyer raising the eyebrow

that was *not* in the warden's peripheral vision. What was Tracy doing? That's what he wanted to know. Tracy didn't need to be a mind-reader to know what he was thinking. She was fluent in the language of eyebrows.

"Who was it then?" asked the warden. "Or do you expect us to believe you immaculately conceived?"

"Kā'eo," she said, invoking the name of her old friend and former guard. It was a lie which would hurt no one, no one alive at least. Kā'eo was dead, his wife was dead, and they had no children. Sure, it was a lie which would fall apart if someone tried too hard to determine the date of conception—given that Kā'eo had died two weeks too early to have knocked her up—but a lot of falsehoods were going to fall apart the moment anyone looked too closely at what was going on here. She just hoped that the old man could forgive her if his spirit was still lingering out there somewhere.

"Kā'eo?" said the warden with a laugh.

The lawyer smiled at Tracy, happy that she'd decided to cooperate. Then he turned to the warden. "She's named someone," he said. "That's what you wanted. So, do we have a deal?"

The warden steepled his fingers in front of himself and considered the pair sitting across the desk from him. He considered them for a good, long moment before he sighed and nodded.

Then Tracy's lawyer turned to her and said, "Congratulations, mama. You're going home."

27

BELINDA

Standing at the front door of her almost-family's home, Belinda considered what she would say after she knocked. What would she say if Dad answered the door, or Mom? And what would she say if Arty answered instead? She couldn't exactly tell a little boy, even one as precocious as Arty, that he didn't exist in the universe she'd come from. So what *could* she tell him that wouldn't prompt a question she couldn't answer?

Was there *anything* she could say in this situation that wouldn't mess *everything* up? Anything at all?

There *had* to be. But if she didn't know what to say yet, was there any point in knocking in the first place? Shouldn't she just walk away right now, before it was too late?

Belinda cast her gaze away from the door for a second, deciding that a good, long stare at the ground might bring her the answer she craved, but she immediately regretted it. Seeing the skirt of her sea-green gown, she felt ridiculous. Who did she think she was?

A goddess, said a voice inside her head. For years beyond counting, that's what she'd proclaimed herself to be. With her ability to read minds and manipulate people with the knowledge her powers gave her, she *had* been like a deity for a while. But it was all just an act. Inside, at the core, Belinda was just a scared kid—the same teenage girl who'd lost everyone she'd ever loved, and who'd dreamed of this moment on her almost-parents' doorstep ever since.

And feared, above all else, how badly it might go when the day finally came.

Belinda returned her attention to the door, to the silver knocker she didn't have the courage to touch. Then her resolve to focus only on herself and her own mind crumbled. Just beyond the wooden door, a mother was trying to run a comb through the wild tangle of her son's hair—and cursing the fact that the boy had inherited her contemptuous curls and not his father's more tamable locks. The boy was delighting in the attention of his mother and in all the potential hiding places this house provided —this house which he'd heard so much about, but which was brand new to him. Mixed in with all that were the thoughts of a father who had just learned, after years of believing himself completely infertile, that he had a son.

Michael, the man who had been Belinda's father in another life, was standing out on his lanai with a paintbrush in his hand. With an easel in front of him and the crashing waves of the Pacific behind him, Michael tried to imagine what he was supposed to do in this moment. He had long ago given up on any notions of being a parent. He had failed spectacularly in his role as a surrogate father figure for his niece. So what was he supposed to do? Scold Arty, tell him to stay put and listen to his mother? Or was he supposed to join the boy and bond with him over driving Jenna nuts? He scratched at his beard and wondered. Maybe he was supposed to do something else entirely?

Michael looked down at the dog sleeping at his feet, as if the beagle might have an answer for him. And yet, the sleepy pooch did not stir. He slept on, relishing the warmth he'd found out there on the deck.

Michael sighed and said aloud, "Thanks, Chuckles. Some help you are." Then he got back to thinking—to *over*thinking, really.

The only thing he seemed certain of was that he shouldn't be doing what he was doing. He shouldn't be standing helpless behind his easel, waiting for his rambunctious son to sit for a portrait. *And yet...*

Belinda smiled at the torturously circuitous nature of Michael's thoughts. That was her dad right there, not her *almost* dad. The only time he was ever certain of anything was when his hands were moving so fast that they outran his mind.

"Are you ever going to knock?" asked someone from behind her, a deep-voiced someone who frightened Belinda as much with his familiarity as with his appearance from out of nowhere.

Belinda wheeled around and looked up at a smiling Kanoa. She'd balled up her fists, ready for a fight, but he set his open hands upon them before she could truly put up her dukes.

"Easy," he said. "You knock my block off and I'm going to have to get someone to sew it back on again."

Belinda unclenched and sighed. Then she returned her attention to the door knocker.

"You're going to tell them," said Kanoa. "At some point, you are. So why not now?"

She looked at him as she nodded her head in the direction of the door. "You been in there?"

Kanoa nodded. "Been getting one of the guest rooms set up for Tracy and me. And the baby, eventually."

Belinda took hold of each of Kanoa's forearms and gave them a hopeful squeeze. "Is she getting out?"

Kanoa smiled and nodded. "Comes home tomorrow," he said.

Belinda threw her arms around him and gave him the biggest hug she could muster. She'd hoped for this particular outcome when Tracy decided to go back to jail, but she'd studied the history of her family too closely and for too long to expect that a happy ending was a foregone conclusion. It was probably this feeling of disbelief that made Belinda squeeze Kanoa all the harder—one gigantic pinch, so to speak, to make sure that he was real, that *all of this* was real.

While they were still in mid-hug, the front door swung open.

"Hey!" said Arty, sounding quite beside himself as he spoke. "What's the big idea?!"

It was only once Belinda and Kanoa parted, only once young Arthur Silver realized who Kanoa was hugging, that the boy's scowl disappeared. In his head, anger gave way to elation—a feeling swiftly made visible by the fresh smile breaking out across his face. Not only was Kanoa *not* cheating on his pregnant wife, Arty realized; he was hugging the person Arty had been hoping would show up on their doorstep for a solid week now.

"Belinda!" shouted Arty.

He was about to run over to hug her when his mother swept him from behind, gathered him into her arms, and said "Gotcha!" with a devilish grin on her face—a wicked smile which betrayed that somewhere inside, perhaps somewhere *deep* inside, she'd been having as much fun with the chase as he had.

"No fair," said Arty, struggling to break free from his mother's clutches—and her tickles—but laughing as he did so. "I was distracted."

Only now did Jenna realize that someone new had arrived on her doorstep. Upon seeing Belinda there, she broke out into a wide smile. "Hey," she said. "I'd offer a hug," but then she held up writhing Arty as her excuse. "Come in?"

Belinda nodded, and she and Kanoa followed Jenna and the suddenly still Arty into the house. Then, as Kanoa closed the door behind them, Arty shouted out, "Dad, we've got company!"

A few moments later, Michael emerged from the hallway which led out to the back of the house. He locked eyes with Belinda for the first time since they'd parted ways in Massachusetts all those months ago.

Months for me, Belinda reminded herself. *Maybe a couple weeks for him.*

"Wow," said Michael, giving Belinda a once-over, "that's some dress."

The casual onlooker might have thought Michael was ogling her, but Belinda could hear what he was thinking in this moment. *She's the spitting image of Jenna from junior year,* he thought. *Yes, she looks just like Jen did for her solo that spring, in that gown she danced in as she told the story of us with her every step and turn.*

Michael turned his attention to Jenna then, who'd sat on the couch with Arty in her lap, and he cried—cried for the love he thought he'd lost, and for the love he'd found again. There weren't many tears, and he wiped them away as soon as he felt them trying to roll down his cheeks, but Belinda saw them before they were gone.

It wasn't accurate to call her the spitting image of Mom. Belinda was far slighter in form—delicate where her mother was built solid and strong—and she was far less freckled besides, but the idea that she'd reminded Dad of Mom in that moment, in the ridiculous getup she was wearing, seemed like the sweetest thing in the world.

Now what if he knew WHY you remind him of her? asked a voice in Belinda's head.

"Okay, Mr. DeMille," said Jenna to Michael, satisfied now with the state of her son's hair, "I think he's ready for his close-up."

❧

AFTER DINNER THAT NIGHT, as she made up the couch for Belinda to sleep on, Jenna asked if Belinda was *sure* she didn't want the other guest room. "Tracy's moms won't be here for another week," she told Belinda. "It's really no hassle."

Standing by Jenna's feet, the dog looked up at Belinda and

tilted his head to one side. That was his way, Belinda decided, of restating Jenna's question.

Belinda shook her head in a silent "no," then reassured Jenna that she just needed a place to crash while she waited for a flight back to Massachusetts that she could afford.

The dog gave a brief, disappointed snort, then padded off to the next room.

Meanwhile, Jenna was thinking *When is she going to tell us?* but that was as far as the thought went. She squeezed the heavy pillow she was still holding and the rest of her musing drifted off as if on a cloud.

Belinda prayed she hadn't blanched when she heard those words in her mother's head. *When am I going to tell them what?!* she thought to herself. Then, in a short-sighted effort to change the subject, she pinched at the fabric of the pajamas Jenna had let her borrow. "Thanks for these, by the way."

Even before she'd finished saying it, Belinda knew her diversion was going to fail. The subject of clothes was only going to bring up *more* questions. Mercifully though, Jenna opted to keep those queries to herself. Instead of saying or asking anything else, she set to work on putting the final pillow into place.

"I mean, they are a little big," said Belinda, tugging up the sleeve that was slipping down her shoulder once again, "but my mother always told me I could stand to put some more meat on these bones."

As she finished fluffing the pillow, Jenna thought, *She IS pretty thin. But I don't know that I'd ever say that to my daughter.* Then she stood upright once more, smiled at Belinda, and said, "I think that's the first time I've heard you talk about your folks."

"I lost them," said Belinda. "A long time ago."

Jenna raised an eyebrow. *How long?* she thought, considering Belinda's age. "When you were little?" she asked aloud.

In the distance, a phone rang. Belinda heard her father mumble a half-whispered curse as he scurried across the hardwood floors, looking for the blasted cell phone so he could answer it. In his head, Michael was thinking, *I literally JUST finished getting the kid to bed.*

"Shit," said Jenna. "I think I left my ringer on." She gestured toward the made-up couch and asked Belinda, "Are you all set?"

Belinda nodded.

"Okay," said Jenna, jerking a thumb in Michael's general direction. "I think I may need to make an assist."

But then Michael came traipsing into the room with Jenna's purple phone pressed to his ear. "Yes," he said to whoever was on the other end of the line, "she's here."

Jenna reached out to take the phone from Michael, but when he said "Hold on" it wasn't Jenna that he held the device out to; it was Belinda.

"It's your boss," said Michael. And when Belinda didn't take the phone straight away, he added, "My cousin. Matt."

Jenna turned to Michael and began to mouth the sentence "Why is Matt calling at this hour?" but had barely gotten started when Michael shrugged, turned, and headed back towards Arty's room to see if the boy was still sleeping.

"Hello?" said Belinda, as she held the phone to her own ear.

"You haven't told them yet?" said Matt, sounding exasperated.

"No," she told him.

Matt groaned. "Do it before Tracy's 'welcome home' party tomorrow afternoon," he said. "Or I'm telling them myself."

"You wouldn't—" Belinda began, before Matt cut her off.

"I would," he said, and he hung up.

Belinda knew it was true. She knew that the last thirty years of her family's story revolved around Matt "ruining" someone else's moment—Auntie Ashley's tenth birthday party—and that he wouldn't hesitate to do what he thought was best.

"Everything okay?" asked Jenna, as Belinda handed her back the phone.

Belinda nodded. Then she said, "I'm gonna lay down if that's alright."

Jenna nodded as she backed off and backed away, tapping her now-darkened phone's screen against her open hand. "Sure," she said, a smile on her face and suspicions in her head.

༺❀༻

BELINDA DREAMT of her last day with her parents, her original mom and dad. She dreamt of the hours before the Pemi flooded their camp in the White Mountains and tore her away from everything. She remembered the look on Dad's face as he came back from town with two bags of groceries and the news of a battle in New York. He was shaking his head and he was smiling, like he couldn't believe it, and though Belinda was doing her best in those days to not read minds without asking permission, she couldn't help but hear the news in Dad's head before he'd even spoken it aloud to Mom.

There was a "sin" monster, an atheist, and a little old lady who'd borne witness to the whole thing—the explosion at the collection facility, the confrontation on Madison Avenue, and the triumph of the non-believer over the creature. The theocracy and the official state news channels were casting doubts on this Mrs. Henderson's testimony, now that she'd mysteriously disappeared —last seen outside of a pub, of all places, a *dive* called The Strumpet's Sister. And yet, everyone up in New Hampshire—the Live Free or Die state where Belinda and her family had been hiding for years—everyone there believed that this was it. This was the beginning of the end.

"Can you believe it?" Dad asked Mom, sitting down on one side of their picnic table. "It might finally be over."

Mom shook her head, laughing and smiling all the while, and said that a celebration was in order.

"Does that mean what I think it means?" asked Dad.

Mom nodded, said "What the hell," and asked Belinda to grab a deck of cards from out of the tent.

"*The* deck?" said Belinda, thinking of the gift Dad had made for Mom so many years before. She blushed as she realized she'd probably sounded more hopeful than she meant to, and she hoped that her hopefulness hadn't ruined things once again.

Mom nodded again. "You heard what your dad said. The nightmare of these past thirty years might finally be over."

And then it was.

The rain poured down; the winds blew in from all sides; and though Dad did his best to guide them uphill to safety, eventually there was nowhere left to go. No high ground. No ground at all.

They lost Dad first, as a rogue wave reached in and tore him away. Belinda and Mom clung to each other after that, but it wasn't long before they were barely holding onto each other by their fingertips. Then they were screaming their throats raw as they each tried to get in one last "I love you."

Then the water, that river or ocean or whatever it was at this point—that uncontrollable *thing*—took Mom from Belinda too. And the last thing Belinda heard in her mother's mind, before that was taken from her as well, was the thought *I'll see her again*. It repeated over and over, a little bit softer each time, until it was gone. *I'll see her again*.

"I'll see *you* again," Belinda screamed with the last of her breath, hoping the sound would carry, and then the water dragged her under too.

Now, a lifetime later and in another world, she sat bolt upright in a cold sweat. And in the early light spilling across the living room from the open doors which led out to the lanai, Belinda *did* see her mother again. There she was, facing the ocean, moving slowly—rhythmically—in some sort of morning routine.

With the edge of her comforter, Belinda wiped the sweat from her brow. Then, fighting off the urge to run to Jenna in a panic, she sat still and took three deep breaths. In and out, and in and out, and in and out. Only once she had steadied herself did Belinda stand. Then she walked gently and with purpose towards the lanai.

She gave her mother a wide berth, trying hard not to frighten the woman and ruin the balance she seemed determined to achieve. This was a consideration which seemed to pay off too. When Jenna's flow finally brought her into Warrior II, when she came face to face to Belinda at last, she didn't seem the least bit surprised.

"Care to join me?" asked Jenna.

Belinda smiled but shook her head in a silent 'no.' "I can't tell exactly what you're doing," she said. "One moment it looks like Tai Chi, the next Yoga."

"Little bit of this," said Jenna. "Little bit of that." Then she moved into a Reverse Warrior, lifting her right arm and looking up into the sky.

Belinda marveled in this moment at the beauty of the woman who had given birth to her—or who would have, had this world been just a touch more like the last one. The strength of her legs and her shoulders, the pliability of her hips and her core, the way her face—often tense out of concern for her family—relaxed as she looked up to the heavens, to the God she wholeheartedly believed in. Then there were the first streaks of silver in her hair, a sign of aging that she wore as a badge of honor—a symbol of all that she'd been through and survived.

Beautiful. Mom was beautiful, and so much more.

How do I tell you? Belinda thought to herself. *How do I ask if there's a place for me in your heart, the daughter you never had but might have if things had been different?*

It was in this moment, as she watched Jenna finish her routine —as thoughts began to flood back into the woman's emptied and quieted mind—that the answer came to Belinda. Because one of the first thoughts that occurred to Jenna in this moment, as she looked at Belinda, was the memory of a dream—a dream she'd had when she was pregnant with Arty.

"Tell me about it," said Belinda, wanting to hear the words aloud. "The dream, that is."

Jenna arched an eyebrow and offered up a smirk. "You reading my mind, Ms. Michaels—?" But before Jenna could finish saying Belinda's surname aloud, the one the girl had adopted oh so many years ago, both her jaw and her eyebrow dropped. It was like she'd just set the penultimate piece into a puzzle, and she was shivering in both fear and anticipation over the complete picture she was about to see.

Belinda did her best to stiffen her upper lip. She kept her chin up, as if remaining stoic would let Jenna know everything was okay—that this was a happy occasion, and that Belinda hadn't minded drifting through history as an orphan. She did her best, but eventually the tears came anyway.

Jenna lifted a hand to Belinda's cheek and wiped away the first tears with her thumb. Then she took her would-be daughter's face in both hands and looked deep into her eyes. In her mind, Jenna asked *When were you going to tell us?*

"I don't know," said Belinda aloud. "How do you...?" she began, then trailed off. "What do you say?"

Jenna smiled, then repeated a phrase she'd said to Belinda on the day they met. "Remember," she said. "I gave up trying to understand what was happening the moment a dead rock star showed up on my lanai to protect me from an undead witch." Then she added, "So, a daughter I never knew I had, from another..." She struggled for the words. "Another what?"

"Iteration of reality," said Belinda.

Jenna nodded. "Yeah," she said. "*That*. If I could accept everything else, why couldn't I accept that too?"

Belinda pulled her mother into the biggest hug she could muster. In the process, through the magic of Belinda's powers, they danced through each other's dreams and pasts and they came to understand each other—or at least begin to—better than they ever could have with words alone.

"Hello?" came the voice of Michael in the distance, a groggy voice still thick with a sleep that the first coffee of the morning had yet to wash away.

Together, Belinda and Jenna turned to face him. And together, they waved him into the hug—deciding that it would be easier to show him than to tell him.

❧ 28 ❧

TRACY

he day Tracy gave birth, she felt the weight of the world on her shoulders. She felt it too upon her bladder—because *damn,* this baby was big—but the weight of familial expectations was, for Tracy, the more pressing concern. It wasn't just the Silvers who had placed all their eggs in her basket, so to speak. No. It was the Hawaiian side of the family now, too. She'd expected the pressure from them to lessen once Kanoa revealed he was back from the dead, but if anything they had gotten even more overbearing—as if his continued existence relied on the safe delivery of the child, as if Tracy and Kanoa couldn't try again if something went wrong this time around.

"What if the witch comes back?" Kanoa's father asked, only half-understanding the story of Ada. "Better get her what she wants now," he said, "so that we're done with her for good."

Though she should probably have stayed in bed, Tracy got up that morning, extricated herself from her husband's snoring embrace, and slipped on a pair of flip-flops. Then she waddled down the hallway toward the living room, toward that makeshift bedroom of her newfound cousin, with only one thing on her mind: *escape.*

Belinda had opted to keep sleeping on the couch for the time being, so that Tracy's moms could have a room to themselves while they were in town for the baby's delivery. It was this sacrifice more than anything else which had cemented Tracy and Belinda's friendship. Even though Jenna and Michael had fully embraced Belinda as their daughter over the past few months, which made this her home now, as much as theirs, Belinda valued the comfort of Tracy's parents more than her own. They were about to become grandmothers. This should have been happening in their home on Cape Cod—and *would* have been, if not for the conditions of Tracy's parole. Belinda felt it was the least she could do to give them their own bedroom.

That's what she'd told Tracy before the moms' arrival: "It's the literal *least* I can do."

When she finally reached the living room, many lumbering steps later, Tracy gave Belinda's shoulder a gentle nudge with her knee. Then, as her cousin stirred, Trace riffed on a line from *Mean Girls* and said, "Get up, loser. We're going walking."

⚅⚄⚅

THEY WALKED, though not very far and not very fast. In fact, it was less than a mile from the house when Tracy plopped herself down on the edge of someone's stone wall, lowered her head, and began to cry.

"What's wrong?" asked Belinda, crouching down and setting her hands upon Tracy's knees.

"I don't know," sobbed Tracy. "Can't you read my mind and figure it out?"

Belinda chuckled. "It's a mess in there," she said.

Tracy sniffled and smiled.

"Have me and Arty being here changed anything?" asked Belinda, who reached up in that moment to wipe the tears from Tracy's cheeks. "Have we made it *any* easier?"

Tracy shrugged. "I still might be the last hope for our *oh-so-important* bloodline," she said with a snicker. "You've been around for centuries without getting knocked up—"

Belinda laughed, dropping out of her squat and onto her behind.

"—and Arty's too young to know if he'll be able or even *interested* in aiding the cause," Tracy continued.

Belinda nodded as she said, "I'm sorry."

Tracy shrugged again. "It is what it is," she said. "The baby's coming, one way or another. The deed is done." Then she rubbed her belly. "Except now it's all on them."

Belinda nodded, then leaned forward and set her own hand upon Tracy's swollen midsection. "I don't think Ada, as angry as she was—as *determined*—would have wanted to pass that burden on. I think all she wanted was a chance."

"What about my great-great-grandfather?" said Tracy, as she and Belinda chased each other's hands in circles over top of the flesh that kept the infant safe, for now, from these concerns. "What about all the harm *he* did to keep the family line going? What if *he* comes back as the villain next time?"

Belinda offered a pained smirk. "You think there'll be a sequel?" she asked.

"*God*," Tracy groaned. "I fucking hope not," she said, but when she looked down at Belinda—hoping to find that her cousin agreed with the sentiment—Tracy found a look on the girl's face that was far more panicked than she'd hoped for. "What?" said Tracy. "Do you honestly hope this shit's going to keep going forever?"

"No," said Belinda, turning her frown upside down with great haste. Then she pointed toward Tracy's groin, toward the wet spot that was blooming there. "It's just that I think your water just—"

Tracy looked down at herself, struggling to see past the belly that was in the way, but then she felt the dampness in her drawers and knew that she didn't need to see to believe—at least not in this case.

"Well, *shit*," said Tracy. "I guess it's time to go."

❧

SEVEN HOURS LATER, in the throes of labor, she said it again. With a contraction bearing down on her, Tracy looked down at the baby in her belly and pled with it. "It's time to go," she said, and though she did not utter the word "please" aloud, she damn well thought it.

There was one mom on either side of her, and Tracy squeezed their proffered hands with all her might as she fought her way through the contraction. Somewhere in the room—she couldn't remember exactly where, with her eyes closed and her mind focused on bending the will of her stubborn cervix—the soothing voice of her husband guided her through the ordeal, his steady baritone a foundation on which she could rest her weary soul in between each battle.

When that contraction was over, Tracy's great aunt Michaela stepped up to the foot of the bed with freshly washed and gloved hands to check on Tracy's progress. Michaela was a pediatrician by trade, but she'd come *this* close to concentrating on obstetrics instead. No one in the family, it seemed, was as excited as Michaela for Tracy's decision to have a home birth. She'd flown in from Massachusetts a week before Tracy's due date, and she'd been at the house from sunrise to sundown every day since—even though her hotel was a mere 10-minute drive away.

"So," said Kanoa to Michaela, doing his best Bugs Bunny impression. "What's up, Doc?"

Michaela slipped her hand out of Tracy and smiled as she pulled off her gloves. "We're getting there," she said, keeping the precise measurement to herself—as per Tracy's wishes that she stop speaking the numbers aloud.

Tracy sighed and plopped her head back onto the pillow, deciding that this particular "We're getting there" was an out-and-out lie, the fabrication of a practiced physician trying to keep their patient's spirits up.

"Get a little rest before the next one," said Michaela, giving Tracy's knee a gentle squeeze.

Tracy nodded weakly, then closed her eyes to focus on catching her breath—on trying to find a second wind, or a third, or a fourth, or whichever wind it was that she was on now.

Someone's fingers found their way into her hair, pushing her matted, sweaty locks up and away from her brow. Whether it was Mom or Desiree didn't much matter at the moment. Tracy was glad for the attention either way. It occurred to her, as a couple of exhausted tears rolled down her cheeks, to wonder whether she'd ever be babied like this again, or if the mere act of giving birth to a child of her own would disqualify her from any future pampering of this sort.

"You'll always be their baby," said Belinda, speaking aloud an answer to the silent question that only she had heard.

Tracy offered a weak laugh in response to her cousin's blunder and imagined in her mind's eye how red Belinda must've turned in that moment. Belinda mumbled a sheepish "Sorry" from across the room.

"Damn right you'll always be our baby," said Mom, and at that moment Tracy felt kisses coming at her forehead from both sides.

❦

IT WAS several hours more before Michaela finally uttered the phrase which had become the mantra of the day. "It's time to go," she said. "This kiddo is ready to make their entrance."

And so Tracy began the ritual: the pushing and the breathing, the breathing and the pushing. Most of it went exactly as Mom had told her it would. Some of it even went the way Grandma had told her it would, though Mom had argued that's not the way it worked anymore. But what none of them prepared her for, perhaps because none of them had ever experienced this part themselves, was the arrival of the ghosts.

At first, Tracy thought it was a hallucination—a brief passing glimpse of someone who wasn't there, but who she desperately wanted to see. When she opened her eyes again after the next round of pushing, she fully expected the translucent specter of Auntie Ashley to be gone. But then Robin was standing next to her—two women who'd never wanted to be mothers themselves, but who seemed transfixed by the beauty and the strength of the act.

Next came Ada, her form un-mangled now—as if the healing of her spirit had also healed her corporeal form. And behind Ada, with her hands upon Ada's shoulders, stood a proud looking woman who must've been the old witch's mother. Then, quite suddenly, the walls of the room melted away to make way for a crowd of women standing behind Ada and her mother—the ancestors Ada had spoken of, who had heretofore been little more than names and dates on a family tree. Dozens of faces, hundreds of features, details Tracy examined in between breaths for some sign of Kanoa.

She turned to Kanoa, standing steady next to Desiree near the foot of the bed—but with one of Desiree's hands set on the small of his back, as if maybe to help him stay upright. He was speaking aloud a mantra of some sort to help Tracy stay focused, but she couldn't hear the words. All she could see in that moment were the tears in his beautiful eyes, tears that he was struggling to hold back—either because he thought he needed to be strong in this moment, that he needed to be "the man," or for some other reason she couldn't fathom.

Then, behind Kanoa in the vast orange space that the room had transformed into for Tracy, dozens of other men appeared— men of his family, and of hers. Polynesians and Europeans, they all broke down in the tears that they'd been too proud or too afraid to cry when they were alive. One of them, Tracy's great-grandfather Eli, clapped a ghostly hand upon Kanoa's shoulder. This, unlike anything else, somehow opened the floodgates in Tracy's heretofore stoic husband. When Kanoa began to cry, Tracy heard the ghost of old Eli say, "That's the ticket."

Pain drew Tracy back to the reality of her body, of her situation. She clamped her eyes shut as Michaela told her, "The baby's crowning," then pushed with all her might.

"Okay, Trace," was the next thing she heard Michaela say—but whether that was minutes later or an hour, she couldn't be sure. "Hold up a second. Deep breaths. The next one should be the last."

Tracy wanted to open her eyes and see the crowd one last time, because she felt as though this might be it, that they would all disappear the moment the baby arrived. So she did. She opened her eyes wide and there they were—all of them she'd seen before and hundreds more, maybe a thousand strong. It felt strange at first—*would you people all stop staring at my gaping vag for a second?*—but then she realized she was deflecting. She was being gross and using humor to keep from feeling what she was actually feeling at the sight of them.

Relief.

They were beaming at her. Hundreds of people whose blood she shared, or who shared blood with the baby she was delivering—all of them were bathed in warm orange light. They wore enormous smiles of joy upon their faces. There were no expectations there. There was no more pressure. Instead, there was love. And pride. And a thousand blessings on a thousand pairs of lips.

As the first cries of a newborn infant filled the room, the ancestors disappeared. In the next moment, when the child was laid naked upon Tracy's chest, everyone else was gone too—not just the ghosts, but everyone who'd been in the room with Tracy until this moment. Suddenly, there was no one left in the world but Tracy and her baby.

Delirious with both exhaustion and elation, Tracy stroked the soft head of her child and marveled at how tiny this little human being was. Then she ran a hand along the shivering newborn's back, aware that she should hand the baby to someone else to be washed and dressed but not wanting to let go just yet. But when her hand reached the child's dainty derriere and she found a dollop of doo-doo waiting for her there, Tracy fought off a measure of revulsion and asked for someone to give her a hand with her little stinker.

Off in the distance, lingering in a doorway, Uncle Michael said, "Actually, baby's first stool is supposed to be odorless. You see—"

But whatever he was going to say next, Tracy would never know. Someone smacked Michael in the arm and he shut up right quick.

Michaela took the baby from Tracy and stepped into the adjoining bathroom to give the infant its first bath and first exam. Mom and Des showered Tracy's sweaty brow with kisses once again. Then Kanoa came out of nowhere with a damp cloth to clean Tracy's dirty hand.

"Did you see...?" Tracy began to ask Kanoa, blushing at her need to know the answer to the question in her head. They had talked back and forth about the question of gender, trying desperately to overcome their own upbringings and be the ultramodern parents they aspired to be, but ultimately—and perhaps ashamedly—they had opted to let the kiddo's genitals dictate their pronouns. For now.

Kanoa nodded. "A girl," he said.

"Did you guys finally decide on a name?" asked Mom.

"Don't rush 'em," said Des playfully. "They only just met her."

"And Dad hasn't really met her at all," said Michaela, returning to the room with the now-bundled baby. "Would you like to?" she said, presenting Kanoa with his child.

Tracy beamed as her husband took their daughter into his arms. She nudged Mom to snap a photo with her phone when she saw Kanoa hold the girl upright against his chest, supporting her head as her grasping hand and hungry mouth reached for the nipple poking through his t-shirt. Then Tracy asked Kanoa if he still wanted to choose the name in the way they'd talked about.

Kanoa nodded, then stepped out through the sliding glass doors and onto the lanai. Tracy watched as he held their child close and closed his eyes to listen to the wind. Then her gaze darted to Kanoa's parents, who seemed genuinely touched at their son's decision to adhere to this old tradition. They were careful not to follow him, however—no matter how proud they were, no matter how much they wanted to wrap him up in their arms at that moment, their own baby grown so big now—and they were careful to hold back anyone who might have ideas of their own. This moment was meant to be a private one.

The dog—having seen Kanoa's parents holding folks back—marched proudly back and forth in front of the small crowd, playing the part of guard dog for the afternoon. Tracy smiled at him, at good ol' Chuck trying to do his part too.

It was a few minutes later when Kanoa returned with the baby and introduced her with the name the wind had given her. "Makana," he said, smiling, and then he translated: "Our gift."

❧

BETWEEN FEEDINGS, a blissfully dreamless sleep swallowed Tracy whole. Though the trials of those first few days were as exhausting as her mothers and a dozen different pregnancy books had warned her they'd be, Tracy felt blessed overall. Between Kanoa and the extended family, she had more than enough help. In fact, most of Kanoa's family had cleared out and Tracy's grandparents, her great aunt, and her great uncle were all flying back to Massachusetts in just a day or two.

Was it a day, or was it two? Tracy had lost all sense of time. They'd warned her about that too, but it was still a jarring sensation. She'd managed time so carefully over the course of her life, especially this last year or two—with the prison and the time traveling—and she'd come to believe that there was nothing in the world as precious. But she knew now that she was wrong.

Tracy rolled over in bed to wrap an arm around her husband, to ask him to grab the baby from the bassinet and bring her over for a cuddle, but she found his side of the bed empty. Warm, but empty.

She sat up and caught Kanoa picking Makana out of her cradle at the far end of the room. "Go back to sleep," he said. "I've got her." Then he started out of the room.

"Wait up," she said, climbing out of bed herself and following him into the hall.

Tracy watched him head towards the living room, stepping deftly over the pile of toys spilling out of Arty's room, and her heart soared as she realized how well fatherhood suited him.

"You should sleep," he told her from over his shoulder.

"I've slept enough," she said.

Kanoa paused at the place where the hallway ended and the living room began, turning to face Tracy and to offer her a playful eye-roll and a subtle shake of his head. Then he returned to his business and brought Makana out into the living room, out into the crowd of family members waiting to play hot potato with her.

Tracy followed him. "It would be nice," she said with a snicker, "to hold my own baby every once in a while." But it was only after she'd said it that Tracy realized the crowd in the living room was much thinner this morning, and that Kanoa was making a beeline toward one person in particular—a rather small person who went pink at the sound of Tracy's sarcasm, not realizing that she was just joking.

"I'm sorry," said Arty. "I don't have to hold her if you don't want."

"Oh no," said Tracy, going pink now herself. "I was just kidding, kiddo."

Arty had been too nervous to hold the baby until now. Every time he'd been offered, often while he was sitting next to his mother or father and examining Makana's tiny toes, Arty had declined. Now that the poor kid had worked up the gumption, Tracy felt terrible for making him nervous once again.

As Kanoa stood off to one side with sleepy Makana in his arms, Tracy grabbed a spot on the floor in front of her cousin and sat down. Then she gave Arty's knee a squeeze.

"Nothing would make me happier," said Tracy to Arty, a kind smile on her face, "than to see you hold her."

Arty looked uncertain still, but then he looked sheepishly up at Kanoa—and at the baby in Kanoa's arms—and he gave a little nod.

"You got this, little bro," said Belinda from her position beside Arty, and she mussed his hair to lighten him up.

Arty rest one arm upon his lap and the other upon a pillow Belinda held in place. Then Kanoa crouched down and handed his child over to the boy—the boy who was still getting used to the fact that he was no longer the youngest in the room.

In the next moment, nothing much happened at all. The sleepy baby slept on in the arms of a kid who suddenly realized he'd had nothing to be afraid of. But in the moment after that, Makana turned her head toward her cousin and nuzzled her face into his armpit. Everyone laughed, even nervous Arty.

Tracy looked around to see exactly who was bearing witness to this moment and found the room emptier than she'd imagined. The eldest members of the family were all asleep, Tracy's mom and her generation suddenly the old folks in the room. Uncle Matt sat in the armchair, asleep himself with a book held to his chest, having dozed off before the big moment. Uncle Michael was on the couch, sleepy Jenna's head resting on one leg while he sketched the scene onto a pad he'd set upon his free knee. Mom was at the piano, ready for her morning practice—as soon as everyone was awake and she knew she wouldn't bother anyone. And off in the shadows at the back of the room, just faintly visible —and probably only because Tracy was looking right at her— stood the ghost of Auntie Ashley.

Ashley nodded her chin toward Arty and the baby, silently telling Tracy to pay attention to what mattered—the lesson she'd been trying to teach Tracy for years at this point. And so, Tracy did as she was told and returned her focus to the living instead of the dead.

"It's quite a story," said Belinda to Arty, "the story of our family. When your cousin asks—"

"*Ahem*," grunted Michael.

When Tracy turned to face him, he had a shit-eating grin on his face.

"First cousin, once removed," he said, correcting Belinda with the same jab Tracy had once used against him—albeit with a far more playful tone.

"When your *cousin* asks," said Belinda to her brother, emphasizing the word to tease her father right back, "where should we start?"

Kanoa took a seat next to Arty and offered up some choices. "With Old Silas' boot?" he said. "Or Ada's wicked potion? Or should we begin with one of the love triangles instead?"

For the first time since Makana had been laid in his arms, Arty looked up to face the rest of them. "What about with Judas?" he said. "Isn't that where Great-Grandpa Eli always started?"

"A story can start anywhere," said Uncle Matt, stirring in his chair. "And at any time," he continued. "The beginning, the middle—"

"The end," said Veronica with a snicker, and Tracy laughed at her mother's attempt to shut down one of Uncle Matt's long-ass stories before it began.

"The point is," said Uncle Matt, dog-earing the page he was

on in his book and setting it aside. "Where you start, Mr. Arty Man, depends on what story you want to tell. And *whose* story. You can fit the pieces together anyway you want, in any order you want, so long as you know where you're going and what you want to say."

The family sat in silence for a moment, deciding whether or not Matt had made a good point or just mumbled the first pointless string of words which came to his mind.

"Well," said Arty, looking down at Makana again for a moment. "What if we wanted to tell her *her* story?" he said. "Where would we start?"

"With her mother's story," said Kanoa kindly, reaching down to give Tracy's hand a squeeze.

And now Arty turned his attention to Tracy and asked, "And where does *your* story begin?"

Tracy thought to say, "with *my* mother's story," which she felt with all her heart was true, but she knew that Mom would be deferential as well and that Arty would never get an answer that way. So, instead, she thought of the day she'd slipped Ada's potion into her mother's evening tea. Then she thought of the story Mom told about her dream that night.

"Tracy?" said Arty.

"Well," said Tracy, turning to face her mother as she spoke, "it began with a piano falling from the sky."

ACKNOWLEDGEMENTS

The text of Chapter 2 was first published, in slightly different form, as "And Again" in the 2019 issue of the University of Hawaii's *Vice-Versa*.

The text of Chapter 15 contains portions of "The Crone on the Common," which was first published in my novella *The Seven Wives of Silver*.

❦

Special thanks to Lissa Brennan, Sarah Buhrman, and Tempest Kwake for their feedback on early drafts of this manuscript. Any remaining errors are the result of my own stubbornness or stupidity.

ABOUT THE AUTHOR

E. Christopher Clark is the author of the Stains of Time series, a family saga with a hint of magical realism and a whole lot of time travel. His other books include the short story collections *Out of the Woods* and *Under the World*, the novella *The Seven Wives of Silver*, and a collection of poems cheekily titled *Bad Poetry Night*. His short stories have been published in *Live Free or Ride: Tales of the Concord Coach*, *River Muse: Tales of Lowell & the Merrimack Valley*, and the University of Hawaii's *Vice-Versa*. A graduate of Lesley University's MFA in Creative Writing program, he lives in Massachusetts with his wife and daughters.

echristopherclark.com

facebook.com/eccbooks

x.com/eccbooks

instagram.com/eccbooks

goodreads.com/eccbooks

pinterest.com/eccbooks

amazon.com/E.-Christopher-Clark/e/B00H0G94T0